P.E. KLEIN

THE INVISIBLE HAND

A PARETO SISTERS MYSTERY

Story Merchant Books, June 2023

All rights reserved under International Copyright
Conventions. Initial Printing in the United States of America
by Story Merchant Books

A Pareto Sisters Mystery: The Invisible Hand

Library of Congress Cataloging-in-Publication Data

Klein, P.E.

P.E. Klein, A Pareto Sisters Mystery: The Invisible Hand

Printed in the United States of America
ISBN: 978-1-970157-39-0

Attribution to **James Bridle** for the technology concepts
and words in Fenton's garden dialogue and to **Axel Munthe**
for the Ohlone judgment day concept

References to **Chuck's Donuts**, Redwood City,
used with permission.

Third Edition Author's Notes

Although this book happens to chronicle the adventures of young characters—eleven-year-old Charlie Pareto and her fifteen-year-old sister Clarke—the following pages are intended for adult readers. Nevertheless, I understand that this and other Pareto books have fallen into young hands. I am told that hostilities in these stories—especially those involving teachers, law enforcement, parents, and other sacred community pillars—could be unsettling to a younger audience. Some reviewers have suggested that this book endorses subversive and criminal behavior. If you are a young reader drawn to delicate subjects, I must point out that the caring adults in your life may prefer you to set this book aside until you are much older. In this moment, please consider the wishes of your caregivers and, given the potential for harm, your wellbeing. It might be best to return this book to its shelf or scroll to the next e-book selection on your list.

On a more upbeat note, this expanded third edition includes 'bonus content' in response to reader requests for technical and contextual details. If you want to read the book quickly and don't want to get bogged down in nitty-gritties, you can skip these tangents. But if you are looking to immerse yourself in the Pareto world, you will want to look them over. I will point out these alternative paths when we reach them.

I remain committed to faithfully preserving the original Pareto family words without simplification, abridgment, or translation. A few readers have commented that I must have misrepresented the Paretos' conversations because, they contend, people just don't talk this way. To this, I can only say the Paretos cultivate many unfamiliar plants in their gardens. Nevertheless, I have been persuaded to remove coarse language from this edition of the book to temper parental grievances and condemnations.

Flight Square

Like many prominent families who live here on the peninsula, the Paretos value their privacy. You will not find their address on any celebrity house map or in any other public listing. No family name or street number appears at their compound's high entryway gates. Their staff refuses all deliveries and turns away unscheduled visitors. Fenton Pareto, the controversial private investigator, has never hosted a neighborhood party, greeted anyone walking past his closed gates, or welcomed a trick-or-treater.

Over the years, the neighborhood rumor mill circulated unflattering tidbits about the investigator. There were whispers that Fenton even involved his daughters, Charlie and Clarke, in dangerous cases. These inquisitive neighbors had not yet learned that the Paretos had added a new member to their support staff. This team member would not only support the sisters' investigation of a sinister scheme but have an opportunity to look behind the veil of secrecy long concealing their family's affairs.

Charlie contends that the mystery began the day she and her aunt met with the school principal to answer questions about her fundraising tactics and the missing money.

* * *

Katherine wagged her forefinger at Charlie, supplying pre-conference instructions to her eleven-year-old niece as they stood outside the classroom.

The classroom doubled as the principal's office. While nodding in agreement with her aunt's counsel, Charlie gazed at a nearby clutch of chatty teachers vacating the school's central office after a long day of classes and after-school paperwork. Charlie's faded green, gold, and white Oakland Athletics baseball cap mostly concealed her straight jaw-length dark hair, with the bill of the cap pulled low. A dark grey t-shirt and camouflage pants completed her ensemble. She shifted from side-to-side while attending to an itchy spot on her right forearm.

With hands on hips, Katherine Pareto stood erect with her head held high as she looked upon her niece. Her face was framed by a brunette twist, with flat braids on the side and back held in place by two gold thistle-leaf pins. A statuesque embodiment of elegance, she exuded a calm, imposing and regal bearing. In her late thirties, wearing a tailored light blue blouse and conservative skirt, her ensemble was better suited for a board room than a teacher conference. She was poised to do battle.

"Charlie, since you've lost your voice again, you can just nod your head in one direction or the other. If your voice should return, I advise you to say even less than last time."

Charlie tilted her head. As she had remained silent during the previous disciplinary conference, she was left to consider arithmetical values less than zero.

Katherine sighed. "We're late. We better get in there." The aunt had arrived at the school only minutes before. She was habitually behind schedule.

The two entered the classroom, which at an earlier point, had been discharged of its students. Late afternoon sun filtered through rows of dusty windows lining the top of one of the classroom walls. Ms. Stiglitz, Charlie's sixth-grade English teacher and acting school principal, was seated at her oversized desk at the front of the room. She looked up as the two entered, peering over reading glasses perched at the end of her beaklike nose. In her late fifties, her sable hair was tightly pulled back from her angular face. Dressed in a checkerboard patterned coral and green blouse, she rose from her desk. Katherine exchanged some pleasantries with the teacher as she pushed aside a few books on a long table, using the table as a chair. Charlie settled into a student chair-desk, with a book basket under the seat. She looked up at the presiding school magistrate.

As she tidied her desk, Ms. Stiglitz remarked that she had just returned from a committee meeting. "Although the school is still in a precarious financial state, at least our anonymous donor is keeping us afloat." Her deep voice suggested a history of tobacco use. "Without the donor, I don't know where we'd be. The last principal didn't handle finances well. He turned everything over to me before following his dream to help the needy in Luxembourg. But enough about our situation. You didn't come here to discuss *our little* financial problems." After a protracted coughing fit, the teacher was able to continue. "Ahem... excuse me. I'm glad we could meet again today and put the post office box incident behind us." Her gaze settled on Charlie.

For nearly two months, school correspondence sent to the Pareto household had been rerouted to an anonymous post office box. During this time, the school did not receive any response to its increasingly urgent requests for parent conferences. School emails and texts sent to the Pareto adults were also never received. Had these messages been delivered, Charlie's caregivers would have been alerted to the school's concerns about her unsanctioned activities at the school and her deteriorating attendance record.

"Naturally, my practice is to meet with the *actual* parents when problems arise with one of our students." The teacher turned to Katherine. "Once again, your brother isn't here. I'm guessing he's attending to a pressing matter. A matter so pressing, that it's taken priority over the welfare of one of his daughters. Fenton's... Mr. Pareto's lack of concern is disrespectful to this school. The school is concerned about his parental competence and the rest. If I'd known what I know now, I would've advised the family court to—" The teacher did not finish her sentence.

Charlie studied the back wall of the classroom, which displayed a sampling of student artwork. There was no indication she was listening to her teacher's impeachment of her father.

"Nevertheless, it's heartening there's at least *some* adult oversight," Ms. Stiglitz said, giving a token nod to Katherine, "in *whatever* form it might take."

Katherine folded her arms, choosing not to respond to the teacher's prickly preamble. This was not the first time Ms. Stiglitz had aired her doubts about Fenton.

The teacher touched the hair on one side of her head to ensure her hair clip had not loosened its grip. "Setting all this aside, there are several concerns I'd like to share today. I understand, Charlene, you've lost your voice. No doubt, an unfortunate consequence of the schoolyard rebellion. Is there any way you can communicate with us today?" the teacher asked in a sugary tone.

Charlie typed into her phone, then passed the phone to her aunt. After reading the note on the phone, Katherine shared that her niece proposed to use a feature on the phone that translated text to voice. This would enable Charlie to respond to questions during her vocal convalescence. Katherine looked doubtfully at her niece.

This communication approach had not been scripted in their pre-conference huddle.

The teacher cleared her throat. "Charlene, although we appreciated your contribution to the school—selling a record 428 beehive cookie jars as part of our door-to-door fundraiser this past term—it's come to my attention that you did so by dishonest means."

Students sold plastic cookie jars in the shape of a beehive, dovetailing with the school's honeybee mascot. Each vessel was filled with cookies fashioned in the shape of the flying insect mascot.

"My source, who I will not disclose, informs me that you offered customers a chance to win a valuable prize if they purchased a cookie jar from you. This marketing approach was not approved by this school. And you doubled the price of the jars—marking them up from twenty dollars to forty dollars—skimming the mark-up for yourself. This was also not authorized and dishonest. Dishonest. Deceitful. Devious. Do you deny any of this?"

Charlie typed into her phone. After a brief pause, the phone translated her message into a soothingly optimistic womanlike voice: "The plastic cookie jars were poorly made. The cookies were stale. The value prop needed strengthening."

"Just answer the question. Did you mark-up the price of the cookies and pocket the profits?"

The educator chose a red pencil from a cup filled with red pencils. She started to rhythmically tap the pencil on the edge of her desk.

After a pause, the mechanical voice answered, "The cookie jars were value-priced at forty dollars." Charlie chose to study her phone rather than make eye contact with her teacher.

"Charlene, *this time* you've been caught with your hand in the cookie jar." Ms. Stiglitz inspected her own left hand, drawing attention to a well-worn idiom. "My source told me that you offered your neighbors and friends a chance to win a $2,500 savings bond as an inducement to buy our cookie jars. Do you deny this?"

"A savings bond raffle prize was offered," the phone responded flatly.

The teacher leaned forward and smiled. "So, you took it upon yourself to... sweeten the pot... by entering people into a raffle if they purchased a cookie jar from you?"

Charlie gazed in the direction of the classroom door.

"My source also told me you called this prize a 'Honey-B Bond,'" drawing air quotes around the unsanctioned raffle prize. "I'm guessing the 'B' was not just referring to our beloved insect mascot, but also represented the bond's rating. In other words, you offered a *'B-rated'* bond as your prize." Ms. Stiglitz's eyes locked on Charlie.

"The bond received a B rating," the phone confirmed.

"And you actually awarded the bond to someone?"

The phone attested that it had.

"So, you tempted people with a speculative B-rated *junk bond*. Have you heard the term *junk bond*?"

"We are acquainted with the term." The phone had switched pronouns.

"And you know that bonds with low ratings are called junk because they're like worthless swamp land?"

The phone did not answer, now able to recognize rhetorical questions.

Ms. Stiglitz smiled as she paused to gaze at the classroom's ceiling, reveling in her laborious interrogative process.

The teacher's smile turned to a frown as she noticed a red pencil embedded in one of the acoustic ceiling tiles. She turned her attention back to Charlie. "To recap, you raffled a worthless prize, swindled your neighbors, and made a profit from a fundraiser. *And* you tarnished the reputation of this school. Did I get that right? Do you think your trickery makes your father proud of you?"

The phone considered the teacher's questions.

The educator turned to Katherine. "I'm just trying to protect... trying to save this school." Her voice dropped to a whisper. "We're having real financial difficulties here. We may need to close the school. Did you know *I* attended elementary school here? I'm doing everything I can to save this special place. You can't imagine..." Her voice trailed off as she dabbed her eyes with a tissue. "Right now, we need to protect the reputation of the school, and avoid any unwelcome attention and..."

In an abrupt persona shift, Ms. Stiglitz straightened up in her chair as she swung around to Charlie. In a stern tone, she said, "And I'm going to need more information from you, Charlene."

The teacher's eyes bore into the girl. "What kind of junk bond did you offer?"

"An ABS," the phone answered mechanically.

"I'm supposed to know what that means?"

"An Asset Backed Security." The phone's answer almost interrupted the question.

"Exactly what type of asset?"

"A package of high interest automobile loans."

"Ah! And, specifically, what type of ȯ-tə-mō-*BEE*-il loans?" Ms. Stiglitz slowly drew out each syllable, showing that she discovered another level of Charlie's pun.

"Loans matching the profile of borrowers in that risk tranche." The phone was unfazed by being thrust into a shrinking corner.

"Oh! I think I see now. These are very risky loans made to people with bad credit. I'm guessing your prize *only* has value if these proven deadbeats decide to pay off their car loans." In a shrill crescendo, the teacher demanded, "Why on earth would you offer a prize like that?"

"Yield." Since the phone's tone was unreliable, it was unclear if the response meant high earnings potential, surrender, or both.

The teacher slammed her fist on her desk. "So deceitful! Like gambling! What will the school board say? They might investigate and negate the *entire* cookie sale, forcing us to retrieve the cookie jars and return all the money."

Turning her attention back to Charlie, "I understand you sold multiple cookie jars to several customers. How many customers bought more than one cookie jar?"

"Several dozen."

The teacher's face reddened. "And what was the most sold to any *one* customer?"

"Fourteen," the phone reported unambiguously.

"What? This wasn't our plan! Troubling. Distressing. Disturbing. What can I do?"

The accused and her counsel sat in silence as the judge resumed her pencil-tapping, drumming the edge of the desk with metronome precision. Abruptly, the magistrate ended the countdown. "Oh! Do you have a list of customers who bought more than one cookie jar from you?"

Katherine shook her head and sighed.

After a pause, the phone disclosed that sales records were available.

Ms. Stiglitz smiled. "Wonderful. Fantastic. Marvelous. In any case, it doesn't make sense to refund your customers their money. But we can't have *you* profit from your dishonesty. I have very little latitude in this type of matter, so... So, you'll need to pay back your ill-gotten gains to our school, amounting to..."

The teacher jabbed buttons of her oversized calculator, testing the resiliency of her peacock blue nail polish.

"After subtracting the cost of the bond, you need to repay $6,060 to the school." She showed Charlie the number on her calculator. If you make this payment now, do not miss one more day of school and–this is really important–provide a list of customers who purchased more than one cookie jar from you, I'll allow you to graduate. You've already been absent twelve days this term, two days over the Section 4820 limit. Our district loses state funding even for excused absences. Your absences have cost us hundreds of dollars. Given your absences, I've submitted paperwork to the district board recommending you repeat the sixth grade. But I'll withdraw that paperwork if you meet these conditions. Can you pay now?"

The mechanical voice responded: *"Non metterai mai le mani sui miei soldi. Mi vedrai tirare fuori un anello di cipolla dal mio orecchio prima che tu prenda un centesimo."*

The phone had switched languages.

The teacher scowled. "What was that?"

Charlie typed into her phone.

"That capital has been deployed," the phone reported.

Castled

"What do you mean deployed?!" Ms. Stiglitz exploded, now surveying the room. "What happened to the $6,060?"

Charlie typed into her phone, but there was no audio response. She gave the face of her phone a couple of hard taps. The phone froze at the very moment the teacher could have learned how the funds were committed and why they were presently inaccessible.

Ms. Stiglitz sputtered, "I'm sure your well-to-do aunt can advance the money until such time you can undeploy or... or... non-deploy your capital."

"Ms. Stiglitz, you need to compose yourself," Katherine purred. She slowly rolled her head, loosening up as she stepped into the ring with the teacher.

Turning to Charlie, Katherine asked, "What's the coupon rate and the maturity of the bond, my dear?"

"Ten percent and fifteen years," the phone promptly replied. The phone was working again.

"It seems my niece has rescued you from an ill-conceived fundraising campaign. You should be thanking her, not subjecting her to your uninformed line of questioning. She said the proceeds from her venture are deployed. And so, they must be." Katherine took a phone from her Bulgari handbag as the teacher dealt with another coughing episode. "But Charlie should've made the school aware of the deficiencies of your campaign much earlier. This is the reason—and only reason—I'm making a $3,030 tax-deductible charitable contribution to this school. This is half of her net proceeds. I will not be party to stifling my niece's ingenuity." Looking up from her phone, she asked, "Venmo, PayPal?"

Ms. Stiglitz did not answer.

"And the historical default rate on B-rated debt is less than 6 percent. Your swamp land analogy is misplaced."

The teacher's face reddened.

Katherine brushed a piece of lint off her sleeve. "If the price of one cookie jar was forty dollars, then the *highest* amount the winner could have paid for the bond was $560. That's the product of forty dollars and fourteen. Do you want to check that on your calculator?"

Ms. Stiglitz closed her eyes.

The aunt continued, "A $2,500 fifteen-year B-rated bond with a coupon rate of 10 percent would be a valuable prize, even for a person who paid as much as $560 for a chance to win it. This bond should generate..." Katherine looked at the classroom's dusty windows. "At *minimum*, the bond will produce a 55 percent net annual return for the winner. If you can tell us where you could match just half that return, I'll double my donation."

The educator's mouth hung open.

Katherine's command of any financial subject was truly dazzling. Years before, she created a financial model that would alter the trajectory of her life.

Katherine crossed her arms. "What's this about a schoolyard rebellion?"

"Charlie... Charlene was observed agitating the lower grades about the partial closure of the playground. You may have heard that the schoolyard blacktop is being resurfaced. We've closed half the playground. Charlene claims this closure is a student rights violation. Her press release accuses us of 'infringing on basic protections involving the right of peaceable assembly and access to sufficient recreational space.'"

The teacher did not comment on Charlie's contention that playground gatherings were afforded First Amendment protection or that her classmates' recreational rights were safeguarded by United Nations CRC Article 31.

Charlie gave her phone a couple of light taps.

The teacher dabbed her forehead with a tissue. "We don't know the full scope of Charlene's campaign, but we do know she bankrolled the protest banners and leaflets, organized the *Occupy-Our-Playground rally*, and indoctrinated student operatives. To prevent the school from plunging into chaos, we mobilized our entire staff to subdue the uprising that swept across all grades. We removed Charlene and her megaphone from the playground demonstration."

Katherine frowned at her niece. "And where was she and her megaphone taken?"

"We had her sit in the administration office. Amid the furor, one of the student leaders—I won't disclose her name—urged me to remove Charlene from the playground to defuse the situation. We still have students who care about the welfare of this school."

"This student recommended you relocate Charlie?"

"Correct." The teacher straightened her shoulders. "Charlene's loud chanting was making the situation worse. Charlie... Charlene was held in the office for about an hour. This is when the school lost electrical power. When it rains, it pours! I'm guessing Charlene lost her voice while stirring up widespread hooliganism and general dissent."

"This is truly disturbing," Katherine said, shaking her head. "This is the first time I've heard of 'widespread hooliganism and general dissent' at an elementary school. Thanks for bringing this to my attention. Until now, I was unaware of my niece's interest in social causes, but she must have her reasons. When she regains her voice, I intend to explore those reasons with her."

The discussion drifted to Charlie's other transgressions and consequent disciplinary actions.

*　*　*

Emma drove across town to the Paretos' home. Everything in her dorm room that had not been given away was crammed in her car. Her battered aluminum poker chip case, her tournament chess board, and lucky backgammon set were stacked on the passenger seat. An empty soda can clanked as it rolled back and forth on the floor behind her seat. Emma had not cleaned her car before packing all her possessions in it.

Weeks before, Emma's life had taken an unexpected turn at the campus spring career fair. Wandering through rows of white tents, she inventoried the collection of prestigious firms. But Emma had no reason to talk with any of the exhibitors. Although she would earn a mathematics degree, she did not have the scholastic measurables or the influential patronage to be considered by any of them. Between the Accenture and Morgan Stanley tents soared a dazzling yellow and white structure resembling a scaled-down fairy tale castle. A crenelated curtain wall framed the display area, straddled by pointy pastel green side towers with orange flags. Topiary boxwood trees in containers were arrayed along the sides of the booth. Carved on a placard that hung above the display area was the name "Pareto." If anyone had a question about the exhibiting employer, the design of the structure or the reason why Aretha Franklin's "Who's Zoomin' Who?" was being broadcast from the battlements, there wasn't anyone to ask. The booth was empty.

Emma decided to take a closer look.

The side of the castle displayed a heraldic crest resembling a coat of arms, with trees, mythological creatures, horned instruments, and acorn studded mantling. On one side of the emblem read: *pati mundum*. On the other: *sed beatus cum parvis*. Had Emma known Latin, she would have been able to read the inscription: Suffer the world but be happy in small ways. A LED screen, attached to the back wall of the booth, displayed a message:

> Greetings! Are you looking for a less traveled path? A gap year opportunity awaits! The Pareto family has an immediate opening for a live-in assistant to help with the transportation and oversight of their two delightful daughters, ages 11 and 15. The Paretos' residence is located nearby. Light house cleaning may be required. All encouraged to apply. The assignment is for one year, with possible extension. Salary negotiable.

Sitting on the booth table was an expensive looking virtual reality headset and large headphones. A note was taped to the top of the visor, which read: "Apply here."

There had been a test. And the results gave Emma a way out of her predicament.

Emma reduced her speed as she entered an affluent residential area. Her playlist transitioned to Club Des Belugas' "A Men's Scene."

The Pareto family lived in a hedged and walled peninsula neighborhood of sprawling twenty-first century mansions interspersed with older one-story ranchers. The new compounds were two-story villas, inspired by European architectural styles. Impenetrable walls and densely planted hedges were punctuated by towering entry gates flanked by decorative lights and surveillance cameras. Beyond these bulwarks, long cobblestone driveways led to four- and five-car garages and arched stone and marble entries. The ranchers, obscured by overgrown trees and shrubs, retained their wood shingle roofs, original brick chimneys, roof antennae, and filigreed wrought iron accents at their entryways. Wealth was locked in land value and in whatever dusty treasures were found within these tired structures. These homes were inhabited by an older generation of residents. Their families had grown up and moved on.

Katherine's directions led Emma to the Paretos' stately two-story Italian inspired villa. The fifteen-foot ornamental wrought iron entry gates noiselessly swung open. Two surveillance cameras followed her car as it passed the gate. After parking her car, Emma trudged up a winding marble slab path leading to the arched entry door. Earth, Wind & Fire's "Boogie Wonderland" was broadcast from a topiaried menagerie of seals, elephants, dogs, and snails eyeing the pathway. An Italian flag hung from a staff mounted on one side of the door entrance. A second flag, bearing a heraldic emblem, hung on the other side of the door. The villa looked like a foreign consulate.

Charlie met Emma at the door with a clipped packet of papers. "Hello, Emma. After introductions, I'd like to review a document with you." Charlie had recovered her voice.

"Can I look at this later?"

"Of course. And, if you don't mind me saying—and I'm sure you hear this often—your face bears a striking resemblance to Goya's muse in *The Marchioness of Santa Cruz.*"

Emma smiled. "Hmm, never heard that before." She brushed back her layered shoulder-length brunette hair.

Katherine joined the two in the entry area, sharing how much she was looking forward to Emma's help with the family. Turning to Charlie, she said, "It's puzzling how your voice comes and goes. I'm concluding this may be a malady of convenience. Next time this crops up, I'm bringing you to a doctor to confirm my suspicions."

Pointing to Charlie's packet of papers, Katherine asked, "What do you have there?"

"These are for Emma," Charlie replied, looking down at the papers.

"Charlie, you will address our new household aide as Ms. Dorner. Ms. Dorner is an adult. You are not. And not her equal. Do you call your father 'Fenton'? Of course you don't. Without a prefix like Aunt or Uncle, children do not address adults by their first name. Do you understand what I've told you and why?"

"Yes, ma'am." Charlie lowered her head.

"What do you have for Ms. Dorner?" Katherine again pointed to Charlie's papers.

"This is for Ms. Dorner."

"Stop being evasive," Katherine snapped.

"It's a non-disclosure agreement," Charlie admitted, studying the Palladian terrazzo entryway floor.

Katherine frowned. "Let me guess: You'd like Ms. Dorner to sign a non-disclosure agreement that would restrain her from divulging certain actions she might see or information she might encounter in your presence."

"Yes, ma'am." Charlie's voice dropped to a hoarse whisper.

"That's outrageous, Charlie. Ms. Dorner will not sign your NDA. If anything, I'd have her sign an FDA—a *full* disclosure agreement—making it an obligation for her to report everything she sees in your presence to your father and me. Let me see your paperwork."

After skimming the document, Katherine said, "I see this is a one-way NDA, which limits Ms. Dorner's ability to disclose your definition of 'proprietary information.' Yet, there are no such strictures on your own disclosures to others. If I ever permitted such a one-sided agreement, I'd demand you substitute your name for Ms. Dorner's. Your motivation to create such a document gives me pause. Apologize at once to Ms. Dorner for your impudence and lack of good judgment."

Katherine's childrearing strategy could be considered multidimensional. She was a fervent defender of Charlie's actions at school. And yet, within the private confines of the Pareto household, Katherine was a harsh critic of Charlie's conduct. Katherine left it to her niece to reconcile the polarity of her approach.

Clarke bounded down the stairs, greeting the group with a broad smile. She was on the tall side with an angular and athletic build. A two-inch white headband pulled her brunette hair away from her face, framing pleasant, well-proportioned features. She wore a purple t-shirt and tight white shorts.

Clarke was a high school sophomore, finishing up the last few weeks of school before summer break. Frowning, she said, "I don't get it, Auntie, my self-phone is borked. Haven't been able to text or call my squad since I woke up."

"You mean your cell phone isn't working? And given your erratic routine, you'll need to clarify when you arose from your latest slumber."

"Let's see, it's almost six o'clock. I've been up for an hour. I've been turning my phone off and on and still no connect-o." Rubbing her eyes, Clarke continued, "My schedule's been thrown off since Daylight Savings. I changed my nap schedule so I can ease into the new time."

"Clarke, that time change was almost two months ago."

"It's been an adjustment." Clarke smiled and stretched her arms to her sides.

Clarke napped at almost every opportunity, supplementing her generous nighttime sleep schedule with extended after-school and weekend slumbers. On occasions when Clarke slept past mid-morning, Katherine wondered out loud how closely Clarke's somnolent lifestyle corresponded to the habits of those relying on public assistance.

Looking at her phone, Charlie said, "My phone has lost its connection, too. This is not good."

Katherine shook her head. "How disturbing, Charlie. Even after accounting for our experience at school today, this certainly rises to the top of this family's concerns. Which brings me to a point. Let's spend a little time together later this evening. Just the two of us. Your phone is not invited. I'd like your help filling in some gaps in your phone's testimony at school today."

Charlie's shoulders dropped perceptibly.

After lugging a suitcase and two moving boxes into her room, Emma unpacked her clothes and belongings. Her ground floor room was divided into two chambers.

A larger salon contained elegant white and gold furniture, with a fancy wrought-iron bed. The top of the walls featured neoclassical pastel frescoes of hunting dogs chasing deer. Several towels were laid out on the bed, each with Emma's monogrammed initials.

The bedroom led to a smaller and even more formal salon designed for intimate social receptions, reading, and reflection. This classically influenced chamber contained four eighteenth-century painted and gilded armchairs and a small table. The walls were covered with a faithful trompe l'oeil of landscapes, draperies, columns, and antique vases. These images served as a backdrop for Greek busts and urns displayed on marble pedestals lining the walls.

Through the wavy pane of an old arched salon window, Emma surveyed the front topiary garden, east wing, and the entryway. The entry flags were still. Emma moved one of the armchairs to the window. From this vantage spot, she would observe the rotation of household, garden, maintenance, and security staff each day.

After unpacking her belongings, Emma explored the house. She found Katherine preparing dinner in the kitchen, which was the size of an average living room.

Katherine was getting down to The Invisible Man's Band's disco hit "All Night Thing." She had moves. Seeing Emma, she straightened up, removed her oven mitts, and turned down the kitchen audio system. "I hope you're finding everything to your satisfaction."

"Everything's been great. But I'd like to know more about the job here."

"My brother will be back tomorrow. When you meet with him, everything will become clearer." She checked on a pie in the oven. "Since the divorce a couple years ago, I've been trying to give the girls a little structure. And I'd like to get to the bottom of Charlie's obsession with money." Katherine sighed. "But I'm only a visitor here. You'll need to hold down the fort when Fenny and I are away. The household orientation will begin on Monday. Coffee?"

Katherine's starched elocution suggested a greater ease with the well-mannered matters of business than the messy concerns of domestic life.

Over coffee, Emma learned that the stylish aunt, who had not married, rotated from one relative's house to another. Her stays at Fenton's home had lengthened over the preceding two years as she attempted to bring order and discipline to a chaotic post-divorce household. Emma did not ask the aunt if these regular interventions were stimulated by her devotion to her nieces, her brother, or both.

Katherine brushed lint from her skirt.

"Fenton is a freelance detective, taking on cases that our law enforcement cannot or will not handle. I don't know much about his affairs, but the girls have assisted him on a few cases." Squinting her cat-shaped eyes, she said, "I don't like my nieces getting involved in dangerous cases. But I suppose it's a net positive they spend time with their father and learn about at least one of the family's businesses."

"There're other businesses?"

"Several. But the girls are only assisting with Fenny's investigative matters. The girls enjoy their amateur sleuthing. In time, the girls will need to learn about these other businesses from the ground up. Eventually, they'll oversee all of them." A hint of a smile formed at the corner of Katherine's perfect lips. "While I prepare dinner, which will take some time, can you please look in on Clarke? You'll find her in *Santa Maria della Concezione*, the entertainment hall, in *Via Veneto*, the north wing. I asked her to attend to a chore. Perhaps you can lend a hand."

Emma did not have difficulty finding Clarke. Chaka Khan's "Ain't Nobody" led her to a large concert hall with seating areas grouped around two identical stages on opposite sides of the space. She found Clarke sprawled on a modular sofa, with her feet propped up on the armrest. She clutched a remote against her midsection. Her eyes were closed.

"Can you turn that down?"

Clarke opened her eyes. "What? Oh, okay, sure." She turned down the volume with the remote.

"Your aunt thought I might help with a chore?"

"The problem is how to get rid of the water." Clarke rose to her feet and pointed to a large circular plastic wading pool on one side of the concert hall. The seven-foot diameter pool had been filled to a depth of almost three feet. A prominent label on its bulging plastic side read: "For Outdoor Use Only."

"Dad, Charlie, and I filled it the other day with a hose from an outside faucet. But we didn't talk about how to deal with the water when we finished using it."

Putting her hands on hips, Emma asked, "Why did you put this thing in the house?

Clarke smiled. "It's been cold outside. Also, Auntie wasn't around."

"Huh, interesting. Have you tried sliding it to the door over there?" At the corner of the hall, floor-to-ceiling frameless automatic glass doors led to an outside patio.

"Let's give it a whirly-whirly." Clarke wind-milled her arms, loosening them up.

They should have done the math first. Weighted down by over six thousand pounds of water, the pool would not budge. Their attempts to siphon the water with a garden hose failed. The two settled on bailing the water, using bowls and empty milk jugs Clarke requisitioned from the kitchen. They made numerous excursions to the garden to refresh the drought-resistant plants closest to the house.

As they shuttled the water from the concert hall to the garden over the next ninety minutes, Emma answered Clarke's questions about herself and her household duties which, she admitted, would need to be clarified.

Clarke stretched her back. "I thought Auntie would be really upset about our indoor pool, but she was more understanding than I thought she would be."

"Why's that?"

"She said our pool would teach me a lesson about the importance of an 'exit strategy.' She said that 'the merits of any enterprise should not only be judged by the strength of the proposition but by the ability to conclude the venture on favorable terms.' She says I act rashly."

Emma's one-year employment contract with the Paretos left little room to initiate her own "exit strategy" if she was unhappy with the job. This agreement did not give her the option to terminate the contract if she disagreed with her employer's parenting methods or objected to relocating large amounts of water.

After completing the water removal project, dinner was served in *Santi Quattro Coronati*, the formal dining room. The four dined on grilled pork loin roast, marinated with minced garlic, brown sugar, white truffle oil, dried fennel, and rosemary. Complementing the entrée were sides of baked apples, cheese-filled tortellini, and steamed broccoli. Charlie dipped the pork slices in barbecue sauce, still transitioning from children's cuisine to fine dining. Katherine's meal was topped off by a homemade chocolate cake. The girls applauded their aunt on her cooking. Balancing a piece of cake on her raised fork, Charlie said, "Brava!" Katherine leaned back and smiled at her nieces.

Baking was one of Katherine's hobbies, and dessert aromas from cookies, cakes, and pies filled the house throughout the day. Between meals, her confections were kept in a locked kitchen cabinet. She kept the cabinet key on a Gucci gold chain around her neck.

Lucy slipped into the room, settling onto a small rug a few feet from the table. Lucy, Charlie's dog, was a regular visitor at mealtime. Lucy was an amalgamation of several breeds, her small frame and cream-colored fur extracted from a mix of Maltese, poodle, and terrier. Lucy maintained excellent eye contact, suggesting a deep understanding and sympathy with each household member. Yet, she was unresponsive to any direction given to her, even if a family member called her name, waved their arms, or pleaded with her.

Charlie turned to Emma, who was handing her dessert plate to one of the kitchen staff. "In my view, Ms. Dorner, there's really no need for Lucy to perform tricks, which are, in fact, little more than degrading contrivances. I've been directing Lucy's attention to higher level pursuits more consistent with her remarkable powers of observation and insight. In time, I think you'll see this."

Emma nodded. "She sounds extraordinary."

Charlie smiled as she leaned back in her chair. "We adopted Lucy from an animal shelter last year. She's probably between one and two years old based on the condition of her teeth. She was found in southern

California and shipped up here. We're told that she was running with a pack of strays. She was the only one from her pack that was captured by Animal Control. The shelter didn't know anything else about her."

Emma waved her hand, drawing the group's attention to the opulent dining room and two staff members standing at the ready. "Looks like Lucy hit the jackpot here."

Charlie nodded. "I've gotten to know Lucy well this past year. I've concluded she was the ringleader of her gang. Lucy's pack relied on her towering intellect to plan their operations. She wasn't as athletic as the other dogs and not fast enough to get away from the dog catcher. Very likely, her records were sealed when she was brought up here."

Katherine folded her arms as she sized up her niece. "Charlie, I was unaware of this dark chapter in Lucy's life. My hope is that she's reforming her ways and redirecting her mental powers to *more constructive* pursuits."

Katherine continued to stare down her niece.

Charlie went on to explain that Lucy was not only a trustworthy companion, but she would show mettle in a future adventure. To prepare Lucy for forthcoming missions, Charlie designed self-improvement programs for her, with a new theme each month. One month's challenge, "It's Time to Shine!" encouraged Lucy to focus on "getting out of her shell" and "exhibiting consistently higher levels of confidence." Another month's campaign, "It's Your Turn Now!" challenged Lucy to take the initiative on two or three important assignments over the course of the month.

Turning to her aunt, Charlie said, "I contend that dogs, like young people, don't need as much guidance or supervision when they have a clear sense of purpose."

"Charlie, you've given us all something to think about," Katherine said. She lifted her water glass a few inches off the table, then slowly set it down.

Lucy left her rug and settled next to Charlie's chair. She licked Charlie's hand as she looked up at her. Lucy was also an admirer of Katherine's culinary talents.

A moment later, loud crunching sounds commenced under the table.

"Don't feed Lucy," Katherine told Charlie. "You can feed Lucy a small portion of people-food after dinner. Remember, no more than one-third of all her food should be people-food. Your dog is up a half pound, at the very least."

After overhearing one of the Spanish-speaking house staff describe Lucy as "*rechoncha*" the preceding week, Charlie looked up the word. Learning that it meant "chubby," she asked the staff to curtail the use of the word in the presence of her dog.

The post-dinner conversation centered on the nonresponsive phones.

Clarke said, "I've replaced my phone three times in the past couple weeks."

Katherine shook her head. "Curious logic, Clarke, given the overwhelming evidence that all our phones are having the same problem."

Charlie rested her chin on extended forefingers. "I wonder why we're experiencing problems now. Perhaps there was a recent ESTHER upgrade or some other system change that's now disrupting our phones."

"My squad hasn't had any of these issues." Clarke's face was flushed. "Without my phone, I'm completely cut-off from the world."

Charlie nodded. "I've set up alerts and reminders on my phones. My productivity has suffered of late. I'll need to play some catch-up."

Clarke pulled her hair into a bun, then inserted a clip to hold it in place. "From what I've heard, you were fortunate your phone was working at school today... Charlene."

*　*　*

Katherine sighed. "Okay, let's get to the bottom of this fundraiser business. What was your motive this time?" She and Charlie sat face-to-face in the middle of *Santa Maria della Concezione*. The other chairs were stacked against a wall of the ballroom.

Charlie rubbed her forehead. "Motive? It was the best way to help my school, the students, the community and–"

"Knock it off." The aunt frowned. "You should've consulted the school first. Given its precarious state, I doubt the school would've approved your... alterations."

"The school's situation is not precarious."

"Oh? And how do you know that?"

Charlie did not respond.

The aunt shook her head. "You don't know, or you're not saying?"

Charlie remained silent.

"You say your ventures are about helping others. But the money trail always leads to you. Is there a point you're trying to make here? Someone you're trying to impress?"

"No, ma'am."

"Are you trying to get your dad's attention?"

"No, ma'am."

"Have you gotten yourself into some type of trouble? You can always talk with us."

"I'm not in trouble."

"Okay, but I can't keep defending you at school."

* * *

After meeting with her aunt, Charlie gave Emma a tour of the family compound. Charlie held Lucy during the excursion, with visits to the fitness center, theater, art gallery, and Rosicrucian library. As the two walked along an arcaded hallway leading to the girls' sleeping quarters, Charlie explained in a matter-of-fact tone that the family added to their property over the years by acquiring adjacent acreage from one-time neighbors–along with their homes. These homes were converted into an entertainment pavilion, guest house, and discothèque.

Charlie said, "It's too late to tour the grounds. There're tennis courts, wading and lap pools, stone fruit orchard, goat pasture, exotic gardens, and an overflow parking area. My mom planted the specimens in the exotics section of the garden. I care for those now. I wish she was here. I can only see her four days each month. And she's moving to Armenia next summer, so I'll hardly see her at all after that."

"I can imagine how much you miss her."

"Well, there might be a way to change all this."

Emma did not ask how this might be done.

"Since I arrived, I've heard this low-level pulsing or throbbing sound. Is there a generator or something that's making that noise?" Emma asked.

"Oh, don't worry about that. You must be hearing ESTHER, our External Synapse Therapy for Healing,

Enlightenment and Realization auditory system. She's a system that produces directional binaural beats from 2.5 to 400 Hz. Dad had her installed years ago to facilitate relaxation, deeper thinking, and physical regeneration. There's scientific evidence that binaural beats promote deeper meditation, creating anti-aging benefits for adults. Embedded within the binaural beats, ESTHER streams subliminal messages of affirmation throughout the house, except the guest room where Auntie stays. She thinks ESTHER is creepy. ESTHER produces soft humming or light rainfall sounds. In a few days, I'm sure you won't notice her anymore. I haven't heard her for a long time."

Emma looked up at the ceiling. "I've never heard of anything like this before. I don't like the idea of being subjected to subliminal messages. I'll ask your aunt how to turn off ESTHER in my room."

Passing one of the staircases to the upper level of the villa, Charlie said, "I've been spending time here with Lucy." Charlie still held Lucy. "We've been working on her confidence. She climbs almost to the top of the stairs, but always stops three steps from the top. She doesn't want to climb past that point." Charlie readjusted Lucy in her arms so she could make eye contact with her. "Lucy, do you fear something? A bad memory? Vertiginous sensations arising from acrophobia? Anyway, Lucy and I have been working on taking the last three steps on her own."

"Does she have a problem going down the stairs?"

"No, she doesn't," Charlie said thoughtfully.

Charlie's tour led to her personal work area, which she called her *bottega*. This area was cluttered with computers, stacks of books, plastic containers, and boxes of zip-lock bags. Hanging on one wall were framed posters of her sister in action on a tennis court, school track, basketball court, and soccer field.

Another wall featured reprints of fifteenth and sixteenth-century paintings. Charlie pointed to a picture of a battle scene showing a confusing tangle of sword and lance wielding horse-backed warriors engaged in desperate combat. "This is a reprint of Rubens' interpretation of Leonardo's unfinished and now lost *Battle of Anghiari.* I can show you how I'm using a program to add colors to a reproduction of another of Leonardo's abandoned works, the *Adoration of the Magi.* I think Leonardo would be pleased with what I've done so far."

"I've never heard anyone refer to Leonardo da Vinci as just 'Leonardo.' You sound like a scholar of his work."

"I'm captivated by his artistic and scientific imagination. Were he alive today, I'd have so many questions for him. I consider him to be the last millennium's greatest portraitist and polymath."

After Charlie put Lucy down, she sprinted out of the room.

As Charlie lectured on "Leonardo's" *chiaroscuro* and *sfumato* techniques, Emma thumbed through several books stacked on a worktable. The titles reflected Charlie's interest in business, economics, art, and political philosophy. As Emma flipped through L.T. Hobhouse's *Liberalism,* a business card fell out of the book. The card was inscribed with Charlie's name, her social media accounts, and the words: "Ventures. Financing. Outsourcing. Discreet." Emma returned the card without Charlie taking notice.

Charlie led Emma to another personal space, containing just a table and chair.

"I use this space for strategic planning. Every Friday, I neaten up in here. But it's often messy. Studies suggest that cluttered spaces encourage higher levels of creativity." Emma's pre-employment discussions with Katherine had not touched on the plots originating in this room. "The NDA was just to protect my interests. The stakes are higher than you might imagine. Anyway, I'm glad you're here."

"I'm happy to be here too."

Deep into the night, Emma was shaken out of sleep by howling, shrieks, and other anguished cries of distressed dogs from the surrounding neighborhood. She sat up in bed, not only unnerved by the hounds' unnatural cries but the unimaginable threat that was terrifying the animals. The outburst subsided after a few minutes, and she eventually fell into a fitful sleep.

Forked

The breakfast conversation was devoted to the late-night dog outburst, which had woken up everyone in the household, and the worrisome status of the mobile phones.

The girls and Katherine and Emma sat at a René Bouchera rectangular glass table located in a space adjacent to the kitchen. The table sat directly under a large pyramid skylight, transforming the morning light into kaleidoscopic forms that made brief appearances on surfaces throughout the room.

"This is the third or fourth time in the past couple weeks the dogs have woken me up," Charlie complained.

"Same with me," Clarke grumbled. "Last night I had trouble getting to sleep anyway. The phone problems have been bothering me. First, it was the smoke detector bird, now the dogs."

"What's a smoke detector bird?" Emma asked.

Frowning, Clarke said, "We have a bird somewhere on our property with a chirp that sounds *exactly* like the warning beep of a smoke detector when it needs a new battery. The bird's tweet can penetrate walls, like an evil superpower. We've been tricked more than once. We wander around like zombies–like at five in the morning–looking for the bad smoke detector."

Katherine frowned. "Why don't you girls shut your windows or use ear plugs?"

"My windows *have* been shut," Clarke said, raising the pitch of her voice. "Why do these dogs start barking at the same time? Then they just stop. Always happens the same way. If it happens again, I'll need to stay home from school to catch up on sleep. People should be fined if their dogs bark at night. What if we left Lucy outside at night?"

Clarke allowed her audience to consider how difficult it would be for Lucy to return to an outdoor life after her fresh start in northern California. Lucy enjoyed the use of several private villas placed throughout the house, each serving as a cozy dog bed, observation post, and fashionable retreat.

Charlie scanned the room. "At least Lucy sleeps through the night. She's been working on being a trouble-free companion in this month's 'Be a Supportive Family Member' challenge."

Charlie leaned back to get a better view of the far end of the room and the central atrium beyond. Accessed through arched glass doors, the arcaded atrium was lined with white and grey hexagonal marble tiles and crowded with ceramic vases, amphoras, and various *objets d'art*. The protected courtyard was Lucy's favorite sunbathing spot.

Katherine said, "Charlie, don't lean back in your chair. That's dangerous."

Raising her eyebrows, Clarke said, "My phone started working again around seven-ish. I've been turning it off and on to try to get service."

Clarke slammed her fist down on a kaleidoscopic shape materializing on the table.

Katherine frowned. "Clarke, since the service problem occurred Friday night, I'm sure the outage interrupted vitally important communications."

Clarke glared at her aunt. "Seems like the phone and dog probs aren't related. They happen at different ticky-tockies."

Katherine shrugged. "Because they occur at different times? Sounds like you've given this some thought."

Lucy trotted into the room, stopping to look at Charlie before darting under the table.

The intercom panel in the kitchen buzzed loudly. "Front gate!" Charlie called out, jumping up from the table. Lucy delivered a couple of reports to confirm that the buzzer had sounded. Switching on a monitor built into the kitchen wall, Charlie announced that Jill Masterson, an elderly neighbor, was waiting at the Paretos' entry gate.

Clarke brought Jill back to the breakfast area. Lucy gave three sharp barks to alert everyone that a visitor had, in fact, entered the home.

The smiling seventy-year-old strode into the room. Jill's curly gray hair cascaded over a white visor. Her puffy black athletic vest, girding a cream long sleeve turtleneck, conformed to the neighborhood's uniform, which allowed only slight variations in composition and color. After sitting down at the kitchen table, she handed Charlie the latest edition of *Gentry* magazine, explaining it had been dropped off at her house. "I know you like reading these. This one features the Women in Tech Conference."

After commenting that Emma needed a cut and color, Jill gave Emma an account of her connection with the Paretos and personal history. Jill was a long-time resident on a nearby street. She lived alone in a ranch-style home, an aging homestead that had seen the passage of three children from birth through high school and the loss of her husband to cancer five years before.

"I'm sure you all have been hearing the dogs barking at night. I'm at wits' end," Jill lamented. "Scrubbles and Ribsy, like all the other dogs, have been barking up a storm. Just a storm! I'd bring them in, but they often need to use the facilities."

"Facilities" represented a stretch of browned-out grass adjoining her patio.

Jill shook her head. "Just exasperating. Once I'm awake, my brain switches into high gear, and I can't get back to sleep. My doctor says I have the metabolic rate of a thirty-year-old. I need regular sleep like an athlete in training."

Jill was a fast talker, not seeing the need to pause between sentences.

As Jill ran down her vitals, Katherine served her a slice of apple pie and an oversized cup of just-brewed coffee. "Thank you so much, Katherine. You're so kind."

"You're so welcome. Just making sure you're taking in enough calories to keep pace with your dynamic metabolism," Katherine said with a smile.

"Anyway," Jill continued, "around two in the morning, Scrubbles and Ribsy start to bark, along with all the other dogs. It's been happening two or three nights a week, starting about three weeks ago. They whimper, snarl, and bark like frenzied feral animals. After a few minutes, they just stop. It's a mystery! A big mystery!"

Charlie said, "At least Lucy sleeps through the night. I don't know about Tank." Tank, a brown and white miniature bull terrier, was Lucy's love interest. Tank lived in an estate neighboring the Paretos' property. A fifteen-foot rebar-reinforced concrete wall between the properties impeded the progression of their relationship.

"Jill... um... Mrs. Masterson, would you be open to hiring Clarke and me to investigate these outbursts?"

Charlie sat erect in her chair as she continued her pitch. "Clearing up this mystery would have the combined benefit of assisting you, one of our favorite neighbors, while bringing a measure of peace to our own household."

Listening in on the conversation, Katherine turned to her niece. "Charlie, I believe Jill understands she's one of our favorite neighbors without it being brought up in the context of your business proposal." Katherine put her apron on the kitchen counter. "And, Charlie, you really don't need to open a case file on this. The best solution might be earplugs or a sleep aid."

"I agree with you, Katherine," Jill said, "but I'd like to hire the girls to get to the bottom of this mystery. Who knows what's causing this? Could be serious!"

Using a deep professional tone, Charlie said, "Mrs. Masterson, can we outline the scope, timing, expectations, and financial arrangements of this engagement now? We can also conduct an initial intake of information."

Clarke started a side-conversation with her sister. "Our standard revenue sharing?"

"I suppose so, but it's not fair."

Clarke sighed. "We've been over this. I'm watching out for your safety. In sketchy ops, your welfare is my numero uno concern. How much is peace of mind worth? Plus, I throw in my advice for free. Full stack."

Charlie frowned at her sister. "The derivation of this lopsided arrangement, which I unfortunately agreed to, can be traced to your unfounded belief in the intrinsic and inalienable benefits of seniority."

Katherine shook her head. "Girls, I suggest you revisit your business arrangement at another time. It's discourteous to invite all of us into this type of discussion."

Charlie turned back to Jill. Using her phone as a recording device, she asked, "Was there anything unusual about the nights the dogs barked? Noises? Changes in routine?"

"Well, no... I can't think of anything special–"

With a wry smile, Katherine interjected, "Was there anything unusual about the nights they do *not* bark?"

Scowling at her aunt, Charlie returned to her line of questioning. She summarized the rest of the interview on her computer tablet:

- Scrubbles is a seven-year-old Bulldog mix and Ribsy is a five-year old Border Collie. These are Mrs. Masterson's favorite breeds, along with the Australian Cattle Dog.

- Dogs are in good health. Mrs. Masterson is in excellent health. Her mother lived to ninety-four.

- Mrs. Masterson traveled by herself in South America last year.

- No sign as to why dogs start and stop barking in the middle of the night.

- Dog barking wakes up Mrs. Masterson. She's been a light sleeper for six years.

- Scrubbles and Ribsy don't have a history of barking. They only barked when a visitor rang her doorbell or knocked on her door.

- Her dogs eat grain-free dog food, purchased in forty-pound bags. No recent changes in diet. When they were last sick, they were given a rice and cottage cheese mix.

- Mrs. Masterson doesn't give her dogs calming treats. She doesn't believe in lots of medications for her dogs or herself. She's only taking Lisinopril for high blood pressure and Lipitor for cholesterol, but just preventatively.

- Once the dogs begin barking, Mrs. Masterson can't calm them down for twenty to thirty minutes. Then they just stop barking on their own and are quiet for the rest of the night. After the barking, she drinks a non-caffeine chamomile tea and works on expert-level Sudoku.

Wrapping up the interview, Charlie said, "That's all for now, Mrs. Masterson. The next step will involve neighbor interviews. Depending on what we find, we may need to examine your dogs and investigate your patio and surrounding grounds."

Jill put her hand on Charlie's shoulder. "I see you have many of the forensic skills of your father. Your questions considered possibilities I never would have considered."

Katherine rolled her eyes.

Clarke returned to the breakfast area after escorting Jill to the front gate. She shared with Emma that Jill often stopped by on a weekend morning and, if schedules permitted, spent a couple of hours with them. She suggested that Fenton was Jill's favorite.

"I agree with you, Clarke," Charlie giggled. "Ms. Dorner, sometimes our dad joins our chats with Jill... um...

Mrs. Masterson. When he makes a comment or raises a question, she looks so... *intently* at him. She obviously appreciates the depth of his thinking. So much so, if not for her quarter-century head-start in life, one might imagine a blurring of intense admiration and romantic attraction." The girls laughed hysterically.

Katherine said, "Girls, there's absolutely no reason to buzz about this like a couple of mud wasps. Time to make a productive use of what's left of the day."

* * *

Several hours later, Emma entered Fenton's dimly lit home office. La Boehme's "Che gelida manina" was broadcast high overhead. After rising to meet Emma, Fenton settled behind his desk. Using a remote, he paused the tenor aria. Emma sat on a simple side chair placed in the middle of the room. Through a narrow side window, a ray of sunlight obliquely knifed across the room, shedding an elongated band of light across the hardwood floor between Fenton and Emma. The light gave the effect of a dividing line, while giving the opposing side of the room an even fainter and obscure aspect.

Fenton was in his mid-forties with closely cropped salt-and-pepper hair extending to a neatly clipped beard of the same color. A long horizontal scar created a small break in his beard at the jaw line. He was, incontestably, a handsome man. Fenton adjusted his slim-fitting navy blazer, which complemented a light-blue shirt buttoned to a forward point collar. Fine lines around his blue-grey eyes carried the weariness of a traveler.

Katherine jogged into the room. She stationed herself next to her brother's desk, not bothering to sit. She wore a thick white turtleneck sweater and dark mid-rise pants.

Finding the perfect outfit was time-consuming. She was late for every scheduled gathering.

Emma had seen a remarkably close likeness of Fenton during her application process at the spring career fair. She had not yet clarified how the Paretos' career fair challenge related to her assignment with the family.

Fenton leaned forward in his chair, resting his chin under his folded hands. He held Emma in a long gaze.

Rather than making eye contact with him, Emma surveyed the home office. Behind the two siblings, soaring to the vaulted ceiling, were bookshelves populated by a variety of travel souvenirs. Next to the desk, a globe balanced on a three-legged wood stand. On the far side of the room was a round meeting table. Five identical Italian marble chess tables, equipped with Staunton design ebony and boxwood pieces, were arrayed along one of the walls. All games were in progress, with pieces deployed. The study was much like a nineteenth-century chamber where long-whiskered Englishmen wearing pith helmets might plot a Zambian safari or Turkish archeological dig.

In a deep voice tinged with an Italian accent, Fenton started the conversation. "Welcome! Your arrival has been much anticipated. Unfortunately, I have just a few minutes. I'm expecting a client. Let's start with any questions you might have."

"Sure. Would you mind reviewing how you'd like me to support the girls?"

Fenton nodded, sanctioning this starting point. "Essentially, there're three parts of your role. With our travel, we'd like you to provide transportation, logistical support and oversight. Oversight may mean offering a helping hand..." and after some hesitation, he added, "or exerting corrective influence." He glanced at his chessboards. "Charlie has four weeks of school before her break. We'd like her to complete the remaining month of school without incident. Charlie's absences are a concern to her school. Please remove any obstacles you might find in her path to her school's commencement rostrum."

Like Katherine, Fenton's tone was professional and flat.

"Our job description suggested light housecleaning. This wasn't meant to be literal. Unless you prefer light or any other type of housecleaning, no housework is required. I have a capable cleaning and maintenance team."

"Thank you, Mr. Pareto. I wasn't looking forward to that part of the job." Emma was left to consider the possible abstract and figurative meanings of "light house cleaning."

"As part of your oversight responsibilities, we would like you to supervise the girls' new community support program." He turned to his sister. "Kat?"

Stepping forward, Katherine outlined the community service plan requirements: "(a) The girls need to formulate their own community service plan which cannot be part of any organized school or public program; (b) no compensation is permitted; (c) each must contribute a minimum of three hours per week during the school year and ten hours a week during the summer; (d) no delegation of duties to a third party; and (e) progress must be posted on the family website beginning in two weeks."

Emma lowered her head to suppress a smile. She did not ask if the children would be required to endorse a contract outlining these terms and conditions.

Katherine clarified that the girls were prohibited from community services that provided personal benefits. Also, any third-party involvement must be scrutinized.

The new community service program for the girls marked a departure from Fenton's laissez-faire approach to his daughters' affairs.

Fenton took off his jacket and rolled up his sleeves. Deep scars crisscrossed his muscular forearms. "By the way, I understand you're proficient in several games. Perhaps you can give Charlie chess pointers. I've found chess provides good preparation for battling real opponents: persistence, logic, intuition, and controlled aggression. And remembering the painful consequences of underestimating an opponent." Fenton gave a sad smile. "But, of course, the true test is to discover our actual adversaries."

He adjusted a framed photograph on the side of his desk. The picture showed a younger version of the investigator standing between two other men. All were in business suits, showing off broad smiles.

Fenton rolled his broad shoulders and rose from his desk. He crossed the room to turn off a standing lamp. Fenton preferred soft, natural lighting. He was never seen outdoors without his sixties style retro tortoiseshell sunglasses.

After clarifying the remaining aspects of the girls' community service plan, Katherine excused herself. Returning to his desk, Fenton asked Emma to stay another minute. "As mentioned, I'm expecting a client. Since I will be traveling again, there's an opportunity for the girls to take the lead on at least one aspect of the case. Also, Charlie has been pushing to get involved in jobs offering recovery rewards. This may be such a case.

I'd like you to sit in on the conference. The girls may need your support."

"I'll do my best, but I didn't know detective work would be part of the job here."

A vein in Fenton's neck became more prominent. He stared at the new household aide as he tapped his fingers together. "If this arrangement is going to be successful, you'll need to be flexible. There will be challenges—and setbacks. This job will not be easy. If you're looking for an easy job, you should leave now."

The investigator paused, giving Emma an opportunity to leave. Emma stayed seated.

"If you decide to stay, you have my full support. In your time here, you might also consider our family's motto. *Pati mundum sed beatus cum parvis.* It means, suffer the world but find happiness in small ways."

Overhead, The Marshall Tucker Band's "Can't You See" rose in volume. The conference had ended.

Minutes later, the girls and Emma were summoned to Fenton's home office. They joined the investigator and a mid-forties woman seated at his round conference table.

"I don't know what happened. I opened my safe yesterday, and all my jewelry was gone," Laura Marcum sobbed. She was slim and attractive, with straight blonde hair clipped behind her head. She wore designer glasses that enhanced her large brown eyes. Laura was a divorcee residing a few streets from the Paretos' home.

She lifted her glasses to dab her eyes. "All my jewelry was stolen, but nothing else was taken. No one else knows the safe combination. I'm sure it was locked."

Laura blew her nose.

"I'm told you conduct your inquiries with discretion."

The investigator nodded. "Naturally."

"Friends and family often stay at my home. I'm afraid one of them broke into my safe. There's no other explanation. This matter needs to be handled carefully... discreetly. I don't want my friends and family to know they're under suspicion. I'll pay your fee and offer a reward for the return of my jewelry."

Laura went on to inventory the various relatives and friends that made periodic visits to her home. She did not advance any theories about possible suspects. Instead, she gave a definitive character endorsement of each visitor.

During one of her visits, Jill touched on the constitution of the Marcum household as part of her unsolicited yet comprehensive weekly status report on the neighbors' endeavors. She volunteered that Laura welcomed an indulgent rotation of male friends.

Fenton shook his head. "I can't take your case at this time. I've taken on a project for an overseas client and will be leaving shortly. But I have a proposal. My daughters have assisted me on several cases. I suggest they inspect your premises. I'll stay in contact with them and offer counsel, but they will be *i miei occhi e le mie orecchie*, my eyes and ears, while I'm away."

"But they're no more than children." Laura shook her head. "I've also heard things about your youngest daughter from my niece. Didn't she have the science fair project with the computer virus that—" Laura glanced at Charlie.

Before Laura could finish, Fenton interjected, "I have complete faith in my daughters. To provide extra assurance, Ms. Dorner will oversee their activities as they look into your case." Fenton rested his chin on his fingers in prayer. "Given the delicacy of your circumstances, consider the advantages of an inquiry *outside* adult channels. A conventional investigation may bring unwelcome attention. Priority should be given to collecting transient clues."

Laura shrugged. "Well, if this is the only option. Girls, you can drop by my house tomorrow. Late morning?"

"Tomorrow is Sunday," Fenton reminded Laura. "The girls are not permitted to conduct this type of work on Sundays between seven and two o'clock."

Fenton's Sunday work moratorium was one of his few rules, otherwise leaving his daughters to manage their own calendars. While the girls' school schedules and organized sports activities imposed a degree of structure, Fenton allowed his daughters to choose when to eat, sleep, attend to homework, engage in recreational activities, and host school friends at their home. Although he discussed joint investigative matters with his daughters and quizzed Clarke about her weekly karate lessons, he did not ask about their other undertakings. Katherine had made only modest inroads in establishing regular schedules for her nieces.

"Well, okay. After school on Monday should be fine."

After showing Laura out, Fenton returned to the meeting table. "After you inspect the Marcum home, develop working theories. I'll check in with you all when I return."

After a pause, Fenton stood up and walked to his desk. He pulled an envelope from a drawer. "Also, plan to attend this wedding at the end of next month, unless the Marcum affair is concluded first. At the wedding, look for Stella Huynh and her aunt, Con mắt who will also be guests. Con mắt is also called Clara. Of course, Clarke, you're well acquainted with Stella. I know you'll look past your history with her."

Clarke shifted in her chair.

"The Huynh family has extensive knowledge of the jewelry trade. Their perspectives will likely be useful in the Marcum case. Your aunt can help get you properly attired for the event." Turning to Emma, "Of course, Ms. Dorner, you'll be the girls' chaperone." Smiling, he said, "*Goditi la celebrazione!*" Somewhere overhead, Róisín Murphy's "Sing It Back" rose in volume, signaling the meeting was concluded.

*   *   *

Using a remote, Charlie rearranged the display tiles on the fifteen-foot-wide video wall system. The Paretos' audiovisual center rivaled technology used by national media newsrooms. Charlie, Clarke, and Lucy lounged in bloated chairs arranged in front of the video wall, flanked by two balloon sofas. The burgundy chairs resembled red blood corpuscles. Peeking over the edge of her concave chair, Lucy stared at the largest display window, featuring a glitzy awards show. Areas of the massive screen were dedicated to other muted programming, including a Latin ballroom competition, Peter Bogdanovich's *What's Up, Doc?* and a roundup of stock movers.

Charlie asked, "Did you know our dad was doing business with Stella's mother?"

"Nope. First I've heard of this. Pretty weird. And in the future, you can drop 'our' when referring to Dad." Clarke scowled. "What the... My phone just lost its signal!"

Charlie confirmed she had also lost her connection.

Clarke threw up her arms. "Ridiculous! I checked with my friends this morning and they haven't had any problems with their phones. It's just affecting this part of town. It's like I'm being punished. Completely cut off. Totally isolated."

"You said *'friends,'* didn't you? I lost the rest of what you said."

"Hush, Charlie. Don't project your social deficiencies on me."

Looking at her phone, Charlie said, "Speaking of being cut off from the world, here's something for you..."

> Model/TV personality Z Lifestyles admits she feels anxiety from being blocked by the President on Twitter. According to Star Daily, Ms. Lifestyles said the presidential blocking has given her anxiety because "every day in America pretty much begins with a flurry of presidential tweets" that she can't look at. When Lifestyles sees people "freaking out" over things our president has tweeted, she has no idea what everyone is talking about. "Do I get in the bunker or not?" she said. A representative for the White House did not respond to our request for comment.

Shaking her head, Clarke said, "I know how Z feels; that's just like me. Wonder what I'm missing. I'm sure lots of stuff."

Turning to the awards show, Charlie gushed, "Those are some fab dresses. *Le donne indossano bellissimi vestiti!* I see myself being a powerful and admired, but mysteriously reclusive, garment industry mogul in my late twenties. I'd attend the most exclusive events, discreetly observing the celebrities at close range. My dreamy escorts would ensure my insulated comfort and security."

After a pause, Clarke said, "You said '*admired,*' didn't you? I lost the rest of what you said."

Initiative

Milo, the Paretos' house steward, flipped through the flashcards, testing Emma's knowledge. The fifty-ish silver-haired staff supervisor worked through the pile of cards, grunting "correct" or "incorrect." Earlier in the day, Katherine reviewed Emma's two-day orientation schedule in *Santa Maria della Concezione*. This initiation, outlined in a two-page syllabus, covered a variety of foundational topics that were critical to Emma's "acclimation and functional effectiveness."

The flash cards tested Emma's memory of the names the Paretos conferred to their villa's common areas, private quarters, corridors, and galleries. Given the compound's numerous rooms and the assortment of structures on the property, one of Emma's trainers explained that it was critical for the family and staff to use common vocabulary to describe distinct spaces in the house and surrounding grounds. With few exceptions, each area was assigned a famous Italian cathedral or street name. Emma had trouble remembering a few of the location tags, such as whether *Viale di Trastevere* was the kitchen breezeway or the hallway to the fitness center.

Emma sat alone in a theatre that could have seated fifty people. The video orientation covered various topics in ten to fifteen-minute learning modules projected on one of the large screens. These short subject productions had Hollywood production values, featuring high-quality graphics, special effects, recognizable actor voices, and stop-motion animated sequences. Topics included:

"Household Security," "Comportment and Personal Standards," "Household Thermal Imaging and Pathogen Detection," "Art, Artifacts and Furnishings," and "Local Restaurants and Entertainment." During the interludes, Emma was treated to a film montage of children from around the world, accompanied by Marni Nixon's "Getting to Know You" from *The King and I*.

House staff proctored quizzes to test Emma's understanding of concepts and details.

Emma was permitted a one-hour lunch break on these training days. The kitchen staff brought stainless-steel chafing dishes and two long tables into the theater for buffet service. After the trainers, proctors, and Emma helped themselves to the food, they chatted a bit before getting back to the prescribed program.

A forty-ish house staff member introduced himself as Karl, the Estate Manager. His thick dark hair was perfectly parted. Life with the Paretos was agreeable to him; his smile was a permanent fixture on his deeply tanned face.

The Estate Manager smoothed his plum-colored vest. "Emma, my role is similar to Milo's, but I'm also responsible for the auxiliary structures and grounds: orchards, flowerbeds, sports fields, and athletic courts. I also oversee the household staff, contractors, service providers, special events, and aircraft."

Emma did not ask what the neighbors thought of the Paretos' air traffic.

Karl clasped his hands. "And I walk Lucy every day."

"This is a big property. What should I check out first?"

Karl beamed. "The gardens are amazing, but you should explore Hadisway Hall. It's reopened now that the water damage repairs are done. There's a large operating model train layout there, with the trains synched with a music and light show. And take the elevator to roof of the Hall. Wonderful views there. Tallest structure on the property."

"You said, Hadisway Hall? Is this a pun for 'had it his way?'"

"Hmm. Could be. Anyway, Miss Clarke and her friends shuffle dance on the flat rooftop of the Hall. Sometimes they use the stage down here to record other routines."

Clarke recruited friends during her father's business trips to produce professional-level music videos, reprising dance videos such as Jason Derulo's "Swalla," Dua Lipa's "Love Again," Normani's "Motivation," and Beyoncé's "Formation."

* * *

Two days after Emma's orientation, Charlie and Emma lounged on the loggia's relaxed linen-covered Ignazio Gardella chairs as the two enjoyed some down time before dinner. The chairs had been oriented to provide an optimal view of the Italian Renaissance gardens. Charlie offered baby carrots to Emma from a small plastic bag she had brought with her to the veranda.

"It's odd that Dad hadn't mentioned his business association with Stella's mother until just a couple days ago."

Emma shrugged. "Don't know. Why don't you ask him?"

"I did, but he didn't have time to talk. He said that there'd be 'a better time to discuss the subject.' Clarke says that Dad is irresistible to women. Maybe he didn't actually have a business association with Stella's mother—and gave dalliance too much the rein."

"Pardon me?"

"You know, maybe there was some hanky-panky going on."

"You mean between your dad and Stella's mother?"

Charlie nodded her head. "But I have no corroborating evidence."

"Then that's quite a leap." Emma stretched her arms. "By the way, why did your dad say that Clarke should look past her history with Stella? Are they enemies?"

"They've had many clashes over the years. I'll tell you how it started."

Zipping up the bag of baby carrots, Charlie started the story.

During a glorious fall campaign, four years earlier, Clarke led her brightly clad middle school soccer team to the regional finals. Clarke's team posted a perfect league record, steamrolling all opponents standing in their path. Along the way, Clarke cemented her standing as one of the top young soccer players in the Bay Area.

Unbeknownst to Clarke, Stella Huynh was leading her inner-city squad on a parallel path of domination in an urban soccer league.

The regional championship was held in a dusty sports field behind an urban school. A crumbling asphalt parking area, situated at a higher level than the athletic field, offered an unobstructed view of the battlefield below. After parking the car and taking off her oversized sunglasses, Ophelia, the Pareto sisters' mother, scanned the field with binoculars. Insulated from dust, noise, and other irritants, Ophelia would remain in her car during the duration of the contest. As the sisters and Ellie, their former dog, started down the hill, Charlie looked back to see her mother tracking their descent through trained field glasses.

During this time, Ophelia worked closely with Clarke's school's coaching staff, supporting the use of sophisticated analytics and predictive modeling tools across a range of sports. She was the leading funding source for the acquisition of these analytical tools. Ophelia would later withdraw her personal and financial support for these technologies shortly before the Paretos' divorce.

With arms stiffly swinging in unison, the high-stepping peninsula team and their crisply liveried band marched in formation onto the sports field – a bare tract of earth with a few patches of grass. The peninsula champions wore their usual fluorescent green and yellow uniforms, matched with knee-high yellow socks and black cleats.

The urban conquerors, attired in a gray and dark blue striped uniform with hand-sewn numbers, huddled on the side of the field. Charlie speculated the uniforms had been passed down by older sisters or donated by a neighboring penitentiary. As drably attired musicians delivered a rendition of 50 Cent's "In Da Club," the urban players showed off hip-hop moves, backflips, and aerials. One girl pulled off a switch leap into a split. With scowls and hands on hips, the welcoming team turned to the visiting crowd, nodding their heads as if agreeing to a question that had been asked. A few of the urban athletes yelled at the visitors while making angry gestures with their hands and forearms.

The urban team fell silent as it divided ranks, allowing its alpha leader to enter the arena. With head held high, Stella Huynh trotted to her team's bench, with teammates following in her wake. Stella, whose features suggested a

Eurasian mixture, was tall and broad shouldered. Her easy gait made it appear she was gliding above the ground.

Clarke's and Stella's dazzling skills were on display throughout the contest, outclassing their teammates. Both had a knack for disguising the direction of their moves, turning their torso one way while legs took them in a different direction. After scoring the tying goal, Clarke looked up at the parking area above the field and smiled.

The game was marred by fights, rough play, name-calling, and injuries. While many factors contributed to the game's savagery, Charlie contended that Clarke's harassment of Stella, her squad's most skilled player and spiritual leader, was at the heart of the hostilities. For Clarke, her athletic doppelganger was the only obstacle to victory. Hemorrhaging players to injury and expulsion, the peninsula coach moved Clarke to goalie in a desperate last stand. She sacrificed her body to keep shots from scoring, with her face, arms, and legs were caked with dirt and blood. The sky darkened, with rolling thunder in the distance.

Not comfortable with this defensive posture, Clarke attacked players at launching points. Blistering shots struck Clarke at point-blank range. With blood flowing down her face from a forehead wound, she challenged opposing players at mid-field. An unguarded net was behind her. Rain began to fall, and spectators scurried off to find cover.

As Clarke and Stella chased a ball near the sidelines, they collided, crashing to the ground in a muddy heap. After picking herself up, Stella flung a handful of mud at Clarke's face as she struggled to get to her feet. Wiping the mud from her face, Clarke glanced at the parking lot. "I'll never let you get in the way of—"

BONUS CONTENT AT THE END OF CHAPTER

After the game, Clarke, Charlie, and Ellie slogged their way through the downpour to the parking lot, not exchanging a word. Ophelia's car's windshield wipers and headlights were turned on. She did not turn around as her muddy daughters and family dog piled into the back seat, remaining motionless as the wipers failed to clear the windshield. Before starting the car, she told Clarke that she needed to spend more time with the VR soccer simulator. Fenton's former spouse did not distinguish between second place and last place.

*   *   *

Three days after Charlie shared the soccer story, Emma met Ophelia. Emma had just left the house to retrieve her car. She navigated the entry path that cut through the topiary phalanx as Ophelia walked up the pathway toward the house, accompanied by Thelma Houston's "Don't Leave Me This Way." Pausing for introductions, Ophelia explained that she was picking up the girls for their scheduled timesharing exchange. She was mid-forties with dark shoulder-length straight hair, sporting her trademark inky lenses.

Ophelia sighed, surveying the topiaried menagerie and the grounds beyond. "Is dees not agree-able? Tempting, no?" Adjusting her sunglasses, she said, "So, you are help-ing Fen-toon and Kath-reen with ze child-reen?"

"That's right. Just driving the girls around and watching them outside the house."

"De-at is good. Fen-toon gives too much free-doom."

Moving her upturned right hand back and forth, as if dealing cards from a deck, she said, "He does not understand what is-es at stake." After a pause, she asked, "May I offer advice?

"Of course."

"Do not be taken in by he-em. He-es not the best way. He sacrifices... to reach goals. Be careful. He-es an angry and broken ma-an."

"Must be going. Need to pick up girls. Charlie has art lees-son in less than an hour. Good luck, E-emma."

The two parted ways before Emma could ask Ophelia to ask about her employer's "way." And Ophelia did not reveal Fenton's goals or what he was willing to sacrifice to achieve them.

A short while later, Charlie met with her art teacher. Ophelia had arranged to have an unemployed art teacher give private instruction to Charlie during the sisters' scheduled visits to her home. Over the preceding months, Charlie sculpted, smeared, rendered, sketched, brushed, dabbed, and spattered. In colorful oils, she completed fifteen portraits of her aunt, reflecting her complicated and contradictory feelings toward her cat-eyed protector and tormentor. Her swirling and disorderly brushstrokes, reminiscent of de Kooning's abstract figural technique, alternated between light touches of admiration and heavier dashes of frustration.

In these seventeen months, Charlie had not produced a creation (including any of the fifteen works from her "*Zia Serie*") she deemed worthy of her mother's evaluation. Undaunted, Charlie privately experimented with computer-generated art techniques. She also studied the commercial intricacies of the art world.

*   *   *

Shortly after Fenton's consultation with Laura Marcum, Emma and the girls met in Charlie's *bottega* to plot strategy. The private investigator had suggested an adult-led investigation might alert Laura's friends and family that they were under suspicion, create clue-spoiling delays, and possibly tip-off the thief. But the girls needed a pretext for three young women, ages eleven to twenty-one, occupying the Marcum household. The subterfuge would not only need to satisfy family members and other visitors but also give the young investigators unrestricted access to all areas of the home.

Charlie supplied an answer: SIPS–*Solutions for Indoor Plant Survival*. Her plan called for the sleuths to pose as a team of budding entrepreneurs testing in-home technology solutions to promote the health of indoor plants. They only needed a few spray bottles, LED light spikes, and phones loaded with an app predicting how much sunlight a household location receives, to pull off their deception.

With a deep confident voice, Charlie said, "Our presence in any room, apart from a windowless basement, can be rationalized as testing for appropriate levels of light." She argued that the team's activities, even if cryptic and improbable, would be incontestable.

Clarke took a deep breath.

"What?" Charlie asked.

"That was me making a weary sigh. It's a ridiculous plan. But I'm going along with it because I want to see what happens."

"Very well, then," Charlie said. "Let's regroup at three o'clock on Monday in *Madonna dell'Archetto*, next to the stairs. We'll then pay Ms. Marcum a visit."

Not bothering to conduct any reconnaissance, the group counted on Laura's household having at least one indoor plant to receive their assistance.

* * *

On Monday afternoon, Clarke and Emma met at the appointed location near the Paretos' grand Sicilian Baroque staircase. Fifteen minutes after the agreed-upon meeting time, Charlie made her dramatic entrance, slowly descending from one of the upper flights of the imperial staircase.

Enveloped in a bulky bright yellow hazmat protection suit, Charlie had difficulty navigating the stairs. Her head was encased in a plastic dome receiving filtered air through a built-in respirator. Tucked under her arm was a metal probe—looking like a straightened clothes hanger—and a plastic grasping claw.

Clarke shook her head. "What the—"

After Charlie reached the bottom of the stairs, Emma asked her how the last-minute flourishes added credibility to the proposed Marcum scheme or helped the team maintain a low profile demanded by the delicate circumstances.

In a muffled voice, Charlie said, "Hold on. I can barely hear you."

Removing her suit's domed head gear, she said, "If we encounter dangerous organic materials, this suit will be indispensable." She held up the claw. "This is for handling hazardous materials. Certain mold spores are dangerous. If there are visitors, I'll unveil our suite of bespoke mold remediation solutions, offered at competitive introductory price points. Visitors will want to consider these services to safeguard their own homes. By the way, Clarke, there's another suit down here for you."

As Charlie put the dome back on her head, Clarke said, "*You* don't have a background in… spores. We're not offering any 'remediation services,' unless you and your minions−"

Before Clarke could finish, Emma chimed in, "We're running late. Let's just see how it goes. By the way, what's that above the door?" Emma pointed to an inscription, carved in stone, above the interior side of the entryway door. Snake and lizard designs were etched into the cast stone surround.

"Oh, it's Latin," Clarke explained. "*Intrabit in mundo dubium* means 'Enter the doubtful world.' Dad says it's a reminder that when we leave the house, not to expect to get the benefit of the doubt." With a wry smile, she said, "When Auntie's here, we need something similar on the other side of the door."

*   *   *

Laura Marcum, attired in a flowing green and yellow tie-dyed kaftan, gave her visitors a doubtful look as she greeted them in her foyer. After Charlie explained that her protective suit and the group's equipment were intended to prevent visiting family members and friends from discovering the true purpose of their appointment, Laura shared that she did not expect the arrival of a handyman for at least an hour. The sleuths would have time to freely investigate the premises without testing their cover story.

After leading the visitors to her solarium, Laura left them to analyze her collection of three indoor plants.

"Just a ficus tree and two cactus plants." Charlie's voice was almost inaudible.

The ficus tree stood over six feet and the spiny barrel cactus specimens were two feet in diameter. The three plants, anchored in heavy pots, were thriving.

"I haven't seen any mold, so I won't activate my suit's respirator. But we'll need to maintain our personas in case there are unexpected visitors." There were no potential buyers of her remediation services in sight.

Ignoring Emma's advice, Charlie insisted on moving the plant trio into whatever room they were investigating.

"I can't lift this any higher," Clarke complained, gasping for breath. "Charlie, you need to pull your weight." The three struggled to move the six-foot ficus tree up a narrow flight of stairs. Only halfway up, they had already pushed past pain tolerance levels. They set the tree down to give themselves a rest.

Emma stretched her back, "Charlie, I told you that we didn't need to do this."

Charlie took the dome off her head. Her hair clung to her face, which was covered with perspiration. She was pale and did not look well. "I don't think I'm getting enough air in the suit... and it's really hot."

Clarke frowned. "It's your fault. You wanted to wear the suit. And you keep hitting the walls with the plants. Watch where you're going."

"I can't help it," Charlie whined. "The shell keeps fogging up."

Shaking her head, Clarke said, "Why don't you just take the suit off? Besides, it's really annoying. Every time you move your suit makes loud scrunching noises."

"That's not an option. I just have pajamas underneath."

Clarke chose not to comment, evidently agreeing that exposing Charlie's undergarments would further strain the credibility of their operation.

Reaching the top of the stairs, the group rested a few minutes before carrying the tree into Laura's bedroom. She was waiting for the investigative team there. Rather than asking about the resettlement of her plants, Laura pointed to her safe, located in a well-lit walk-in closet adjoining the bedroom. After positioning the tree at its first test location, a few feet from the closet door, the girls began their investigation. The safe occupied the center shelf of her closet, straddled by smaller shelves and rows of drawers. The safe had been left open for inspection. A stack of papers was inside.

Folding her arms, Laura said, "Only I know the combination of the lock. There's also a key that can open the safe."

Clarke slowly turned the combination dial as she studied the mechanism. "No sign of tampering. The wheel pack and drive cam look okay."

Charlie moved behind her sister. "Did you examine the drive pin?"

"Hold on. I haven't gotten to that yet. Mm, seems okay." Clarke straightened up. "Mind if we look around, Ms. Marcum?"

"Not at all."

Clarke inspected the area around the safe and opened a few drawers. Reaching into one of the drawers, Clarke withdrew a key. "Is this the key to the safe?"

Laura confirmed that it was.

Using her deep voice, Charlie interjected, "The security of this arrangement seems to be compromised by the key being placed in close proximity to the safe."

Shaking her head, Laura said, "No one else knew I put it there."

Clarke reached behind the safe and pulled it toward her.

"Check this out! I moved the safe! See, I moved it a couple inches." Clarke turned to Laura. "Should've been bolted to the shelf. Somebody messed up."

"I suppose so. I didn't know about this."

Clarke said, "But even if the safe had been bolted down, the shelf could've been pulled out. Maybe the thief found the key, unlocked the safe and returned the key." Clarke scratched her neck. "No other things... incidents in your house?"

"Well, no." The homeowner looked at her ceiling.

"You're sure? Something out of place? A noise? A smell? Could be a dinky thing."

"Oh, there was *one* thing... I found something by the stairs. Hold on. I'll get it." After she returned, she handed Clarke an "Inter-Department Delivery" pouch.

Clarke turned over the large envelope. "You've never seen this before?"

"Right. And there was nothing inside."

Clarke checked the pouch. "Yep, empty. Didn't schools use these once upon a time? Speaking of papers, did you go through the papers in your safe?"

"Of course. All the important papers are still there."

"Would you mind checking again? Just a random thought."

Laura pulled the papers from her safe. "Strange. Didn't notice this before." She picked up a blank envelope that lay on the top of papers. She opened the envelope, pulled out a sheet of paper and handed it to Clarke. "There's a QR code on this."

Clarke scratched her head. "You've never seen this before?"

Laura shook her head. "Never."

"Huh. Let's see what it opens."

Laura waived her arms. "Wait! You need to give this to a police officer right now!"

"Uh, what? Why?" Clarke asked.

"I... I just know. The police should scan the code." Laura rubbed her forehead.

"I think it'll be okay." Using her phone, Clarke scanned the QR code. A banner titled "You're Served" popped up. "Looks like a restaurant menu," Clarke said with a smile. When she tapped on the banner, the link disappeared. "The site's no longer working." Clarke handed the paper back to Laura. "Guess this was nothing."

The group entered Laura's Moroccan-inspired bedroom, colonized by more than thirty sequined and fringed throw and floor pillows of various Kilim and Fez designs. Colorful suzanis hung from the walls. Incense and cannabis aromas permeated the room.

With a deep sigh, Laura said, "Guess I should've hid the key. But I always keep the windows and doors locked. It's really hard to keep up with everything." With a trembling voice, she continued, "The outdoor lights are always going out. The appliances are conking out. I'm at war with these weird beetles." Laura pointed to a large can of lemon-scented ant and roach spray on her dresser. "And you're telling me somebody made a mistake installing the safe. It's just me here." Laura wiped away a tear.

Charlie nodded sympathetically. "I'm sorry to hear you've been caught shorthanded, Ms. Marcum. Alas, I'm no stranger to such difficulties. There have been occasions when I've also suffered hardships arising from understaffed endeavors."

Laura gave Charlie a puzzled look.

The girls checked all possible entry points to the room, including Charlie's careful inspection of areas behind the suzani wall hangings. These areas did not reveal any recent plasterwork.

With Charlie sending her wire probe into the soil around the ficus trunk, Laura inventoried the purloined items, which by her memory, included two brooches, six rings, three necklaces, eight pairs of earrings, two pendants, and six bracelets. She was uncertain when the theft occurred, admitting that the articles could have been stolen weeks before.

Wrapping up their investigation, the four moved to the homeowner's kitchen. They were joined by the ficus and the two cactus plants. As Clarke spritzed one of the cactus specimens, Charlie asked Laura about recent visitors to the home. Their communication was encumbered by the impermeable plastic shell encasing the young sleuth's head.

After accounting for family members and others who had visited the home, the interview shifted to Laura's reflections. "I just have this feeling I'll see my jewelry again and that everything will turn out okay. I've been getting more sleep and feeling more emotionally centered. I've also cut down on alcohol. But I've been having strange dreams, some about my jewelry."

While rubbing her forearm, showing indications of an allergic reaction to cactus spine punctures, Clarke asked, "Ms. Marcum, have you been able to sleep through the dog barking in the middle of the night?"

"Not at first, but now I've been getting better sleep by using relaxation techniques and earplugs."

Spotting one of her school's beehive cookie jars on the kitchen counter, Charlie said, "Ms. Marcum, thank you for your generous patronage of my school. Are you enjoying the cookies?"

"Honestly, they're a little stale. But Ben, my handyman, doesn't seem to mind. He's been helping himself to the cookies. Who won the savings bond grand prize?"

"The bond—" Before Charlie had a chance to volunteer information about the prize-winning recipient or touch on a related investigation initiated by her school, the smiling handyman stepped into the kitchen. Mid-fifties with a broad clean-shaven face, Ben was thick around the middle, perhaps owing, in part, to an undiscerning taste in cookies. He sported faint tattoos on the side of his neck. The handyman's unannounced entry suggested a friendly relationship with the homeowner.

The young investigators had noted numerous areas of Laura's home needing minor repair. There was an open question of why this tradesman, presumably making recurring visits to the home, had not supplied the much-needed maintenance.

Ben accepted the premise of the girls' visit, not questioning the placement of the household plants in the kitchen, Charlie's preparation for biohazard threats, or Clarke's continuous irrigation of one of the cactus plants.

*   *   *

Returning home, the girls made a dismaying discovery. All personal files stored on their home computers, tablets and phones—including all files backed-up on the cloud—had been encrypted. The girls were no longer able to access any of their social media accounts, photos, school accounts, personal contacts, emails, music, or investigative notes.

——— Bonus Content: A Stormy Game ———

The peninsula league's rosters, including Clarke's talented team, were comprised of a few recreational players. Some of these carefree teammates hailed from the walled-and-hedges part of town, with the sport representing the least traumatic athletic choice—a default option to be enjoyed in the merry and frolicsome company of high-fiving friends. At the other end of the spectrum, Clarke and a few other combatants saw sports fields as dark arenas to unleash primal aggression and claim dominion over weaker adversaries. Where their bouncy teammates chose pizzas, these warriors opted for circular saw blades.

Charlie supported Clarke's team on weekends and after school, "helping with equipment maintenance." Charlie's support role gave her an opportunity to observe coaches and players at close range, including the peninsula coaching staff's preparation for upcoming opponents. Charlie's sharpened ears detected the coaches quietly scouting Stella's team at the mid-point of their own season, evidence that the coaches had privately concluded that the teams would meet at the regional finals. These scouting reports not only assessed a team's schematic approach but dissected player tendencies.

Minutes into the game, a swirling wind kicked up clouds of dust.

The urban team not only enjoyed an athletic advantage over the visiting team but was more aggressive, using shoulders and forearms. Playing forward, Stella's mesmerizing skills were on display, dribbling the ball around Clarke's proud teammates like roadside cones. She threw in a few head fakes for good measure. Stella taunted one peninsula player after another, calling the peninsula players "Karen." Clarke's team did not have a "Karen" on their roster.

In the swirling dust storm, Stella scored the first goal of the game.

To celebrate the goal, two urban players hoisted a third teammate to shoulder level so that the elevated girl's stiff body formed a limbo bar. To Usher's "Yeah!" Stella shook her torso and bent backwards as she ducked under the teammate, enacting a limbo dance.

After Stella took down one of Clarke's teammates using a hard-sliding tackle, pent-up frustrations boiled over. The players' benches emptied, and the teams collided in the middle of the field. Opposing players shoved each other, traded profanities, and threw punches. In the middle of the melee, Clarke and Stella exchanged heated perspectives, with Clarke reinforcing her points by repeatedly jabbing Stella's sternum with her forefinger. Stella grabbed Clarke's finger and gave it a sharp twist. Officials separated the teams as the urban band played The Black Eyed Peas' "Shut Up." This marked the first of eight stoppages of play. Six yellow warning cards and five red expulsion cards were dispensed during these breaks. Local law enforcement was called to restrain agitated parents, with one arrest recorded in the local newspaper police blotter. This contest was, by any measure, the most violent middle school soccer match in district history.

Toward the end of the first half, with the urban team holding a 4–0 advantage, the peninsula coaches unleashed their analytically-driven strategy to shut down Stella. Data showed that once Stella passed the mid-field line, with 68 percent certainty, she would move to her left to position a cross to another forward or to continue up the field. The analysis further showed that when Stella was met by a defender, there was an 87 percent probability she would turn counterclockwise, momentarily turning her back to her opponent's goal. The analytics suggested that a second defender could slip in from Stella's blind side and make a play on the ball.

Clarke was quickly briefed during a time-out and assigned to Stella.

After joining a defensive teammate who had already engaged Stella, Clarke repeatedly and ferociously separated the ball from Stella using hard sliding tackles or stripping the ball as Stella made her 87 percent predictable counterclockwise rotations. Clarke's team evened the score at four with ten minutes left in the game: four goals scored by the inner-city kids, four goals tallied by computer science.

Eventually, the law of averages prevailed. Slipping behind the overextended goalie, Stella received a teammate's pass and put her fourth and winning goal into the net.

After the final whistle sounded, Ellie, the Paretos' Golden Doodle and Lucy's venerable antecedent, sprinted onto the field in search of Clarke. Ellie zig-zagged through the throng of rejoicing players and Clarke's fallen teammates, either writhing in soggy heaps of despondency or coiled in motionless masses of distress. Ellie found Clarke as she staggered to the sidelines. After giving her a few licks here and there, both quit the field of battle.

Stella climbed to the top of a ladder that her team erected in the middle of the muddy field. Bathed in steady rain, Stella held up the championship trophy in one hand while pumping her fist with the other. The victorious team serenaded her with an uncensored version of Outkast's "The Way You Move."

Quiet Moves

Fenton scratched his beard. "Girls, this reminds me of the 'Cryptolocker' cyberattack in '14. Files were held for ransom. Victims who paid three hundred dollars in bitcoin were given access to an encryption key. Those who didn't, lost their data forever."

Clarke's face reddened. "So, our files are being held for ransom?

"Looks like it. I expect you'll receive a ransom demand very soon."

Charlie asked, "Do you think this had something to do with the QR code Clarke scanned at Ms. Marcum's house?"

"Likely. The site you opened probably attacked your phone."

Charlie frowned. "Ms. Marcum told us that the police should scan the code."

"She said that?"

"She insisted," Clarke said. "Guess I should've listened to her. But no problem. Right, Dad? You'll just trace the QR code to the site and catch the crooks. Don't you do this sort of thing all the time? And when you find them, I'll grab them by their—"

Fenton responded before his daughter could describe the criminal's punishment. "This may have been a single-use QR code. If so, once this QR code was used, the code would disable itself. This will make it almost impossible to trace. Since all your files were encrypted, this looks like a well-designed hack."

"But why's *my* phone affected?" Charlie asked.

Fenton shrugged. "Hard to say. The attack program probably found a connection in a device you both use. ESTHER's Aegis program probably prevented more damage."

"What do we do now?" Clarke asked.

"I'll send someone to pick up the QR code from Laura. You should replace all your devices and set up new passwords. Beyond that, I'm afraid we'll just have to wait until the hacker sends their demands." Fenton rubbed the back of his neck. "It's strange that this thing was in Laura's safe. I wonder if it was kept there for safekeeping. Or maybe it was meant to be found. The QR code link could've been a tripwire, alerting someone—somewhere—that Laura was going through her papers."

*   *   *

Later in the week, the girls visited Jill Masterson and her two dogs, Scrubbles and Ribsy. Pausing in her entryway, Charlie asked Jill about her dogs' nighttime barking.

"Still barking up a storm. And they're probably even *more* stressed now they've lost their walker, who can't afford to live here now. The Bay Area is *so* expensive." Jill sighed. "If it's not one thing, it's another. I'm now taking an all-natural sleep aid to help with the barking." Looking at Charlie, she asked, "No Lucy today?"

"I decided Lucy should stay at home. Her schedule this past week was quite taxing. Overstimulation can be a problem in dogs, leading to a buildup of cortisol, a dangerous stress hormone. I'm having her recuperate the next few days."

The elderly neighbor beckoned the girls to follow her. "I think you'll enjoy *immersing* yourselves in my humble South American-influenced *la residencia*."

Jill welcomed a pageant of artwork to the public areas of her home. Much like temporary exhibitions at a museum, displays were rotated every six to twelve months. Furniture, artwork, floor coverings, wall paint, and even Jill's vocabulary made transformations to promote each new theme. Past decorative motifs included Asian Eclectic, Scandinavian Minimalistic, African Tribal, and Greek Revival.

As the girls followed Jill through various display alcoves, Charlie asked questions about how Jill acquired her artwork, suggesting more than casual interest or mere gestures of civility. She was particularly interested in Jill's views on the direction of market prices in the art world.

The centerpiece of Jill's recently installed Indochristian art collection was an oil portrait of a missionizing nun, crowned in a wreath of colorful flowers. Half the ascetic subject's face was missing where a piece of paint chipped off. In one hand, she held an elongated wood crucifix. In the other, she grasped a silver scepter with a flame-shaped finial. The proportions of the hands were wrong and mismatched.

Jill turned to Charlie. "I see this piece has caught your eye. Since you've been asking me about my artwork, a question for you. What can you tell us about this portrait? If you don't have much to go on, just give your general impressions."

Charlie stepped back to give the painting some consideration.

Smirking, Clarke said, "Cue the minstrel music."

Charlie frowned. "Well, ah, I'm not familiar with this particular work."

"Please, Charlie. Share your thoughts."

"Well, the Christian subject matter and the informal style point to a blend of European and South American artistic traditions. I'd surmise it's a mid-seventeenth century original, judging by the darkened vermillion pigment and brushstroke patterns."

"*¡Increíble!* That's very impressive, Charlie. As far as I know, everything you've said is accurate. Is there anything else you can tell us about the portrait?"

Charlie shifted her weight from side-to-side.

Licking her lips, she said, "Mrs. Masterson, you're already familiar with the piece. You don't need... my perspectives." She avoided eye contact with the elderly neighbor.

"Go ahead, Charlie. What else can you tell us about the piece?"

The young cognoscente wiped perspiration from her forehead.

"Well... there was an artistic tradition in Peru that used native flora in these types of pieces... creating their works anonymously." Charlie moved closer to the painting, checking for an artist signature. "There was a group of Spanish artists in Cusco, Peru that founded a school to teach indigenous and mestizo groups to paint in European styles, such as found... in your painting." Charlie was losing her voice. "These artists were sent to Cusco to aid in the conversion of the Inca people to Catholicism. I'd say your piece... is an early work produced by the Cusco School." Charlie's voice was almost inaudible. "Important works... in this subcategory... are housed... in the Museo de Arte de Lima, Cusco Cathedral and..." Charlie did not finish. She had lost her voice.

Jill's mouth hung open. Taking a deep breath, Jill said, "Charlie, that was amazing! You remind me so much of your father."

Clarke yawned loudly. "Now that you've lost your voice, Chuck, we won't learn how you picked up these little nuggets. What a shame. But I'm guessing you and your minions are cooking up another flimsy scheme. Regardless, maybe your research will pay off one day. If you ever make it on *Jeopardy!*—who knows—'Roman Catholic Artistic Traditions of South America' could be a category."

Charlie had a history of losing her voice when receiving attention outside the Pareto home. This condition was transient, generally resolving itself a few minutes after relocation to a less stress-inducing setting. Ms. Stiglitz reported that Charlie used a megaphone during the demonstration. On that occasion, there had been no problems with her voice.

The group moved outside, allowing the girls to inspect Jill's dogs and their play area. Charlie walked around the dogs, pausing to record observations on her computer tablet. Clarke settled onto a patio chair and closed her eyes.

In a confident clinical tone, Charlie reported her findings. Her unreliable voice had returned. "We've conducted a preliminary examination of your dogs and they appear to be in excellent physical condition. Nevertheless, we advise that the animals be examined by a local veterinarian to provide a confirmatory opinion. We also noticed you have azaleas and a sago palm in your backyard. These can be toxic to dogs. We suggest dog-friendly alternatives such as daisies, hibiscus, and snapdragons."

Jill shrugged. "I've been thinking about relandscaping anyway."

Charlie pursed her lips. "Let's schedule an outdoor overnight stay with the dogs. Although the dogs' play area is otherwise in good order, there's evidence of mole activity. You may want to consult a licensed pest control professional. We recommend Victor ultrasonic spikes as a nontoxic solution. But be advised: Moles are highly intelligent and can find ways to defeat conventional remedies—particularly in this area. After all, this is a university town."

Clarke opened her eyes. "Who's we?"

As the girls reentered *la residencia*, Charlie turned to Jill. "Do you have any friends or neighbors needing any type of complimentary assistance?" Charlie did not mention that she was short community service hours.

Jill adjusted her visor. "One of my friends in the neighborhood, Roberta, might need—how should I say—a little household decluttering. I'll get back to you after I talk with her. You'll enjoy her. *And* she knows *everything* there's to know about dogs! *Absolutely* everything. Maybe she can help you with the dog barking investigation!"

"Sounds like she could be a valuable asset."

"Roberta is a descendent of an Ohlone tribe. I've been reading all about the Ohlone. Before you go, I've something to share with you. Might be helpful background if you visit Roberta. Really fascinating..."

Finding a computer tablet on her coffee table, Jill read:

c. 1750 CE: The height of Ohlone prosperity and influence. The Ohlone, a group of Native American tribes populating the northern California coastal area, was composed of approximately 40,000 members dispersed over a land area equivalent to the state of New Jersey. Adept in hunting and fishing, the Ohlone inhabited thirty-three villages and collectively spoke six distinct languages. They lived in a complex mystical world, populated by spirits residing in all living and nonliving things. Shamans interpreted the undertakings of these invisible animistic forces. Through dreams, the spirits informed the most important edifices of their civic sphere, including the manner of economic exchanges, social interactions, leader selection and daily decisions.

Charlie stood motionless next to the homeowner's elbow. Clarke sat down on the sofa, leaned back and closed her eyes. Neither asked the esthete if a Native American decorative motif was being considered for her home. Jill continued:

The shamans assured their fellow citizens that if they placed their faith in the sacred rituals and dream messages, the spirits would help guide the Ohlone to a glorious future. Dreams informed the shamans that the Spanish explorers, who visited their shores from 1602 to 1769, were delivered by their mule god to enrich their culture. The explorers were succeeded by the Franciscans in 1770. The Ohlone would learn that the Spanish had their own plan: the Franciscans would soon establish their own version of an 'idyllic religious community' for the Ohlone.

Now briefed on the early Ohlone history—including the allusion to the tragic turn it would take during the ruinous missionizing era—the girls departed Jill's house.

* * *

Katherine blocked the front door, with hands on hips. "You girls cannot leave this house! You both look like you've just rolled out of bed. Pointing at Clarke's footwear, she asked, "What are *those*, bed slippers?"

There was a fine line between the girls' daytime loungewear and pajamas.

Clarke threw up her arms. "Auntie, everybody dresses like this!" Pointing at her footwear, Clarke said, "These aren't slippers. See, they have rubber soles. This is the way people dress now. At least younger people. I doubt you could–"

"Oh really? Even if Gen Z means zzz, you'll both adjust your clothes and, Clarke, your attitude."

Although Katherine took little notice of the girls' clothing choices within the home, she ruled on the appropriateness of the girls' public attire, insisting on her own conservative fashion revisions before allowing them to leave the house. Her verdicts involving *la bella figura*, the proper decorum of dress, were immediate and final. She stocked the girls' wardrobe from her Veronica Lodge collection, consisting of dark tones, plaid skirts, and solid long-sleeve tops with crisp white collars. She gave extra credit for a pearl necklace, brooch pin, or some other stylish accessory.

In their upgraded attire, the girls expanded the scope of their dog barking investigation, interviewing twenty-three households impacted by the barking. Over the week, they visited sixty-three families. Residents were also asked to complete a questionnaire on the Paretos' website. To encourage participation, those who completed the questionnaire were entered into a drawing for a pet grooming, dog treats, and pet store gift cards.

Winners could roll over their prize to be eligible for a yet-to-be-disclosed grand prize. Their research found:

- The barking problems started five to six weeks ago.
- Barking occurred between 2:00 a.m. to 3:00 a.m., three times per week.
- Barking episodes lasted fifteen to twenty minutes.
- Both indoor and outdoor dogs were affected.
- The few dogs that had long-standing habits of night barking continued to bark in the most recent four to six-week period.
- Owners concluded that other dogs were causing their dogs to bark.

However, there was no discernible pattern explaining why some dogs started their recent nighttime barking while others had not.

* * *

The girls convened in *San Lorenzo Fuori le Mura*, the Paretos' technology center, to test statistical associations between surveyed "independent variables" and the newly acquired nighttime barking "dependent variable."

BONUS CONTENT AT THE END OF CHAPTER

The girls squabbled about study method design, selection of statistical tests, nonlinear relationships, and categorization of dependent and independent variables. After Clarke routed her sister on a technical matter, Charlie stormed out of their work area. A few minutes later, she returned, resuming her efforts without a word.

"Where were you, Chuck? Did you suddenly remember that you needed to redeem your SPACs or trade one of your meme stocks?"

Emma entered the room, with a pitcher of lemonade and glasses balanced on a tray. "I'm told this is safe to drink now." Katherine's lemonade was staggeringly tart. Over time, the family had informally agreed that her concentrated mixture should only be served after one o'clock.

Charlie sat in front of four monitors, arranged on two levels for ease of viewing. She cut and pasted blocks of numbers. Clarke turned her swivel chair away from her workstation, folded her arms, and closed her eyes.

Emma asked, "Clarke, where did you learn about the tests and software?"

Clarke yawned and stretched her arms over her head. "What? Oh! Pops emailed the stats pack awhile back. He also forwards links to college lectures on stats, AI and other stuff that he thinks will be handy when we help with cases."

Charlie stared at her screen. She muttered, "VLOOKUP is a godsend."

"What if you have a question about something he shares with you?"

Clarke rotated her torso back and forth. "He keeps office hours on Thursdays from 7:20 p.m. and 8:50 p.m. when he's not traveling. His content is legit."

"I concur," Charlie said, emerging from her shell. "Dad's resources have been invaluable." She kept her eyes on one of the monitors, cascading lines of code. "I'm currently wading through a lecture series on differential equations. Of course, the utility of these methods is axiomatic. After all, the essence of calculus lies in its applicability."

Clarke shook her head. "Chuck, it should be axiomatic that there's no utility in sharing your calculus commentary with us, or anyone else I can think of."

* * *

That night, Emma was woken up by knocks on her door.

"Yes, who is it?"

"It's us," Clarke said. "Put on a robe and slippers, quick. Follow us to Santa Maria del Popolo." From her orientation, Emma had learned that Santa Maria del Popolo was one of the villa's many terraces.

Emma slipped on a robe and trudged behind the girls as they made their way across the compound.

Clarke said, "Cosmo is starting to serenade her again. Good thing I woke up in time. He sets up a ladder outside the wall that's closest to her room. He must park on that side. Auntie and backstreet boy won't see us on the veranda."

Emma yawned. "Who's Cosmo?"

"We found out he's a fifty-ish bachelor," Clarke said. "But we don't know anything more about him. Last month, he sang an a cappella version of Styx's 'Lady' to Auntie in the rain. Fleekin' fairy tale."

The group tiptoed onto the dark chianche stone patio. Cosmo was singing. Katherine was standing above them on a balcony outside her room. Emma identified the song for the girls: Babyface's "It's No Crime." Cosmo's tenor voice was pitch-perfect and soulful. In song, Cosmo declared that if love was a crime, he was prepared to be incarcerated.

Katherine chuckled a few times during the performance.

After Cosmo finished, Katherine clapped, then called out, "Very impressive, Cosmo. Now you need to get down from that ladder. Be careful, don't hurt yourself. It's late... get on home now."

Without alerting Katherine of their presence, the three tiptoed back into the house.

—— Bonus Content: Test Variables ——

Questionnaire responses were loaded into a linear regression program to test the statistical associations between the following surveyed independent variables and acquisition of nighttime barking:

- Size of dog (Small/Medium/Large)
- Location of dog at night (Inside/Outside)
- Color of dog (Light/Medium/Dark)
- Age of dog (Young/Adult/Senior Citizen)
- Length of fur/hair of dog (Short/Medium/Long)
- History of nighttime barking (Yes/No)
- Prong collar restraint to curb pulling (Yes/No)
- Dog socialization or any formal training (Yes/No)
- Regular professional grooming (Yes/No)
- Good citizen or emotional support certification (Yes/No)
- Special commendations (Yes/No)
- Non-professional dog walking at least once/week (Yes/No)
- Professional dog walking at least once/week (Yes/No)

- Food eaten in most meals (Dry/Wet/Mixed)
- Changes in appetite in last six weeks (Yes/No)
- Health issue(s) requiring vet care in past six months (Yes/No)
- Disabilities or infirmaries (Yes/No)
- Changes in other (non-dog) household pet routines/ behaviors (Yes/No)
- Multi-dog household (Yes/No)

Deployed

"We've been at this for over an hour," Fenton said. "Quite obviously, my daughters have been framed."

Fenton, his daughters, Katherine, four family lawyers, and six FBI agents sat at a large round table that had been set up in *Santa Maria della Concezione*. The curtains had been drawn, with a 1920s multi-tier crystal chandelier providing the only light.

The mid-thirties FBI lead investigator, dressed in a smart black pantsuit, pushed herself away from the table. "While I'd like to believe this, the evidence points in another direction." She had a strong nasal tone. "Shall I recap? We traced the attack to your daughters' phones, using their IP addresses subpoenaed from their ISP. Just like the 'Melissa' virus, this virus hijacked Microsoft Outlook. But this attack targeted only federal offices, with a message from a 'Rex Odus.' Odus' message demands an increase in pay and benefits for local, state, and federal law enforcement and their staff. The virus is spreading by tempting recipients to open a virus-laden attachment called 'Sign This Petition.' We take this very seriously. *Your* team contends that the girls did not originate this attack, but—let me get this straight—that when they were investigating the loss of a neighbors' jewelry, the girls opened a QR code. This code not only launched the attack but encrypted all their devices. This QR code no longer functions. *Quite* convenient, I'd say. And their phone records and other files—which could clear them of all charges—have been encrypted. Also, *quite* convenient. No one has the encryption key.

Again, *amazingly* convenient. Do you understand how improbable all this sounds?"

Fenton laughed. "Don't you see what happened? The QR code was a trap to delay law enforcement's pursuit of whoever stole Laura Marcum's jewelry. The thief knew that the Melissa-style virus would quickly be traced to its origin. If a police investigator *had* launched the QR code, the virus would've been traced back to *their* phone. That's why the attack was designed to look like the work of a disgruntled law enforcement officer. The QR code was shut down and the devices encrypted so the officer wouldn't be able to use their phone records in defense. My daughters were caught in a trap meant for a member of law enforcement. Rex Odus? Is anyone familiar with Exodus?"

Charlie raised her hand.

"No, Charlie. I'm asking the *federal agents* if they see any similarities between this cyberattack and the story of Exodus in the bible."

During the pause, Fenton clenched and unclenched his jaw.

"No one went to Sunday school?" Fenton sighed. "After God parted the waters of the Red Sea, Moses leads the Israelites across the parted sea while being *followed* by the Egyptian army. Once the Israelites have safely crossed, Moses drops his staff, closing the sea and drowning the *pursuing* army. The jewelry thief's plan, from the beginning, was to pin the cyberattack on whoever investigated that safe–thwarting any pursuers."

Curtains on one side of the ballroom billowed from a gust of wind.

"And the staff that Moses drops? What's another word for a staff?" The audience did not respond. "A rod!

In law enforcement, doesn't a 'ROD' mean a Relieved of Duty order? Don't you see? Whoever is behind this is toying with us."

The lead investigator shrugged. "An interesting theory, but we're moving forward with the prosecution of your daughters within the computer delinquency framework codified at U.S.C. §§ 5031 to 5042 of Title 18, governing the criminal prosecution and adjudication of minors in federal court. While this may appear retributive, several factors tip the scale for us. One, this involves a serious matter involving federal agencies, putting this squarely within federal jurisdiction. Two, the current event, when considered within the context of your youngest daughter's 'science fair project' last year, suggests a pattern of serial cyber misconduct. Three, your oldest daughter has replaced her phone five times in the past month, apparently to conceal her IP address. Four, 'criminal trespass to create havoc'—clearly present here—is a common juvenile cyber offense. This agency has *significant* experience in prosecuting and adjudicating minors in this area. Five, juveniles are obviously not afforded several Fifth Amendment protections, including right to a trial by jury. The 'guilt' phase of the upcoming delinquency proceeding will be conducted in a bench trial. The case against your daughters can be handled efficiently and cost effectively, from a taxpayer's perspective. Six, this agency is unimpressed by this family's attempts to deflect responsibility for this incident—failing to produce one shred of evidence that would exonerate these juveniles."

Fenton shook his head. "I'm relieved this agency is sensitive to how taxpayers might look at all this."

The federal agent shifted in her chair. "Here's what happens next. A hearing will take place in ninety days. At that time, we'll consider a discretionary transfer for your oldest child. Regardless, expect the court to give no quarter to your daughters. As time is short, I suggest this family focus on the hearing, dispensing with these other— let's say—flights of fancy involving criminal conspiracies. And, by the way, this agency has been following this family's business interests for some time now. We're unimpressed."

After the meeting, Fenton and his daughters debriefed at the round conference table. Clarke stared at the chair that had been occupied by the lead FBI investigator. Charlie's head was lowered, with tears rolling off her cheeks.

Clarke crossed her arms. "At least we now know what 'You're Served' means. *We've* been served."

Fenton nodded. "Obviously, you two shouldn't be held responsible for this virus. Our legal team will do spadework, but *none* of this should distract us. The criminals want to slow us down. We're not going to give them what they want. When we bring the jewelry thief to justice, we'll get the encryption key and clear your names. There are only ninety days before the hearing. After that, our options will be... limited and unpleasant."

Wiping her eyes, Charlie asked, "What was the 'Melissa' virus?"

Fenton looked at the ceiling of the room. "About twenty years ago, there was a cyberattack targeting Outlook users. It was one of the most damaging email worms of all time—impacting dozens of businesses and the military. More than a million email accounts were hijacked by the virus. The FBI caught and prosecuted the perpetrator."

Charlie scratched her head. "Why was it called Melissa?"

"The architect of the attack claimed that he was inspired by a Florida stripper named Melissa. The vulnerabilities exploited by Melissa were thought to have been addressed decades ago. If this virus is anything like the previous one, this will be damaging to not just commercial interests but our government."

Time Trouble

"Some very noisy, high-variability data," Charlie said, peering over her sister's shoulder at the graphical output. "The shotgun data pattern really accounts for the low r-squared value." Charlie's deep and steady tone gave the impression she possessed the credentials of a seasoned academic researcher. After updating Emma on their meeting with the FBI, the sisters and Emma continued their dog barking statistical analysis in *San Lorenzo Fuori le Mura*. As instructed by their father, the girls pushed ahead with the dog barking case, ignoring as best as they could the fate that awaited them in eighty-nine days.

Emma shook her head. "You're deconstructing data from, what, a total of sixty-three households? I wouldn't be too sure about the validity of any correlations you might find. Even big data samples can have validity problems. Somebody found a strong correlation between Nicholas Cage film appearances and swimming pool deaths."

Charlie scratched her head. "Nicholas Cage?"

Clarke smiled at her sister. "No, Chuck. Nicholas Cage hasn't been in movies with dangerous underwater scenes that people try to reenact."

Statistical credibility aside, the girls' software package showed associations between:

- "Past history of nighttime barking" and recent nighttime barking;
- "Professional dog walking at least once/week" and recent nighttime barking; and

- "Multi-dog household" and recent nighttime barking.

Clarke leaned back in her chair. "The first correlation's a no-brainer. Long-standing barkers—LSBs—still bark. But the second and third correlations are sketch."

While rubbing her hands together, Charlie said, "I concur. Conclusions drawn from these low coefficient values have the foundational integrity of Tacitus' *Agricola*."

Clarke shrugged. "Okey-dokey, Chuckie... Anyhow, let's ask Auntie to look at this. She's a stats wiz. Wait... maybe we should first kick this around. We can run all this by Auntie later if we come up dry." Katherine's harshly articulated self-service policy compelled the girls to take their academic and other projects as far as possible before asking for adult assistance. Fenton also encouraged his daughters to work things out for themselves. Two years prior, Clarke retained an academic tutor. In a show of anger, Fenton overturned their worktable as he cast the tutor from the home.

Emma asked Clarke about her aunt's background in statistics.

"She jammed in finance at the big U."

Charlie added, "With a specialization in econometric models."

Clarke frowned at her sister. "No cap, Ace. And I'm sure you're itching to tell Emma how Auntie made coin."

"Very well. She developed an algorithm that identified markets offering the best potential for speculators to flip residential properties. Her model used historical transaction data to predict the degree to which sellers on average would lower their asking price and, conversely, the degree to which buyers were willing to increase their bids in the same market. The greater the market elasticity, the more likely a speculator could profit from short-term buying and selling opportunities."

"What happened to her business?" Emma asked.

"She sold her firm, along with her arbitrage model, about five years ago."

It went without saying that Katherine retired a wealthy woman.

What the girls did not know was that Katherine's professional success had come at a price. Her long-time romantic partner, a struggling entrepreneur, had difficulty coping with the attention she was receiving from the business community, media, and friends. He ended the relationship. Heartbroken, Katherine sold her business to remove the source of their problems. But her concession did not bring back her man.

Emma asked, "By the way, why does she wear a kitchen cabinet key on a chain around her neck?"

"Why don't you take this one too, Scout."

Charlie lowered her eyes. "Well, let's just say that Aunt Katherine was unimpressed I had identified a robust secondary market for her baked goods."

Smirking, Clarke said, "I think you and your little minions called your food business 'The Greater Goods.' Pathetic... *CP*."

Clarke loosened up her shoulder by practicing some tennis serve motions. "Okay, LSBs have continued to bark. Makes sense. But why would professionally walked dogs be more likely to have started barking than other dogs? Gotta be bogus. Maybe we should look to see if professionally walked dogs are more likely to fall into swimming pools."

"Hold on," Emma said. "Let me go over the math. Show me the algorithm and data." After checking the numbers, she said, "It's weird, but the second association seems to check out."

"Thanks, Emma," Charlie said. Furrowing her brow, she said, "Perhaps professionally walked dogs are distressed, *angosciato*, because they don't know where their walkers are at night. Conversely, family-walked dogs have the comfort of knowing where their family is sleeping..." Charlie's words trailed off.

"Are you anxious about where your teachers are at night?" Clarke countered.

"No, I'm generally more concerned about where they are during the day."

"Makes sense, given what I've been hearing–*Charlene*." Turning to the third association, she said, "Hmm, I don't get why multi-dog houses would be more likely to have an RB, a recent barker."

"*Ascolta*, perhaps the dogs that are part of larger dog families are, *allora*, unhappier and more likely to bark," Charlie said, mixing in more Italian vernacular.

"You might be onto something, Flash. Consider how blissfully ignorant your life could have been without the guidance of an older and much wiser sister."

Redirecting the deteriorating sibling dialogue, Emma asked, "What if a dog is more likely to bark if another household dog starts to bark?"

"Lightbulb!" Clarke announced. "I'll look at the overlap between multi-dog households and professionally walked dogs."

After a few minutes, Clarke said, "Sick! Not all multi-dog families have an RB. But all multi-dog families that *have* an RB *also* have at least one that's professionally walked. It's freaky, but the best predictor of an RB is whether a dog has been professionally walked. We should look into who's been walking these dogs."

* * *

Emma passed the kitchen on her way to meet Charlie in the Golden Vault. As she navigated *Vialedi Trestevere*, the passageway adjoining the kitchen, she paused to listen to Katherine's rendition of "Abrázame." While attending to kitchen matters, Katherine sang romantic Latin standards such as "Cuando Pienso En Ti," "La Historia De Un Amor," "Bésame Mucho," and "Quién Será." The mezzo-soprano passages mixed with kitchen clatter. On occasion, Emma lingered in the hallway listening to these recitals.

Clarke was out with friends, leaving Charlie and Emma to their post-dinner gaming in the Golden Vault. Emma spent many evenings with the girls in the vault, conferring with Clarke on social matters while playing backgammon or chess with Charlie. Charlie said little, not just a testament to her competitive focus but a corollary of an unexecuted NDA. Nevertheless, there were occasions when Charlie emerged from the cover of her psychological refuge to engage in conversation. When she did, she raised a hypothetical situation for discussion. Such a topic could often be traced to a personal concern.

Charlie and Emma played their chess game in silence. When not focused on the game, Charlie flipped through Dvoretsky's *Endgame Manual* or scanned the octagonal room. The Golden Vault, or *Volta Aurea*, was accessed through two heavy crystal doors embellished with gold and bronze leaf, grape, and sprig accents. The vault's coffered dome was supported by fifty-foot granite pillars, each with a nine-foot-high niche. The pillars framed high windows. Gold leaf bands ringed the vault, accenting a Pantheon-style glass oculus at the apex of the cupola.

Looking at the chessboard, Charlie frowned. "Regardless of the opening played, you always gain the upper hand, gradually and ineluctably choking off available squares for my pieces. What's your strategy?"

"I use my intuition to find, as they say in chess, provocative moves that create strong continuations that cannot all be defended."

"That's fascinating. You use your intuition to select your moves? I don't do that. I just calculate what happens if I play different moves."

"I've been playing chess a long time, so I have a sense of what will work and what won't. Before making a move, I calculate what happens if I play my intuitive move. If my intuitive choice has a problem, I then analyze my next intuitive choice, and so on."

"Could your technique have applications beyond chess?"

"We're talking about a game with rules. It's tricky to know how to balance intuition and calculation. But my intuition tells me you have something in mind that doesn't have anything to do with chess."

"From my research, I've learned you were once an elite chess player."

"I play many games."

"I read that when you were sixteen, you were ranked fourth in the world in the 'Girls under Age 21' division, the top American in that division, and an International Master. Why don't you play competitively any longer?"

"I needed a breather after some bad stuff in high school. Also, being known as a tournament player in

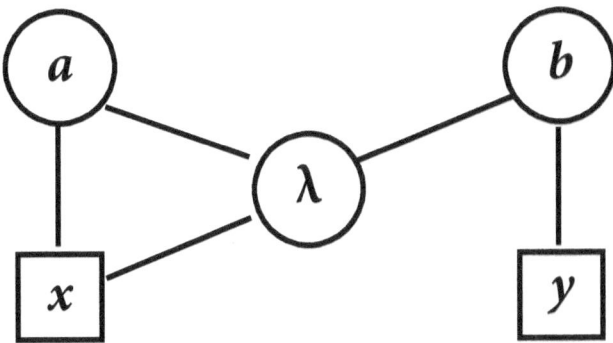

college would have—how would *you* say—precluded other lucrative pursuits."

"Would you mind elaborating on your negative experiences?"

"Okay. One example. I played a tournament in Lyon my senior year. To prep for it, I studied games that AlphaZero, the strongest self-trained AI chess program, played against another strong engine. AlphaZero places higher value on bishops controlling key squares than human players. Using what learned, I won my first four matches. One against a Grand Master. The problem was that I played too much like a computer and not enough like a human. Two Latvian opponents, both men, accused me of cheating. They said I was getting transmissions in my lip balm tube from someone with a computer. I didn't need to put up with that... that sort of thing any longer."

"Thanks for sharing that unfortunate, but captivating, account."

Emma pointed to a figure in one of the semi-circular niches.

"I notice these niches have diagrams. What do they mean?"

"They're physics and engineering diagrams. Depending on the time of year and the hour of the day, such as the March equinox, the sunlight from the oculus illuminates a certain niche or mosaic symbol on the floor."

"Interesting. And your dad designed all this?"

Charlie nodded. "The niches and lancunaria provide structural support, a bit like corrugated cardboard. They make the vault's supports and dome lightweight and more resistant to earthquakes, moisture, and temperature swings. There are also hidden relieving arches to dissipate the weight. Although the voids make the supports look weak, they actually strengthen them. I can run through the math later if you like."

The bands in the dome were accented with rows of precious gems. A version of the room might have been found in Nero's *Domus Aurea*. The highpoint of the dome resembled a giant eye.

"Charlie, can we switch subjects? I heard about your latest conference with your teacher. If you don't mind me asking, do you think Ms. Stiglitz treats you fairly?"

Charlie sighed. "Let's just say that Olivia draws her inspiration from notorious oppressors of the past who were unencumbered by pesky concepts like due process. During conferences, her multi-part questions are intended to ensnare me in any contradictions she might find. She invokes the testimony of unnamed sources, who are naturally unimpeachable. Inevitably, she metes out her judgments under the cover of implicit academic canon or pedagogic theory, alleging 'institutional directives' demand harsh judgments. But her dialectical maneuvers are just riggings dredged from her dungeon, designed to enforce compliance. Her real aim is to enlarge the frontiers of power, for reasons I cannot fathom. This thirst for power denies me the latitude to test ideas that might one day improve the life of others and make the world a better place."

"Wow. Sounds like you and your teacher haven't been on the same page."

Emma did not ask Charlie to elaborate on why this elementary school administrator would be expanding her sphere of power. And she did not explore the particulars of the sixth grader's world-improving hypotheses or how they were being tested.

After a pause, Charlie said, "To sum up, Olivia's nature could be best depicted by Gris' charcoal portrait of Germaine Raynal. The picture's heavily articulated shapes and forms suggest the steadfast conviction and calculated bearing of the subject. And the portrait's abstracted Cubist elements—the misaligned eyes, nose and mouth—arouse suspicions of contradiction and duplicity."

"I get that you don't like your teacher. But I don't understand why you're so intent on making money." Emma waved an arm over her head, drawing Charlie's attention to the ornate vault. "What else could you possibly want?"

"The most important thing in the world to me." Charlie's eyes filled with tears.

"What's that?"

"I want my parents together again—the way it was. Everyone was happier. If I could only turn back time..." Charlie wiped her eyes. "Can I share a secret?"

"I suppose so."

"I call it Operation RECLAIM. No one else knows about it. I'm giving my parents a romantic one-week private chartered Adriatic cruise next spring to get them back together. I'll recreate their honeymoon, with a few minor differences. I've raised $126,000 of the $265,000 that I need. I only have nine months to raise the rest. Fortunately, the cyber freeze didn't impact my accounts."

Emma shook her head. "Not a good idea, Charlie. You need to respect your parents' decision and accept that the marriage is over. There's nothing you can do. And I doubt you could even get your parents on the same boat."

"Once they understand what has gone into this project, it'll be difficult for them to turn it down. About 12 percent of divorced couples end up reconciling. I need to do everything I can to improve those odds. My simulation predicts that I can push the 're-pairing' probability to 32 percent. But this window of opportunity will probably close forever when my mom moves back to Armenia next summer."

"Your parents are people, not math equations you can manipulate. And you're talking about lots of money here."

"This is the going rate for a fifty-five meter fully-crewed super-yacht and the other arrangements. I've made a €70,000 nonrefundable down payment for a yacht departing from Dubrovnik. It'll cruise the coastlines of Croatia and Italy. All passengers will disembark in Rimini, one of Italy's hidden gems."

"*All* passengers? Are there other passengers?"

"I'm lining up some onboard entertainment my parents will enjoy. I'm trying to book Nicole Scherzinger, Anastacia, or Róisín Murphy."

"Even if you pull this off, which I seriously doubt, a week on the water with a little music won't get your parents back together."

"I agree. That's why one of the world's top independent mediators will also be onboard. I'm evaluating Chris

Coleman, Deborah Compton, and C.D. Veenker. They have deep expertise in mediating disputes involving tech development, corporate finances, and a range of commercial matters. Any one of them can support this type of negotiation. You see, Operation RECLAIM is my shorthand for Romance and Entertainment while Cruising Leisurely on the Adriatic *with* an Independent Mediator."

Charlie clasped her hands "And did you know that Adam Smith asserted that the presence of children in a household acts as a morally positive and restraining influence on their parents? Reuniting my parents will be best for everyone."

Emma shook her head. "Restraining influence? What a load of... You don't know what's best for your parents. We often don't know what's best for ourselves."

The two resumed their game without exchanging a word. As Charlie tested her instinctual inclinations, Emma gazed at the trees and shrubbery through the glass panes of the vault. The foliage twinkled with hundreds of lights, simulating summer fireflies.

Charlie broke the silence. "Let's say, individuals are left alone, without government oversight or regulation. Do you think those individuals will spontaneously form a social and economic structure superior to any type of centrally organized plan?"

"*Spontaneously* form a social and economic structure? Do you think that people are capable of spontaneously creating anything but chaos? And why does this interest you?"

The ensuing conversation covered classical and neoclassical economic theories, with Charlie drawing heavily from the tenets of Adam Smith. Months before, Charlie quietly induced one of the house staff, in

Katherine's absence, to make last-minute alterations to her own birthday cake. The sheet cake not only commemorated her big day, but featured a newly-added mint green icing inscription of a favorite passage from Book IV, Chapter V of Adam Smith's *The Wealth of Nations*:

> The natural effort of every individual to better his own condition is so powerful, that it is alone, without any assistance, not only capable of carrying on the society to wealth and prosperity, but of surmounting a hundred impertinent obstructions with which the folly of human laws too often encumbers its operations.

Eventually, the discussion led to Charlie's objections to her aunt's encroachment in one of her operations involving the exchange of retail gift cards for neighbors' accumulations of spare change, which her associates collected door-to-door from residents. Katherine investigated this venture. Charlie drew a comparison between her watchful aunt and an oppressive government.

Switching topics, Charlie's voice became strained. "Do you think it's possible to identify the point in which a company's market intelligence gathering activities passes from legitimate information-gathering to unlawful corporate espionage?"

"I do, Charlie. But can you give me an example?"

"Let's suppose *a person* finds out that someone else has been eavesdropping on conversations. How would *a person* determine their motives?"

"I'm guessing *this person* does not know how the other party has used the information they've acquired?"

"That's correct."

"Where did *this person* find the evidence of spying?"

"Well, let's say the venue is a central area that houses administrative and other data."

"Administrative and other data? Does this have something to do with the time you spent in your school's administration office?"

Charlie's eyes grew wider.

"Come on, Charlie. What did you find in the school's office?"

After a pause, Charlie admitted that her question was stimulated by her stay in the school's office. Since Emma was unencumbered by an NDA, there was no obstacle standing between Charlie's confession and her aunt's and father's ears. Charlie must have concluded that the burden of her secret outweighed the unpleasant consequences to come.

She confessed that this was not her first unsupervised visit to the central office. This excursion involved routine system maintenance and surveillance software upgrading. Charlie shut off the electricity to reboot a router, initiating her upgrades.

"The objective of my efforts was *purely* defensive. Maintaining unfettered access to parental contact information has been an ongoing priority. System maintenance is essential."

While conducting her routine system work, Charlie made a stunning discovery: Someone else was conducting their own surveillance operation in the central office.

Charlie brought Emma up to speed with the patience of a seasoned instructor. "A photocopier often falls outside the aegis of an organization's data security architecture, particularly early generation digital copy machines." Emma would not have to be told that Charlie's budget-challenged elementary school had an early generation copier.

Charlie cleared her throat. "Nearly every digital copier built since 2002 contains a hard drive, like the one in our personal computers, storing an image of every document copied, scanned, or emailed by the machine. A typical copier hard drive can store up to twenty thousand documents. Newer copiers run routines to periodically wipe the hard drive. But earlier machines have no such protections. These older copier disk drives retain data indefinitely."

In a wistful tone, Charlie ruminated on the golden era of copy machine infiltration, roughly spanning a ten-year period from 2002 to 2012. This gilded age had long passed. Copy machine technology had evolved, complicating the extraction of data. "I've employed a more elegant method to monitor the school's data flow. But somebody has been secretly extracting data from the copy machine, inserting a connector between the machine's hard drive and their own data storage device."

Emma asked her how she was able to discover the eavesdropping competitor.

"One of the tasks on my punch list was to remove a short run of cabling along the base of a wall behind the copy machine. I'm *finally* 100 percent wireless. Anyway, when I pulled the cable, it brushed against the back of the copy machine, dislodging the hard drive compartment panel plate, normally attached with four Phillips screws. When I peeked into the compartment, I immediately saw what was done."

"Immediately?" Emma sighed. "Why do you think the panel was loose?"

Charlie looked up at the glass oculus high above. "I surmise that the party that installed the surveillance device was interrupted, and the panel was replaced in haste. Perhaps they didn't have time to reattach the screws."

"Do you know who installed the spy device?"

The young entrepreneur paused. "I haven't advanced any theories. But to be perfectly candid, I'm shaken by this development. I wonder if my own activities have been under surveillance. I downloaded the contents of the storage device. I'll give my dad a copy of all the stored files, but they're encrypted. And someone wiped the hard drive. Unless the storage device is decrypted, we'll never know what was copied. Can I share something in confidence?"

"You're putting me in a difficult position, Charlie. But go ahead."

Charlie whispered, "I made my own copy of all the data on the storage device, which I'll try to decrypt using my APREE program. I'm conducting my own, off-the-record, inquiry into this matter."

Overloaded

Ms. Stiglitz adjusted her glasses as she sized up Charlie and Katherine. Following the school hearing denouncing Charlie's fundraising tactics, the Pareto adults sought to avoid another conference before summer recess. They had set their sights too high. This was the second disciplinary conference since the cookie sale indictment.

Once again, the aunt had run late. The conference was delayed fifteen minutes.

"Charlene, while we've appreciated your initiative in founding the art club a couple years ago—particularly with the cutting of non-essential programs here—unfortunately I've learned you've been using your club as a front to sell our students' artwork to private collectors. Two students, who were operatives in your art trafficking network, have admitted to being part of your scheme. This time you've really crossed the line."

Katherine smoothed the sleeve of her plaid tweed jacket. She quietly said, "I agree, Ms. Stiglitz. Charlie has discussed the specifics of this matter with me and her endeavor, on the surface, would appear to raise a few legal questions. Consequently, I've taken the liberty to consult our family's counsel. I'm prepared to divulge all pertinent information shared by our counsel and can give you access to our advisor."

Once again, the teacher employed her trademark Crossing-the-Rubicon prologue, with Charlie fated to suffer the painful consequences of her rule-breaking transgressions. But something was different here.

Katherine's opening statement raised the *possibility* that there could be valid questions involving her niece's conduct. This uncharacteristic acknowledgment was not an ideal starting point for Charlie's defense team. A conciliatory strategy had been selected after a careful weighing of options.

Sighing, Ms. Stiglitz said, "Katherine, I don't see we need to consult our counsel at this point. We can do that later if needed. I'm gratified your family has taken this matter seriously. But it would be more convincing if Fenton was here."

Although Fenton had failed to appear in any of the previous eleven conferences, the teacher had not yet realigned her expectations.

The teacher continued, "Rather than at least *acting* like an engaged and caring parent, he uses delegates to frustrate our attempts to hold Charlene accountable for her actions. But Mrs. Pareto is *legitimately* unable to attend today's conference due to an unavoidable conflict. Even so, she made it a priority to discuss this latest concern directly with the school." Rubbing her temples, the teacher said, "It's been said that one can find some Matisse in children's art, but I would never have *dreamed* that our students' art would actually be sold as Matisse."

Katherine brushed lint off her jacket sleeve. "My niece has briefed me on her art club's undertakings. In the interest of time, it might be best for me to cover the major points, so we can quickly clear up this unfortunate misunderstanding. Let's discuss the art club's goals and accomplishments. We can then address any specific concerns the school might have about her club."

Katherine was the consummate counterpuncher. In past conferences, she waited for the teacher to enter Charlie's offenses into evidence before unleashing her withering response. In this case, she took the initiative, already steering toward her hand-picked arguments and exculpatory strongholds. She was not waiting for the teacher to slog through her usual ponderous process.

The teacher nodded. "Alright. But as discussed before, no media coverage! I don't want anyone snooping... disrupting the school's operations." She turned to Charlie. "No leaks to the press! Nobody's constitutional rights have been violated!"

"Given that condition, let's get started." Katherine rolled her shoulders. "As you've mentioned, Charlie founded the art club two years ago. The club's original charter, reviewed and approved by this school, is two-fold. First, to cultivate creativity and artistry in your students. Second, to recognize and support students showing extraordinary artistic talent. I believe my niece's art club has met both goals. One of the club's major accomplishments was the creation of the after-school Art Clubhouse. Overseen by local teenagers, the Art Clubhouse has given many of your students an artistic outlet as they've waited for parent pick-up after school. This has been a valuable program for working parents. All parents have registered, in advance, for this after-school artistic supervision. Charlie also organized the semi-annual art showcase, exhibiting the talents of your students. You were one of the judges at a recent showcase."

"Yes, yes, but none of this involves selling our students' art." The teacher plucked a red pencil from her cup of red pencils. She tapped the pencil on the edge of her desk. Perhaps dissatisfied with the pencil's performance, she returned it to the cup.

In an even tone, Katherine said, "For now, let's set aside the issue of selling art and focus on the club's efforts to recognize students exhibiting extraordinary artistic talent. You've heard, Ms. Stiglitz, that 'one can find some Matisse in children's art.' This seems to be true. My niece has confirmed *some*, or shall we say a little, Matisse is found in virtually all children's art. But she's also ascertained the probability of finding any more than a *little* Matisse-level artistry in children's work is almost zero. It's extremely rare to find compensable value in children's artwork."

"If the probability of finding commercially valuable children's artwork is zero, you've just made a case that Charlene has been swindling buyers into thinking they have been acquiring valuable art."

"Not at all. I said that the probability of finding any more than a little Matisse-level artistry in children's artwork is *almost* zero, not actually zero. In fact, my niece has found roughly one-tenth of one percent of children's art has commercial value."

"If true, that's only one in a thousand art pieces. I doubt our students produce that many pieces of art in a year."

"From my niece's records, you're underestimating the volume of art created at your school. On average, each child produces three art pieces a week. You have 360 children in grades one through six. This means that your school produces about 1,080 compositions *per week*. There are eighteen weeks in each academic term. This means your students are producing almost twenty thousand artistic compositions each term." Katherine summarized, "So, my niece has found that, on average, your school produces twenty art creations having commercial value each term, or one-tenth of one percent of twenty thousand."

"How does Charlie... er... Charlene know twenty pieces have value?"

"I've learned that my niece retained a New York art appraiser, some time ago, who evaluates all the artwork produced at your school."

"How's this possible?" She shook her head in disbelief.

"I believe you already have part of the answer to that question. The two students you detained for questioning were using their phones to take pictures of the art in their classroom, as each Art Club Monitor agrees to do *every* day in *every* classroom that produces art in your school. The appraiser only requires a digital image to conduct a preliminary evaluation of a composition. A better high-resolution series of digital images is made of those works selected for commercialization."

"How much value does twenty pieces of art have?" The teacher shifted in her chair.

"I've learned that there's a high loss rate in children's art. Of the commercially viable creations, half of this art is lost or misplaced before a better image of the piece can be obtained. The loss rate is highest in the first through third grades."

"So then, how much value do the ten pieces have?"

"These works have values ranging from $300 to $1,800, with an average market price of $900. Your students have produced about $36,000 of art since the inception of the art club two years ago."

Not being able to contain herself, Charlie reported that the fourth-grade jellyfish art project the preceding term was a triumphant artistic and commercial success. The jellyfish project inspired a few of the school's artists to produce work echoing the organic and spontaneous characteristics of Abstract Expressionism.

Turning to Charlie, Ms. Stiglitz said, "Charlene, your little venture overlooked a couple of important things.

First, copyright laws protect creative works, including artwork produced by children. Since our students are obviously minors, you would have needed to obtain their parent's permission to sell, reproduce or otherwise use their art. Legally, when a child creates a piece of art, they also become a copyright owner of the image. Copyright lasts for *life plus seventy years!*"

The teacher extended her arms, giving Charlie a visual of this lengthy interval.

Ms. Stiglitz had done her own legal research.

"And, Charlene, there's another problem. Even with permission, any contract involving a minor's work product is voidable because minors lack the legal capacity to enter into an agreement. In simpler terms, another party would not have dealt with you if they were aware our students could arbitrarily break a contract involving their art."

After Ms. Stiglitz's barrage of legal challenges, the three sat in silence. Breaking the calm, Katherine quietly suggested, "Let's take each of those points separately. In fact, all parents *did* give the art club authorization to license the artwork produced by the students."

The teacher frowned. "I sincerely doubt that. How might that have happened?"

"You may want to review the after-school Art Clubhouse consent language the parents signed. You'll find contractual language that not only gives the clubhouse permission to provide after-school supervision but gives Charlie's club authorization to license and commercialize all artwork produced at your school. It's true that minors cannot enter into non-voidable contracts to sell goods and services. But, in this case, only the images of the artwork, not the *actual* art pieces, are licensed to a third-party distributor. The pieces are not actually sold to the distributor. The distributor has an exclusive license to place images of your students' art on coffee mugs, posters, jigsaw puzzles, pillowcases, print advertisements, and so on. Your students retain full ownership of the *original* art pieces, including all the copyright protections you've mentioned. The licensing agreement terminates the earlier of (a) the child's or legal caregiver's written request, (b) the child's eighteenth birthday or (c) the dissolution of the funded trust."

"Wait, the what? Funded trust? The children don't understand any of this!" Ms. Stiglitz expostulated. Her face was crimson with her eyes darting from side-to-side.

In a cool tone, Katherine said, "There's actually no legal obligation for the children to be even advised of the licensing agreement. That's been for the parents to decide."

Ms. Stiglitz's breathing became labored. "But the students haven't been paid for their work."

"That's true. However, there are no laws governing artist compensation involving copyrightable matter. The Clubhouse parental consent terms state that 23 percent of the net proceeds generated by each licensed art piece is placed in trust for the student, up to age eighteen. Charlie secured legal, trust, and tax advice and the necessary documents from one of your student's parents, a well-regarded trust attorney. He's expecting your call."

Katherine handed Ms. Stiglitz the attorney's business card. Reaching under her chair, Katherine lifted a bundle of papers containing trust documents and bank account statements. She handed them to the teacher.

One of Charlie's most gifted artistic contributors—the son of the well-regarded trust attorney—had amassed a sizable Art Club trust account. Puzzlingly, this young artist's advanced artistic technique and mature compositions could not be traced to any formal instruction. The student worked in the Surrealist idiom, with several abstract pieces exploring synthetic representational styles, such as found in Miró's *Head of a Catalan Peasant* series. After ruling out conventional explanations, the student's parents, with the assistance of a parapsychological researcher, were investigating the possibility of a psychically induced or telepathic agent.

Charlie was conducting a background check on this parapsychologist.

Quickly flipping through the documents, Ms. Stiglitz asked, "Why only 23 percent?"

"Charlie tells me there is significant business overhead, with 67 percent of revenues paid out in appraisal and distribution fees. Nevertheless, 23 percent is well above the customary 8 percent artist commission for licensed images."

Ms. Stiglitz did not have to ask about the remaining 10 percent.

"Charlene, this seems like a lot of trouble for $3,600," Ms. Stiglitz said with a sigh.

Speaking for her niece, Katherine added, "Charlie informs me that she franchised the art club model, including the after-school Art Clubhouse, to four other elementary schools. These art promotion franchises are now fully operational. Of course, this significantly increases the number of talented artists that will be recognized over time."

Ms. Stiglitz bit her lip. "We'll let the other schools deal with these parasitic... these affiliated... art clubs." The teacher fell into a coughing fit.

After the coughing subsided, the educator turned to Charlie. "Ahem... as in all criminal schemes, there's always some important detail that's been overlooked. We'll find that detail! For instance, if a newer student has not been enrolled in your Clubhouse *and* you've licensed their artwork, your entire scheme comes crashing down. You'll suspend all art licensing operations at this school until we finish our investigation."

Charlie's empire was the target of four other ongoing elementary school probes.

Although Charlie's fine art operations at the school were now paused, Katherine knew all too well that the majority of her niece's assets were still in play across the district, if not beyond. The school's attempts to police Charlie's diverse commercial interests were like battling a giant squid. A tentacle or two would make a brief appearance above the surface, catching someone's attention. The acting principal tried to dispatch the beast but ended up lopping off just a few regenerating appendages. There were many more probing arms deeper down, with numerous tentacled feelers attaching themselves to a defenseless host.

Damage control was exhausting work for Katherine.

From her pre-conference interviews with Charlie, Katherine learned that the art club operation was at risk when a student's art piece was licensed without a corresponding clubhouse registration. The registration form contained critical parental disclosure and release language. Her niece needed to keep track of new students. Katherine did not yet know about Charlie's administration office surveillance activities or how these clandestine efforts enabled her to keep the clubhouse registration list up to date.

Yukon gold miners run thousands of tons of dirt, gravel and rock through their sluicing plants, only to capture a few scant ounces of gold. This same basic business model was in operation here. With five schools operating full tilt, Charlie could mine at a rate of two hundred thousand pieces of appraised student creations per year. Even with one school now off-line, her enterprise was still sluicing at a rate of one hundred sixty thousand pieces per year.

* * *

Three days after the art club interrogation, Charlie stood in the middle of the soccer field with her hands on hips. She looked down at her black cleats, tapping the ground with the toe of one shoe before testing the other as if there had been a footwear malfunction. Taking a deep breath, she looked up at the gloomy late afternoon sky as she fought back tears. The score was now tied 2-2.

Emma sat between Clarke and Katherine on the school's rickety bleachers. Ophelia was somewhere in the packed stands of parents, students, and teachers. Since the divorce, Ophelia chose not to sit with the Pareto family at any of the girls' school functions or sporting events. During the girls' stays with their mother, they had heard her make a couple of angry references to their father's "betrayal." The girls speculated that their mother's detachment was a consequence of this nameless treachery.

Ms. Stiglitz, wearing an elfin yellow and black propeller beanie, paced next to the bleachers. Earlier in the day, Emma gave Katherine an overview of Charlie's administration office activities. Katherine would address the matter when Fenton returned from his travels.

Over the course of the season, and the two preceding it, Charlie recognized the shortcomings of her own play. Coaches pointed to her carrying a few extra pounds. But she loved the intricate choreography and subtle strategies of the game. Charlie's passion only repaid her with pain and humiliation.

The first fifty-eight minutes of this game encapsulated Charlie's soccer career. Playing goalie, she did not challenge the opponent's center forward's shot on goal, leading to the first score. She surrendered the tying goal by giving too much leeway to the opponent's left midfielder, who raced by her for an easy goal. For the final two minutes of regulation, Charlie moved to defensive center back. By this time, teammates were giving her a wide berth and avoiding eye contact.

With play restarting after the tying goal, the opposing team's speedy blonde forward pushed the ball to the middle of the field. Easily shedding Charlie, the forward passed the ball to an unguarded wing. The wing smoothly placed the ball—representing the winning goal—in the back of the net.

With her head hung low, Charlie joined her family on the sideline. Charlie admitted that she, and she alone, had been the source of her team's schematic breakdowns. She turned away from time to time to wipe away tears. A few of her teammates and their families looked over at the Paretos as they loudly recapped the derivation of the afternoon's debacle.

Ms. Stiglitz came over to the group but not to share her condolences. She informed the family that Charlie's absences had been undercounted by one day. Shaking her head, the acting principal broke the news that Charlie would need to repeat the sixth grade.

Pawn Storm

The exposure of her adventures in the school's administration office, and the district's verdict on her attendance record, hung over Charlie like the Sword of Damocles as she waited for her father to return from his trip. The Pareto household was uncharacteristically quiet following the soccer match. Charlie made only brief appearances at meals. She was suffering.

Katherine showed signs of fatigue and sadness. Her face was drawn with dark circles under her eyes. Her clothing choices were simple and reserved. Emma did not hear romantic Latin songs as she passed the kitchen. While the recent art club defensive stand could be considered successful, this fiercely fought campaign had come at a price.

After a few days, Charlie emerged from her refuge. The wheels of household life turned again, and the regular rhythm of the girls' activities resumed. Charlie was resilient. And, after all, she needed to get back to managing the affairs of her empire.

After Fenton returned from his travels, Emma was summoned to meet with him and his sister in his office. Fenton and Katherine sat at the small office table with their backs to the door. They were unaware that Emma had entered the room.

Sighing, Katherine said, "You might have your suspicions, but the girls need more time with her. It's time to forgive. Remember, you set all this in motion. I've played a part in all this, but now... Oh, hello Emma. Please sit down."

Emma took a seat across from the siblings. Fenton pulled on the collar of his worn blue t-shirt. His wardrobe selections were drawn from an assortment of conservative business shirts and slacks or, in a jarring contrast, a collection of faded and tattered t-shirts and shorts. The investigator did not select apparel falling between these endpoints. Katherine and other family members made repeated attempts to fill his wardrobe gap at gift-giving holidays with no detectable results.

Emma reported Charlie's confession about her eavesdropping and the copy machine. She did not divulge that Charlie made her own copy of the data on the storage device.

Nodding, Katherine said, "This explains how Charlie has been keeping up with new students. Remember, Fenny, I told you and the lawyers that I didn't know how Charlie got this information."

"You did, Kat. You certainly did." Fenton lowered his chin on pointed index fingers.

Katherine frowned at her brother. "With the franchising, Charlie's team has been eavesdropping on teachers and administrative staff at five schools. God knows how many privacy laws are being violated." Katherine sighed. "Charlie's trust attorney and our counsel discussed a breakup of her syndicate this morning. Each school's art club will be reincorporated as an independent nonprofit limited partnership. They're protecting themselves from actions the school may take against her art business. These other clubs are raising their drawbridges. You can't allow this. Time to act. Are you listening?"

"Yes, time to act. Time to... Kat, let's you and I discuss how to proceed later today. Emma, thank you for bringing this to our attention."

Katherine dropped her head.

The follow-up actions and disciplinary measures would not be discussed with Emma.

* * *

Later in the day, Katherine asked Emma to meet with her on her private veranda.

"Thanks for taking time out, Emma. I'm not sure how much of the conversation you overheard earlier but want to discuss a few things with you."

Emma looked up. "I only heard the last few words when I walked into the office."

"Nevertheless, I'll share a few concerns I raised with my brother today. I want you to understand what's happening. Since the divorce, I've been helping with the girls. Fenton is away quite often and, to be candid, I've told him for quite some time that they need to spend more time with their mother."

"And he doesn't want this?"

"No. There are long-standing issues, and he doesn't want to give Ophelia more time with them. It's odd saying this because I think he still loves her. Anyway, I want you to know this because I'm making a push for Fenton to allow the girls to spend more time with Ophelia. I'd like this to happen as soon as possible. This might change your role."

"I understand."

"It's even more serious now. Depending on the outcome of the FBI case against the girls, they could be placed with Ophelia. The court will not look favorably on his parenting abilities. And there's Olivia... Given how my brother has treated Ophelia, I'm afraid she'll push for sole custody. If this happens, I'm not so concerned about Clarke. She just has a couple more years of high school. But Charlie needs her dad."

* * *

Emma and the Pareto family sat down the following Sunday morning to enjoy another one of Katherine's culinary masterpieces at the René Bouchera rectangular glass table under the mammoth pyramid skylight.

Charlie helped herself to her aunt's epicurean extravaganza, featuring oversized baking powder biscuits, crispy bacon, scrambled eggs (infused with cheddar cheese, chives and red pepper flakes), fruit plate, and two-shot cappuccinos with steamed milk. Leaf designs were etched into the cappuccino foam.

After taking a few bites, Charlie closed her eyes. "*L'appetito vien mangiando.*"

"What does that mean?" Emma asked.

Fenton smiled. "She said her appetite grows stronger with each bite."

Over breakfast, the girls and their father discussed the Marcum and barking dog investigations. He leaned back in his chair. "Happy to hear you're not letting the FBI problem to interfere with your investigations. The hearing is in eighty days. Remember, I'll be traveling. Also, your aunt is leaving tomorrow for her meditation retreat. Emma will be in charge the next six days. Clarke, don't forget your karate class on Tuesday. One more thing. The storm is arriving this evening. No mud sliding with your friends. We had to replace all the topsoil and reseed in that area."

Clarke frowned. "Spending time with friends is normal. Don't you want at least one member of this family to be normal?" On rainy nights when her father was traveling, Clarke sometimes invited her friends for impromptu co-ed mud sliding. The activity was held on a poorly drained expanse of grass behind Hadisway Hall. With running starts, the scantily clad teenagers took turns launching themselves onto the muddy runway.

Fenton did not respond, choosing not to challenge his daughter's contention that nighttime mud sliding was critical to cultivating friendships.

A cloud moved across the sun, dimming the breakfast area and the adjoining arcaded courtyard. The courtyard overflowed with plantings of camellias, flowering ash, azaleas, and Chinese wisteria. Niches showcased Roman bronze heads, dating from the fourth and fifth centuries. A large Roman puteal, cut from a single block of marble, occupied the center of the loggia. This wellhead bore a carved depiction of Somnus, the mythological Roman God of Sleep, and his twin brother, Mors, the God of Death.

Charlie asked Emma if she could meet later in her *bottega* to discuss a question.

Lucy slipped away from her prescribed mealtime waiting area rug. She sat next to Charlie's chair, enjoying a scaled-down version of Charlie's meal.

After breakfast, Katherine asked Charlie to hold up. "Before the storm arrives, take your dog for a walk. Maybe this will partially compensate for those surplus calories."

* * *

Later in the day, Emma visited Charlie in her *bottega*. Lucy sat on top of Charlie's worktable, with wires extending from electrode pads on the side of her chest to a small device. The subject's body was rigid. Charlie's phone was turned up to a high volume. A mechanical voice slowly recited female names beginning with the letter "E," pausing between each name. "Emilia. Eloise. Elina. Elaina..."

Emma asked Charlie what she was doing.

Turning down the volume on her phone, she looked up. "I'm monitoring Lucy's heart rate. You see, I discovered her heart increases 2.5 pulsations in the five seconds after hearing her name. I'm endeavoring to learn her former name, the one she was called *before* we adopted her. My premise is that Lucy's autonomic nervous system will respond similarly to her original name."

"Why do you want to know her old name?"

"Once I discover it, I'll be able to delve into a broader range of subjects with her, including her early life. But there may be hundreds more names to test."

Emma did not ask Charlie what aspects of her dog's early life would be examined.

Charlie gave Lucy a hug. "I'm interested in your views on Ben Aberdeen, Laura's handyman. Given the backlog of chores in Laura's home, he might be just posing as a handyman. His online service ratings are low. Do you agree he's a prime suspect?"

Emma frowned. "Not really. Maybe he just hasn't gotten around to the repairs."

"Why not? What's he been doing?"

Emma looked away as she considered the question. "Oh, boy. Who can say? But he doesn't seem too suspicious. I'll let you know if I come up with a better answer."

*　*　*

The storm raged into the night, with sheets of rain lashing against the windows of the Pareto home. A static hum of a steady rain was joined by the somber cry of a wailing wind. Rooms were intermittently illuminated by lightning or shaken by peals of thunder.

The mobile phone interruptions continued. While these interruptions affected each member of the household, they had a more profound effect on Clarke. What began as an annoying splinter of inconvenience festered in her mind, swelling to an angry obsession. While other family members looked for environmental or mechanical explanations for the outages, Clarke fixated on the notion of a malevolent agent at work.

The evening after the Pareto adults' departure, the girls and Emma sat in the Golden Vault. Through the vault's arched entryway, they watched Lucy race back and forth on *Viale di Tresteuere*, her favorite recreational run. House staff stood at each end of the hallway and played keep-away with her toys. Lucy enjoyed this game, regularly depositing her favorite toys in this indoor avenue to get the game started.

Clarke pulled her hair into a bun. "A couple weeks ago, I asked Pops if he could get the lowdown on the phone hiccups. He told me yesterday that one of his sources spilled sundry deets on what's going down."

Fenton was well-connected with a variety of individuals who supplied intelligence to him, including a telecommunications insider.

Clarke stretched her arms over her head. "Pops learned that the service providers are having '*challenges*' with our local cell tower. The operator can't figure out what's messing with the signals. Service breaks are vanilla, but the so-called experts don't know why they're happening around here. Guess their Google searches have come up empty."

She rotated her shoulder under her chin. "The techies said '*certain obstructions*' like trees, concrete, glass, and metal can cause glitches. I'm surprised they didn't include tall people on their list. Or the tower could be the problem. Their geniuses have been rerunning diagnostics on the frequency settings and signal switching functions."

Emma asked, "What do you think is happening?"

Clarke shook her head. "I'm not buying any of this. I asked Pops if someone might be blocking cell signals to the tower. He said that's probably not happening. But he said the tech is out there. A jamming thingy can send a radio signal on the same frequency as the phone, messing with the phone's connection to the tower."

Emma shrugged. "Sounds far-fetched. I'd guess this is just a reception problem."

"That's what I thought at first. I tried a signal booster, but it's done jack." Clarke sighed. "I learned a jammed signal raises the noise floor, drowning out even the strongest signal. I downloaded an app that measures background noise. When my signal bar drops from four bars to zip, the noise floor spikes. I seriously doubt that's a coincidence."

"Wonder what's happening," Emma said.

Frowning, Clarke said, "Guess it's up to me to find out who's messing with our phones."

Charlie smiled. "I've often wondered, Clarke, if your determined mindset contributes to your sports competitiveness or if it's the other way around."

Not bothering to wait for the local tower operator or the FCC to resolve the intermittent phone outages, Clarke conducted her own research the following two days on how to root out a jamming device.

And she developed a plan.

* * *

Over dinner, Clarke updated Charlie and Emma on her research. With a mouthful of gnocchi, she said, "Mumph... It's simple. To prove the phones are being blocked, we just need to find a strong, steady transmission across the cell bands—700 megs to 3.8 gigs—when phones aren't working." She paused to swallow. "This'll be the smoking gun."

She speared a Gorgonzola-coated gnocco and held it to her eye level.

"To find the jamming signal, we need to check signal strength at various spots. That'll help us triangulate on the jammer." Clarke took a long drink from her water glass and continued, "To do this, I downloaded scanner software to measure signal strength and to send GPS coordinates to my phone. Three cheers for the public domain."

Pushing aside her empty pasta bowl, Charlie said, "Clarke, you're certainly invested in this pursuit. Although I fail to see the commercial value of your search, I'm curious where it will lead."

* * *

The following evening, the three regrouped in the Golden Vault, sorting through their supplies. After a series of false starts, Clarke issued the "go" order for the operation to proceed at twenty-one hundred. Rain pounded the oculus high above. Explosive bursts of thunder shook the vault. A flash of lightning illuminated the east-facing niches, giving Emma a quarter second to decipher a closed-loop transfer function etched into the wall of a nearby alcove.

Clarke yawned as she studied her computer tablet. "It's getting late, but it's time to go. I just checked the

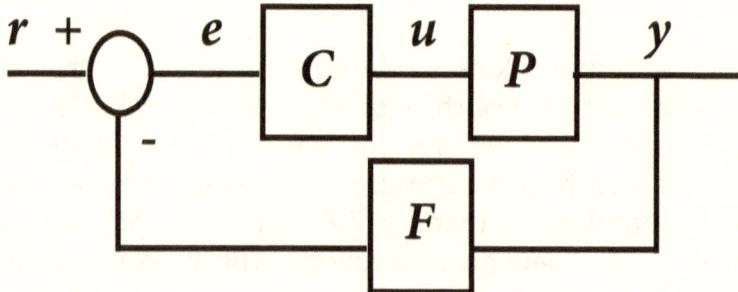

forecast, and the storm is expected to blow over within the hour."

Charlie nodded. "This should open a favorable navigational window." Clarke had won over her sister. She looked at Emma. "You don't think this is a very good plan, do you, Ms. Dorner?"

"It's late and stormy. Do you *really* think this is a good idea?"

The girls nodded enthusiastically.

Emma folded her arms. "Well, I don't. But I suppose we can always turn back if there's no break in the storm. I doubt we'll be out there long."

The troop wore rain jackets, rainboots, and headlamps. The girls filled their backpacks with supplies piled on the floor of the vault. Provisions included umbrellas, flashlights, backup batteries, computer tablets, walkie-talkies, phones, and other electronics. Charlie anticipated a protracted campaign, packing eight energy bars, a cluster of grapes, six boxes of raisins, four energy drinks, and dog treats. Charlie placed the tablets, phones, and electronic gear in large zip-lock bags. Clarke's personal provisions included rubber gloves, a mace sprayer, a compact toolbox, and bolt cutters.

Emma told the girls that the weight of these supplies would likely pose problems.

Clarke reviewed the campaign details and field map one last time. The expedition leader explained that the team would work their way eastward, leading to the faulty cell tower located near a highway. Along the way, Clarke would check for strong, constant transmissions around the cell bands. Emma would serve as her aide-de-camp, providing diplomatic assistance in the event of adult encounters. Charlie would offer logistical support. Lucy rounded out the team, supplying Charlie with operational support and reconnaissance. She was sheathed in a hooded pink rain jersey spanning the length of her body and safeguarded by a high-powered blinking beacon light on her collar.

Overcoming the torrential downpour and gale-force winds, the expeditionary force enjoyed early success. Within the first half-hour, Clarke acquired an unexplained strong and steady transmission across all the major cell bands. The next step involved locating its source. The girls sang Verdi's *Libiamo ne'lieti calici*, with Charlie reprising the male role in the happy duet.

From that point, their progress slowed to a crawl. Over the next two hours, the group took readings at various spots in the neighborhood, zigzagging through private properties as they proceeded in an easterly direction. Their advance was hampered by needing to access locations protected by fences, walls, and large guard animals.

Clarke angrily turned to Charlie. "Your flashlight keeps blinding me. Point it down. And pick up your feet. You're shuffling."

The predicted pause in the storm had not materialized. Instead, the ferocious thunderstorm turned umbrellas inside out, drenched clothes, and threatened Clarke's sensitive electronic equipment. Since the phones and tablets required direct touch, the plastic bags needed to be opened.

Charlie grumbled about the problems with the plastic bags. "I should have tested this use case. This arrangement has proven unwieldy." In a shaky voice, she added, "Let's go home. We should have turned back a long time ago."

The girls struggled with the increasing weight of their water-logged provisions. The party was taking frequent breaks under trees or house eaves, with Lucy sniffing around muddy gardens during these pauses. Her legs were caked with muck. Charlie repeatedly held up the group so Lucy could conduct her reconnaissance. Lucy failed to return after each errand, and Charlie was forced to hunt her down.

Turning to Charlie, Emma snapped, "Put a leash on Lucy! When she wanders off, she could get bogged down in a place where you won't be able to find her."

Raising her voice so she could be heard over the steady rain, Charlie said, "It's important for Lucy to conduct her own recon."

"Come on, Charlie, you're wasting time. What do you expect her to find?"

"If Lucy encounters a threat, I've trained her to run back to us and start barking."

Charlie continued to put her faith in Lucy's training. Lucy had not taken time away from her garden survey to offer any cautionary barks.

Charlie knelt to establish eye contact with her dog. "Although it's past her bedtime, at least her morale remains high." Lucy's tail wagged as Charlie supplied her assistant with vital sustenance from her own provisions.

Well past midnight, the troop trudged on. Despite the group's increasing fatigue, Clarke urged Charlie and Emma forward. She reminded them that their struggles would be for naught if the transmission source moved to another location in the future. From dozens of readings, Clarke created a heat map, showing the intensity levels of the transmission at different locations. A clear pattern was emerging: the further they moved in an easterly direction, the stronger the interference signal. The signal was gaining intensity as the group moved closer to the cell tower.

The exhausted team did not discuss the possibility of an error in Clarke's calculations or that the signal might be related to the routine operation of the tower.

The radio signal breadcrumbs led the team to the foot of Macro Cell Tower 2173. Rising over one hundred feet, the tower's lattice outline was barely discernible against the night sky. Charlie's powerful flashlight beam revealed dripping surfaces of the colossal structure. Attached to the lattice work were dense clusters of antennas, panels, microwave dishes, and other strange mechanical appendages. At the base of the tower, cabinets housed generators and other equipment. The installation was encircled by a chain link security fence, with strands of barbed wire ringing the top of the fence. No trespassing signs discouraged visitors from approaching this menacing spectacle. The tower was unmanned but monitored by unseen security cameras.

Lightning knifed across the sky, followed by a crash of thunder.

This location did not agree with Lucy. She snarled and barked at something on the other side of the security fence. It took a few minutes for Charlie to calm her.

Looking up at the structure, Charlie suggested, "Let's come back tomorrow morning when we have the benefit of light and better weather conditions. Can we wrap this up? Now would be a good time." She made little effort to disguise her quavering voice.

A sudden cloudburst brought a roaring deluge. Turning to her sister, Clarke shouted, "Nonsense, Charlie, we're here at the perfect time. We've come so far. You need to step off the sidelines... and get into the game!"

Looking up at the tower, Clarke assumed the role of tour guide. Wiping the rain from her face, she shouted, "Macro cell sites form the core of the cellular network, enabling providers to deliver voice, text, and broadband communications." In a higher pitch, she said, "This tower has a 4G service radius of six miles and a 5G service radius of fifteen hundred feet." Clarke's audience did not ask her why these statistics were needed at this moment.

Emma held an umbrella over Clarke as she fine-tuned her attenuator, dampening the amplitude of the mysterious and now overwhelmingly powerful signal. Once the equipment was calibrated, Charlie, Lucy, and Emma set off to inspect the fenced perimeter of the installation, leaving Clarke to pinpoint the location of the jammer.

With a security fence between themselves and the tower, the group had not discussed how they would proceed if the signal source was found on the other side of the fence. Clarke acknowledged that she did not know what type of jamming device was being used. She might not even recognize the jammer if she found it.

Following the fence line, the recon team reached an entry gate secured by a new padlock. The original door lock looked like it had been attacked by a drill.

Lucy turned back to Charlie, confirming the direction and logic of the errand.

The team walked past caches of industrial supplies, large liquid tanks, and equipment. They passed another gate with a mangled lock and a new padlock.

"Did you see that, Charlie?"

"What?" Charlie asked, shouting over the rain.

"There was something near the tower, on the other side of the fence. It looked like a yellow light. It darted away. I don't see anything now."

Charlie wiped rain off her face. "I didn't see anything. Let's get back."

Completing their inspection of the fenced perimeter, they returned to where they had left Clarke.

She was gone.

Lucy put her muddy front paws on Charlie's leg and started to bark.

They called to Clarke, but their cries were drowned out by the heavy rain.

A flicker of lightning revealed Clarke's silhouette lithely scaling the tower. She had found the central access ladder at the trunk of the structure. Water cascaded from the upper levels of the tower, creating a series of waterfalls that spilled down to the branches of panels and antennae below. The slick rungs of the access ladder would be unforgiving. An ill-chosen handhold or misstep would result in a long and likely fatal plummet.

Every ten feet, Clarke stopped and scanned the tower with a hand-held device. She then climbed higher, still looking for the jammer. At sixty feet, Clarke slipped. She dangled from the ladder, holding onto a rung with one hand. Her feet flailed, desperately trying to find the ladder.

Clarke swung her free arm to grab a rung. She missed. She tried again, this time latching onto the ladder. At last, she was also able to find her footing. She hugged the ladder for a few minutes before resuming her climb.

Two jagged streaks of lightning grounded nearby, followed by an explosive roar.

At seventy feet above the ground, Clarke stopped. Rather than climbing higher, she descended to a lower spur. After completing her scanning procedure, she moved to the next lower limb. This process was repeated at each ten-foot interval. At forty feet, she took extra time to scan the area. After a moment of hesitation, she stepped off the ladder and crawled onto a two-foot-wide horizontal limb with a cluster of panels and antenna. She inched her way along the spur, working her way around cables and other obstructions. Halfway out on the bar, she scanned the area. She then took off her backpack and took out a few tools. A moment later, a ten-foot arc of sparks sprayed out from her work area. Clarke slumped over. Like a lifeless marionette, her head, an arm, and a leg limply dangled over the narrow spur.

Charlie, Lucy, and Emma raced back and forth along the security fence, trying to find a way to get to the other side.

Clarke lay still. Her dripping hand, clenched in a fist, held two exposed wires. From the ends of the wires, sparks trickled to the ground, forty feet below.

Outpost

Emma found Clarke's backpack near the fence. Throwing her body against the enclosure, a flap of fence fell away. This was where Clarke used her bolt cutters. She sprinted to the tower, leaving Charlie and Lucy behind. Charlie called out to Emma, but her cries were lost in the driving rain. Emma had missed Charlie's warning about rainwater being an excellent conductor of electricity. And Emma did not hear her screams about water magnifying the severity of electrical shock.

After scrambling up the ladder, she slid onto the spur. The acrid aroma of burning wires led her to Clarke and the central problem. Emma could not help Clarke if she was also electrocuted.

In darkness, she reached Clarke's limp body. She held her breath as she touched Clarke's neck. It was cold.

She checked for a pulse. Clarke was still alive.

As Emma pulled her toward her, Clarke's body began to shake violently. She hung onto Clarke's arms during the seizure, preventing her from slipping off the spur. Emma cried out and sobbed as she held onto Clarke. She had not cried since her mother's death four years earlier. After the paroxysm subsided, she dragged Clarke to the access ladder. Holding her by the waist, Emma supported Clarke's entire weight as they descended the tower. Still thirty feet up, Emma leaned against a heavy cable that straddled the ladder.

As rain beat down on the two, a flashlight beam from below searched the tower.

Clarke extended arms and lifted her head. With her eyes still closed, she wrapped her arms around Emma's shoulders. It would be easier to carry her. Several minutes later, they reached the ground. Charlie and Lucy waited for them there.

Clarke's senses were returning. After resting for a while, she was able to lift herself to her feet. Stumbling and limping, Emma supported her as they made their way to the fence. Clarke held her right hand, which had suffered second-degree burns. Leaving the enclosure, Clarke muttered, "I found it... it was there."

The rain abated, and ground mist rose. After resting again for a few minutes, Emma suggested to Clarke that it was time to leave. Charlie slipped off with Lucy. With her dog, she stood in a grassy area; her hooded head hung low. The back of Charlie's rain jacket shook from sobs of relief. Lucy stood in front of Charlie, gazing up at her downcast hood.

Their campaign would end here. They would first withdraw to the Paretos' home before making a trip to urgent care to check on Clarke's condition.

*　*　*

Late the next morning, the girls and Emma convened a conference in *Volta Aurea* to discuss the grim implications of their night's adventure. With her sandaled feet, Emma traced and retraced part of a pattern of the obsidian blue rug anchoring the seating area as they replayed their visit to the tower and sorted through their limited options.

Shaking her head, Emma said, "Clarke, you were lucky you weren't more seriously hurt. This was totally my fault. I should've never let you two to go out in the storm."

Clarke frowned. "It wasn't your fault. I pushed you into going out there."

"I wasn't *pushed* to do anything. I was hired to watch over you. But I don't think I'm the best person to protect anybody, including you girls." Emma wiped away a tear.

Charlie raised her hand.

Emma rapidly blinked her eyes. "Yes, Charlie."

"I disagree with your contention. You rescued Clarke after she was electrocuted. And if you hadn't helped us lift Ms. Marcum's ficus tree, I could've been crushed."

Emma sighed. "None of this matters now. We're in trouble. The question is what to do next."

Their deliberation was brief. Emma insisted they throw themselves on the mercy of local authorities. They had unambiguously trespassed on federally leased grounds and recklessly damaged valuable property. Although their shrouded attire might conceal their identities, she pointed out that just one unflattering facial image captured by a surveillance camera would lead investigators to the Paretos' doorstep.

If the matter could be settled quickly and quietly, Emma might even be able to sidestep child endangerment charges.

The group decided to wait several days to confess their crimes. Fenton would return in three days. Emma thought that he might be needed for posting a bond. And there was an unspoken reason to delay the confession. Like many criminals finding themselves in similarly desperate circumstances, the group hung its hope on a yet-to-be-revealed reversal of fortune.

In the next few days, there were two developments. First, the family and neighbors would no longer experience phone interruptions. Whether Clarke disabled a jamming device before her electric shock remained a hotly but privately debated topic. Clarke argued that she discovered a jammer on the tower. When she cut the wires protruding from the contraption, she received a shock. It was also plausible that Clarke had simply disengaged a hazardous component of the tower. Perhaps the tower operator finally fixed the cause of the signal interruptions, remedying a mundane malfunction in the tower.

A subsequent development caused the three to postpone their police station confessional. Two days after their nighttime campaign, the local media reported an early morning propane depot fire. The depot abutted Macro Cell Tower 2173. The fierce repository fire spread to the tower. The heat of the conflagration compromised the structural integrity of the tower, leading to its complete collapse. A later report raised the possibility of arson.

The three hoped the investigators would focus on the cause of the propane tank repository fire instead of the cell tower surveillance footage. They agreed they were not yet in the clear. An arson investigator or police detective might knock on the Paretos' door at any moment. The girls did not discuss the possibility that the fire was somehow connected with evidence Clarke found on one of the limbs of the tower.

Over the next few weeks, Clarke sighted a multitude of cell towers along the Bay Area highways. For her, this raised a troubling question: Had they popped up overnight, like some type of new mushroom, or had they been there all along?

It was also unclear if the community needed Tower 2173 after all. The other towers—new or old—absorbed the service demands of their area. Clarke dispensed regular, albeit unsolicited, reports of uninterrupted and high-quality phone service.

*　*　*

Emma needed to talk with someone about her escalating problems at work. Her hair appointment, the week following the tower escapade, provided an opportunity for a confessional. As with past appointments, Emma could tell that the hairdresser paid little attention to anything she said. In her one-way conversation, Emma described her murky assignment with the Paretos and her difficulties, including the cell tower misadventure. She admitted that the nighttime mission had nearly become an unspeakable tragedy. Her poor judgment, beginning with her consent to allow the girls to leave the house during the powerful nighttime storm, was indisputable, at least by any standard that could be applied to decisions involving children. She conceded that the truth about the night's proceedings would remain sealed pursuant to an unspoken covenant with the sisters. Wrapping up her confession, she pledged to convert her temporary reprieve into actions more fitting of her station and consistent with the level of her employer's misplaced trust.

*　*　*

Charlie turned her attention to "Tuscany," her three-day semi-annual business symposium for eight exceptionally promising young female entrepreneurs. This highly selective invitation-only retreat brought together her school's captains of industry and intellectual elite, spanning ages eight through eleven.

Although the FBI hearing loomed and the dog barking mystery needed her attention, for Charlie, the symposium was one of the professional highpoints of her year and simply too important to postpone.

The name of Charlie's conference reflected several influences. Major economic forums like Davos and Jackson Hole borrow their conference names from their host location. Charlie's kick-off plenary session and several breakout gatherings were held in the Paretos' expansive wine cellar. As the Paretos' cellar reflected the family's taste in Italian wine, "Tuscany" was a logical moniker for the event. The conference's appellation also conveyed an aura of polished sophistication if not global significance.

The upcoming event represented the third edition of the symposium. In keeping with tradition, the event would be held from Friday afternoon to Sunday noon. With Katherine's assistance, Italian themed meals and periodic snacks were served during the event. Lodging was available to attendees. Charlie charged participants a registration fee corresponding to the significant value she placed on the forum's provocative content and richness of the overall experience. Clarke performed a vague offstage function, commanding a sizable share of the registration revenue. Although Katherine supported her niece's information-sharing mission, "inappropriate and regrettable" conference content had surfaced in the inaugural convention. From that point, Katherine made it clear to Charlie that, so long as she used the family's household for her retreat, all collateral materials were subject to advance inspection. Given the substantial volume of conference material, Katherine asked Emma to help review symposium content. She also asked her to conduct a "pre-conference walk-through" of the parts of the house that would be used, and to monitor the proceedings—not necessarily with notice.

BONUS CONTENT AT THE END OF CHAPTER

Since most of the conference sessions were held in the wine cellar, maintained at a constant fifty-five degrees, guests had been advised to dress warmly.

Although on the chilly side, Charlie saw the advantage of this area being insulated from household distractions. Sensitive matters could be considered without inopportune interruptions and, for the most part, unwelcome intrusions. The only oversight at this spot was found on the walls of the cavern. Religious figures rendered in the eighteenth-century oils of Tiepolo, Amigoni, and Canaletto gazed upon the young visitors, unmoved by their secular deliberations.

Other breakout sessions and networking events were held in warmer parts of the household. To assist attendees in finding their way to these locations, Charlie provided a map of the house and grounds, highlighting meeting rooms and social areas. Breakout rooms bore temporary signage, such as Sangiovese, Barbera, and Primitivo.

Emma was able to review all conference material in advance, except for a breakout session titled, "YOLO and The Prosperity Inflection Thesis." Emma repeatedly asked Charlie to submit the session content for pre-conference review as demanded by Katherine's disclosure decree. However, the material was never quite ready for inspection. Emma made a point to attend the session, slipping into the wine cellar behind the last guest as the cellar's glass doors closed. She stood in the shadows between two towering wine racks stocked with Shafer, Paul Hobbs, Harlan, and Rivers-Marie wines.

Charlie unveiled her thesis: Rule-breaking was a precondition of personal achievement and prosperity. For contrast, she supplied "rule-following" examples: acceptance of traditional scholastic achievement metrics, adherence to adult rules and standards, and reliance on any "wisdom" not validated by first-hand experience.

Charlie summed up: "The most absolute and widely embraced rules must be broken most repeatedly."

Emotions overflowed, with several girls shouting down Charlie's theory. An agitated attendee jumped up and rattled off her objections. How could serial rule-breaking possibly lead to anything other than strife, incarceration, and personal ruin? During the commotion, Charlie removed two eighteenth-century portraits from a wall and placed them on the tasting table. After the group settled down, Charlie switched on a small projector. To correct the group's thinking, she projected a chart on the wall of the cellar."

Charlie explained that she formulated her Prosperity Inflection Thesis (PIT) after considering the implications of dozens of scholarly journal articles. She patiently explained that the chart's vertical lines represented a standard error from the predicted path of her rule-following and rule-infringing peers to age fifty. She suggested that the rule-breakers would see, around age thirty-one, the strategy really start to pay off.

Emma tiptoed out of the wine cellar. On her way to the loggia, she asked a staff member where she could find Katherine.

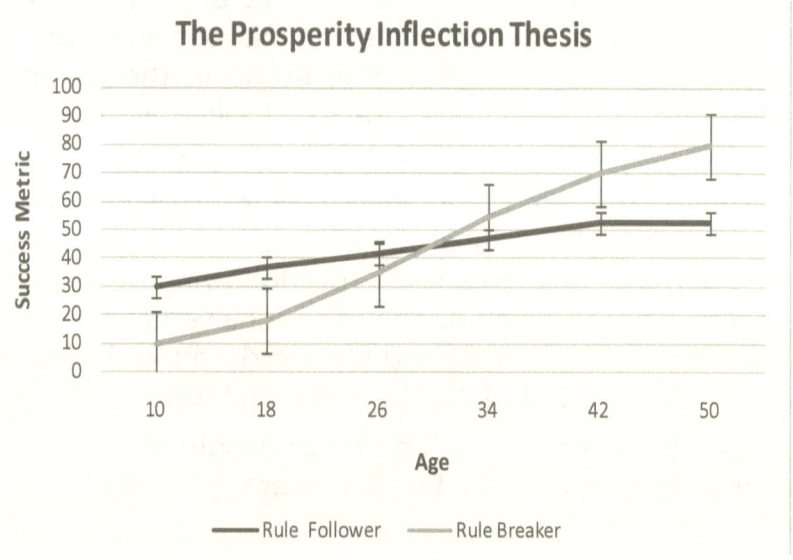

The Prosperity Inflection Thesis

Charlie privately interacted with each attendee during break-out sessions or meals. Rather than joining the larger group, she and Emily Hayek enjoyed their meal at a table for two. Katherine's Saturday dinner featured thin slices of pan-fried veal scaloppini, topped with a lemon butter, brown sugar, Madeira, and minced garlic sauce.

Charlie refilled Emily's glass from a large Pellegrino bottle.

Emily was the youngest member of the group. She had just celebrated her eighth birthday. If Emily made the cut, she could expect to play a small role in one of Charlie's future endeavors. This would give her an opportunity to demonstrate her value, opening the door to increasing levels of responsibility. Emma edged closer to their table. Emily talked about the unusually small stature of her six-year-old sister, Scarlet, and the challenges of getting her diminutive sibling onto a more successful path.

Charlie inventoried the special skills and traits of each guest, and others she might hear about, during the conference. Charlie made a note of Scarlet's unique attributes.

After dinner, the girls congregated on the veranda, enjoying a view of the Paretos' gardens. The grounds were illuminated, much like a resort. At the far end of the property rose the shining edifice of Disco Pareto, spotlighted for the occasion. Like the colonnade surrounding St. Peter's Basilica, the domed building was ringed with Tuscan order columns. Marble statues of disco, funk, and R&B icons stood on balusters flanking the structure's roof. Lighted fountains occupied the square adjoining the discothèque. The central fountain featured a marble statue of Toni Braxton with outstretched arms. The sculpture, clad in a shimmering alabaster Tom Ford Gucci gown, was inspired by a transcendent moment in the contralto's "Un-Break My Heart" official music video.

The evening's highlight was a thirty-minute professional aerial fireworks display launched from a remote part of the property.

— Bonus Content: Charlie's Symposium —

At the start of the conference, members of the house staff worked the registration table, which was set up in the Paretos' entryway for guest check-in. After the young VIP picked up her bulky conference packet, the visitor was escorted to the welcome reception on the loggia. Charlie greeted each arriving guest there, as circulating waiters dispensed Martinelli's Sparkling Cider in champagne glasses and hors d'oeuvres on small plates. A hired pianist treated guests with stylized versions of classic rock songs.

Lingering near the registration table, Emma's attention was drawn to a well-dressed young visitor engaged in an excited conversation with two tuxedoed staff members.

"This is outrageous! *I am* Lira Klezmer-Ross. I'm a registered guest, influencer, and member of the conference's steering committee." (A steering committee helped Charlie create conference content, with a perfect overlap between committee members and conference attendees. Committee titles included: Senior Event Director, Intellectual Property Director, Lead Professional Excellence Officer, Head Technical Advisor, Lead Project Director, Creative Director, Media Relations Liaison, and Chief Futurist.)

Looking at the two remaining name tags on the registration table, Milo, the silver-haired house steward, shook his head. "I am sorry, but we do not have a name tag for a Lira Klezmer-Ross. Perhaps, you're at the wrong conference."

An older female staff member, who joined the group, chimed in. "I admitted Miss Klezmer-Ross earlier. She's wearing her name tag and is inside."

Turning to the visitor, Milo frowned. "Miss, as you've heard, a Lira Klezmer-Ross has already been admitted. In the absence of another name tag bearing the same name, we are unable to admit a second Lira Klezmer-Ross to this event."

The youngster was on the verge of tears. "But I am *the* Lira Klezmer-Ross!"

Emma inserted herself into the conversation, eventually sorting out the mix-up. One of the other girls picked up Lira's name tag by mistake.

Charlie was the featured speaker at the plenary sessions, designed to meet didactic and inspirational objectives. Following these impassioned group gatherings, participants would be turned loose to facilitate break-out sessions, host networking assemblies or simply attend the rich array of colloquia. Two thirty-minute afternoon recesses allowed participants to penetrate more abstruse subjects, catch up on emails and text messages, follow QR codes to supplemental enrichment material, and reexamine break-out session selections. These adjournments, held on an airy veranda, not only offered the young guests an assortment of gelato flavors and temptations, such as an apple strudel with almonds, but rewarded the guests with a panoramic view of the Paretos' captivating Renaissance-inspired Italian gardens.

The conference theme was "Taking the Helm." Session topics were selected to address the pressing concerns of these grade school dynamos: "Influencing without Authority,"

"Monetizing Personal Assets," "The Dangers of Past Success," "YOLO and The Prosperity Inflection Thesis," "Women Hedge Fund Pioneers," "The Women Winemakers of Piedmont Italy," "Parents and Caregivers–Managing Up," and "Beyond Wealth: Redefining Financial Power."

Past conferences predicted notable divergences between the syllabus topics and the actual discourse of the attendees. Regardless of the starting point of a conversation, the conference discussions gravitated to subjects involving young actors, musicians, current fashion, food, parents, and classmates.

A generous fifteen-minute break after each session would give participants an opportunity to share reflections and transition to other symposium venues. A popular session was held over from the prior conference: "What to Expect Next?" Each participant was matched with another guest to discuss the demands of the next grade level. For the oldest students, a guest speaker was brought in from middle school to share first-hand perspectives on the rigors of the seventh grade.

While Charlie was the architect of Tuscany and the featured speaker in one of the general sessions and two breakouts, she was satisfied to let her acolytes direct many visible aspects of the conference. From the sidelines, she would watch her devotees lead discussions, facilitate information exchanges, formulate plans, and weave new social networks. Once again, the conference would give Charlie an opportunity to quietly vet new business propositions and assess emerging talent.

Later, Emma joined Charlie and one of the conference guests who were having a quiet discussion in a corner during one of the unstructured networking breaks.

Brooke appealed to Charlie: "There's a real opportunity to make money, CP."

While looking at Emma, Charlie shook her head in disagreement. "Let's not talk about money. How much is a nurturing family worth? Can you count a father's love? Can you spend a mother's kiss? What price do you put on a friend's... or an important caregiver's support? Insofar as your proposal, you haven't articulated your differentiated value prop. We can keep our powder dry for the right opportunity."

The piano player changed up the tempo with a soulful version of Guns N' Roses' "Sweet Child O' Mine."

"Maybe you're right, CP, although I think it was a good idea," Brooke said.

Charlie gave Emma a thoughtful look. "Brooke, although I find aspects of your proposal appealing, I'm currently channeling my time and resources into nascent projects that I can help guide and nurture, elevating their yield. It's all about helping people."

Charlie would disclose only the most general outlines of a proposed commercial undertaking in the presence of an adult.

Charlie clasped her hands. "Specifically, I'm attracted to endeavors that harness the labor capacity of our classmates. Allow me to illustrate using a sharecropping example. You're familiar with the sharecropping concept, no doubt?"

"I think so..." Brooke said, lowering her eyes.

"Good. Well, the centuries-old Italian *mezzadria* system took its name from an arrangement whereby a landowner provided the land and resources for planting in exchange for half, or *mezza*, of the yearly crop. Like Tuscan landowners of the past, my portfolio is weighted toward business ventures where I can furnish resources or other assistance in exchange for labor and a share of the proceeds. As a rule, I avoid ventures susceptible to low inventory turnover, third-party interference, and negative carry. But I will be launching a talent tracking system that you can help me stand up and..."

A chime sounded, prompting the guests to move to the next event venue.

Charlie and her apprentice suspended their conversation as they made their way to the wine tasting area. The girls' conversation did not reveal how Charlie's favored labor exchange model had been deployed in the past or, more specifically, whether this commercial template facilitated the sale and distribution of 428 beehive cookie jars.

Emma followed Charlie and Brooke to the wine tasting area, featuring two skill-building activities. The girls first challenged each other to identify wine related scents from a 54 bottle *Le Nez du Vin* aroma sampling kit. Using their finely tuned palates, the young connoisseurs took turns describing and rating a dozen non-alcoholic grape juice mixtures. One of the Paretos' uniformed housekeepers stiffly doled out the juice mixtures in precise two-ounce pours.

Brooke vigorously swirled one of the juices in her nine-ounce wine glass. In one swift motion, she drained her glass. Nodding appreciatively, she said, "This was a good one. Really fruity. Tangy."

"Hmm... I'll give it a try." Charlie said, then picked up the glass by its stem and held it up to the fading evening light. After taking a small sip, Charlie rendered her verdict. "I detect red cherry, licorice, and rose petal notes. I would say that it's medium to full-bodied, rich, and layered. Its stunning depth of fruit conceals a velvety tannic structure, all buttressed by succulent acids.

Try this other one, Brooke."

Riverworn's "Exotic Night" was broadcast during the pianist's break.

After taking a big gulp, Brooke said, "This one is totally lit, CP. More refreshing than the last one."

Charlie sampled the second pour. She closed her eyes. "To me, it's deeply communicative and articulate, boasting immense power and persistence. It is chiseled and sharp with blackberry, ripe cherry, grilled herb, and barbecue spice."

As Emma asked if there were different vintages of the juice mixtures, Katherine walked up to the group. Handing Emma a glass of actual wine, she fanned out the floor-sweeping hem of her full-length gold brocade Andrew Gn gown. An inlaid jewel yoke accented a crew neckline and three-quarter balloon sleeves of a vestito lungo that could have been commissioned for royalty. Winged eyeliner accented her cat shaped eyes.

"I think you'll enjoy this, Emma. It's one of our finer brunelli," she said with a dazzling smile.

During their pre-conference walk-through of the wine cellar, the two had discussed the Paretos' extensive collection of 2010 Brunello di Montalcino wines.

Charlie joined Katherine and Emma. "Auntie, can Regan and a few other guests swim after dinner? By the way, Regan wanted me to convey to you that 'this is the best event ever—great food.' You met her. She's the conference's senior event director."

Katherine nodded thoughtfully. "Rare indeed to receive such a positively unqualified endorsement... and from a disinterested party, no less. Yes, your friends may use the rognone pool after dinner if one of the staff is available to watch them."

Preening a sleeve of her dress, she turned to Emma. "I'm looking forward to your post-conference report." She then steered toward a constellation of rising stars nearby.

Antipositional

The girls touched base with their father in a video conference the Monday following Charlie's Tuscany event.

Fenton stroked his beard. "The FBI is pushing forward with their case. The prosecutor has brought formal charges against you both. Clarke, you may be tried as an adult given 'enhancements' in the government's case. Most likely, though, you'll both be tried as minors. The prosecutor wants you to enter guilty pleas. There would be court-ordered counseling, informal probation, detention, or possible placement with your mother. And there will be a demand for restitution, likely in the $5-10 million range."

Clarke scowled. "This is bunk. I'm not pleading guilty to anything."

"I won't either. Pleading guilty won't unlock our files," Charlie said with a sigh. "Without access to those files, I'm losing control on many fronts."

"Try to get through this as best you can. But get ready to jump back into the Marcum case. I've been following a promising lead. And something else. When I talked with Laura a few days ago, she didn't seem concerned about her stolen jewelry. She believes her jewelry will be returned to her. Her mindset is very strange. Need to sign off now."

After the conference call, Clarke said, "Wonder what Pops found. Something good, no doubt. One slammin' criminal catcher!"

Charlie nodded. "Indeed. Dad's investigations have ended with the 'slamming' of many jail cell doors."

* * *

Each morning, pairs of fast walking women traversed the walled and hedged neighborhood. Emma occasionally spotted these neighborhood walkers, dressed in matching long sleeve turtlenecks and puffy athletic vests, as they stopped to look through the Paretos' wrought iron entry gates, swapping the latest rumors about the investigator. Although Fenton conducted his business with discretion, stories about him had surfaced. Clients engaged the investigator to recover stolen property and to track down the perpetrators of identity theft, social media blackmail, email scams, and ransom schemes. These crimes often carried sizable recovery rewards. Fenton's specialty was tracing cybercriminals. Once accomplished, there were whispers that he found ways to empty criminals' bank accounts and appropriate their other assets.

It was no secret that Fenton's investigations brought him in contact with all manner of lawbreakers. It was rumored that, once confronted with their crimes, these perpetrators did not freely relinquish their ill-gotten goods, offer a heartfelt apology, and make solemn promises of reform. With intransigent wrongdoers, Fenton's team was known to apply indelicate methods of encouragement.

The investigator had made many enemies. Enemies that had *not* heard the clang of a closing prison cell door.

* * *

The next week, the girls returned to the dog-barking case. Since the girls' statistical analysis showed a correlation between nighttime barking and the use of a professional dog walker, they decided to visit the thirty-seven surveyed households that used a professional dog-walker. Charlie brought along Lucy.

Two problems became evident. First, only eighteen of the thirty-seven households were available for a follow-up interview. Of the households that shared information about their dog walking, ten families did not have problems with a nighttime barker. This left just eight households with professionally walked barkers. Second, the interviews revealed little commonality in the dog-walking rituals: the timing, duration, pack size, and pit-stop frequency varied by household. The dogs were walked by different dog walkers.

The breakthrough the Pareto team needed was found in a small detail. Although the dog-barking families were using different dog walkers, these households had once shared the *same* dog walker. This was the very dog walker Jill had used (who had recently relocated out of state). Adding significance to the finding, the ten families that did not have a nighttime barker had *not* used this enigmatic dog walker.

The girls asked the owners about the shared dog walker, who Charlie designated as "a person of interest." Charlie's journal summarized these findings:

• The dog walker's name is Jay; no last name was provided

   • Jay is described as "handsome," but might be getting too much sun. He is twenty-eight to thirty-five years of age, muscular, long light brown hair with blonde highlights and wears a blue and white San Diego Padres baseball cap

   • Residents hired Jay two to three months ago; advertising online

   • Clients did not ask for references

- Jay's self-reported Net Promoter Score (NPS) was 82 percent
- Jay's rate was ten dollars per dog per walk; other walkers charge fifteen to twenty dollars per walk
- Services were paid through Venmo or PayPal (accounts no longer active)
- Dogs were walked thirty to forty-five minutes in late morning or mid-afternoon
- Side note: Lucy had a tense stand-off with Olive, a large dark-brown Labrador; Lucy has a history of responding poorly to large Labradors
- Jay did not have keys to any of the clients' houses
- Jay sold plush toys to his clients. He said that they would make perfect fetch toys. Customers thought his sales approach was too pushy. Two clients gave Clarke four of these plush animals for future study, including a large orange gorilla
- Jay carried blue plastic bags to pick up after the dogs
- One of the residents ran into Jay while shopping in Santa Cruz (a nearby beach community) the previous month. They thought Jay lived in Santa Cruz
- Jay walked several dogs at once
- Discounts were provided for monthly dog walking packages
- Customers shared Jay's telephone number (no longer in service)
- Jay resigned three weeks earlier. All residents reported the out-of-state relocation due to the high cost of living in the Bay Area

- Jay did not provide his new address to his customers
- Jay had a pilot's license

BONUS CONTENT AT THE END OF CHAPTER

As the girls trudged home after a long day of neighborhood interviews, Charlie recapped their findings and open questions. "Our efforts have led us to the dog walker, the presumptive key to the mystery. Now we find out he's disappeared without a trace. This is like searching for the Ninth Legion. How was the dog walker connected with the barking? And why do the dogs continue to bark after he moved away?"

Clarke shrugged. "No idea. But you've missed the most important question."

Charlie scratched her head. "Why nobody bothered to ask Jay for a client reference before hiring him?"

"Incorrect, my gullible guppy. The question is: Why was Jay trying to unload these plush animals? This is sketch. This gigantic gorilla doesn't look anything like a dog toy." Clarke looked at her armful of toys. "I'll take a closer look at these later. Argh! These shoes that Auntie picked out are killing me."

*   *   *

The next day, Charlie gave Jill a status report on her case, including the disappearance of a key witness, if not prime suspect. As the two chatted in Jill's entryway, two men in bib overalls measured an adjoining alcove.

Charlie cleared her throat. "Unfortunately, Mrs. Masterson, the dog walker's trail has gone cold. We'd like to turn our attention to what's making the dogs bark. May we schedule a sleepover with Scrubbles and Ribsy in your backyard next Saturday night? By observing your dogs at night, maybe we'll expose the catalyst of the outbursts."

Jill folded her arms. "I don't know... I'd like to talk with your father."

"Unfortunately, he's traveling and unavailable for consultation."

Jill frowned. "That's too bad; I'd like to talk with him. But if your aunt supports this plan and Emma comes along, then no problem."

Charlie clasped her hands. "Excellent! I'd also like to bring along Lucy for observational support. So far, Lucy has been immune to the DOGGY syndrome. I'm sorry, I should clarify. DOGGY is my shorthand for Disturbing Outbursts of Growling, Gnashing and Yapping. I wonder whether Lucy will succumb to the barking fits in the presence of other dogs."

The following Saturday afternoon, Charlie made eight trips to Jill's backyard, shuttling equipment and supplies. Charlie's mission checklist included a large tent, air mattress, dog supplies, night vision goggles, binoculars, flashlight, several cans of bug spray, split cordwood, lighter fluid, canned goods, marshmallows, and snacks.

A social obligation precluded Clarke from supporting the field research. The overnight mission would disrupt sleep, a nonstarter.

In the fading evening light, Emma unpacked her backpack next to their tent. The campsite, located near the backfence line of the property, was camouflaged with large conifer branches, ferns, and other shrubbery Charlie had removed, without permission, from neighboring properties. At the mouth of the tent, obscured by leafy vegetation, Charlie set up her surveillance area, equipped with giant ultra-zoom binoculars on a tripod for daytime observation and night vision goggles for thermal imaging.

Much like a young Jane Goodall stealthily surveying chimpanzees in the Gombe River Reserve, Charlie sought to minimize the impact of her intrusion. From her well-camouflaged location, she would be able to observe her subjects' behaviors and social interactions. Notwithstanding Charlie's preparations, Scrubbles and Ribsy sniffed around the edges of the tent, sensing the presence of Lucy, who had settled in the enclosure.

Somewhat later, Jill discouraged Charlie from having a campfire on her property. There would be no need for cordwood, lighter fluid, or marshmallows.

In the absence of a campfire or other scheduled activities, the two turned in early, setting an early morning wake-up alarm for 1:45 a.m. to prepare for a possible canine outburst.

As Emma drifted off to sleep, Charlie asked, "Why did you take this job?"

"What do you mean?"

"Didn't you have other options after college?

"I did."

"Then why did you take this job when you could be immersing yourself in more rewarding professional or academic pursuits?"

"They didn't pay as well." Emma was now fully awake.

She did not reveal that her employment options were limited by her marginal grades and lack of marketability. Faculty interpreted her silence as apathy. She needed these same faculty members to write endorsement letters and to give an extra push with top employers. Her peers knew how to gain the support they needed.

Emma did not try. Her detachment also showed through in her interviews. What her instructors and prospective employers did not know, however, was that she had not always been this way. Before her mother's illness, Emma was a bubbly teenager with many friends. During the illness, these friendships fell away as she cared for her mother. Shortly after she entered college, Emma's mother died. She then further withdrew from the world. During this time, the school facilitated two rehab stays for her substance abuse. Through all this, she retained her abundant analytical skills—skills she successfully deployed in poker, chess, and other games involving directed aggression and money exchange. Her college transcript would not show that her winnings, extracted at the hands of monied and resilient classmates, had funded more than half her tuition over the years. Her father was not impressed. Early on, he learned of Emma's gambling and threatened, more than once, to disown her. Tired of criticism, she broke off all communications with him.

The Pareto career fair challenge demanded rapid problem-solving, not an engaging personality.

"You must have been an exceptional student to be admitted to a top university. What did your parents say when you told them that you accepted this job?"

"I didn't talk with my dad about it. But I know what he would say. He thinks I make poor choices and lack direction. The reality is he's disappointed that I'm not who he wants me to be. I don't talk with him anymore. My mom died four years ago."

"I'm so sorry." After a pause, Charlie asked, "What type of person does your dad want you to be?"

"He wants me to follow his path: work for a prestigious firm then move on to grad school. He thinks anything that doesn't fit this mold is either a pipedream or a dishonest shortcut. He'd go nuts if he knew about this job. Things have gotten off to a rocky start, but everything will go much smoother from now on. I need time to block everything out and think about my future. This is the reason why I'm here."

"Well, I'm glad you're here. I don't know if you realize, but you're my only true friend. The rest are business associates and family."

"I'm glad you consider me as a friend. I admire many things about you. You have an impressive work ethic."

After a pause, Charlie said, "I've felt alone for a long time. I'm afraid I'm fated to lead a solitary life, like one of those lonely souls in a bleak Edward Hopper composition. People don't understand me."

"I don't completely understand you. But is it even important for us to fully understand one another? Personal relationships can be built on just one or two important connections." Emma did not mention that, in the case of a curly-haired engineering student, she had not found the courage to test her theory. Emma turned on her side. "Don't you admire Leonardo da Vinci?"

"I do."

"I read that he had many friends throughout his life. And he was amazingly talented. You can be talented, or just different, and still have connections with people. Doesn't need to be a tradeoff. By the way, how come you were absent from school so much?"

"I've had health challenges over the years."

"Sorry to hear that. Anything serious?"

"Doctors haven't been able to pin anything down."

Charlie had been plagued by a myriad of mysterious asymptomatic syndromes. These maladies eluded detection and were transitory. After a day or two of uninterrupted rest at home, these flareups resolved themselves. Although no professional diagnosis had been rendered, Charlie's self-reported ailments bore a resemblance to fibromyalgia, subclinical synovitis, interstitial cystitis, and an uncommon regional pain syndrome.

"Mm, I thought you just didn't like school."

"I haven't had any health problems since you've been here. Mom's taking me to Dr. Farcas next week to get a diagnosis on why I haven't had any problems lately."

"Never heard of anyone seeking a diagnosis for good health."

"As an aside, contrary to the pop culture cliché, it's difficult to hack into students' scholastic and attendance records."

"Good to know."

Charlie sighed. "Another year of Stiglitz. She said that repeating the sixth grade will give me an opportunity to raise my grades. If I really apply myself, she believes I can do better in geography and history. She also said that my PE teacher told her that I've 'just been going through the motions,' so there's room for improvement there too."

*   *   *

Charlie's screams woke Emma. Charlie wailed, "I fell through a hole in the mattress!"

The air mattress was underinflated, leading to dramatic shifts in its elevation. Charlie was a restless sleeper. Repositioning herself, she created a new peak or trough in the mattress, accompanied by whooshing and hissing sounds. Lucy continually walked over the two as she looked for a comfortable resting spot.

There was another problem. Despite spraying insect repellent around their tent, Charlie's camouflage foliage introduced a host of bugs into their sleeping quarters. These pests produced an endless succession of prickly and itchy vexations.

Emma was wide awake when her phone alarm sounded at 1:45 a.m. Exactly twenty-two minutes later, a long mournful baying pierced the early morning air. A moment later, Scrubbles and Ribsy leapt up and started howling, barking, and whining. Charlie tracked the commotion on the patio through her night vision goggles, detecting variations in heat. Her infrared goggles interpreted the dogs' structural make-up as semi-translucent blobs of shifting colors. Other neighborhood dogs joined the ruckus, adding their own distinctive cries of anguish. Lucy was awake but quiet. She preferred to stay in the tent, licking Emma's hand.

Charlie advanced to the distant patio, crawling on her belly, commando-style in her camo pajamas. A few minutes later, Emma joined her, observing the dogs at closer range. Both dogs yapped and howled, shaking their heads and making corkscrew body spins. As suddenly as the uproar started, it ended. The night was quiet once more, with the dogs settling down and resuming their normal sleep routine. The two were at a loss to explain what had precipitated the dogs' distress or brought about their relief. The only clear-cut finding was: Whatever had disturbed Scrubbles and Ribsy did not have an effect on Lucy.

As Charlie and Emma sullenly broke camp early the next morning, Jill asked Emma if she could pick up her dogs after their grooming appointment later in the day. Jill realized she had scheduled a hairdresser's appointment at the same time. Emma agreed to pick up the dogs. Charlie asked to tag along, as she wanted to interview the groomer "to uncover any nexus between the dogs' upkeep and their nighttime behaviors."

Charlie had just left with an armful of provisions when Jill came over to talk with Emma. "Is everything going okay at the Paretos' house?"

"All of this is kind of new. It's been a struggle."

Jill adjusted her new green plastic visor. Resembling a welder's mask, the visor covered most of her face. "Fenton and Katherine come and go, so I'm sure this means lots of work for you. And Charlie gets into lots of trouble at school. You know, like that science fair project. It's a shame she's being held back. Olivia Stiglitz and Ophelia are friends. I'm sure Ophelia hasn't had nice things to say about Fenton's parenting style."

"I didn't know about Ms. Pareto's and Ms. Stiglitz's friendship."

"They're close. And that child timesharing agreement is unusual. Very unusual. Courts generally award most of the time to the mother. Not in this case. Fenton wanted the time. And he gets what he wants."

The elderly neighbor went on to say that, despite her limited time with the girls, Ophelia imposed her strong work ethic on her daughters. Ophelia's unbending standards also demanded categorical excellence and measurable results.

Emma had also noticed that, like planets ceaselessly tugged by their faraway star, the girls' orbits were influenced by their mother. The girls grumbled about their mother's dogmatic mandates, dictating lofty levels of achievement if not perfection. But Emma chalked up these complaints to—as commonly found in divided families—the children's attempts to shape adult perceptions in one household. Ophelia's assertive parenting style clashed with Fenton's hands-off parenting approach. The stresses and perturbations of this parental binary system were as obvious as they were inevitable.

"Yes, Fenton is tough and clever." Jill squinted at the brightening sky. "That abduction case, ages ago, hardened him. During his recovery, he told my late husband: 'I awoke only to find the rest of the world asleep.' Whatever happened, he's been driven since. He doesn't let anything stand in his way: diabolical criminals or a tough ex."

Jill rubbed her hands together. "Anyway, Ophelia never saw it coming."

"Saw what coming?" Emma asked, shifting her weight to her other leg.

"Well, Ophelia hired a high-powered divorce lawyer to make sure her interests would be protected. Fenton is a powerful man. But it didn't work. He outsmarted them all. As the plaintiff, Ophelia had to submit a declaration... you know, saying why she wanted a divorce. These days, though, the reasons are unimportant. Just a formality. California is no-fault. The spouse filing for a divorce doesn't need to prove the other spouse did anything wrong. But Ophelia's lawyer added a couple paragraphs disparaging Fenton, making sure the court wouldn't be sympathetic to him. Just insurance in case he pulled something out of his hat. But he did anyway!" Jill surveyed her garden. "Very few people know that all divorce declarations are a matter of public record. In this county, files can only be viewed in person in the records room of the courthouse basement. Fenton's team spent day after day in that basement, digging through all the past cases handled by Ophelia's lawyer. What they found there still haunts Ophelia to this day."

"What did they find?"

"They found that Ophelia's lawyer used the same couple paragraphs, word-for-word, in vilifying other male respondents in five other court cases. The lawyer just recycled these declarations. From that point, Fenton had the upper hand. Yes, he did."

"If the lawyer was tainted, why didn't Ophelia just hire another lawyer?"

"Well, Fenton's team threatened to bring the lawyer's conduct to The State Bar. But the really smart thing they did was to threaten the court with a public investigation. You see, the court should have caught onto what the lawyer was doing long before—if they had bothered to read any of the declarations. To avoid embarrassment, the court encouraged a quickie settlement. Fenton certainly had the upper hand during those negotiations. The upper hand. The court couldn't risk denying Fenton what he wanted."

"What did Mr. Pareto want?"

"He wanted to raise the children his way, not Ophelia's. He also wanted to manage other decisions, like keeping them in public schools and—"

As Charlie walked up to the two, Jill turned to another subject. Emma did not have an opportunity to ask Jill how much the girls knew about the divorce. And there was another question that could have been asked: Had the girls learned that their father had pointedly kept them from their mother?

*   *   *

Released from the groomer's caged area, fluffier and fresher smelling versions of Scrubbles and Ribsy charged at Emma. As she settled them down, Charlie interviewed the groomer, asking about the health of Jill's dogs, the quality of fur, and unique behaviors. The conversation drifted to the difficulties of the flea season in full swing. The groomer asked if the chip on their collars emitted a high frequency to drive the fleas away. Not being familiar with this technology, Charlie removed Scrubbles' collar. Attached to the underside of his collar was a small chip, about the size of a blouse button. Ribsy also had a matching gadget on the underside of his collar.

Charlie stepped back. "Emma, would you mind taking the device off the collar?"

The groomer handed Emma tweezers and a small bottle. "Feel free to use these."

As Emma gently pulled on the chip with the tweezers, tiny twitching pins, like insect legs, extended from its body. The legs dug into the collar, reattaching itself. The device was like a stubborn tick. It did not want to let go of the collar.

Emma frowned. "What the—"

Charlie moved further behind Emma.

Taking a deep breath, Emma plucked the chip off the collar. Helplessly caught in the tweezers, the chip's tiny legs searched for something to grasp.

As Emma was about to drop the electronic insect into the small bottle, Charlie asked if she could examine the insect. Using the tweezers, Charlie studied the top and bottom of the chip. As she commented on the wriggling legs, the tweezers lost their grip and the insect fell. Instinctively, Charlie caught the chip with her other hand. She cried out as the insect dug itself into her palm.

___ Bonus Content: Charlie's Analysis ___ of Jay's Financial Situation

Charlie concluded that Jay's financial situation was precarious if not untenable based on assumptions in her income and expense pro forma:

If Jay walked fifteen dogs five days a week, his monthly income was $3,375. The average rent for a one-bedroom apartment in Santa Cruz is $2,504. With average food expenses, dining out twice per week, "moderate" alcohol consumption, average utility and insurance costs, no dependents, and one (owned) car, Numbeo's cost of living calculator for Santa Cruz estimates living expenses of $1,413. Jay's total expenses: $3,917 per month ($2,504 + $1,413). Estimated income shortfall: $542 per month ($3,375 - $3,917).

Charlie reviewed her cost-of-living analysis with Clarke.

In a scholarly tone, Charlie said, "Jay interacted with many of our affluent neighbors. This meant Jay was constantly reminded of his income disparity, likely affecting his outlook and actions."

"Obviously, Slick. He couldn't make ends meet, so he moved away."

"I've read that the greater the income inequality within a community, the higher the incidence of certain crimes, particularly property crimes. I adhere to Gary Becker's thesis that all crime is economic, and all criminals are rational."

Clarke shook her head. "Who says there's been a crime? And I don't remember signing up for this lecture series."

Sacrifice

As Charlie winced in pain, Emma used the tweezers to detach the insect. She dropped the insect into the bottle. Using direct pressure, the groomer stopped the bleeding from two rows of tiny puncture wounds. The groomer dressed the wound, using several layers of surgical tape and gauze. It looked like Charlie was getting ready for a one-handed boxing match. Instead, the hand would be out of commission for three days.

Using her functional hand, she conducted an internet search for a flea-suppression gadget matching the squirmy little device. She came up empty.

Charlie held the small bottle at eye level. The pin legs were still twitching. After handing the bottle to Emma, she called Jill, using her phone's speaker.

"My hair appointment is going well, but it's taking longer than I expected."

"I understand, Mrs. Masterson, but we…"

"I've been coming here for years." Jill's voice rose so she could be heard over Charlie's words. "Some of the girls have been here for years. They're *fantastic*! Maybe they can do something with Emma's hair. They take even the worst cases."

"That's very thoughtful of you, but I…"

Jill pushed forward with her salon soliloquy. "They do it all. The new girls are also topnotch! My hairdresser understands that my style needs to be classy and sophisticated."

After Jill exhausted her inventory of hair styling requirements, Charlie asked about a flea suppression device installed under her dogs' collars.

"I suppose I'd buy one of those flea doodads, but I'd need to check out the prices."

For the rest of the call, Jill elaborated on her purchasing criteria for flea control products. Charlie concluded that Jill did not know anything about the electronic parasites.

* * *

"What you have here is both a radio signal receiver *and* transmitter," Owen explained, holding the device between his thumb and forefinger. "There's also a tiny amplifier and battery in this little thingy. Wish I could have seen it wriggle."

Emma had dropped off the devices with Owen the previous day, asking Owen to share his findings with the girls. The two had shared the same dorm their sophomore and junior years. While Emma rarely interacted with other students, she struck up conversations with him on occasions when they met at the dorm entry. They shared a few laughs about eccentric professors and the irrationality of various class assignments. Although attracted to him, she had not found the perfect time to test the presence of reciprocal feelings. To Emma, Owen was one of the many missed opportunities comprising her private mountain of regrets.

Owen parlayed his newly minted electrical engineering degree into a technical role at a local start-up. Although he had entered the professional world, his hippie bad-boy vibe remained strong. His shoulder-length curly dark hair, worthy of a hair care product commercial, fell forward over his brown almond shaped eyes. A few strands slid down the sides of his face, only to be joined by a progressively expanding cascade of thick locks and ringlets. In a swift stroke, he pulled back his hair to restart the sequence.

The visitors searched for a place to sit. Owen's living room was crowded with camping gear, cardboard cartons, a dining table resting on its side, a racing bike, and a full-sized standing cardboard picture of Gandalf from *The Lord of the Rings.* Sidling up to Owen on his sofa, Charlie asked him a string of questions, greeting each response with a nod of appreciation.

Owen pulled back his hair and said, "It's pretty clever. A high-frequency radio signal turns on and off this little gizmo. When actuated, the transmitter then broadcasts an amplified signal on a lower frequency."

He rose from the sofa and resettled on an orphaned dining table chair on the opposite side of the room. Charlie followed.

Owen juggled the device from hand to hand. "Quite a little beastie."

"What do you think this 'little beastie' was intended to do?" Charlie asked, standing over Owen's shoulder.

"I don't know, but I have a theory." He pushed back his thick hair and continued, "Based on the circuitry, I found the frequencies of the incoming and outgoing signals. Its *receiver* is set at a frequency of 52.350 megs. Its *transmitter* is set at 35k hertz, a much lower frequency but still much higher than people can hear."

Owen turned in his chair, looking over his shoulder at Charlie. "Emma told me these were found these on dog collars. From what I read last night, people can hear frequencies up to 23k hertz. But dogs can hear sounds up to 45k hertz. Frequencies between 30k hertz and 45k hertz can bother them. The louder those sounds are, the more painful for them. They bark, whimper, or run away if they're near a frequency in this range."

Owen said, "Charlie, can you give me a smidge more space? Scoot back just a bit. Thanks." After Charlie took a small step back, he returned his attention to the electronic device. "This *receives* a high-frequency signal of 52 megahertz. It then *sends* an amplified signal of 35k hertz, which would be painful for dogs. Since you found these on their collars, I'm guessing they're meant to irritate them. Can't imagine why."

Clarke asked, "Does this device transmit at the same frequency of mobile phones?"

"Oh no, Clarke. Cell phones use much, much higher frequencies, from 700 to 3,800 megahertz. Dogs can't hear frequencies that high."

Clarke asked, "What's the range of a signal on this frequency?"

"A VHF signal broadcast from a low power home station might have a range of twenty to thirty miles."

"Is there a way to find the source of the signal?" Charlie asked.

"Now we know the frequency, you can use a scanner to zero-in on its source."

Charlie edged closer to Owen. "Will this be difficult?"

"Nah. Easy to do."

Owen lobbed the transmitter in the air, tilted his head and opened his mouth, like he was about to catch an airborne snack. He deftly intercepted the device midflight with his other hand.

Charlie smiled. "Easy to do? That's a relief. So often I navigate troubled waters. A report of fair weather and straight passage is welcome."

Clarke smiled at her sister. "Skipper, yer anchor's snagged on somethin'!"

As they walked to Emma's car, Clarke teased Charlie about her new crush, referring to Owen as Charlie's "mane man."

*   *   *

This was Charlie's and Emma's second late night expedition to Chuck's, the Paretos' favorite all-night donut shop. The previous night had conveyed an influx of calories but no high-frequency signals. Nearing two o'clock, Charlie rechecked one of the cables connected to the receiver, dialed to 52.350 megahertz, before turning her attention to the frequency wave modulations on her laptop.

Clarke had opted out of this late-night research project. For her, sleep was a protected and inconvertible resource, a bank available for deposits but not withdrawals.

The previous week, Charlie consulted an expert who advised on the equipment needed for transmitter hunting. She found this technical adviser from a posting on a ham radio hobby site:

Have you tried transmitter hunting on the six-meter band? A group of hams in the Woodside, California area holds Saturday afternoon mobile hunts on 50.5 MHz FM simplex twice a year. This is intended to be an easy hunt with the hiders waiting within a fifteen-mile radius of the tavern. Most hunters use simple loop antennas. More information and results of the April hunt are now in this site. The next hunt will be held in October.

Charlie had found the dog transmitters, acquired the tracking equipment, and was leading the chase to find the signal's origin. If Charlie could bring Jill's case to a glorious dénouement, her name, and no other, would appear on a dazzling marquee of triumph.

Although two glazed doughnuts, a cinnamon twist, and two bear claws kept Emma's blood sugar at an elevated level, her eyes were drooping. Shifting in her chair, she found a spot where she could stretch her legs.

Satisfied that all was in order, Charlie leaned back in her chair and adjusted her new oversized tinted glasses. Katherine brought Charlie to an optometrist the preceding week for a routine exam. She was nearsighted. Charlie chose a 1970s tinted retro style, reminiscent of the outsized shades worn by Bernard Edwards, legendary disco songwriter, producer and Chic bass guitarist.

A handful of customers were seated at booths, including two members of local law enforcement. Charlie's and Emma's booth looked like the others, except for items Charlie placed on their table: a rotating two-foot-wide loop antenna, squawking top-of-the-line receiver, two laptops, and bundles of thick cables. If the police officers had questions about Charlie's equipment, they didn't ask.

Emma yawned. "*So* late. Your aunt gave you permission to stay out late these two nights, but I doubt she thought we would be here *this* late. After I visit the restroom, I'm taking you home. Start packing up."

"I just need a few more minutes. I believe I'm on the cusp of a breakthrough."

Emma sighed. "What makes you think so? You've been at this for hours."

"The dog outbursts have occurred at this time."

"Why's all this so important to you?"

"If I can acquire the signal source, I'll be one step closer to solving the dog barking case. When Dad asks us to help with cases, Clarke always makes more valuable contributions than I do. But if I can crack this one, Dad will see I'm a top-notch investigator." Charlie straightened a cable connecting her antenna and receiver. "And perhaps he and Auntie will give less attention to my recent setbacks at school."

On her way to the restroom, Emma passed a middle-aged man examining the contents of a dusty pink carry-out box at a nearby table. He had short gray hair, broad face, and large brown eyes accented by thick eyebrows. He looked up at Emma.

He tipped his head toward Charlie, who was turning dials on her receiver. "Don't you think she's a little *young* to be out at this hour?"

"Her aunt gave her permission to stay out late to do some detective work."

He raised his eyebrows and leaned forward in his chair. "Detective work? By chance, is she related to the Paretos, the famous detective family?"

"I'm Emma Dorner. I'm helping the Paretos with the girls this year. That's Charlie, Fenton Pareto's daughter... and niece of Katherine Pareto, who hired me to—"

The man jumped up, clutching his head. "You said, *Katherine*? I know her! She's wonderful! What a saint. And so beautiful. I'm so sorry, I should have introduced myself. Cosmo Tal. I'm a family court judge. Pleased to meet you."

The late-night serenader.

As Cosmo settled into his chair, Emma asked, "So, how do you know Katherine?"

"I first ran across her a couple years ago in my courtroom. Naturally, I can't get into the specifics of the case..."

The judge smiled and closed his eyes.

"Katherine came to my court to apply for co-guardianship of a minor. The parents could no longer care for the child. Troubled circumstances. She pledged her financial support to a close relative of the child, who applied to become the new caregiver. You see, the relative needed financial assistance to qualify as the new guardian. Without Katherine's help, the child would've been moved into the foster care system."

Emma did not ask what motivated Katherine to help this family, accepting financial responsibility for the child.

"It was incredible what Katherine did for this family, keeping them together."

The judge shook his head in awe. "Katherine presented the family's arguments to the court. She was very persuasive, and the court ruled in her favor. She's such an intelligent and caring person. I have the utmost admiration for her. And, of course, she is an *incredibly* attractive woman. When I occasionally see her, she makes me want to be a better man."

High praise for Katherine. Yet, there was no admission of his repeated visits to the perimeter wall of the Paretos' property.

As Cosmo collected his doughnut box, the two exchanged good-byes. A minute later, the judge swung out of the parking lot and steered toward the Paretos' compound.

Emma did not share her conversation with Cosmo when she returned to the table.

Rather than packing up, Charlie had been busy acquiring backup power. An industrial electrical extension cord snaked its way across the shop, climbed the back of a seating bench and bridged an adjacent booth before dropping to their table. A second loop antenna and a receiver were set up in the Pareto house. The two receivers would triangulate a signal, sending the broadcast location to Charlie's laptop. Her equipment required a quarter-second transmission to pinpoint the signal source.

Charlie's receiver crackled loudly before issuing a series of high-pitched chirps.

At 2:32 a.m. Pacific Daylight Time, the broadcasting coordinates were displayed on Charlie's laptop. The young transmitter hunter pumped her fist in victory.

* * *

There was a mix-up on when the group would meet at the transmission location. Clarke and Emma were sure that they had agreed to meet Charlie at the broadcast coordinates at three o'clock Sunday afternoon. However, Ophelia had dropped off Charlie, Lucy, and a young friend nearby *an hour earlier*, following an extended mother-daughter-dog brunch. Charlie had begun her operation at the stroke of two o'clock, the cessation of her father's Sunday curfew. She did not wait for Clarke and Emma.

Earlier in the day, Charlie took it upon herself to expand the brunch party to include the Hayek family, including Emily and her wayward six-year-old sister, Scarlet. During the meal, Charlie unveiled a magnanimous proposal to babysit Scarlet for the remainder of the afternoon at a nearby park. Her stated aim was to give Scarlet's weary mother a measure of relief while giving the youngster an opportunity to enjoy some fresh air. The substance of this proposal was fiction. Charlie did not intend to give Scarlet a chance to enjoy any fresh air.

Following the necessary parental approvals, Ophelia dropped off Charlie, Lucy, and Scarlet at the park, three blocks from where Charlie had agreed to meet her sister and Emma. This forsaken location featured hazardous play equipment, graffiti-covered hardscape, accumulations of rusting car parts, fresh excavations near a maintenance shack, and mammoth black birds that patrolled a littered grassy area. Park visitors were given an unobstructed view of a scrapyard across the street.

To put her mother's mind at ease about this recreational venue, Charlie shared that supervision, in the form of Emma and her sister, would be arriving momentarily. This was also an untruth.

An hour later, Emma and Clarke arrived at the agreed-upon meeting spot, three blocks from the park. Charlie's software had pinpointed the signal source within a residence located in a large development. However, the source of the signal, and the house that contained it, was enveloped in a colorful fumigation tent. The rubber tent had broad yellow, red, and blue stripes with warning signs on each of its sides. The notices cautioned visitors that inhalation of sulfuryl fluoride is hazardous, potentially leading to respiratory irritation, pulmonary edema, nausea, abdominal pain, central nervous system depression, numbness in the extremities, muscle twitching, seizures, and death.

Charlie knelt at one of the corners of the tent, threading a line through a flap in the colorful canopy.

As Clarke and Emma sprinted to the tented structure, Emma yelled, "Charlie, get away from there!"

Charlie looked up. "You missed Scarlet's insertion by less than ten minutes. I'm monitoring her on my phone. She's tethered for her welfare."

"Cue the ominous music," Clarke said.

Although Charlie's young assistant was out of sight, the contours of Charlie's plan were coming into view.

"Charlie, you need to bring her back right now! What were you thinking? This is dangerous! Scarlet could die in there!" Emma shouted.

Charlie's shoulders slumped. "Okay. I'll instruct Scarlet to return. But she's quite safe in her protective gear. And she hasn't completed her mission."

Using her phone, Charlie instructed Scarlet to abort her mission and retrace her steps. Charlie's assistant did not respond.

"Base to Scarlet. Return to Extraction Point Alpha. Please respond... please respond." Charlie's confident military tone gave way to alarm.

Emma grimaced. "Give me your phone, Charlie."

Charlie's phone revealed a view from the dark interior of the tented house. Scarlet's flashlight cast a pale beam on an interior ceiling, displaying an unmoving scene as it rested in a prone position on the floor. All was quiet.

Emma whipped out her own phone. Between shallow breaths, she explained the situation to emergency services.

Charlie tugged on Scarlet's safety line, consisting of a chain of linked dog leashes. But the line had become tangled, a predictable consequence of pulling the leashes through rooms containing an assortment of obstacles. She dropped the safety line.

Charlie looked at Lucy, then at the small tent opening. She snapped a leash on her dog then looped the other end to the safety line. Despite Lucy's reluctance, displayed by the rigidity of her body, Charlie pushed her through the opening in the tent.

Pinned

Charlie and Clarke frantically called Lucy's name on Charlie's phone, hoping their voices would lead Lucy to Scarlet's phone and the imperiled child. Pausing after each appeal, the three stared at the phone, straining to see any sign of movement.

Clarke left the two to look for a sharp object to expand the opening in the tent. Meanwhile, Charlie and Emma continued to call Lucy's name.

Clarke returned to the tent, carrying a metal signal flag removed from a neighbor's mailbox. Charlie motioned to her sister to look at the scene on the phone.

Lucy's head filled the screen. She gave Scarlet's phone a quick sniff before turning away. Scarlet's phone moved, followed by rustling sounds. Lucy barked. There was a cough and crackling noises. After pause, Lucy barked again. Scarlet's phone showed a flashlight beam making its dizzying path through several rooms. Charlie picked up the line and collected the slack as her assistant returned to Extraction Point Alpha. Moments later, she dropped the line and pulled her assistant through the opening of the tent.

The discussions with emergency services and the Hayek family were tense and protracted. Katherine responded to Emma's call, serving once again as her niece's defense counsel and the family's lead negotiator.

Ophelia arrived at the site. With her head down, she listened to the conversations.

Charlie recapped her actions, culminating in a near tragedy. She admitted to retaining a drone surveyor to map the broadcast location and surrounding area earlier in the morning. From the high-resolution images, Charlie ascertained that the signal source was inside a house enveloped by a fumigation tent. Charlie saw this as a stroke of good luck, giving her unrestricted access to the dwelling. She only needed to find a means of entry and, if the house had been fumigated, an answer to the sulfuryl fluoride fumigant, a colorless, odorless, and potentially lethal gas.

Charlie found an answer to the means of entry. Her research revealed that most fumigation tents have a small opening in the event a cat or small animal becomes trapped under the tent. If an opening could permit a small animal to exit, it could surely allow a small child to enter. From the Tuscany event, Charlie learned that Scarlet was the embodiment of a small child.

Arriving at the site, Charlie deduced that the lethal vapors had likely dissipated from a posting on the tent. Although the gas had been pumped into the tent days earlier, Charlie took precautions to ensure Scarlet's safety. Since Scarlet was too small to fit into her hazmat suit, Charlie outfitted her with a painter's mask and goggles. Carrying a flashlight and phone, she would be Charlie's eyes and ears. A linked dog leash safety line was fastened to Scarlet's waist to facilitate her return to Extraction Point Alpha.

The group was disappointed to hear how Charlie was able to coax Scarlet to enter an unfamiliar, pitch-black house recently filled with lethal gas. Charlie had invited her assistant to consider the similarities between a fun-filled circus tent and the colorful canopy that stood before them.

In the darkness, Scarlet tripped over a rolled-up area rug and landed heavily on tiled flooring. Charlie credited Lucy's valiant action, along with a few licks to the face, to reviving Scarlet. She saluted Lucy's valor in this desperate moment, announcing a future celebration "to fête Lucy's gallantry."

Clarke smiled at her sister. "Astounding work. Is it just my imagination, or are your underlings getting younger and younger?"

Ophelia and Katherine stood side-by-side as they watched an army of police officers and emergency responders re-secure the tented house. Katherine stood erect with her arms folded. Ophelia's hands were at her hips before dropping them to her side.

They stood in silence.

Ophelia turned to Katherine. "Dees is out of hand. Your new girl vas supposed to watch over my daugh-ters. Since Fen-toon has broken our agreement, I will bring back to the court. He dinks he can bully me. We'll see about dat. Custody needs review and..."

Ophelia broke off the conversation, realizing that Emma had walked up behind them.

Ophelia had pushed to expand the girls' support team, leading to Emma's employment with the family. If Emma had heard Ophelia's comments, she would have learned that not only was her employment in jeopardy, but the custody arrangement hung in the balance.

* * *

Two days later, the Pareto sisters and Emma returned to the fumigated house after the tent was removed and the emergency response and law enforcement paperwork completed. This time, Owen joined them. Under close homeowner supervision, Owen climbed to the roof to inspect an ancient television antenna.

"What do you see up there?" Clarke yelled.

Owen called down to the girls. "Just a TV antenna. Not much else. Ugh... there's a dead squirrel next to it. Looks like this little beastie has burns on one side of its body."

"What do you mean?" Clarke asked.

"Looks like an electrical burn. Like it was electrocuted."

"Be careful," Charlie advised.

"Wait a second. Something's attached to the aerial. It's an electronic thingy. Looks new. I'm going to take it off..."

Later that afternoon, Owen shared with the girls the results of his analysis: The device found on the antenna was an electronic relay, operating as a link within a chain of transmission links. This relay was controlled by an omnidirectional transmitter located elsewhere, the actual source of the signal sent to the dog collars. Owen explained that this pirate radio-linked broadcast tactic is used to conceal a signal source, at least long enough to give the operator a chance to get away.

Owen and the girls did not discuss another possible implication of Owen's discovery. When detaching the device, could Owen have tripped a silent alarm? If so, the operator now knew the Paretos were in pursuit.

* * *

Sitting at Fenton's home office side table, the girls updated their father on the dog barking affair. During the preceding week, the girls removed seventeen transmitter bugs from dog collars. However, the dog transmissions had ceased. Charlie's scanning receiver, still tuned to the

52.350 frequency, had not acquired a signal in a week. Nights were no longer interrupted by dog outbursts. The girls reasoned that "Jay" attached the under-collar devices during his dog walks. Once the installations were complete, the dog walker skipped town. They were skeptical that "Jay" was even the dog walker's name.

Charlie presented Jill with an itemized invoice for her team's time and expense charges. The invoiced time charges were broken down in ten-minute increments by date, investigative professional, and billable activity. Charlie's invoice contained a fifteen percent friends-and-family discount applied to all time charges, including consultations with "subject matter experts," such as the ham radio club hobbyist, the groomer, and Owen. Remittance options included e-payment and discretionary gratuity.

Although Jill had questions about the expense charges—including doughnuts, insect repellent, dog leashes, painter's mask, lighter fluid, and mileage charges—and, of course, the motive for the dog attacks, she was delighted with the outcome of the investigation. The Masterson household was once again at peace.

Placing his hands on his daughters' shoulders, Fenton congratulated his girls on their detective work. However, he reminded Charlie that she should have exercised better judgment at the tented house. He did not have to point out that Charlie's proceeds from the Masterson case were about to be reduced by municipal fines and penalties. She would need to compensate Santa Clara County for emergency response and pay fines for violating several safety ordinances. After a complete expense accounting and her sister's contractual allotment, Charlie contributed only $118.75 to Operation RECLAIM.

The conversation turned to theories about why the dogs had been harassed. Fenton suggested the girls consider several questions: What could be gained by having dogs bark in the middle of the night? Could the nighttime assault be an act of retaliation? Was the barking intended to trigger or cover-up something? Could the dog collar tampering be related to the earlier cell phone reception problems?

It was clear that the dog barking mystery had not been solved.

Fenton's question about a possible connection between the dog collar tampering and the phone problems was troubling to Emma. She had created some fiction for the adults that explained Clarke's urgent care visit the night of their cell tower outing. And, without the adults' knowledge, Emma had taken Clarke to a couple of check-ups to ensure there were no lingering health effects. If any part of that night or the follow-up care was revealed, Emma would be looking for a new job.

As the group wrapped up the discussion, Fenton reported, with dismay, that the Marcum case had stalled. The FBI hearing was only five weeks away.

* * *

Charlie turned down the volume on her laptop, which was transmitting the day's late afternoon financial news. She smoothed her London School of Economics t-shirt as she rose from her work bench, the central work area of her *bottega*.

"Thanks for meeting, Emma. Clarke will be joining us shortly. She said she has something to share about the plush toys she collected from Jay's clients. She asked me to inspect the fetch toys too, but, sadly, I've come up empty."

Charlie pointed to the remnants of four plush toys. Each polyester animal had undergone a complete forensic autopsy. The animals lay on their backs, with white hand towels covering their heads. Large T-pins, functioning as thoracic retractors, pulled the polyester fur away from the surgical sites. The postmortem examinations exposed disemboweled body cavities, with heaps of synthetic stuffing piled next to each carcass.

Clarke sauntered into the room. She picked up a handful of stuffing and sighed. "Ah, my floundering flounder, what have you learned?"

"The manufacturer tags have been removed. And something stitched onto two of them—maybe patches—has also been removed. The purpose of these modifications eludes me. My analysis is inconclusive."

Clarke smiled and shook her head. "*Such* promise. *Such* potential. And yet, such a disappointment. Why, my underperforming Padawan, would Jay remove the identifying patches and tags?"

"He didn't want anyone to know where they were purchased or, perhaps, where they were stolen?"

"Have you considered the possibility they weren't purchased or stolen?"

"I don't understand. Did Jay *make* the plushies?"

"No, my simple sprout. The point is that if he *hadn't* removed the tags, it would have been harder for him to sell them. I've discovered from my internet search that these are no ordinary plushies. They're *not* offered for sale. Can you guess the one spot in the Bay Area where they're found?"

"I confess, I'm at a loss."

"Jay cut off the Seaside Park logo that had been stitched onto them. He was selling midway game prizes. He probably thought his customers wouldn't buy stuff that's pretty much given away. I'm guessing he, or someone close to him, spent time at the park, winning all those plushies. If he hasn't moved away yet, maybe we can find him there—or maybe someone who knows him."

"*Lavoro ben fatto*," Charlie said, nodding appreciatively.

"And it gets better." Clarke raised her chin and swept back her hair. "This big orange gorilla you autopsied was like two others the neighbors showed us. This prize was given away at just *one* midway game. That's it for now." Clarke strode out of the room.

Turning to Emma, Charlie said, "When we work together, she always makes the most important contributions. And she doesn't even take detective work as seriously as I do." She sighed. "Anyway, would you like to see how I've repurposed my strategic planning area?" Emma followed Charlie to an adjoining space. Charlie's stick legs made her Gucci "Tennis 1977" sneakers look implausibly large. "Using our chess conversation as a jumping off point, I'm working on techniques to unburden my mind, acknowledging my intuitive impulses. Boosting my intuitive abilities will improve my detecting skills."

Yoga mats, foam rollers, and cork blocks were scattered on the floor of her room.

"I now use this space for yoga and meditation. I'll demonstrate one of the techniques. My goal is to clear my mind, focusing on *feeling* my upturned palms. You can try it too. Pick a mat and meet me in a Padmasana position, choosing your own relaxation posture or expressive position, acknowledging whatever body you're in today. Focus on being a physically and emotionally connected and awakened woman."

Emma settled next to Charlie in a lotus position. She did not ask her instructor why, in this moment, she should focus on being a physically and emotionally connected and awakened woman. And she did not ask if Charlie's technique was appropriated from an online source or the organic byproduct of an eleven-year spiritual journey on the planet.

"Now activating a cleansing Ujjayi breathing technique, I find it is helpful to visualize two cotton balls resting on the palm of each hand. Feel the air move across your palms. You might even feel a tingling feeling…" Charlie's voice drifted off. She had fallen into a deep meditative state.

A company's earnings call drifted from Charlie's *bottega: "U.S. subscription revenue increased by 16 percent sequentially and 42 percent compared to the year-ago quarter. The stronger dollar lowered dollar-denominated revenues, slowing sales…"*

Charlie opened her eyes. "Emma, let your eyes flutter open. Take the time you need to acknowledge this moment of observation. After honoring yourself, option to follow me into Utkatasana and Shavasana. If these detoxifying movements are not fully available to you, find an engagement layer that works for you."

Not seeing a need to honor, inspire, or detoxify herself, Emma declined to follow Charlie's lead. With some unexpectedly sharp movements, Charlie progressed through a few undemanding body positions.

"We can wrap up with a final stretch. Opportunity to confront any residual tensions."

Charlie did not supply an example of a possible stressor.

"Option to make your way to your own relaxing posture of humility and trust, celebrating the flow of giving and receiving. Hands to heart-center. Namaste."

* * *

Lucy's parade was coupled with activities on the last day of school before summer recess. Charlie would not be graduating with her classmates. Nevertheless, she attended the graduation ceremony to support her fellow students. The parade, consisting of dozens of her classmates and seven members of Stanford University's marching band, wound its way through the surrounding neighborhood following the ceremony. Charlie had organized the parade, instructing students to bring their dogs. Parents and onlookers were surprised to see row after row of regimented young signifers bearing banners and standards emblazoned with Lucy's name along with pronouncements of her great deeds.

The hero led the procession. Lucy was seated on a four-wheeled garden cart pulled by a young student draped in a white toga with a plain headwrap. Her wagon was trimmed with Independence Day bunting and streamers. Rather than gazing upon her many admirers, Lucy was focused on reducing a supply of dog treats she was finding in her chariot. Wearing fishing bucket-style hats, the Stanford sax, brass, and drumming septet performed Pérez Prado mambo classics and rock standards, including "She's Not There" and "All Right Now" on a slow-moving flatbed truck. Onlookers cheered and danced along the parade route.

With the legion beginning to string out and pets breaking from formation, Charlie sauntered along with a small pack of processioners. She had the glow of pride and contentment. This day not only represented an endorsement of her patient tutelage, but the elevation of a friend.

Charlie's parade was modeled on a Roman triumphal procession two millennia before. Such a spectacle acclaimed the return of a victorious general and army to the Capitol City from a far-away land. The garland-decked and gilded pageant not only celebrated heroic deeds and fruits of victory, but eternal glory.

*　*　*

Three days after Scarlet's rescue, Jill told Charlie that Roberta Ru't would welcome any assistance in removing "a little household clutter." Arrangements were made for Charlie to spend a few hours each Wednesday and Saturday to help Roberta dispose of papers and other build-up. Although the project met the criteria outlined in Katherine's community service plan, she asked Emma to accompany her niece on the cleanup days.

Jill had mentioned that Roberta was an expert on dogs. Charlie looked forward to hearing Roberta's perspectives on possible motives for the high frequency dog attacks.

Charlie and Emma arrived at Roberta's residence Saturday morning. The deeply shaded house, just a few streets from the Paretos' home, was screened from the street by a bewildering tangle of overgrown and intertwined trees and shrubbery. Bordering the property were mounds of ivies and creepers suspended by the skeletal remains of generations of Christmas trees, shopping carts, and hazardous debris. What was once a sunny yellow-and-white cottage had fallen into disrepair, with sagging rafters, peeling paint, and ubiquitous wood rot. The roof was blanketed with a two-foot layer of leaves, pine needles, and other organic material in various stages of decomposition. Ivy, creeping fig and potato vines clung to the sides of the house. The *Lacrimosa* sequence of Mozart's Requiem in D Minor drifted from the direction of the house.

Roberta stepped out her front door to meet them. She had a kind, round face, large playful dark eyes, and white hair pulled into a bun on the top of her head. She was just under five feet in height. She wore a dark smock with a necklace of shells, beads, and feathers. Roberta was a descendant of the Muwekma Ohlone Native American people that populated the northern California coast through the late eighteenth century.

With Charlie sliding next to Roberta on a porch swing, and Emma testing a rickety chestnut rocking chair, they spent a few minutes getting acquainted on her veranda. Roberta shared that her great great grandmother, Summer Rain, was a tribal healer. Although successive generations celebrated marriages and children, the Ru't line faltered: premature disease and smaller families whittled the clan to a few members.

Roberta's voice ebbed and flowed like soft waves on a beach. Each sentence started with a rolling deep tone, then flowed into a soothing murmur.

Roberta lost both parents at an early age and was raised in a series of foster homes, eventually joined by a younger foster brother Silas. Roberta was the last of the Ru't line and one of 397 known descendants of her aboriginal clan. She shared that her people suffered through relocation, subjugation, and brutality during the Spanish missionizing and Gold Rush eras. A mistake would have disastrous consequences for the tribe over the following decades. In 1927, a UC Berkeley anthropologist declared the tribe extinct. Since that time, the Ohlone had been unable to convince the federal government to recognize their tribe. Roberta's life had been shaped by a world that did not recognize her existence.

Roberta was a ward of the state. Although she lived with her younger foster brother Silas, he had declined to serve as her guardian. June Hatcher, a county social worker, spent ten hours each day at the house to support Roberta.

As the three entered the dim entry area, Roberta commented that she had socialized with Charlie's father decades earlier, adding that the investigator had contacted her the preceding month. Charlie admitted that she had not heard about their friendship. Beyond the entryway were dusty stacks of paper, heaped in dozens of piles, many soaring to the ceiling. There was little leeway to skirt the paper mounds in the cramped rooms. A resonant passage from Mozart's liturgy shook the paper towers. The visitors were unaware of the delicate balance that kept the stacks standing.

Theory

The piles were comprised of decades of newspapers, magazines, telephone books, utility bills, advertising flyers, bank statements, instruction manuals, letters, flattened cereal boxes, paper shopping bags, sheet music, cardboard food packaging, warranty information, notebooks, scrapbooks, tax returns, maps, and greeting cards, both received and never sent. Based on the National Study Group on Compulsive Disorganization's Five-Level Clutter Hoarding Scale, the Ru't's house could have been categorized as Hoarding Level One or Two, with clutter inhabiting more than two rooms, but with all doors and stairways accessible and the home generally safe and sanitary.

Roberta asked Charlie if she would be interested in hearing an old Ohlone story. The decluttering could wait. Not bothering to ask for Emma's opinion, Charlie endorsed the idea. The youngster settled on a short stack of papers, folding her hands in her lap.

While unfolding two lawn chairs, Emma said, "Charlie, be careful when moving around the stacks of paper. If one falls on top of you, you'll be flattened."

Roberta's fable featured a menagerie of anthropomorphized wildlife, including coyote, eagle, falcon, hummingbird, badger, and possum. The story carried a thinly veiled moral lesson about finding friendship in unexpected places. She then recounted the story in Tamien, one of the dialects of Costanoan, the Ohlone language. For Roberta, Costanoan was the language of nature; its regular cadence echoed the rhythm of the world: the flapping of a hawk's wing, the whisper of a June breeze, the swish of a marsh reed, and the chatter of a night cricket. "*Wa's xi's i'nix ti'ius...*"

Roberta was the last surviving fluent speaker of the language. The Tamien language and the original tribal stories would die with her. But the word, Tamien, would live on as the name of the Caltrain commuter station in San Jose.

Following the story, Roberta asked Charlie about her interests and personal goals. This discussion left no time to declutter or discuss motives for the dog harassment.

The next visit to Roberta's home followed the same pattern: Roberta's storytelling and questions did not leave time for household clean-up or a dog discussion. She acted as if the goal was to provide Charlie with pre-teen counseling rather than being the recipient of her assistance. Silas, Roberta's foster brother, dropped in on the storytelling. June Hatcher, the county social worker, also made brief appearances.

Emma reported to Katherine that her niece's visits to the Ru't household had little to do with the approved plan. Katherine asked her to continue to monitor the visits but was not concerned with the postponement of the decluttering campaign. It was unclear if she anticipated an eventual return to the original proposal.

During a later visit, Roberta told a story about a three-legged dog that protected an Ohlone family from wolves. Roberta believed that dogs could speak in ancient times. But dogs lost the power of speech when it was given to man. In former days, all animals, plants, stones, and lifeless things possessed the power of speech because they were created by the same Great Spirit that created man. Man should treat all animals and lifeless things as if they could still hear and understand.

At the end of a man's life, when his afterlife hung in the balance, the Great Spirit first called upon the animals to give evidence against the man. Only after this was done would the Great Spirit ask for testimony from his fellow creatures.

"Are you afraid of dying, Ms. Ru't? I know I am," Charlie asked.

"No, Charlie. There is no death, only a change of worlds." Her words flowed like lapping waves in an ocean cove.

Charlie learned that Roberta's paper files were part of an organized filing system. The elderly woman said, "My paper-based filing system is the best way to protect my personal information. Any system can be penetrated, given time and inclination. Electronic systems are vulnerable after a breach. Once compromised, it's easy to extract information from an automated system. My system has no such flaw." Roberta's voice rose and fell in an entrancing rhythm.

Roberta did not disclose the key to her system and enjoyed Charlie's attempts to find her secret. As Charlie studied the paper piles, they chatted about the dog barking case. Ruling out savant powers—Roberta claimed to have an unexceptional memory—Charlie tried to decipher the paper filing system based on document age, subject, context, length, physical size, condition, type style, language, and color—along with combinations of these elements. She also considered each hoarding pile's height, girth, and location.

Charlie pursed her lips as she probed a paper pile with her WiFi endoscopic camera. "Your NP-complete system is truly impressive. Although I don't have a background in metaheuristic functions, I'll keep plugging away."

Roberta ran her finger down a paper pile. "Consider the possibility that mathematical rules can apply in some realms but not others. The term mathematics–in the plural–connotes the multiplicity of contexts that must be considered, such as time, place, and purpose. The answer to 2+2 is obvious. Or is it? In the base-4 number system, 2+2=10." Roberta smiled. "Your inquisitiveness reminds me of your father as a younger man."

"Has my dad ever consulted your cryptographic expertise on any of his cases?"

"No, he hasn't. But I'm flattered that you think he might have."

"We've talked about possible motives for the dog attacks. It sounds like you're as baffled as we are. But do you have any advice?"

Roberta frowned as she crossed her arms. "Advice? Ah, let me see... How about: Beware of the man who does not talk and the dog that does not bark."

"I'll consider that. By the way, how did you and my dad meet?"

Roberta's face brightened. "We met decades ago. We both love gardens and classical music. It was so nice seeing him again. If you don't mind, please tell me what's happening in your gardens. Share every detail."

Roberta asked about the woodland area. How dense were the oak tree canopies? Were there vines growing on the oak trunks? Were there mushrooms near the oaks? She did not disclose how or when she became acquainted with the garden but spoke knowledgeably about the leafy residents found there. She mentioned that parts of the garden were ancient, long predating Ohlone elders she met as a child.

After reporting on the status of the grounds around the Paretos' home, Charlie asked, "Ms. Ru't, what was my dad like when he was younger?"

Roberta adjusted her shell and bead necklace. "I met your father when he was in his mid-twenties and he—" The aged woman paused, looking at the palms of her hands. "He had just launched his PI firm with two partners. He hasn't changed much, just a bit grayer hair. And I know something about that myself! He's always been a very handsome man."

Charlie adjusted herself on her paper chair. "But what was his personality like when he was younger? Was he serious about his business then?" Charlie did not ask Roberta to elaborate on her father's appearance as a young man.

Roberta smiled. "He's always been a wonderful man." There was no mention of the investigator's past or current standing in the community. Roberta crossed her arms. "He wasn't so focused on business. He was light-hearted and social. His friends came first."

"Really, *my* dad?"

Roberta clasped her smooth hands as if in prayer. "His business partners were also close friends. I don't recall a love interest. Anyway, he enjoyed bocce. He played with his two partners and another person. Who was the other bocce friend? A judge? Maybe—" Roberta trailed off in thought. "Anyway, the abduction case changed all that."

"I've heard parts of the story, but my dad doesn't like to talk about what happened. What did you hear about it?"

"Only the little your father shared years ago. I suppose it wouldn't hurt to tell you—" Roberta paused as she looked over her left shoulder. "Early in your father's career, a banker hired your dad to rescue his kidnapped son. The banker refused to pay the ransom or involve the police. He hired your dad to find his son. Your dad and his two partners chased the kidnappers across the country in the depths of winter."

"I've heard that part," Charlie nodded.

Roberta surveyed an area where one of her paper towers met the ceiling. "The search continued for weeks. In the end, your father and his partners caught up to the kidnappers, holed up in an abandoned warehouse." She sighed. "In Connecticut, I think. The three staked out the building, waiting for the right moment to make their move. One of the partners thought he saw smoke through the warehouse windows, and the three rushed in. Only your father knows what happened next. Five men lost their lives in that building, including your dad's two partners. Your dad rescued the banker's son, but your dad was severely wounded. The police didn't find evidence of a fire."

"I hadn't heard *why* they went into the warehouse."

"Your aunt went back east to care for him. There was suspicion that the kidnapped son was actually in league with his 'abductors' to extort money from his father. The banker knew this all along. For that reason, he didn't want to involve the police."

"The banker should have shared his suspicions with Dad. He probably felt betrayed."

"Most certainly. In any case, when he returned, he was a different man."

"In what way?"

"Hmm... A personal subject. I'll just say that his heart was heavier. I'll tell you another story that might help you understand. But before I do this, young lady, consider our teamwork conversation. Giving ourselves to others is the only way to give our lives meaning. Remember, if you want something in life you've never had, you'll have to do something you've never done. Have you been trying out what we've discussed?"

Charlie's shoulders dropped. "I've been swamped of late. But your suggestions are on my punch list."

Without commenting on Charlie's punch list, Roberta recounted one of her stories.

BONUS CONTENT AT THE END OF CHAPTER

Silas also listened to the story. He was a rickety professorial type, with long and angular limbs, like a praying mantis. During the storytelling, he rocked back-and-forth on a stack of paper, grasping his shins with his elongated bony arms. After the story ended, he unfolded himself as he rose to his feet. Without a word, he looked over the visitors with his bulging eyes before tottering out of the room.

June had not appeared since their arrival. Charlie asked, "How long has Ms. Hatcher been visiting your home, Ms. Ru't?"

"She's been with us about a year, helping with chores, meals, and running errands. It was thoughtful of Silas to bring her here, but I can still keep the house running. This has been good for him, though. Before she arrived, I think he was lonely and needed someone to talk to. They spend lots of time together."

June was mid-fifties, with a blotchy face framed by a chin-length brunette bob. The social worker would greet Emma and Charlie with a scowl before rushing off to attend to a chore. Taking a break from dusting or sweeping, June would sometimes linger nearby, watching over her ward and the unwelcome visitors. Charlie occasionally caught June eyeing them through one of the narrow aisles of the paper maze. After one of their visits, Charlie told Emma about another instance of June's eavesdropping: June had flinched when Charlie asked about the elderly host's dreams.

"Can you tell us about your foster brother?" Charlie asked. Sitting on a paper stack, she looked up at Roberta who was inventorying one of her towering archives.

Roberta slowly ran her index finger down the side of a paper tower. "Silas and I have lived here many years. Before retiring, Silas conducted research at the university, specializing in acoustic design. He set up our wonderful sound system!" The household's audio system broadcast Bach's B Minor Mass, Vivaldi's Gloria, Hayden's Lord Nelson Mass, and Roberta's other classical choral favorites during their visits.

Repositioning herself on her paper stack, Charlie said, "I understand you were a scientist too. Did you work together?"

Roberta sighed. "Only on one occasion. But unfortunately, it didn't work out..." Roberta's voice trailed off. "A long time ago, we had a disagreement involving our work together. This has been a longstanding issue between us." Roberta's eyes filled with tears. "Silas is still angry. I hope he will find peace... and we'll be friends again one day."

Charlie pursed her lips as she slowly nodded in agreement, suggesting profound empathy. "I think I understand. It's been challenging to collaborate with others on my projects, especially during the discovery, design, development, testing, and deployment stages of an endeavor. Anyway, at least your foster brother appreciates your stories."

Roberta nodded and smiled. "He does seem to enjoy them. I wish he would come up more often. He spends too much time in the basement with his experiments."

"What type of experiments?"

"I don't know. I haven't been down there for some time. I avoid shadowy and creepy places below ground."

Charlie nodded. "I do too, along with shadowy and creepy places above ground."

Roberta laughed. "At least the stories get him out of the basement for a little while. I was disappointed we didn't see him today."

Charlie gave Emma a puzzled look. Rather than contradict Roberta, she remained quiet. Roberta had overlooked that her foster brother was in plain sight minutes before.

There would be another strange occurrence a week later. Charlie offered Silas baby carrots from a plastic bag she brought to Roberta's story-time. Silas rocked back-and-forth on a paper pile, waiting for the story to begin. Roberta looked directly at him and told Charlie that her brother was in the basement. Silas put his bony forefinger to his lips. June, who was standing next to Roberta, glared at Charlie while remaining silent.

On their walk home, Charlie and Emma discussed this curious episode. Charlie's conclusions: Silas and June could not be trusted and, whatever they were up to, it was not good for Roberta.

* * *

Roberta shared more about herself in their next visit. Since her tribe was declared extinct, it stood to reason there could be no living members of such a tribe. Based on this premise, she concluded at an early age she did not exist. Since she was nonexistent, there could be no actions in her life that would elevate or lower her value. Rather than becoming dispirited by the negation of being, she saw the liberation of nothingness, forming a fearless philosophy that invited her to leapfrog the limits of conventional thinking and explore novel and sometimes controversial academic theories.

Had Roberta acknowledged her own existence, she might have celebrated a doctorate in botany, five scholarly books, a thirty-year career, and a Copley Medal.

The Ohlone generally considered dreams a form of reality, revealing deeply perceptive psychological insights. Roberta admitted that her sleep was disturbed over the past year by Wiwe, or "Body of Stone." Body of Stone was the underground Earth Lord, a man with a stone body. He fed Ohlone to his servants with his subterranean domain littered with their bones. She took these visions seriously, fearing a malevolent force was at work. She had not visited the basement of her house since the dreams began.

As the three discussed the possible meaning of Roberta's visions of the underworld, several tall paper stacks behind Charlie teetered ominously, with the middle of the piles slipping and buckling. Charlie jumped to her feet as an avalanche of rumbling ceiling-height mounds of paper pitched forward and cascaded down on her.

— Bonus Content: The Three Bird Fable —

Ma'tcan, the coyote leader, addressed the animal council on a chilly autumn evening. The assembly was composed of other land-dwelling representatives, such as badgers, bears, possums, skunks, elk, and deer. Avian delegates included eagles, falcons, hummingbirds, blue jays, geese, crows, and a variety of songbirds. After making the necessary ceremonial address to the esteemed body, Coyote Ma'tcan moved to the point of this emergency gathering. Tci'pil's six-month badger cubs had been missing for almost a week. With winter coming on, it was vitally important for the two cubs to be found to secure their safety in the family's wintertime burrow. Without such protection, the badger cubs would certainly perish in their first winter. Ma'tcan and Tci'pil were close friends and hunting partners when pursuing tunneling prey, such as gophers, moles, and field mice. The elder badger could be relied upon to share a good story, especially after eating fermented fruit. Ma'tcan had grown very fond of the badger cubs, with the three seen roughhousing on several occasions—and he had become an honorary uncle to the two youngsters.

Coyote Ma'tcan turned to the winged representatives of the group to help organize a search party. Ma'tcan argued birds could cover the most ground in a search and could bring intelligence back to the council. Once found, the council could arrange a land-based party to retrieve the badger cubs.

Kerome, the head of the falcon clan, hopped forward. Puffing out his chest, he declared, "The speed of the falcon is unmatched in this world. We are also the only winged animal with a sharp tooth to complement our strong talons. I offer my fastest and most ferocious soldier. Speed and courage will likely be needed on this quest."

At this point, Uci, the leader of the hummingbird clan, flew to the center of the gathering. After making a few circles around the group, he quickly said, "The maneuverability of the hummingbird is unmatched in this world. We can fly forwards, backwards, and upside down. We are also cooperative, working well with others. I offer my most agile, creative, and clever soldier. Maneuverability and creativity will likely be needed on this quest."

Tuxi, the leader of the eagles, extended his broad wings. Speaking in a solemn and commanding voice, he bellowed, "The eyesight and strength of the eagle is unmatched in this world. We have the vision to see the edges of this land and have the strength to carry a mule deer fawn. We are the king of birds; we do not look back over our shoulders when we strike our prey. I offer my sharpest-eyed, strongest, and commanding warrior. Vision and strength will likely be needed on this quest."

The coyote addressed the three winged leaders. "Your words have both wisdom and generosity within them. Indeed, there will likely be a need for speed, courage, flexibility, creativity, vision, strength, and leadership on this desperate mission. However, I believe there may be additional qualities found to be equally important during this pursuit. The trials of this journey will bring forth these hidden attributes; these cannot be measured, weighed, or described as the strengths so evident in your warriors. Do not look for these. Kerome, Uci, and Tuxi return to each of your clans and find the one truly unremarkable, undoubtedly common, and eminently average representative of your group. Once found, please send your clan's representative to me to prepare for the search."

The birds looked at each other in puzzled amazement. Coyote Ma'tcan was known to be an unconventional thinker. While he could be wise, he was just as often found to be rash, irresponsible, and even duplicitous. Why would Ma'tcan put the badger cubs at risk by substituting the most qualified and elite members of the winged kingdom for a ragtag band of mediocre and unproven searchers?

Shortly after the conclusion of the animal council, Kaknu, U'mun, and Ci'irx reported to Ma'tcan for their mission briefing. Kaknu was the representative of the falcon group. He was not a soldier or even a good hunter. While he was a fast flier by many standards, he was average at best for a falcon, barely reaching half the speed of the best fliers. He had practiced his diving month after month but had not improved at all. While Kaknu did not mention his thoughts to others, he saw himself as a failure. U'mun was the representative of the hummingbirds. Both parents and her two siblings were acrobatic, being able to maneuver in impressive ways to the amazement of other hummingbirds. However, U'mun did not have any distinguishing aerial skills. Although she tried, she could barely fly backwards, often clumsily colliding with a flower or branch. She dreamed of effortlessly jumping in any direction faster than the blink of an eye but had resolved to simply become a competent nectar gatherer for a future husband. Ci'irx was the representative of the eagles. Although he was large and broad winged, he was clearly not the strongest of his peers. He had the unfortunate habit of dropping his prey mid-flight. Others laughed at his incompetence. Compounding his weakness and clumsiness, Ci'irx was slightly near-sighted. Unlike his cohorts, he could not see to the edges of the world. His prosaic field of vision could only see fine details within two miles. He certainly didn't see himself as a member of the distinguished bird kings. He would settle for fitting in with his friends.

Coyote Ma'tcan briefed the three on their mission and equipped them with provisions for their search. Details and contingencies were covered. The birds would be on their own, with Kaknu returning once every three days to provide a status report to Coyote Ma'tcan. This would continue until the cubs were found.

Over the next three weeks, the birds searched in expanding rings around the badger's home. Every three days, Falcon

Kaknu would report their failure to find the cubs while asking Coyote Ma'tcan to send their love to their families. With each passing day, the level of urgency rose. They were still hopeful of finding the cubs; they would find small tracks that could have been made by the elusive youngsters, only to lose them again. The three searchers worked well together. Ci'irx would often spot a promising clue with his eagle eyes. If there was animal movement in the forest below, Falcon Kaknu would swoop down to immediately evaluate a new location. Hummingbird U'mun's contribution was indispensable. She navigated in tight areas, investigating hollow logs, dense thickets, and impenetrable brush. Now in the fourth week, the birds searched a quarter-day from the badger's home. After a long flight, Falcon Kaknu reported to Coyote Ma'tcan they had followed a pair of tracks that could be the cubs. Ma'tcan agreed to allow the search to continue, but the snow had settled on the mountain peaks; the dimming days were becoming colder and shorter, and many of the animals had either taken refuge underground or had flown to warmer southerly locales. Coyote Ma'tcan asked Kaknu to inform U'mun that her hummingbird family had already left for the winter. Coyote Ma'tcan also shared that he would be expanding his own foraging radius and would not be able to meet for future status reports. He advised Falcon Kaknu and the others to use their judgment as to how much longer to continue the search. Now in the sixth week of the search, winter held a tight grip on the world, bringing icy rain and snow. Clear nights chilled the search party to their bones. The three birds were in a state of exhaustion. Falcon Kaknu and Eagle Ci'irx needed to spend increasing time and energy to find rapidly dwindling game. To allow time for search on the shorter days, they would need to become increasingly adept and efficient hunters to even come close to meeting their nutritional requirements. Suffering from starvation and exposure to the extreme elements, the falcon hallucinated, telling the others the cubs had been found and it was time to return home. Meanwhile, Hummingbird

U'mun's condition was desperate. Her regular flower diet had long disappeared; she now relied on honey caches and a rare winter lily to sustain herself. She had already lost one-quarter of her weight, and she was adding to this deficit each day. As her relative caloric requirements were the greatest, she was in great peril as she habitually sacrificed energy conservation for her desire to maximize her search area. A persistent cold strained her already depleted reserves.

Ten weeks into the search, in the heart of January, the desperate search party retraced their search pattern, slowly working their way back to the starting point of their journey. It was increasingly difficult to focus on the task, and they would become lost. But their thoughts were clear enough to know they would not survive much longer. Friends and family would not have recognized the three. Falcon Kaknu's and Eagle Ci'irx's tattered plumage was thicker and much darker than before. Their eyes now were deeply recessed with a trace of something formidable and even frightening. Hummingbird U'mun's colorful plumage had been replaced by shorter mottled feathers, flecked with mud and grime. Her once colorful crown was now a ring of white. Although she was just a shadow of her former self, she moved with the efficient grace of a queen.

It was now the fifteenth week of the search. Suffering from exhaustion, the eagle dropped from the sky, making a long spiraling fall into a half-frozen river. With the falcon and hummingbird making panicky circles above, the river tossed Eagle Ci'irx along with slabs of dangerous ice, with the eagle barely having enough strength to stay afloat. Mercifully, the river current eventually deposited Eagle Ci'irx on a sandy shoal where the three were reunited. Eagle Ci'irx was unhurt but was in immediate need of rest and a warm shelter. Seeing evidence of a badger colony further up the riverbank, the birds collected their strength and conveyed themselves to the nearest borough. Rubbing sleep from her eyes, an elderly badger sow was surprised to see such unusual guests. Over the next few days, she helped stabilize the condition of the three beleaguered travelers and shared an important revelation. Two badger cubs meeting the exact description of the missing youngsters had wandered into their village three months earlier and were lodging with a neighbor. Unable to find their parents, the neighbor initiated adoption proceedings; these would be finalized if the parents failed to materialize by summer. The elderly sow admitted her own relief to a biological family reunion, conceding the neighbor was more interested in the future products of the cubs' labors than a happy enlargement of their family. Shortly thereafter, there was a happy meeting with the young badgers. After further recuperation, Hummingbird U'mun flew south to try to find her family. Two days later, the falcon and eagle reported the joyous news to Badger father Tci'pil who, naturally, had been in great distress. After arrangements were made to transport the cubs home, Kaknu and Ci'irx rejoined their families for the remainder of winter.

When spring arrived, Hummingbird U'mun returned to her home. Her family celebrated their reunion with great fanfare. Although she had searched far and wide for her family in the southern gardens, she had not found them. Over the remaining weeks of winter, she had been self-sufficient as she healed herself and fattened on southern tropical flowers. However, her kaleidoscopic plumage had not returned. She was now cloaked in lustrous white feathers. The hummingbird saw that her friends had also made radical springtime transformations: Falcon Kaknu and Eagle Ci'irx were now much larger and more formidable specimens than when they had left the village the preceding autumn. Oddly, both now sported iridescent jet-black feathers but retained their solemn deep-set eyes. Over the next year, the three would meet regularly, recounting the desperate and even lighter moments of their four-month trial. However, all confessed to persistent if not increasing feelings of uneasiness and restlessness. They had returned to their friends and family, but they no longer fit into the rhythm of social life and felt at odds with family and community activities. Notably, their skills had somehow risen to a high level: Eagle Ci'irx could now see a rabbit stick its head up at the edge of the hunting ground, Falcon Kaknu could now dive faster than his friends, and Hummingbird U'mun could gracefully navigate in any direction. However, none of these skills mattered as they once had.

It was the second anniversary of their departure when the three friends met with Coyote Ma'tcan. The three told him they would leave their homes and devote their lives to looking for animals that had strayed from their families. Their enduring mission would be to return these strays safely home. The next day, the three friends bid farewell to bewildered and saddened friends and families. The three searchers would not return home again. However, over the years, a forest animal would occasionally report seeing one of the three on an errand. They were not difficult to find. Falcon Kaknu's dive was accompanied by a thunderclap. Hummingbird U'mun's backward maneuvers were so rapid it is said she could jump to a moment earlier in time. Eagle Ci'irx's keen vision allowed him to see the providential spirit dwelling in all things.

Trap

Emma shoved Charlie away from the bulk of the paper slide, representing hundreds of pounds of debris. It was a close call. Charlie could have been crushed. The most powerful part of the avalanche missed them.

A double choir delivered the climactic *Dies Irae* from Verdi's Requiem as they dug themselves out of the papers. Although Charlie and Emma were covered with dust, there was no serious damage. Roberta had not been in the slide's path, so she was able to give assistance to Charlie, brushing off her back.

The elderly homeowner was shaken by the mishap. She profusely apologized, bewildered by the cause of the avalanche. As Charlie continued to dust herself off, June called out from behind a wall of paper, pronouncing the house too hazardous for visitors. She asked Emma and Charlie to leave, insisting that she and Roberta would restore order to the house. The two said their farewells to Roberta, without making return plans.

Later in the day, Charlie shared with Emma her suspicion that the mishap at Roberta's house might not have been an accident.

"I agree," Emma said. "Something fishy is going on there."

Charlie frowned. "It's as if Roberta is being controlled by her foster brother and June. It's really depressing. And I've been feeling low lately. Seeing those people—who don't seem to like each other—makes me think that some people aren't meant to live together. I'm wondering if Operation RECLAIM was ever a good idea."

*   *   *

Three days after the avalanche at Roberta's house, Emma and the sisters set off to Seaside Park. Clarke had revealed that the orange gorillas were prizes given away at the midway's high striker. Their plan was to observe the game throughout the day, looking for the dogwalker. The girls would pass the day with two school friends they would meet there. Emma would provide the transportation and accompany the girls.

Before heading to the amusement park, the group made a stopover at Chuck's Donuts. Charlie ordered her usual powdered sugar doughnuts. These white sugar doughnuts, called Sweet Snowballs, left a trail of white powder in their wake. Running late, Emma asked the girls to eat the donuts on the way to the park. Charlie used zip-lock plastic bags as gloves and as receptacles to catch the spilled powdered sugar.

Emma had not cleaned her car in months. Since the seats and floor of her car were crowded with empty soft drink cans, free-floating vitamin pills, candy, fast-food wrappers, a couple of unpaid parking tickets, and small sheets of foil, she told Charlie that she was not concerned about the sugar further degrading the interior of her vehicle.

Emma was relieved to find a mostly-legal parking space close to the entrance of the amusement park. The girls met their friends, Yinyue and Aurora, next to an antique carousel. Yinyue was Clarke's peer and Aurora was Charlie's age. Charlie shared Aurora's name when debuting the amusement park plan with Emma. Before this, however, Charlie had not mentioned the friend. Emma did not ask Charlie if Roberta's counseling reprioritized her punch list. If she had, she might have learned about a bond between the girls: Like Charlie, Aurora would be putting middle school on hold for another year. But for a different reason. Aurora's parents had decided that their daughter would benefit from a gap year, giving her an opportunity to unwind from the stresses of elementary education and recharging before undertaking the rigors of middle school.

Lingering near the carousel, the girls reviewed the day's itinerary. The carousel horses took little notice of their small group, their resolute and solemn features displaying the import of their enduring pageant. The girls ironed out a few final details as the carousel's band organ provided a cheery accompaniment. The girls would split up: One team would watch the high striker while the other enjoyed the park. After thirty minutes, the teams would switch.

The party grew to seven, once two other youths, Jack and Leo, attached themselves to the group in the early afternoon. Both were the same age as Clarke and Yinyue. These additions reshuffled the surveillance assignments, with Emma and Charlie spending more time watching the high striker.

Throughout the day, the group enjoyed rides, arcade games, snacks, and conversation. Clarke won a large yellow plush narwhal in a ring toss game. Charlie replaced her Oakland cap with a red Bartholomew Cubbins hat with a long yellow feather purchased from a vendor. However, the girls had not seen anyone resembling the dogwalker.

Evening arrived, and it was time for the company to disband. An exchange of contact information pointed to the possibility of the girls seeing the young gentlemen again. Clarke and Yinyue's farewell partings with Jack and Leo were drawn-out, indicative of profound attachments and suggestive of the difficulty of managing painful separations. In turn, Clarke and Charlie bid farewell to their girlfriends. Clarke's sendoff was filled with hugs and teary proclamations of plans together.

Before leaving the park, the girls and Emma decided to try a small attraction near the high striker. As they waited in line, the high striker's bell clanged. Charlie tugged on her sister's arm. She pointed to a muscular man holding a gigantic mallet, accepting praise from a group of admirers. "Could that be Jay?" The high striker winner was thirty-ish, with neck length brown hair pulled back behind a San Diego Padres baseball cap.

Clarke frowned. "I'll ask him if his name is Jay and see what happens."

Clarke pushed through a small group surrounding the winner. The moment she spoke to the stranger, he bolted. Sprinting away at top speed, he weaved in and out of the late evening crowd. Clarke took off after him, jettisoning her plush narwhal. Charlie and Emma chased the two, with Charlie clutching her feathered hat.

After she and Emma lost contact with the two in the crowd, they anxiously waited for Clarke to reappear where they had last seen her.

Twenty minutes later, Clarke limped back to the two, the side of her face smeared with blood. She had caught up with Jay at the boundary of the amusement park. Tackling the suspect, the two thrashed about, but Jay was able to struggle free. The dog walker sprinted onto the beach, away from the park lights. He vanished into the night.

Purple bruises started to appear on Clarke's neck and forearm.

As Emma wiped blood from Clarke's face with a tissue, Clarke touched her cheek. "This isn't mine. There still might be time to get Jay."

"We need to leave," Emma urged, shaking her head.

"I agree with Emma," Charlie said. "You need medical attention. We can come back to the park tomorrow and interview concessioners. Maybe someone else saw our suspect. We may be able to take a casting of one of his footprints on the beach or find other clues to ascertain his identity and the location of his hideout."

Clarke wiped her nose with her shoulder. "We may not get another chance to get Jay. This is a golden opportunity. Charlie, you have to take a risk once in a while."

Clarke's risk-welcoming stance contravened her security pledge, the foundation of the sisters' revenue sharing agreement.

"I don't like this," Emma said. "But let's hang out here for a half hour. If we spot this guy, I'll ask park security to help. If we don't, I'm pulling the plug."

The three leaned against a wall, watching guests leave the park. Just as they were ready to give up, Clarke pointed to an area down the street from the park entrance.

Charlie squinted her eyes. "What? I don't see anything."

Their suspect darted across the street, momentarily exposed by a nearby streetlamp.

Clarke smiled. "Security won't help us outside the park. Wheels up! Let's go."

Clarke took off, with Emma and Charlie at her heels. "Be careful!" Emma called out. The pursuers ducked behind parked cars, suspecting Jay was likely on the lookout for an oddly hostile young female in pursuit. Trailing him along a string of parked cars, Clarke turned back to look for her sister. She found Charlie clinging to a car bumper.

Jay stopped to use a key fob, unlocking the driver's side door of a black commercial cargo van having no windows or markings. The man stepped into the cab and shut the door. Standing behind the van, Clarke took a picture of the license plate.

"Emma, get your car," Clarke whispered. "I'm going to try something. If we get separated, track my phone." Without giving Emma the opportunity to review the details of her plan, Clarke tested one of the cargo doors at the rear of the vehicle. It was unlocked. Clarke jumped in, pulling Charlie through the cargo door behind her.

Emma screamed, "No!" She dove at Charlie but missed, landing hard on the asphalt. The cargo door slammed shut as the van pulled away from the curb.

Emma stumbled to her feet. After a few shaky steps, she shifted into an all-out sprint.

Panting, she arrived at her car. As she reached for her key fob, hands grabbed her back and shoulder, slamming her face against the side of her car. Her phone and key fob were ripped from her hands. Warm blood dripped from her chin. As the recent college graduate's arms and legs were forcibly repositioned, six flashlight beams converged on her. Ten law enforcement officers surrounded her vehicle with weapons drawn.

En passant

Emma briefed the arresting officer on the precarious state of the Pareto siblings. As she wiped the blood flowing from her chin with the back of her handcuffed hands, she urged the officer to consider the incalculable benefit of contacting the girls.

The officer nodded but took time to review the various elements that drew law enforcement's attention to her vehicle. Although Emma's not-actually-legal parking choice, expired registration, outstanding parking citations, and the numerous pills sprinkled throughout the vehicle had drawn their notice, it was the significant volume of white powder, both on the seats and wrapped in plastic bags, that had rallied five squad cars to these coordinates.

A drug test would be administered shortly.

Questions involving drug trafficking needed to be resolved before the officers could turn their attention to helping the girls. Emma suggested that the officers draw upon their experience to identify the doughnut sugar, arguing that a simple taste test would remove the most serious charge against her. The arresting officer removed his cap and scratched the side of his head.

The other officers weren't moving. Losing her patience, Emma screamed, "They're in trouble! They need help! They could die!" The police stirred, shaken from their daze. The senior officer motioned for a stout subordinate to open one of the zip-locked baggies. After gingerly inserting his pinky finger into the powder and placing a sample on the tip of his tongue, the hefty officer closed his eyes and dropped his chin in thought.

The subordinate opened his eyes and rendered his verdict: "This is powdered sugar, most likely from a Sweet Snowball from Chuck's Donuts in Redwood City." As Emma's handcuffs were removed, the stout officer explained that doughnut sugar is like a fingerprint, allowing a skilled investigator to pinpoint a doughnut's place of origin and to deduce batch characteristics. The officers did not ask Emma if her faith in law enforcement had been restored.

Emma used her phone's speaker feature, allowing the officers to listen to Clarke's status report.

"We're in the van." Clarke's voice was muffled, with a humming sound in the background. "The van's rocking from side-to-side. I think we're on a mountain road, maybe in the Santa Cruz Mountains. We can't see outside. There're no windows."

Cracking and crunching sounds were coming through the phone. Clarke was moving around in the van. "It's pitch black in here. I'm using the light of my phone. There's a partition, so we can't see the driver. I don't think Jay knows we're in here."

One of the officers instructed, "You two need to disembark from the vehicle as soon as possible."

"We will." The pitch of Clarke's voice was much higher than normal. "As soon as the van stops, we'll jump out. Oh! I took a picture of the van's license plate. Emma, I'm sending it to your phone."

A moment later, Emma shared the image of the license plate with one of the officers.

Clarke continued, "It's hard to move around in here. It's cluttered with lots of cables and electronic stuff.

There are stacks of manuals. Charlie... Charlie! Stand up! Move over there and look at those manuals. Pull yourself together."

One of the officers cut in. "Clarke, we've dispatched pursuit cars using your phone's coordinates. When the van stops, exit the vehicle." The officer did not mention that an AMBER alert had just been broadcasted to 1.2 million mobile phone users in the area.

Clarke continued her status report. "I'm taking a few snaps of the equipment. Don't know what all this stuff is."

Charlie was saying something, barely audible. Her voice intermittently cut out: "Amazing... can't believe... manuals... you need to..."

Charlie had found something important in the pile of manuals.

Not responding to Charlie, Clarke said, "There are cables connecting the equipment. Can't get to the electronic stuff. There's a wire blocking the way. I'll disconnect it."

One of the officers yelled into the phone, "No! Don't touch anything!"

A moment later, the phone broadcast a roaring sound from the van's cargo area. The girls screamed. The police and Emma called out the girls' names, but the deafening noise made it impossible for them to hear anything. The cargo area was being filled with an earsplitting rendition of Sister Sledge's "Lost in Music."

When Clarke detached the wire, she triggered an alarm intended to repulse unwelcome visitors to the van's cargo area.

Through the commotion, the girls pleaded for help. The officers turned to Emma with matching blank expressions. Getting out of the van was all that mattered now. But there was no escape while the vehicle barreled down the mountain road. One of the officers reported that the van had picked up speed. No doubt Jay had become aware of the intruders in the cargo area.

Joni Sledge's ode to melody and rhythm played on.

The girls' muffled screams coincided with each shift of the vehicle, heaving from side-to-side as it traversed the mountain road curves at break-neck speed.

The officer pointed out that the increase in the van's speed likely meant that the driver had no intention to free the girls. He did not mention that the passengers were *likely* being taken to a remote location for interrogation. And he did not share his perspectives on what would *likely* happen when this interview was concluded.

As Emma fought back tears, Clarke's phone went dead.

*　*　*

A half an hour later, one of the officers reported that the girls had been found in a commercial district of Los Gatos, a town at the foot of the Santa Cruz Mountains. The officer asked Emma to follow a police cruiser to that location. No additional details were provided. Although an officer assured Emma that there would be a future court date to sort out her vehicle infractions, she was granted the use of her car. Emma followed a police car to a service station, joining several police vehicles obliquely parked at the front of the shop's service bays.

The girls, wrapped in reflective Mylar rescue blankets, were in the middle of a police huddle. Pushing through the officers, Emma reached the girls. Each gave her a big hug.

Clarke pointed to Emma's bandaged chin. "What happened to you?"

"Nothing, really. How did you get out of the van?"

Clarke rubbed her left ear. "I unjammed the cargo doors. When it stopped, we jumped out. It took off, heading in that direction," she said, pointing to the rear of the service station. "The police tracked my phone here. They said that the license plate on the van was stolen so it's of no use. But I hid my phone in the van so the police can keep tracking it. I lost the connection with you, but my phone still has plenty of juice."

One of the officers chimed in. "We're tracking your phone, miss, but our tracking system is showing it's still here."

Clarke scowled. "No, it's not! My. Phone. Is. In. The. Van. Full stop."

The officer rubbed the back of his neck. "That's just it, miss. We're showing your phone is still at this location, here at the service station. Can you double-check your pockets? Maybe you didn't actually leave it in the van."

Patting her pockets, Clarke said, "Can't you see I don't have it?" She grimaced, rubbing her left ear. "*Maybe* you should *double-check* your training manual on basic observational skills. Cross-reference 'blockhead.'"

"Settle down," Emma said with a frown.

Charlie joined the conversation. "Clarke, may I have your blanket? Due to supply chain problems, I have an urgent need for Mylar."

Clarke shrugged. "Huh? Always jonesing for something."

As the police and the girls headed off to search the area around the service station for Clarke's phone, Emma called Katherine. She outlined the evening's events, offering an expurgated version of the circumstances leading to the delayed police response.

Although the police tracking system continued to show the phone was at the service station, their search came up empty. Twenty minutes later, the police lost contact with Clarke's phone for good. Raising her voice, Clarke shared her opinion about the quality of the police tracking software with the surrounding officers.

Emma cornered Clarke after her rant. "Can't you see this isn't helping?"

Clarke pointed to the officers. "*They're* not helping. And now I need to buy another phone." Clarke would purchase her sixth replacement phone in seven weeks. Clarke replaced her phone, on average, every 8.2 days since Emma joined the Pareto team.

After a debriefing with the officers, the last police car drove off. As the three walked to Emma's car, Charlie grabbed her sister's arm. She pointed across the street, lined with shops and a large a private banking center.

Clarke turned to her sister and asked, "What? The bank? Why do you always get so jacked when you see one of these fancy shoe boxes?"

"There! Do you see it? Something moved in front of the bank."

A semi-transparent object eclipsed the building, distorting the financial center's lighted sign and other features as if a large lens was moving in front of it. The edge of the lens revealed a blockish object drifting down the street. Clarke sprinted to the front of the building in pursuit, but she was too late. With a whoosh of air Clarke was thrown to the ground, and the diaphanous dreamlike thing dissolved into the night.

* * *

Fenton moved from behind his desk, giving his antique globe a quick spin before joining his daughters and Emma at a small round conference table at the side of his dimly lit office. He brushed the shoulder of his faded t-shirt, mistaking a small hole for a piece of lint. If this shirt caught his sister's attention, she would transfer the garment to the staff's cache of cleaning rags. He leaned back in his chair with his long fingers forming a prayer gesture below his neatly clipped salt-and-pepper beard.

The girls took turns recapping the amusement park adventure, apart from their casual convergence with Jack and Leo. From time-to-time, Fenton asked for a clarifying detail. He rose from his consultation table and picked up a stack of playing cards from his desk. As in other conferences, he invited the girls to consider broader meanings and implications, with his meditations resonating with philosophical or spiritual tones.

As he returned to the table, he invited his daughters to consider a dynamic that went beyond their pursuit of the dog walker. What larger design connected Jay's dog walking with the Sister Sledge performance? "All things are implicated in one another and in sympathy with each other. These events are consequences of others. Things push and pull on each other, breathe together, and are one."

Returning home after the van chase, Katherine shuttled the girls to an urgent care center to attend to Clarke's contusions and to have the girls' ears examined. Clarke was still experiencing intermittent ringing in her ears. The ear specialist explained that a soft conversation hovers around 50 decibels. A rock concert can reach 100 decibels. A rocket launch is in the 180 decibel range. The music in the van likely reached 130 to 150 decibels.

Charlie had sidestepped the effects of the noise. Clarke was not so lucky. Tests indicated permanent auditory damage, resulting in a ten percent hearing loss in her left ear. Although Clarke had not suffered any long-term effects of her electrocution weeks before, she would live with the consequences of her latest actions.

Concluding that the elusive Padres fan was much more than a humble dog walker, the girls bestowed "Jay" with a new sobriquet: "San Diego."

Shaking his head at his oldest daughter, Fenton said, "I doubt that sneaking into an unmarked van of a suspected criminal was the best choice among all available options for you and your sister. We'll review this matter later, but let's be thankful you both were able to extricate yourselves from a tight spot."

Emma's face and neck reddened. Fenton had not taken the opportunity to point out that Clarke's actions could have cost the girls their lives.

With a steady hand, the investigator erected the first level of his playing card house.

Fenton said, "I believe a cloaking technology may have been deployed to conceal the van. If this was the case, on one side of the vehicle, there were dozens of high-resolution cameras; on the other, hundreds of LEDs. The cameras and LEDs would be concealed within the body of the vehicle, likely in the interstitial space between the exterior and the interior walls of the van. The cameras on one side of the vehicle transmitted images to the LEDs, camouflaging the vehicle by projecting what was behind it."

Fenton erected the second and third levels of his card tower. He paused to look at his creation. Each level was narrower than the one below.

"I think I saw this tech in a Bond film. You know, the one with the bad guy who couldn't sleep?" Clarke said.

Fenton nodded. "This technology is also used in some slow-moving military aircraft, projecting the sky or clouds above the airplane to the underwing, concealing the airplane from observers below. Most likely, the driver suspected you girls left your phone or another tracking device in the van to assist the police. The driver knew there wasn't time to search the cargo area for a phone. Knowing he couldn't outrun the police, he deployed the cloaking technology, gambling the police would conclude you dropped your phone when you exited the van. *Stratagemma intelligente.*

The driver was probably parked very close to where you girls exited the van, observing you and the police the entire time!"

Fenton completed the fourth and fifth levels of the card tower. The cards on each level were placed in oblique groupings, creating a lattice design.

Crossing his arms, Fenton said, "By the way, you girls will be spending more time with your mother. There's a new arrangement. We'll review the details later." Fenton frowned at his tower, then at Emma. Still glaring at her, he pulled a card from the first level. The tower collapsed, with the cards spilling onto the floor.

Emma picked up the fallen cards. The playing cards doubled as business cards. Printed on the back of the cards were his contact details and his service offering: "Recovery. Recompense. Retribution. Discreet."

Shaking his head, Fenton said, "Last night's events speak volumes about the acumen of our adversary. Our foe *anticipated* there might be an unwelcome visitor to the van's cargo area, so a countermeasure was developed for that possibility. This same adversary *anticipated* there might be someone trying to trace the source of the dog collar transmissions, so a radio signal relay system was developed to frustrate any attempts to pinpoint the signal source. And our foe *anticipated* that a phone would be left in the van to help the police, so the cloaked van likely remained nearby to confuse anyone tracking the phone. *La mossa migliore*. Most likely, we're dealing with a sophisticated criminal organization. These criminals now know who you are and likely why you're in pursuit." The private detective tore the playing cards in half, one after another, as he clenched and unclenched his jaw. He turned to Emma. "In fact, the perpetrators likely became aware of your activities the moment your friend disabled the relay on the roof of the house."

Emma's face reddened. "Owen was just trying to help. We wouldn't have gotten this far without him."

"Emma's right," Clarke chimed in. "And these crooks may know who's chasing them, but they have *no idea*, what they're up against." She showed off a series of bodybuilder poses.

Fenton took his daughters' hands in his own. "I don't want to alarm you girls, but you can expect there will be an unpleasant response or even reprisal if your further inquiries are seen as a threat. Even when we win in chess, we lose many pieces. All worthwhile endeavors involve loss. To bring this adversary to justice, you'll each need to make sacrifices. What are you prepared to sacrifice?"

The investigator paused to allow the girls to absorb the gravity of his message. During this interlude, a conga line of house staff passed by the open door of his office. Karl led a procession of six cleaning staff singing "Ai No Corrida." Other performances featured "Oye Cómo Va," "Dónde Estabas Tú?," and "A Mi Me Gusto Asi."

After the cavalcade passed, Fenton turned to his daughters. "You girls now see part of a chess board that represents your shadowy adversary's field of operations. This board was meant to be concealed, along with the dark pieces being played. To discover the identity of your opponent, you must first understand what they desire. *Il cuore è verità.*"

"How do we find out what they want?" Charlie asked.

"Methods betray intent. *I metodi rivelano l'intento.* Consider the tools they use."

Fenton leaned forward. "You've become aware of one of the actors in a criminal design. Your adversary is heavily invested in keeping the rest of their pieces from view. But I expect that your opponent's eyes fixed upon you for some time. Anger and fear will guide the hand that moves the dark pieces against you."

Fenton stood up again and walked over to one of his chess tables. He looked down at the board. "Your thoughts and actions should not be restricted to the single-minded and steadfast pursuit of your objectives but should dynamically consider how your moves could trigger a range of responses. Setbacks will invite frequent and sobering reassessments of your underlying strategy and vulnerabilities."

Clarke frowned. "Exactly what are you saying, Dad?"

"Boxing champion Mike Tyson once said, 'Everyone has a game plan until they get punched in the face.' That pretty much sums up my point."

Fenton switched to another topic. "I agree that the dog walker and the man at the amusement park are likely the same person. Nevertheless, you girls should confirm this theory by corroborating the suspect's description with those who employed him."

Fenton moved a piece in one of his games. Another piece moved in response. "This man's panicked actions are not likely dispositive of any question involving the canine conspiracy, but they hardly support his probity."

Emma interjected, "Sorry, I don't understand what you just said."

"I was making the point that San Diego's actions at the amusement park and in the ensuing van chase—as reprehensible as they were—don't necessarily mean that he's also guilty of tampering with the dog collars. Proof is required."

Charlie raised her hand as if she wanted a schoolteacher to call on her.

"Yes, Charlie," her father said.

"The manuals in the van were related to one subject."

Smirking, Clarke asked, "Are you going to tell us, or do we need to move to *Santa Maria della Concezione* for your formal presentation?"

Charlie rubbed her hands. "The manuals were related to cell tower architecture, with schematics and technical specifications of tower components. I wonder if San Diego and his confederates have been blocking or rerouting signals to one or more towers."

Charlie's revelation raised a question: Were the earlier phone service interruptions somehow connected with the high frequency dog attacks?

Back Rank Problems

Fenton smiled as he looked up from one of his chess boards. "That's certainly an important discovery, Charlie. So, you found literature about cell towers in the van? Hmm, intriguing." Fenton returned to the table. "It would be challenging to interfere with cell phone service over an extended period. Such tampering would draw the immediate attention of the FCC. And yet–"

Fenton was enjoying the chase. Weeks earlier, he supplied intelligence to Clarke about the problems experienced by the late Macro Cell Tower 2173. He recently raised a question about the possible connection between the use of a high-frequency band on the dog collars and the earlier cell phone reception problems.

Crossing her arms, Clarke said, "Dad, let's say that the same criminal was blocking the phones *and* messing with the dogs. What would be the point?"

"Very well," Fenton said, tracing an edge of the table with his index finger. "Setting aside motives for the moment, an analysis might consider the *impact* of these disruptions. Cell interruptions disrupted human communications while the dog collar transmissions unsettled dog *and* human sleep routines. The common denominator is the disruption of *human* routines– our communication channels and sleep schedules. I'll have my research team look into possible connections between phone problems and sleep interruptions. There may be academic research or other perspectives that could help us."

A few days later, he shared that a survey of academic studies and papers revealed an intriguing finding. His team uncovered a 2013 study published by Stockholm University's Stress Research Institute that concluded:

"... women suffering from stress-related exhaustion exhibit hypersensitivity to sounds when exposed to stress. In some cases, a sound level corresponding to a normal conversation (as low as 60 decibels) can be perceived as painful..."

Science Daily, which generalized the study, suggested women who are emotionally exhausted from some type of stressor should pay attention to changes in hearing, including sensitivity to loud noises. The mechanisms producing higher sound sensitivity for women are not fully understood.

* * *

The girls discussed their father's research during a morning stop at Chuck's Donuts. Emma invited Owen to join them. He was taking the day off from work. Emma had been exchanging periodic texts with him about the dog collar mystery.

Charlie stacked Sweet Snowballs in a square pyramid on her plate. Past visits to the shop predicted she would reduce the mound from top to bottom.

Emma turned to Charlie and said, "You always stack the donuts. Just a habit?"

"When balls are stacked within a square frame, Emma, the quantity of spheres is a square pyramidal number. During his expedition to America in 1585, Sir Walter Raleigh asked Thomas Harriot, who was his scientific advisor on the voyage, to find the most efficient way to stack cannonballs on the deck of the ship. Harriot's ensuing theory about the close packing of spheres bears a striking resemblance to modern atomic theory. I can run through the math later if you like."

Nodding, Emma said, "Thanks for the offer."

"I've been extending this theory into other domains such as our investigative methods. Dalton's atomic theory tells us that all atoms of a given element are identical in mass and properties. Since San Diego is likely part of a larger criminal enterprise, I'm considering what his 'properties' might suggest about his circle of confederates."

Owen chuckled as Charlie deepened his appreciation of the principles connecting donut-stacking, molecular geometry, atomic theory, and investigative techniques.

But this public display was out of character for Charlie.

Clarke shook her head. "Charlie, your theory is baloney. Or should I say, *bologna*?"

Returning to the topic of Fenton's research, Clarke said, "Pretty obvious that the phone problems caused lots of people to stress out." Clarke did not acknowledge the stress-induced compulsive behaviors leading her to the top of a macro cell tower.

Without taking her eyes off the stack of doughnuts, Charlie nodded in agreement.

Clarke stretched her arms and yawned. "Maybe someone was messing with the phone signals to stress out women, making them even more sensitive to the barking. But why make women extra-sensitive to noises in the middle of the night?"

Charlie balanced her chin on sugar-coated index fingers. "I find your query raises both provocative and troubling connotations. While I cannot tender any theories, there's a discernible pattern in which electronic sounds are being weaponized, from dog collars, vehicle defense systems and, possibly, cell phone signal blocking."

Owen chimed in, "You girls better watch your step. Let me know if I can help." Turning to the Pareto sisters, he said, "You know how much I care about your guardian. Don't do anything rash that puts Emma in danger."

Emma smiled. "What a nice thing to say, Owen. But how do you know that I don't regularly put the girls in danger?"

Somewhat absently, Charlie said, "I'd bet doughnuts to dollars that all of this leads to someone who has acoustic expertise." She had a sugar ring around her mouth.

"Charlie, the expression is to 'bet dollars to doughnuts,' not the other way around," Emma corrected.

"Emma, that aphorism is no longer true. When purchased individually, the average price of a doughnut in the Bay Area has risen to $1.29. If one is confident in their wager, they would stake their higher-priced doughnut against a dollar. And why are you pointing to your mouth?"

Owen chuckled.

Clarke said, "Charlie, I'd bet a cannonball to a doughnut that your inability to censor yourself stems from a breathtaking lack of self-awareness."

The group sat in silence as Charlie examined a couple of sweet snowballs at eye-level, inventorying the slight differences between the two.

* * *

Later in the day, the two girls and Emma sat in the kitchen, enjoying a mid-afternoon snack. During this interlude, Clarke elucidated on the occasions that united, and the shared values that sustained, a tightly woven social circle of friends that included herself, Yinyue, Leanne, and two other high school girls. One of the five would briefly fall from the graces of the group. However, the exiled young woman would inevitably redeem herself, regaining admission into their select society.

Another crisis was testing the resiliency of Clarke's group. Leanne had become entwined with a young gentleman who, according to Yinyue and the corroborating reports of another friend, suffered from the absence of a single redeemable quality. During the visit to the seaside amusement park, Clarke counseled Yinyue on the rewards of sympathetic friendship and compassionate tolerance that, in due course, might reveal the hidden qualities of the suitor and the mutual benefit of their affiliation.

Clarke's reflections were cut short as Katherine entered the kitchen, carrying a grocery bag. She set the groceries and a table tennis paddle on the marble pastry and candy making island.

With a smile, the aunt announced, "Hello all. Stopped at the market after my lesson."

She pulled two loaves of bread from her grocery bag and stuffed them into a freezer. Virtually all food items under her charge were subjected to a frosty initiation, including an emergency supply of Chuck's donuts, stockpiled in large plastic bags.

Turning to Charlie, Katherine said, "I'll be preparing a marinade for Shaking Beef tonight. I need a one-gallon zip lock plastic bag for the marinade. Although I didn't find any here earlier, I'm confident, Charlie, that you have at least one to spare from your inventory. Given your wide-ranging application of these bags, I'm having difficulty keeping a supply in the house for, how would you say, more prosaic domestic uses."

Charlie shrugged. "My stock is running low, but I have a box I will bring to the kitchen. I'll need to reorder more from my regular online supplier. I can give Dad a friends-and-family discount for a few boxes from my next shipment."

"Before you sell back household supplies to your father, you might consider the overall balance of payments under this roof," Katherine advised, unleashing an acerbic tone reserved for private counsel with her nieces.

A one-gallon zip-lock bag found in Charlie's inventory was later used to marinate the filet mignon in a mixture of sesame oil, mushroom soy sauce, garlic, sake, chopped onions, sugar, salt, and black pepper. The family enjoyed the one-inch filet mignon cubes, coconut-scented rice, and Brussels sprouts, prepared in an oil, garlic, and balsamic vinegar mixture. Molten brownies completed the aunt's culinary triumph.

Later in the evening, a staff member asked the girls to meet their father at *St. Peter's Basilica*. The colonnaded square was the backdrop for his early evening Spanish guitar recitals. He sat on the edge of a fountain, strumming the final measures of "Asturias."

Turning his sad eyes to his daughters, he said, "I received two important calls this evening. First, Laura reported that her missing jewelry reappeared on her dining room table last night. Apparently, her unwavering optimism has been rewarded. *Sarà il tempo a dirlo.* Please visit Laura tomorrow to find out more about the reappearance of her valuables. Second, a prospective client wants help recovering jewelry removed from a reportedly 'impregnable' vault. *Un altro mistero!* I'll interview the client tomorrow and share what I hear.

We're running out of time—just five weeks to the FBI hearing."

While Fenton's reputation might be unsavory, his services were in high demand. There was a steady stream of distressed parties petitioning for help. If Fenton accepted a new case, the client was subjected to an extensive background check. Visitors to the compound were carefully screened to guard against vengeful criminals. Cases often led to travel for the investigator, as his tracing technologies led him to the sources of electronic fraud across the globe.

* * *

Seated at Laura's dining room table the following afternoon, the girls waited to hear about the reappearance of her jewelry. Before broaching this topic, Laura insisted on hearing about the events leading to Clarke's battered condition. Clarke's face, hands, and exposed arms bore expansive black and purple bruises. The young combatant's neck and right forearm were wrapped in large surgical bandages, arousing suspicions of even more severe injuries. She was unable to grasp why Clarke had been "the victim of a monstrous assault." She finally turned to the topic that had brought the girls to her home.

"I woke up at my regular time yesterday morning. After breakfast, I walked past my dining room. Something on the dining room table caught my eye. I found all my missing jewelry there. Everything was neatly arranged. All the rings in one pile. All the earrings in another pile, and so on."

Charlie asked, "Were any family members or visitors occupying your house when your jewelry reappeared?"

"No. Hector Estrada visited earlier this week, but he wasn't around when the jewelry was returned. Hector is helping out around the house." There was no mention of Ben Aberdeen, the handyman they encountered during their previous visit to Laura's home.

"May I examine the jewelry?" Charlie asked.

"Of course. I just had a *feeling* that, from the beginning, everything would turn out fine."

Charlie unwrapped an enormous magnifying glass from its original packaging. The first use of this instrument represented a definitive moment in the career of an aspiring sleuth. Its proportions ensured that the significance of its deployment would not be lost on the casual observer. Peering through the enormous lens, Charlie assayed each piece of jewelry. She drew a deep breath before turning to Laura.

"Ms. Marcum, have you worn these pieces of jewelry?"

"Of course. I have worn them many times over the years."

"Then I find it strange, indeed, that there's a paucity of wear marks on several of the pieces. They are pristine, without a single blemish. It makes me wonder if these are the original articles. May I have your permission to borrow a few of these—including this unusual bracelet—for a more expert evaluation?"

Laura nodded, but her vacant expression revealed signs of shock and distress.

Zugzwang

In a video conference, Ms. S furnished additional details to Fenton about the theft of her jewelry. She explained that she was a widowed actress, residing just a few streets from his home. She asked for his help, offering a reward for the return of a precious necklace.

Three nights earlier, a nightmare had left her feeling uneasy about her valuable family jewelry, which was housed in a heavy vault in her home. Although kicking herself for allowing a dream to rattle her, she decided to check her vault the following morning to make sure all was well.

Her jewelry was gone. The nightmare was real. And yet, there was no evidence of a break-in. The safe had been closed and locked. Everything looked as it always had. Only the jewelry had been taken; documents and cash in the safe had been untouched. The vault antechamber, monitored by a surveillance system, had not been disturbed. Only Ms. S had been in the house.

Ms. S told Fenton that she wanted to handle the matter quietly. Police involvement would likely bring unwelcome public attention. One of the stolen articles was an iconic necklace used in a suspense film. The media would feed on the uncanny parallels between the film and the disappearance of her necklace. There would also be uncomfortable questions about how the piece came into her deceased husband's possession and its murky provenance.

The following day, Fenton investigated Ms. S's home. There was no envelope with a QR code in the vault. He explained that another high-priority jewelry theft case would delay the next steps. He suggested his daughters fill in for him until he could give attention to her case. Although Ms. S expressed misgivings about turning over any part of the case to children, she agreed to meet with them the next day.

* * *

Seated on the loggia overlooking the Paretos' gardens, Charlie took another sip from her glass of sparkling grapefruit water. She unzipped a plastic bag filled with baby carrots and offered them to Emma who sat next to her.

Charlie rotated the bill of her Oakland A's cap from front to back. "Next weekend we're meeting with Stella and her aunt at the wedding. From his dealings with Stella's mother, Dad said the Huynh family has insights that may help us with the Marcum case."

Charlie frowned. "All this is mysterious. We've been researching the Huynh family to prepare for the meeting."

"We?"

"My research team." Charlie did not elaborate on the constitution of her team.

"What's your team trying to discover?"

"The Huynhs' connection with the jewelry trade."

"Found anything?"

"Nothing about Clara Huynh, Stella's aunt. Tay Huynh, Stella's mother, has had some scrapes with the law, but no known connection with the jewelry trade."

Charlie downed the rest of her grapefruit water. "Aside from this, I don't understand why my dad had *any* connection with this family. I have this gnawing suspicion that there's a deeper association between the Huynhs and our family. Over the past few weeks, I've been developing my VMPFC and –"

"VMPFC?"

"My ventromedial prefrontal cortex. The region of the brain that governs intuition." Charlie closed her eyes. "I've used yoga and meditation to increase my sensitivity to intuitive impulses. I've amplified those impulses through VMPFC boosting exercises."

"Really? What does your intuition tell you?"

"Somehow, Clarke's and Stella's battles hold the key to this puzzle. But it's not clear how. And there's something else. An incident at one of Clarke's tennis matches three years ago might provide a clue about the Huynh's connection to the jewelry business."

Emma helped herself to a few more baby carrots. "I'm not following you. But why don't you tell me what happened at the tennis match."

While surveying the Paretos' gardens, Charlie brought Emma to the courtside of a championship tennis match between Clarke's middle school tennis team and Stella's urban netters, which occurred three years earlier. This tennis clash occurred one year *after* the violent soccer match that crowned Stella's team as regional champions. During these years, there had been collisions between the two schools, with Clarke and Stella directing their respective squads across other theaters of battle, including contests arbitrated on the basketball hardwood and softball diamond.

Clarke's and Stella's sentiments toward the other could be considered unfriendly. Likewise, Charlie reported that the dispositions of their respective squads might correspond to the attitudes of warring red and black soldier ants in a seething territorial battle. Charlie summarized: "Between the teams, the last battered bulwark of civility had been swept away. Through this shattered levee of forbearance flowed a venomous tide of acrimony, etching its corrosive effects on contestants and spectators alike."

"Charlie, let's play *Scrabble* one of these nights," Emma suggested.

While the tennis championship was hosted by a private peninsula racquet club, the Friday afternoon affair had acquired a carnival atmosphere. Courtside stands overflowed with parents, families, students, school bands, and media. Adults tried to restrain younger family members and pets from entering the courts during play.

Charlie recalled, "Opposing groups of parents traded unbecoming imprecations, protesting umpire rulings in patterns corresponding to their allegiances. These ebullitions were amplified by the availability of adult beverages at the nearby clubhouse."

To stimulate interest in the event, Charlie awarded a raffle entry for a generous gift card to each parent who nominated a synthesizer-created telephonic on-hold music selection. She convinced the peninsula middle school band leader to integrate these refrains into the band's repertoire. These compositions were performed during stoppages of play to the delight of parents who appreciated regular reminders they were not at work.

The event's attendance eclipsed all but two professional circuit tournaments hosted by the club in its sixty-eight-year history.

Charlie admitted that her sports promotions had once served a broader agenda. Her campaigns sustained a bookmaking operation, managed by one of her grade school operatives. After discovering this gambling enterprise, Katherine supervised its dissolution. At the time of this tennis championship, the aunt had not yet severed this corrupted commercial tentacle.

Charlie shook her head. "I was shocked to learn that one of my associates accepted a pawn ticket for a wager. My policy is to accept only cash wagers. Although the amount financed by a pawn shop is typically about 25 percent of the value of the pawned item—and my associate credited only half of that—we needed cash to cover bets."

"So, you're saying you didn't have enough cash to pay out the winners?"

"Precisely."

"But 12.5 percent of the value of a pawned item couldn't amount to much. Right?"

"My associate took a $2,500 bet. The pawn loan was $5,000, plus interest."

Charlie pursed her lips. "Given the size of the bet and the handle, we stood to lose our juice and more. The term 'handle' means the total amount wagered by bettors and 'juice' was my take for offering odds."

"Thanks, Charlie. I'm familiar with these terms."

"We offered a straight-up plus-minus 150 money line. Our customer placed $2,500 for Stella's team to win, which was favored. There was already heavy action on Stella's team. And no time to reset the odds. The money we needed was tied up in inaccessible property. A perfect storm. Our only hope was for Clarke's team to win. My personal and financial interests were completely aligned."

"I can imagine. What happened?"

"Clarke's team lost three of the first five matches. Another loss would give Stella's team the championship. Clarke and Stella, their teams' number ones, played next. Stella was higher ranked than Clarke. In their forecast, Clarke's coaches conceded this match—calculating a 37 percent Match Winning Probability (MWP) based on a Monte Carlo simulation."

If the underdog somehow prevailed, the final match— that would decide the team championship—would pit the doubles team of Huynh-Pashov against Pareto-Marsh. Computer modeling gave even odds for this lineup.

*   *   *

BONUS CONTENT AT THE END OF CHAPTER

Emma shook her head. "All this is interesting, Charlie, but I'm not seeing how any of this is helping you find the connections you're looking for."

"Hold on. Just before Clarke's singles match, my associate gave me the pawn ticket. There were two items of note on the ticket. First, the pawned item was described as 'thirty-eight cut gemstones of various types.' Second, the borrower's signature was... Huynh."

"Then what?"

"As I pondered my dilemma, a tough-looking man came up to us and asked if we had advanced a wager against a pawn ticket. He said that he would buy back the ticket plus pay us $500 for our trouble."

"What did you do?"

"Naturally, I sold him the ticket."

"What do you make of all this?"

"I would deduce that the thirty-eight cut gemstones were once set in a variety of jewelry settings or were cut for new settings. The pawned gems were likely worth far more than what we credited. The tough-looking guy bought back ticket because he, or someone he was working with, knew their actual value."

"Could be. Or... maybe it wasn't about the value of the stones..." Emma smiled. "Maybe the guy bought back the ticket because there was something at the pawnshop that wasn't meant for your eyes."

Charlie nodded thoughtfully. "I hadn't thought about it in that way. You've reframed the value construct for me. Thank you for challenging my binary... my base-2 thinking."

"What happened next?"

Charlie brought Emma back to the doubles match.

Clarke and Sloan handily won the first set 6–1 and had cruised to a 3–1 advantage in the second. During her dominant run, Clarke looked up at the stands from time to time. In addition to picking on Kasserine Pashov, Stella's weaker partner, Clarke found that Stella was having difficulty with sharply angled shots that drew her wide off the court. "Like Clarke, Stella used a two-handed forehand and two-handed backhand, making it difficult to reach balls landing just inside the sidelines."

Charlie paused, creasing and re-creasing the bill of her Oakland A's cap on her lap.

"Charlie, is something wrong?"

"I'm not sure." She closed her eyes and dropped her head.

After finishing the story, Emma asked Charlie if her retelling offered fresh insights about the Huynhs.

"Yes, I believe I've found something. But it wasn't what I was expecting. Perhaps next weekend will help answer a few questions that are surfacing."

Without asking Charlie what she found, Emma considered her own theories on the loggia.

*   *   *

Ms. S, a mid-eighties former actress, leaned back in her chair as the girls ate pastries in her kitchen. Pushing her silver hair away from her face, she shared that she lived alone. Housecleaners made weekly visits to her large home, but she had not welcomed other visitors in weeks.

"Although you girls may be helping your dad with his investigations, my case is for a professional investigator. I would go to the police, but that's not an option."

Charlie nodded, conveying her understanding of Ms. S's plight. "Yes, our dad told us there are sensitivities involving the loss of a particular necklace."

"That's right." Ms. S shared pictures of the necklace and other stolen jewelry.

Charlie opened her mouth in surprise. "It can't be. *The* Carlotta?"

Nodding, Ms. S said, "The one in the film was a prop. This is the original. The gemstones are real. Aside from its legendary aura, it has significant intrinsic value."

To prepare the girls for their visit with Ms. S, Fenton asked them to screen a classic thriller set in the Bay Area.

Ms. S closed her eyes. "I'd give anything to get the necklace back. But I have this strange feeling it's being put to good use. And somehow it will be returned to me."

The homeowner reviewed the features of her state-of-the-art burglar alarm system, which included motion, pressure, and heat sensors. Security had been important to her late husband. The windowless vault antechamber was monitored by a surveillance camera and secured by automatic self-locking doors. The vault was protected by a combination lock and heavy doors.

Bins of packaged food and water bottles were stacked against the antechamber wall.

The girls inspected the security room. "Have you noticed any recent changes in this room or in the vault?" Clarke asked.

"It's been this way for months. I haven't touched anything."

Clarke rummaged through one of the tubs of emergency food. "Ah, what do we have here?" she asked with a smile, then removed wire cutters from the bin.

Ms. S shrugged. "I don't know how they got there. They could be mine..."

"And you don't know how this got here either?" Clarke pulled a crowbar out of the container. "Or this?" She turned on a battery-powered drill. With theatrical flair, Clarke removed other items from the bin, including leather gloves, wool cap, and calipers.

"I don't remember leaving these tools here. They could be mine. I don't remember."

Clarke asked, "Did you have a chance to review your security camera records?" During Fenton's visit, he had asked the homeowner to review the antechamber surveillance records.

The actress shook her head "I'm embarrassed... confused... by what I found."

Charlie nodded sympathetically. "You'll find no judgments here."

"Well, I skimmed ten days of records. The daytime stuff looked normal. But the records showed me... ah, showed me entering the vault on three different nights."

Charlie tilted her head. "Don't be embarrassed. Some of our other clients keep unusual hours."

"I'm not embarrassed about that, Charlie. The problem is that I don't remember visiting the vault on any night."

In this climactic moment, Clarke stretched her arms and yawned.

The girls reviewed the surveillance footage. They watched Ms. S visit the vault on three mornings between 3:41 a.m. to 3:59 a.m., 2:16 a.m. to 2:30 a.m. and, finally, from 3:01 a.m. to 3:06 a.m. On each occasion, she entered the room, unlocked the vault, entered the vault, exited the vault, closed the vault, and departed. During each sequence, the stationary camera captured only the side of her face and back. She had not made any nighttime visits after discovering the disappearance of her jewelry.

The actress shook her head. "And there's something else. Earlier this morning, I discovered part of a pane in one of my rear windows was cut out. This must have been the way the thief got into the house. Somehow, your dad and I overlooked this."

Ms. S led the girls to a sash window at the back of the house. With tears welling in her eyes, the homeowner excused herself.

"How odd." Charlie stepped back from the window. "A perfect five-inch round hole has been cut in the glass. Looks like the hole was cut to give the burglar access to the inside window lock. But look at these strange smaller holes that have been drilled into the glass near the edge of the pane. There are four of them. They've been freshly made too. Any theories about these tiny holes?"

"Don't have a clue. But all this doesn't add up," Clarke concluded.

Charlie adjusted her cap. "What do you mean?"

"To begin with, Padawan, there's no evidence of forcible entry or that the tools I found were used in the robbery."

Charlie pointed to the window. "You don't call this forcible entry?"

"No, my tender little weed. Whoever messed with this window did so after Dad's visit. I seriously doubt he missed this when he inspected the house or forgot to tell us about it. Whatever happened to this window, I'd bet it wasn't related to the robbery. And observe, my simple tadpole, the paint on the sash. The paint looks old. See where the paint dripped into the channel, locking the sash in place? Looks like the window was painted years ago, the last time this window could possibly have been opened. The burglar didn't use this window to enter the house."

"Very observant." Charlie examined the window sash with her oversized magnifying glass. "What do you think happened here?"

"I'd say, either there was an aborted second burglary after Dad's visit or, more likely, the window is a red herring meant to throw us off. After he investigated the house, someone doctored the crime scene."

Clarke lifted her arm and dropped her imaginary microphone.

— Bonus Content: A Clash on Center Court —

Clarke and Stella were all business as they strode onto the court, radiating the self-possessed aplomb of champions. They wore oversized headphones and toted enormous sports bags, each holstering five racquets.

Disregarding the United States Supreme Court's 1962 ruling on the unconstitutionality of public school-sponsored prayer, Clarke's coach, Dr. Mwangi, and Clarke knelt on the side of the court for a pre-match prayer. Waves of heat radiated off the court. Dr. Mwangi's Bear Bryant-inspired hounds tooth fedora was pulled forward, shielding his face from the sun. A towel was draped over Clarke's head. She was still groggy from a three-hour nap.

Recognizing the gravity of the moment, Dr. Mwangi appended his usual prayer with a gravelly extract of the King James Version of Psalm 144 for inspiration:

... Blessed be the Lord my strength which teacheth my hands to war, and my fingers to fight;

My goodness, and my fortress; my high tower, and my deliverer; my shield, and He in whom I trust...

Even as Clarke and Stella exchanged warmup groundstrokes, it was clear that the two were only nominally playing the same sport as their teammates. Balls were hit precisely, producing loud reports. These rifle cracks silenced the crowd.

Stella's game featured a nasty slice serve and deep backhand slices. She held a number two national ranking in her age group at the time.

Perched on the top row of one of the spectator stands under a large dark gray umbrella, Ophelia gazed upon the proceedings through oversized sunglasses. She used two portable "mini-helicopter" fans to form a personal cool air cocoon. She arranged her phone, binoculars, and two computer tablets (streaming match statistics and graphics) on either side of her seat. Through a headset, she maintained a communication channel with a coaching team that included Dr. Mwangi and two other professional advisors.

Charlie was at court level, giving her "an immersive experience." Looking up into the stands, Charlie observed her mother rebuffing male visitors who, she surmised, were trying to find a cool spot or to inquire about her mother's technology.

During this middle school match, the Pareto and Huynh coaching staffs made use of eight automatic cameras, with at least four cameras covering every ball bounce. The data mined from this surveillance network informed the coaching given to the players during breaks in play.

The first set of the match was tied 6–6. Failing to find a weakness in the other, the first set had become a slugfest, with the girls taking full swings with hard-hit balls landing just inside the baseline. The girls went toe-to-toe, like two galleons exchanging close-range broadsides. The frenzied crowd gave the girls call-outs and standing ovations.

Sweat streamed off the contestants, requiring constant hydration and reapplication of sunscreen. Between points, the girls toweled off arms, hands, and racquet grips.

Before the first set tiebreaker, Dr. Mwangi shared his heated perspectives with Clarke about her tactics. Clarke lost the tiebreaker and the first set.

During the second set, Clarke unraveled, losing her first two service games and trailing 0–3. She missed shots she should have put away for winners. Her face was deeply flushed. Charlie's financial predicament had become even more precarious. Stella was on the verge of closing out the match, clinching the championship for her team.

Clarke came to the sidelines for a scheduled change-over break. Standing over the seated Clarke, who had a white towel draped over her head, Dr. Mwangi assessed the condition of his athlete.

Using her state-of-the-art compact electret condenser microphone, Charlie captured Dr. Mwangi's rasping ringside counsel through her headphones: "Clarke, you're doing fine, but stop trying to be perfect. If I wanted to see perfection, I would have just stayed home with Mrs. Mwangi!"

Clarke was able to regroup, playing faster and more relaxed as she strove for personal imperfection.

She roared back, winning six straight games and the second set 6–3.

The girls had been on the court for 105 minutes. The air temperature soared to ninety-four degrees, with the playing surface reaching a scalding 103°F.

In the third set, Clarke found herself again at 0–3 game disadvantage. Stella's camp had discovered Clarke's winning shot percentage was 31 percent higher with faster play. Stella was instructed to make Clarke wait longer for each of her serves and hold up play during Clarke's service games.

The girls knelt after long points. They had been on the court for 155 minutes.

With a hushed crowd, Clarke served at triple break point—one point away from what would surely be an insurmountable 0–4 game deficit.

In this desperate moment, as Clarke started her second serve wind-up, someone shouted from the stands: "Hang in there, Clarke!" Clarke halted her serving motion and turned to her anonymous patron. For all to hear, she said, "I got this! Nothing else I need to do today!" The crowd's cheers rose above the tennis complex.

Tears welled in Charlie's eyes as she explained that such unexpected and seemingly inconsequential occurrences had decided the outcomes of sports contests. And so it was in this case. Clarke was able to salvage her service game. Feeling the crowd's support, she elevated her play. Clarke emerged with a 6-7, 6-3, 7-6 victory. The team score was now tied at three matches apiece, with the deciding doubles match up next.

The doubles match had gone well for Clarke and her partner, Sloan. Clarke saw the artistry of the sequence that began with a hard-hit ball to Kasserine's side of the court. Although Kasserine was playing exceptionally well, she was only able to launch hasty lobs in defense. Clarke finished off the points by directing an overhead smash at some part of Stella's body. Clarke reasoned that Stella should bear the brunt of her partner's imperfect shot selections. In other matches, she found this sequence would inevitably create a rift between the opposing partners.

Tiring of the pummeling, Stella delivered a message of her own in the form of a head-shot at Clarke who was playing at the net. This brought the players to the net and at least two dozen overheated spectators to the perimeter of the court. As angry adults flowed out of the stands, there was a question if the match would continue.

During the melee, four automatic courtside cameras, along with Charlie's directional microphone, were aimed at the unladylike conference at the net. Charlie noted that Stella's profanities were graphic and inventive.

After numerous warnings and penalties, the players were ordered to resume play, and the spectators were enjoined to return to the stands. Holding a 5–2 advantage, Clarke served out the match. No longer needing to drive a psychological wedge between the opposing players, Clarke directed all shots to Stella's side of the court. The last point of the match ended with Clarke's overhead smash, with a ninety-four mph ball hitting Stella on her left wrist. The applause was mixed with fiery adult exchanges.

Dr. Mwangi rushed Clarke and Sloan off the court as spectators, representing a range of dispositions, poured onto the playing surface. Charlie caught up to the three at the edge of the parking area outside the complex. From this location, the four heard agitated crowd noise mixed with the peninsula band's celebratory on-hold music.

Dragon

Charlie and Clarke looked wobbly in their platform-heeled shoes as they trudged up the gravel path leading from the parking area to the lushly landscaped retreat. Nestled in a grove of redwood trees in the Santa Cruz Mountains, this sanctuary offered a romantic location for the late afternoon wedding. At their father's direction weeks before, the Pareto siblings would meet Stella and her aunt, Clara, at the wedding to discuss topics connected with the still unresolved Marcum affair. With the assistance of a local jeweler, Charlie confirmed the items returned to Laura were not the original articles; they were cheaply plated imitations of little value.

Reaching the entrance of the retreat, Charlie turned to Clarke. "I suppose this would be a good time to share the results of my research. It's obvious that Dad and the Huynhs are mutual friends or business associates of the bride, groom, or both. Unfortunately, I've been unable to ascertain the Huynh's connection with the jewelry trade, the significance of this meeting place, or how any of this can be useful in the Marcum affair. But I've learned that Stella's mom, Tay, is called 'The Hand.' Evidently, The Hand operated in the criminal underworld and is serving time in a low-security federal correctional facility in Dublin, called FCI. By the way, FCI's more notable inmates include Patty Hearst, Sara Jane Moore, Heidi Floss, Felicity Huffman, and Lori Loughlin."

Sighing, Clarke said, "Low-security? Don't even think about it, Charlie. But really, all this is relevant because...?"

Charlie pursed her lips. "In many domains, judgments about relevance can only be made after the passage of time. I'm happy to furnish the exegetical underpinning of my contention. Anyway, there are various theories about how The Hand earned her moniker. Some suggest she imprinted her undertakings with a skilled touch. Others say that she had her hands in an assortment of questionable enterprises. And it's rumored she managed her affairs with an iron fist. We should also consider that The Hand was, and perhaps is still, an important appendage of a criminal family. We better watch our step."

Smirking, Clarke said, "You and your little helpers did some digging."

"Indeed, my explorations consider a multiplicity of contexts, so often revealing layered and ambiguous properties. The answer to 2 and 2 is not always obvious."

"It's not 22?" Clarke straightened her dress.

Katherine helped attire the girls for the event, outfitting Clarke in a Carolina Herrera hibiscus floral sleeveless dress with a slight bateau neckline and Charlie in a Valentino navy lace short-sleeve dress with a jewel neckline, flutter sleeves, and flounce hem. Although the ensembles had been expertly tailored, the girls continually tugged on some part of their attire. Leaving the haute couture to the girls, Emma wore a comfortable floral print dress she purchased the year before.

Four large Asian men stood shoulder-to-shoulder at the side of the registration area, observing the incoming guests. All wore unbuttoned dark suits and sunglasses. Two of these gentlemen held cigarettes by their sides. Their jackets were too tight at the arms and shoulders, giving them the look of nightclub bouncers. Other men were stationed at the perimeter of the lush grounds.

This was an outdoor wedding. The surrounding area provided a stunning backdrop with luxuriant gardens, two large ponds, and waterfalls. After the girls picked up their welcome gifts (a tiny bird cage with a tea candle inside), they circulated through the crowd, clustered in gender-specific groups. Many guests smoked cigarettes and drank Hennessy from short water glasses, using friendly salutations like anh, co, em, and bac.

Men were smartly dressed in suits with colorful ties and pocket handkerchiefs. Women wore backless dresses, displaying elaborate tattoos extending from their neck to lower back and from their shoulder to hand. As the girls surveyed the scene, they commented on the designs adorning the backs and arms of these young women. The illustrations featured serpents, dragons, phoenix birds, Centaurs, and other mythological creatures. One young woman's back showed a dragon wrapped around a chrysanthemum stalk, with the dragon peering around her neck. The reptile's body extended down the length of her back, with the dragon's tail found at a location under the plunging garment.

At two tables, guests were engaged in wagering games, including Mạt Chược and Tiến lên. "Taki Taki" drifted from the direction of the resort lodge.

The girls listened to the guest exchanges before engaging in discussions. Both the subject matter and language was coarser than might be expected at a gathering of family members and business associates. A tall, middle-aged man with a dyed blonde ponytail and a much darker, closely trimmed beard joined the girls' huddle with three other guests. Although specifics were not provided, he explained he rendered legal services to the groom's family. These duties were limited to clearing up periodic misunderstandings with law enforcement. Most recently, the family's counsel had assisted the groom and his business associates resolve a mix-up involving their generous lending practices.

Moving onto another guest scrum, the girls met a stocky redheaded guest who provided "security services" to the groom's family. He shared extracts from his military career in which he had served under several nations' flags. The conversation drifted to firearms. To provide visual aid for a point being made, the redhead reached behind his back, pushing back his bomber jacket, and produced a nine-millimeter handgun. This was a cue for several nearby guests to commence a show-and-tell of semi-automatic handguns they had brought to the nuptial celebration.

Emma pulled the girls aside. "Might be a good time to get out of here."

Charlie nodded in agreement. "I'm struggling to recall if I've seen so many firearms at a past wedding."

Clarke crossed her arms. "Not down with the jailbird jamboree? Let's hang a little longer." Turning to Charlie, she said, "Pro tip: Be polite to all the wedding guests."

A few minutes later, a small group of guests gathered around Charlie. She asked the assembly of firearm experts to recommend a weapon that most optimally balanced ease of firing and stopping power. The redhead, and several other guests, appreciated Charlie's grasp of more technical topics, such as recoil buffering and muzzle suppression, with the redhead dubbing her "Hotshot." Charlie reminded the group that recoil is a result of conservation of momentum, according to Newton's third law. As Charlie turned over one of the firearms in her hands, Stella and her aunt Clara walked up to their group.

Clara was a middle-aged woman with a round face and straight short black hair, precisely parted on one side. She had the look of an imposing and unyielding matriarch. She pulled on her tight Jonathan Simkhai deep sea ribbed dress. Holding her chin high, she looked the girls over as she fiddled with a chain that showcased an impressive white gold diamond ball pendant.

Stella, the co-star of Charlie's sports chronicles, stood next to her aunt. She had a serious face, hazel eyes, and straight dark hair with sharply formed and mature features. Although only a year older than Clarke, her stern demeanor gave the illusion of Stella having an even wider lead in their race to adulthood. Her shoulder-length straight hair was clipped behind her head, except for a platinum ringlet that hung on the side of her face. She wore a simple sleeveless yellow dress, revealing sculpted shoulders and arms. Like the Pareto sisters, Stella was ill at ease in her outfit, repeatedly adjusting the neckline and sides of her dress.

The group traded introductions. After Emma introduced herself, Stella said, "Pleased to meet you... Miss Emma..." She drew out the salutation with a snicker, drawing attention to the street name of a brown opiate.

Clarke and Stella stepped away for a private conversation.

Stella crossed her muscular arms. "So, if it isn't Clarke Can't, Superscam. I'll just say that your dad and my aunt might be friends, but that doesn't mean anything else has changed. I see you for who you really are: just a spoiled second-rater who has nothing better to do than try to keep up with me. Good luck with that."

Clarke smiled. "Nice dress. Did you find it at Kohl's?" Looking up while pointing to an area above their heads, she said, "*I'll* just say: Scoreboard."

As Clarke and Stella chatted, Clara shared with Charlie and Emma that she was a good friend of the groom's family, with many mutual friends attending the wedding. Charlie placed herself slightly behind Emma for protection from the intimidating and presumed doyenne of the Huynh clan.

Clarke and Stella rejoined the group. Turning the conversation to the object of their rendezvous, Clarke said, "Ms. Huynh, our father didn't give us much information about this meeting. But he thought you and your niece might be able to help us with a stolen jewelry case we're working on."

Abruptly, Charlie interjected, "What's your profession, Ms. Huynh?"

Turning to Charlie, Clara quietly replied, "I have two primary businesses, Charlie: personalized outsourcing and jewelry resale."

"The outsourcing business sounds interesting. What type of business is that?"

Clara crossed her arms, revealing a jade, ruby, and diamond serpent bracelet. "Charlie, your father has always been fair to our family and has helped us. Tay and I hold him in the highest regard. We consider him family. So, I'll answer your questions about our businesses. And we can talk about what's brought us together today. But to protect our interests, this conversation should not be repeated to anyone else. Do you understand?"

Charlie vigorously nodded in assent.

Clara repositioned her diamond ball pendant necklace. "An outsourcing model transfers job functions from one party to another, with the goal to get the job done on a more cost-effective basis. We also perform an outsourcing service, but with a... personalized twist. Let's say our client, Percy, is a software developer employed by a technology firm, with a salary of $170,000 per year. We provide a private service to Percy so that a third-party contractor performs most, if not all, his job duties as a software developer. Percy's employer would not... know about this arrangement. Percy's job, for example, could be performed by a coder in Shenyang for less than one-third of Percy's salary to produce code for his employer. The contractor's work product is reviewed and confidentially transmitted to Percy each day—on time, with the strictest quality standards. Percy's employer continues to pay him his salary. Clients like Percy have received raises and promotions as their employers have rewarded the quality of their work and output. Percy pays us a fee for our contractor's work. With more free time, our clients can engage in more fulfilling pursuits. You can use your imagination."

Charlie's ensuing interrogation of Clara delved into numerous aspects of Clara's outsourcing enterprise.

BONUS CONTENT AT THE END OF CHAPTER

Like a child visiting Disneyland at the perfect age, Charlie responded to Clara's magical revelations with wide-eyed trembling delight.

Not only was Charlie in awe of Clara's manifest entrepreneurial vision and virtuosity, but perhaps how Clara's Carnegie Hall-level performance bore little resemblance to her own grade school recitals. Of course, there could never be a public airing of Clara's talents.

Clara turned the conversation to her jewelry resale business. "At first, we bought jewelry from distressed sellers, reselling the pieces at trade shows or online. But now we're just buying pieces for the scrap value, reselling the setting stones. We've been selling gold and silver to 'additive manufacturers' which use design software to make custom jewelry. Using a 3-D printer, they create a thermoplastic wax mold. They melt down the metal we sell them, pouring the metal into templates. This rapid prototyping allows them to produce jewelry at a lower cost than overseas operations. Thanks to printing tech, our business is helping bring back American jobs!"

Clara squared her shoulders and smiled with pride.

"Our business eliminates the need to carry any inventory. I've brought Stella along, and she's been helping with back-office admin and customer service. She's even been assisting with the smelting process, flux-mixing, and ingot-pouring!" Clara smiled at her niece. "Stella needs to learn about our family's businesses from the ground up. Some day she will oversee all these businesses."

Clara flipped open a diamond encrusted compact mirror and touched up her lipstick with her forefinger.

Clara did not need to explain that her suppliers were highly motivated to minimize their jewelry inventories, which constituted an occupational hazard.

Charlie nodded, approvingly. "Impressive. Is jewelry reselling a cash business?"

Smiling, Clara said, "Good question. Our suppliers and associates often... prefer... alternatives to cash–alternatives that can also be used as an exchange of value. By coincidence, Charlie, you nearly became a remote party to one of our transactions." Looking at her niece, Clara recalled, "I understand a couple years ago, one of our overly confident... overly enthusiastic associates sold you her pawn ticket to fund a wager involving a tennis match. We needed to step in and stop the transaction. I'm sure all this was quite mysterious to you."

Charlie nodded. "I must confess, I found the episode puzzling."

"I'll try to clear this up. Many pawn shops issue 'bearer' tickets. Whoever holds such a ticket can pick up the pawned item after paying off the modest loan. This gives the ticket value. Parties can exchange this ticket over and over, creating an asset-backed currency to purchase... services."

"Ms. Huynh, your business acumen and vision are inspiring. If you have time later this month, I'd be honored if you could give me advice on how to quickly raise money for a...ah, a worthy cause. But why did your colleague buy back the ticket?"

"Usually, we don't care who holds a ticket. But if you had retrieved the loan's collateral, Charlie, there might have been complications for your father and me."

Changing subjects, Charlie recapped the jewelry theft cases—and the evidence that jewelry was being copied. Charlie showed her Laura's recast bracelet.

"I don't know who made this. But I got a call a few months ago from someone asking if we could make low-cost reproductions. The caller said they'd sell us the original articles for melt value. But I told them we don't make jewelry."

"Do you recall the name of the caller?" Charlie asked, raising her eyebrows.

"We don't ask for seller names. But I doubt we've worked with this person. The caller was a woman with a low voice. She was impatient. Had lots of questions."

"What did she ask about?"

"Questions better directed to a manufacturer, like: How quickly could copies be made? Could someone, who was acquainted with the original piece, spot a replica? Was there a volume discount?"

"Did the caller mention how many articles?" Charlie asked.

"I don't remember, but I was under the impression there might be hundreds."

"Ms. Huynh, did you refer the caller to one of the manufacturers?" Clarke asked.

"I would have asked Stella to handle this." Clara turned to her niece. "Stella, did I ask you to share our referral list? You've been taking care of these requests."

Stella crossed her arms. "I remember this lady. You asked me to call her back. But when I did, the lady said she changed her mind and didn't want... ah, any referrals."

"That's weird. When I talked with her, the woman wanted the names of companies that could help her. Stella, you're sure you didn't give her any referrals?"

Stella tugged at the neckline of her dress. "No... no, I didn't."

Charlie shook her head. "Pity. The caller might have ended up working with one of the companies on your list. That would have narrowed our search."

In a high-pitched tone, Clarke said, "Our dad mentioned he's done business with your sister. Would you mind sharing a little bit about her? Anything you can tell us about their business relationship? If this is not too forward–"

Since Fenton's and Tay's respective clientele often had opposing interests, the Pareto and Huynh association was delicate. If their alliance became visible to others, there could be difficulties. This conversation made it abundantly clear that Emma and the Pareto sisters were playing an intermediary role between Fenton and the Huynh family.

"I would be happy to share, Clarke, but let me give you a little background about my sister, Tay. She earned advanced degrees in philosophy and literature. Always a top student. But she couldn't find a way to use her education. She ended helping underserved parts of our community. She's so selfless and so giving! My sister provided project management, document drafting, and business planning services to her clients. She was a savior to those who, for the first time, had access to a high caliber business professional."

Clara pushed down the sides of her dress. "In a few cases, her clients were involved in pursuits deemed to be... let's say, legally discordant. Yes, legally discordant. But Tay took no sides in ethical debates. She offered impartial professional services to those who were free to accept or reject her counsel. My sister is a good person."

Clara's lips trembled.

Raising her forefinger, Charlie said, "I believe your sister might find support for her non-judgmental stance in Adam Smith's meditations on the merit or demerit of actions: 'The only consequences a person can be answerable, or by which a person can deserve either approbation or disapprobation of any kind, are those which were some way or other intended.'"

Charlie liked to quote from Adam Smith's *The Theory of Moral Sentiments* to support her opinions. She memorized large sections of the Glasgow edition of that work.

Shaking her head, Clara said, "Unfortunately, Charlie, the judge probably wouldn't have accepted that argument.

He wanted to hold my sister accountable for one or two little missteps. Legal technicalities, really."

It was not clear which "little missteps" Clara had in mind. Tay was serving a five-year sentence in a federal penitentiary for mail fraud, identity theft, second-degree forgery, racketeering, and copyright infringement. Sentencing considered past convictions for several Ponzi schemes, cybercrime, tax evasion, mail tampering, obstruction of justice, and gambling violations under the RICO Act.

"Anyway, she was skilled in helping her clients refine a concept to make it more commercially successful. Gather round. I'd like to show you some of her work!"

Clara decrypted Tay's portfolio on her oversized phone. "Check this one out! You're looking at a red-line version of a letter my sister marked up for a client. Just by correcting a few grammatical, logical, and other errors, she increased the response rate by 450 percent! She's always been good with details. Notice the sender of this letter was changed from the bank to a law firm *representing* the bank? *So* much more credible. *Such* a nice touch. The actual letter—I don't know how many were sent—was printed on law firm stationary with an *actual inked signature.*

Remember, girls, there are no shortcuts in producing a quality product!"

* * *

Dear Mr. Snuckle,

My name is Derrick Tan, **with the law firm of Gray, Stratham, Hong and Oren**, representing Bank of Singapore Hong Kong **(The Bank)**. ~~I am currently in the U.S. on a five days official assignment. I am getting in touch with~~ **We are contacting** you regarding the estate of a deceased client with ~~a similar~~ **your same** last name whose portfolio ~~we had the pleasure of managing about~~ **The Bank managed approximately ten years ago.** ~~a decade ago.~~ **This letter contains** information about the estate of **Mr. Lockni Snuckle.** ~~I hope to establish some level of trust and understanding with you.~~ **We** respectfully request ~~that~~ you keep the contents of this ~~mail~~ **letter confidential as this intestacy process is protected by privacy laws.** ~~I'm contacting you independently, no one knows about this communication.~~

The current balance of these funds is approximately $13.5 million. **After numerous** inquiries by our risk department, we determined ~~that~~ **Mr. Snuckle** ~~Lockni had~~ passed away ~~around~~ August 25, 2013. **Subsequently, we were informed** ~~we also discovered~~ he died intestate with no known relatives. ~~In~~ Hong Kong ~~the~~ intestacy laws ~~will~~ determine how ~~your~~ assets are distributed if ~~you have~~ **there are** no known family members **at the expiration of** ~~after~~ the "seven year no claim rule." ~~expires.~~ **Our research indicates you and one other individual have legitimate claim to these funds.** ~~What I propose is quite simple, I have exclusive access to Lockni's file and can place you in a benefactor's position and instruct HAM to make payments to you after~~ **We can release funds to you after** ~~all necessary~~ verification **process** is ~~done~~ **completed.** ~~as long as no one gets greedy we can have a fair and equitable share by splitting the funds evenly.~~

~~It's a lifetime opportunity if we can act~~ swiftly. ~~I would like to meet on a one on one before I head back to Asia,~~ **We expect this transaction can be completed within sixty days. I am sure you have many questions.**

I assure you the statements in this letter are truthful and you have a legal claim to a portion of the aforementioned funds. I look forward to having a more in-depth conversation about this **matter**.

Kind Regards,

Derrick Tan, **Esq**.

* * *

Clara did not have to explain that the recipient of such a letter would never see funds from the bank or the law firm. The beneficiary would be asked to periodically pay legal and other administrative fees to secure the release of the funds—a jackpot waiting to be claimed, but always just out of reach.

Turning to Clarke's earlier question, Clara explained that Fenton and Tay found it useful to exchange information that might be helpful to their respective clientele. She did not share details. If she had, Emma and the girls would have learned that, in some cases, Tay encountered certain useful information remote to her business interests and protected relationships. Correspondingly, Fenton was well-informed about local law enforcement activity, including the resources expended on cases, the direction of investigations, and even investigative theories. Fenton's insights could help Tay's clients evaluate their risk management strategies. The two conducted their private conversations while strolling through the Paretos' gardens.

Two events elevated Fenton to an honorary Huynh family member. Although not providing specifics, Clara shared that twenty years earlier Fenton served as a defense witness involving a criminal case brought against Tay. Unsurprisingly, there would be questions about the integrity of Tay's clientele. There were instances when a legally ensnared client found it expedient to shift culpability from themselves to Tay. Fenton's testimony was key to the dismissal of charges against Tay in one such case. She had not always been so fortunate. Clara suggested that her sister's current incarceration was the consequence of an unfortunate entanglement with a client who, when facing serious criminal charges, retroactively promoted Tay's role from occasional advisor to operational mastermind.

A personal episode, fifteen years earlier, further strengthened their bond. Tay, age forty-two and unmarried, yearned to start a family. However, her advancing age combined with her lackluster romantic prospects ruled out traditional conceptions. She would happily adopt a child, but her growing list of felony convictions spoiled the adoption agency's assessments of the stability of her household. Fenton provided the answer: he had a client with an infant baby girl available for immediate adoption.

With the other guests, the group moved to the outdoor chapel, a lakeside amphitheater flanked by trees and ferns. The bride and groom would exchange their vows under a wisteria-laden pergola. Patches of late afternoon sunlight accented the forested areas and the congregation of well-wishing friends and family.

Seated on a long redwood plank, the group waited for the ceremony to begin.

Charlie asked Stella about her nail polish. After comparing Stella's hands with her own, she commented on the similarity of their fingertips. In the past, Charlie and Clarke had discussed the uniqueness of their stylus-like fingers, with Clarke advancing a theory that their narrow fingertips represented an evolutionary leap to meet the technological demands of the modern age, such as texting and precise touchscreen manipulation.

Clara motioned for a group huddle. She whispered that, years before, Fenton helped the groom's mother, Joan, resolve immigration challenges concerning a few of her restaurant employees. Joan and Fenton remained friends.

The time arrived for the bride and groom to exchange vows. The bride wore a shimmering white lace and beaded backless dress, exposing a dense tapestry of fruiting plants and mythological animals extending the length of her back. Turning to the bride, the groom professed his love.

Bun-bun you're somebody I can be real and such

You-know chill'n and so on Boo

Be'in together all day and night now

It's 'cause of you girl, crazy none of the other _ _ _ _ _ matters

The way you shake your hips gets me jump'n

Right now I could get it goin' with you and stuff

You got me addicted to your _ _ _ _ _, tak'n those _ _ _ _ _ and _ _ _ _ _

You give me the insight and the light

My Boys be'n all jealous of home skillet and new Donna

'Cause of all we got together...

Several guests dabbed their eyes, responding to the groom's heartfelt and tender affirmations of adoration and devotion.

*   *   *

"I didn't know my dad was a criminal," Charlie said.

Charlie and Emma sat at Charlie's *bottega* worktable the day after the wedding.

Emma shook her head. "I don't think he's a criminal."

"But he exchanged information with Tay, a convicted felon." Charlie frowned.

"Sometimes, Charlie, things aren't so straightforward. I'm sure your dad thought that this was the best way to get information he couldn't have gotten otherwise. As far as we know, he didn't break any laws."

"Perhaps Mom knew about all this. And that's the reason why she left him."

"Maybe, but we don't know that."

"Or maybe there was something going on between my dad and Tay."

"Romantically? Perhaps, but it sounded like they were just good friends. He helped her out in that case against her. And he helped her with that adoption."

"I can tell most people don't like my dad. Maybe he's just not a good person. Maybe Operation RECLAIM is just a bad idea."

"People always have opinions. You never know why. Could be jealousy. Anything."

"I don't know. I still feel like there's something that's right in front of my face that I don't see."

*   *   *

Five days after the wedding, Charlie asked the family to convene in *Santa Maria della Concezione.*

Even though Charlie was standing on a stool, only the top of her head was visible over the podium that the house staff had set up for her on the stage. Clarke, Katherine, Fenton, and Emma sat together in the front row of the concert hall. Dozens of empty chairs were arrayed in straight rows behind them.

Charlie switched on a small reading light on the lectern so she could refer to her prepared remarks. Glancing at her notes, she cleared her throat and said, "Thank you for gathering here this afternoon. I know your time is valuable. So, to paraphrase Henry VIII, I'll make this brief." Her voice was clear and confident.

Fenton said, "Not a problem, Charlie. Take your time."

"Thanks, Dad. No doubt you are all aware that DNA ancestry testing, which relies on thirty-five distinct genetic markers, is shown to be over 99 percent accurate. I will return to this point in a moment."

Charlie turned a page of her notes.

"Over the past few weeks, you all are undoubtedly aware that I've adopted a yoga regimen and have designed VMPFC exercises to strengthen my intuitive abilities. These heightened abilities led me to suspect that there was some aspect of Clarke's and Stella's sports rivalry that held a deeper and more profound implication for our family. Clarke, I recently recounted for Emma your doubles match with Stella from a couple years ago in the hopes of uncovering some detail or clue to disentangle a riddle that had been gnawing at the edge of my consciousness."

Clarke yawned. "This is fascinating. When do we get to the point of this lecture?"

Charlie ignored the question and turned another page of her notes.

"Over the years, I've noted many similarities in Clarke's and Stella's athletic abilities. Here's a brief recap. In soccer, both have similar skills, using body control to disguise the direction of their moves. In basketball, both use the crossover dribble more than any other player I've seen. In softball, both are switch hitters and throw with their left hand. In volleyball, they're better setters than blockers. Their pre-service rituals are almost identical. And there are many other commonalities. But let's turn to tennis. Both gravitated to an unorthodox two-handed forehand stroke. Very few high-level players now use this stroke. My analytical program red-flagged this anomaly, which I've dubbed SWAT: A Suspicious Willingness to Adopt a Two-hander."

Charlie reshuffled her notes, turning pages so they could be read right-side up.

"Taking all this into account, an idea began to coalesce in my mind. Could these skills, traits, and preferences be the byproduct of a common physiological attribute?"

Fenton and Katherine looked at each other.

"At the wedding, I made a point to look for other similarities between Clarke and Stella. I was not surprised to find that the shape of Clarke's, Stella's and my own fingers were similar. Following the wedding, I was able to procure saliva and hair samples from all family members. These were submitted to a reputable DNA testing firm. One more point before I share the results of this analysis: Mitochondrial DNA, which is exclusively inherited from the mother, is associated with elite athleticism."

Charlie lifted a pitcher from a lower shelf of the podium and topped off her water glass. She took a small sip before returning to her prepared remarks.

"Unsurprisingly, the results confirm Clarke and I are biological sisters sharing the same parents." With a quavering voice, she continued, "More significantly, however... the analysis shows approximately 25 percent of Stella's DNA matches Clarke's and my genetic material, making Stella our half-sister. Based on Mom's hair sample, all three of us are Mom's biological daughters. Stella has a different biological father of Asian lineage."

The audience was quiet. The speaker turned off the lectern light, stepped down from the stool and, with head lowered, walked off the concert hall stage.

*   *   *

The test results provoked highly emotional discussions within the Pareto and Huynh households. Two days after the chromosomal revelation, Fenton held an emergency briefing with Ophelia's three daughters to explain the DNA results. Fenton's narrative omitted the understandably delicate interpersonal dynamics among the adults.

While living in Pokr Vedi, Armenia, Ophelia Artashat, then in her mid-twenties, struck up a remote friendship with a gentleman residing in the United States. While they had never met in person, they enjoyed many video exchanges. Over time, the substance of these interchanges also encompassed emotions of greater depth; and a marital engagement ensued. Ophelia arrived in the Bay Area on a bitter January day with the intent to marry and take up permanent residence. But Ophelia was six-months pregnant. The fiancé, unimpressed by this development, broke off the engagement. Ophelia was now alone in an unfamiliar country, at least until her baby arrived.

It was at this time, Fenton and Ophelia met. Fenton was providing immigration services as a sideline to his expanding PI business. (One of his customers was the mother of a groom who would much later deliver impassioned vows at an outdoor wedding.) He could help Ophelia with the immigration process, establishing dual citizenship. Ophelia wanted to put her child up for adoption. By good fortune, Fenton had a client looking for a baby to adopt.

What began as a business relationship between the two evolved into mutual admiration, deeper sympathies, and blossoming love. Ophelia gave birth to Stella in April of that year. Tay welcomed the infant into her household in May. The identities of the birth mother and the adoptive mother were not publicly disclosed: Neither Ophelia nor Tay learned the identity of the other. One month later, on a June afternoon heavily scented with star jasmine and blue moon wisteria, Fenton and Ophelia would marry. The following April, the couple welcomed Clarke into their household. Ellie, a Golden Doodle puppy, was added to the growing Pareto family that same year.

Thirteen years later, Tay "The Hand" Huynh was sentenced to a lengthy prison term for her felony convictions. Tay's sister, Clara, agreed to serve as Stella's legal guardian through the completion of high school. However, the county family court found Clara "demonstrably unfit" to serve as Stella's guardian. In the absence of other viable Huynh family members, the court would have no choice but to place Stella in a foster home. Tay turned to Fenton for help.

Fenton wanted to assist her but did not want to alert his wife about his more personal association with the Huynh family. He asked Katherine to quietly serve as Stella's financial co-guardian to allow Stella to stay with Clara. This would satisfy the court, presided by the Honorable Cosmo Tal. No one else would need to know about this private court arrangement. This plan would have succeeded if a court document, intended for Katherine, had not been sent to Ophelia by mistake. A predictable series of painful events would follow.

It is not known how Tay reacted to the birth mother revelation. However, there was no doubt that Ophelia was puzzled and sickened by any motive that would place her biological yet unfamiliar child so close to her home. She saw Fenton's decision to select a nearby household as a monstrous act of betrayal. The adoptive mother of her child had conducted business with her husband in their Italian Renaissance gardens. Her child had been repeatedly placed in the crosshairs of her own advanced sports weaponry and tactics. It would then come as little surprise that the Paretos' marriage would wilt from the intense emotional heat aroused by these exposures.

—— Bonus Content: Clara's Outsourcing Business ——

Clara shared the following details about her outsourcing business:

- Several customers have been using personalized outsourcing services for many years.

- Work-from-home jobs are best suited for personalized outsourcing.

- Clara's business mission is to preserve and bring back American jobs, serving U.S. clients and using domestic contractors when possible.

- A suite of such outsourcing services is available to privately held company executives, including positions as CTO, VP Finance, VP HR, Treasurer, CMO, CFO, COO, and CEO.

- Individuals named in a proxy statement (of a publicly traded firm) may not participate in the program as a client or contractor.

- Higher security fees are charged to executives for an additional layer of protection.

- A full suite of personalized outsourcing services can be delivered for approximately 30 percent of take-home pay.

- Financing options are available. A recently introduced product allows clients to use retirement assets as collateral.

- Clara is exploring ways for her business to securitize their financing options; her vision is that someday counterparties might privately buy and sell these securities, with hedging mechanisms to mitigate counterparty risk.

Discovered Attack

In the two weeks following her *Santa Maria della Concezione* presentation, Charlie avoided conversations about Stella. Concerned about her emotional state, Emma asked her how she was feeling from time-to-time. On those occasions, Charlie referred to her half-sister as her "mezza-sister." Not only had the DNA test results lifted the parental veil of secrecy that concealed the true identities of the actors in her sports anthology, but they exposed the catalyst of her parents' disengagement. A survey of half-sibling relations predicted Fenton's daughters would find it difficult to give their half-sister a warm reception. Queen Mary imprisoned her half-sibling Elizabeth in the Tower of London, placing her under house arrest. In *King Lear*, Edmund fabricates stories about his half-brother, Edgar, leading to the latter's exile. Biblical Joseph's half-brothers cast the young Joseph into a pit to die. After reconsidering their plan, the brothers sold Joseph as a slave.

Although such historical, literary, and even more contemporary examples of half-sibling discord might arouse disturbing conceptions, Emma's frequent check-ins with the girls did not uncover any malicious intrigues or even anxieties above usual levels. Nevertheless, Katherine launched a four-pronged strategy to facilitate the realignment of the family. Katherine encouraged Stella to have regular outings with her biological mother. She also invited her to join a few dinners in their home. And she asked her brother to have Stella assist Clarke and Charlie in their investigations, encouraging interactions that might help temper the rough edges of the recently forged sisterly bonds.

The final prong of the integration strategy involved a third-party intervention. The adults agreed that Charlie would benefit from professional counseling. Given Charlie's role in uncovering her parents' secret, Katherine thought her tender psyche might be at risk. Katherine conceded to Emma that her youngest niece would not likely see the merit of counseling.

Although Clarke was spared a therapeutic intervention, she faced difficulties on another front. She needed more hours to meet her aunt's community service quota. Nursing homes, community daycare centers, and hospitals had given Clarke ample volunteer opportunities. (In a stroke of luck, she found a three-week university-sponsored community sleep study the preceding month.) But she ran into trouble: the reservoir of available hours from her usual sources had dried up. She found her answer by recalling the abundance of worthy causes and the many socially conscious residents who contributed to them. One of her favorite causes was a local guinea pig rescue operation, with the motto: "No guinea pig left behind." This nonprofit organization provided rescue, medical care, sanctuary, boarding, grooming, bonding, and respite care services to guinea pigs in need. Clarke simply needed to sponsor a walkathon or another time-consuming activity to raise money for these abandoned "starter pets."

One of Clarke's soccer coaches recommended she concentrate on improving her endurance over the summer, so she was running two to three miles each morning. So, it was quite natural for her to decide to raise money for the guinea pigs by finding sponsors for a personal runathon. There was no theoretical limit on the number of miles that could be funded, but Clarke's plan was to run as many miles as she could comfortably fit into a four-hour session.

She found fifty-five sponsors sympathetic to the guinea pigs' plight. To avoid the heat of the day, she would start her run at six o'clock in the evening at her high school track. Stella asked Clarke if she could join the run so she could raise money for her school's film, improv, and cooking clubs. Stella's participation prompted two changes to Clarke's original plan. First, two other friends from Stella's school would join the half-sisters for their run, also raising money for their school clubs. Second, the fundraiser was moved to Stella's high school. As the track and surrounding grounds were illuminated at night, her school would be an ideal event venue. Katherine approved Clarke's proposal but asked Emma to provide transportation services and oversee the evening's activities. Although Katherine allowed Charlie to join the group, she made it clear that her spectator status disqualified her from community service recognition.

Since Clarke diligently protected her sleep quota, Katherine did not impose a curfew for the outing. However, she asked Emma to send periodic texts if the proceedings extended beyond ten o'clock. Stella was given permission to spend the night at the Pareto compound after the fundraiser.

*   *   *

Emma steered her car into the high school's vacant parking lot. The car bounced along, rolling over mounds of loose asphalt and stones. Emma parked her car near a chain link fence. There was no shade anywhere.

Clarke and Charlie collected their belongings from the trunk. Charlie hoisted a large duffle bag over one shoulder. She held Lucy under an arm, protecting her paws from the parking lot asphalt that had been baking in the mid-summer sun. After locking the car, the three made their way to the closest building, with gravel and asphalt chunks crunching under their feet.

Reaching the building, Charlie put Lucy down so she could look through one of the windows of a dark classroom. Satisfying herself that school had not been in session for the previous month, she and Lucy sprinted to catch up with the rest of the group, sidestepping remnants of picnic tables, bicycle parts, computer equipment, and school furniture they found in their path. The school had opted for a minimalist *cotto al sole* asphalt motif. Dusty heaps of litter ringed the school's exterior walls. There were no signs of life except for a large rat that scuttled along a windowless, sunbaked stucco wall etched with a web of large cracks. The rat turned into a dark hallway. Lucy dawdled, collecting olfactory data from this unfamiliar venue.

With a trembling voice, Charlie started, "Given the school's neglected state, I'm not feeling good about this. And, Emma, we won't be able to see your car from the track. Perhaps we should reschedule this fundraiser, relocating it to a more hospitable venue."

Clarke turned to Charlie. "Fix your hair, leash your dog, and pull yourself together."

Charlie scratched her forearm. "But I'm concerned about our security. You told us the school keeps its lights on all night. But how could an impoverished school justify the expense of all-night lighting? The implication of the school's decision is unsettling."

Clarke shook her head. "Unsettling? No, I don't think so. Have you considered... Ah, there they are!"

Clarke trotted ahead to meet Stella, and her two classmates, Isabella and Catalina, who were stretching on the cinder and dirt track. The girls wore sweats, tee-shirts and athletic shoes. Catalina's boombox broadcast The Cult's "Love Removal Machine," ensuring that anyone within a mile radius of the school would be alerted to their presence.

As Charlie emptied the contents of her large duffel bag, Lucy set off to explore the moonscape of gopher and mole holes cratering the track's infield. Charlie ensured that her sister would be well supported during her trial, unpacking fourteen energy bars, ten plastic bags of trail mix, fifteen water bottles, six sports drinks, four bananas, and twenty dog treats. Her provisions also included flashlights, a picnic blanket, a portable chair, pepper spray, roadside flares, and a digital lap counter. As the boombox blasted Nazareth's "Hair of The Dog," Charlie struggled to activate the lap counter that she placed at the side of the track. The counter would subtract each lap from a starting value of ninety-nine.

The four girls settled into a comfortable trot. Having left her directional microphone at home, Charlie was unable to overhear the teenagers' exchanges. She and Emma lounged on a picnic blanket in the infield portion of the track. Lucy excavated a gopher hole with only her hindquarters visible at field level. Charlie turned her attention to Stewart H. Holbrook's *The Age of the Moguls*. Emma lay next to her phone, churning through a backlog of episodes from a medieval fantasy series featuring rolling verdant hills, commanding castles, open fireplaces, winsome maidens, and handsome liegemen.

The mixture of her phone's lackluster content and the heavy evening air proved overwhelmingly powerful. Emma lapsed into a deep sleep.

She woke with a start. The sun had been replaced by a pale yellowish light cast from elevated lights near the track. She checked her phone. It was 8:55 p.m. She had been asleep almost two and a half hours. Charlie stood next to the track, re-inventorying her supplies with Lucy. Clarke and Stella were circling the track.

After Emma joined Charlie at trackside, Charlie updated her on the evening's events. Isabella and Catalina jogged for approximately two hours, covering ten miles. They reached their mileage goal and departed. At a much earlier point, Clarke and Stella pulled away from the original pack, dissatisfied with the leisurely pace.

The lap counter now showed twenty-nine laps remaining from a starting value of ninety-nine. While Emma napped, the girls had run seventeen miles. No doubt, Lucy's own assessment confirmed that Charlie's provisions were dwindling. Energy bar wrappers, empty water bottles, and banana peels were strewn along the track's infield.

Charlie stepped onto the track to take pictures of the two runners with her phone.

Charlie ran with the two athletes for brief stretches, supplying them with hydration and nourishment so they would not need to pause for refueling. During one of these relief efforts, Charlie overheard Stella urging Clarke to disengage from the run. Stella broke the news that Clarke's heart was on the verge of catastrophic failure: An egg yolk-like structure, composed of hardened cholesterol and calcium, dislodged from a vascular wall. The mass was making its way to Clarke's heart.

Charlie relayed this conversation to Emma. Emma told her that, although she understood her reenactment was verbatim, she did not have license to use profanity.

During another refueling, Charlie learned that if by some miracle, the yolk-like structure passed through Clarke's heart muscle, she would suffer another running-related ordeal. Stella predicted her half-sister was minutes away from a brain aneurysm, ruptured spleen, pulmonary hemorrhaging, or intestinal strangulation from an acute sports hernia.

Clarke ignored her myocardial crisis and other dire medical diagnoses, saving her strength to respond to a health threat that might materialize.

At ten o'clock, Emma texted Katherine, advising her that the group was still at the track and all was well. She informed her that the girls would be wrapping up their run soon. Her report did not have any factual support. The girls showed no sign of stopping.

The lap counter reset itself. The girls approached twenty-six miles—the marathon distance.

The half-sisters continued to run together over the next hour. Miles of lactic acid buildup shortened their strides and tightened their arms. Both wore determined and tortured expressions. If Stella was still convinced that Clarke was about to suffer a catastrophic failure, she kept it to herself.

The lap counter showed seventy-two laps remaining. The two girls were approaching thirty-two miles. At eleven o'clock, Emma texted Katherine again, acknowledging she was now uncertain about the finer points of the girls' fundraising campaign. Emma asked her for guidance. The girls had been running for five hours.

At 12:32 a.m., Stella drunkenly weaved across the track lanes, arms flailing and torso rotated to the left. She no longer controlled her legs, which had acquired minds of their own. As her legs took her on a meandering path across the infield, her efforts were no longer being credited by the lap counter.

Clarke stumbled every few steps, falling to her knees or catching herself with her hands. As she stood up, an unseen force tossed her back. Clarke's arms wind-milled as she fell backwards. As she struggled to her feet, once again, she was pushed back.

Emma yelled, "_____ that's enough!"

With the athletes on opposite sides of the circuit, Charlie raced onto the running track. Lucy was at her heels. As Charlie made one clockwise lap, with tears streaming down her face, she cried, "Stop it! Stop it! Stop it! Stop it! Stop it!" Lucy paused to give each exhausted athlete a few disapprovingly sharp barks for good measure.

And so ended the evening's fundraiser.

The girls tallied a total of 36.3 miles in six and one-half hours. As the group collected their belongings, the school lights turned off. The group used flashlights as they left the track area in silence. Charlie ignited a roadside flare, assuming rearguard duties.

"The flare should ward off any threats as we walk back to the car," Charlie said. She did not clarify what specific dangers she had in mind.

Emma sighed. "Come on, Charlie, put down the flare. You can't bring it with you."

"There might be something dangerous out there."

"I doubt that. But from what I've seen, this group poses a serious threat to itself."

Charlie shook her head. "You sound like Aunt Katherine. You're so different than when you started here."

Reaching the car, Emma pointed her flashlight at the driver's side door. "That's strange. I was sure I locked the car after we arrived. Now it's unlocked. Is this where we left the car? I thought it was further down, closer to the entrance. It's dark. Maybe I'm just confused. Do you smell gasoline?"

Charlie pulled on Emma's arm. "Hold on. Did you see something move on the other side of the fence?"

"No. Where?"

"Down there." Charlie trained her flashlight on a spot on the fence thirty feet from where they stood. "I saw a yellow orb. The size of a golf ball, moving behind the fence. I don't see anything now..."

Clarke sighed. "Honestly, Charlie. *A yellow orb*? It's really late..."

With a quavering voice, Charlie said, "We should get into the car. Now."

Poisoned Pawn

Clara met Katherine, Clarke, and Stella in the Pareto's entryway to retrieve her niece later that morning. Stella casually mentioned the 36.3-mile run during the sleepover. She asked her aunt if she could spend a minute with her half-sister.

Stella and Clarke stepped away from the others. Stella quietly confessed that she had, in fact, shared the Huynh manufacturing referral list with the mysterious deep-voiced female caller months before. She would pass along the referral list to Clarke. The list contained three operators. Stella did not indicate if her change of heart had occurred during the endurance test at her school.

*   *   *

After parting with her wearied half-sister and her aunt, Clarke met with Katherine in the kitchen.

Crossing her arms as she leaned against a kitchen counter, Katherine said, "I didn't feel well yesterday and turned in early. You can imagine my surprise when I picked up Emma's late-night texts earlier this morning. I'd like an explanation."

"Well, we kind of got caught up in the run and..."

Katherine frowned. "I imagine the miles just flew by."

"It was a way we could raise money for the guinea pigs..."

Katherine placed her hand over her heart. "Those poor guinea pigs. I'm touched by your solicitude."

"And the clubs at Stella's school need help..."

"Almost too distressing for words."

"I logged lots of extra community service hours and..."

"And found an intelligent way to acquire them." Katherine closed her cat eyes.

Clarke lowered her head. "Alright, I really don't know what happened."

Nodding in agreement, Katherine brushed a speck of lint off her sleeve. "Now we're getting somewhere. Give this some thought. Perhaps you'll learn something about yourself." She folded her arms. "I trust your self-examination will lead to a restoration of sensible thought and action. I don't want to hear about another obdurate ordeal with your half-sister. My hands are full here."

* * *

Before lunch, Charlie and Clarke relaxed in a seating area outside their father's office, waiting for him to open his door. As they waited, the girls were treated to a soft orchestral version of Gerry Rafferty's "Baker Street." Just as Clarke closed her eyes, the door opened. The investigator led his daughters to his consultation table. Adjusting the sleeve of his olive t-shirt, he asked the girls to summarize what was known or could be deduced from the jewelry thefts. The girls took turns inventorying facts and theories, supplying a probability for each hypothesis.

BONUS CONTENT AT THE END OF CHAPTER

Smiling, Fenton said, "You two have provided a comprehensive summary of what is known or could be deduced about the robberies. Well done."

Clearing her throat, Charlie said, "For the components of the mystery that have received my attention, it's been a captivating thought experiment. I've reinterpreted several conventional modeling techniques, representing—in my humble opinion—a novel use of synthetic reasoning and probabilistic design."

Shaking her head, Clarke eyed her sister. "We'll alert the media. Should we also let them know you have additions to the periodic table?"

Smiling, Fenton stretched his arms. "Why don't you team up with Stella to interview the manufacturers on the Huynh referral list? Lots of ground to cover there. Since manufacturers have ways to identify their handiwork, I suggest you bring along one of the replica pieces—perhaps the Marcum bracelet. I've been getting calls about other jewelry thefts. Please compile a list of ways to either remove jewelry from a residence that would not require forcible entry or ways to conceal a break-in. And I suggest you canvass the area to find homes with single women who are anxious about their jewelry. You might find houses that have been burglarized and even ones targeted for a future robbery! Ms. S had a premonition about her jewelry before she discovered the theft. If you find a house targeted for a future crime, this will turn the tables in our favor. *Ricorda, ogni cosa ha cagione.* Remember, everything has an underlying reason."

Charlie said, "Sounds like we have our work cut out for us. Without access to my files, it's been debilitating." She dropped her head. "I...I don't know how much longer I can keep this going. I feel like I'm just limping along."

Fenton scratched his beard. "I understand, Charlie. This has been difficult for you both. And, of course, Stella." The investigator paused. "We all need to push through the pain." Fenton shifted in his chair. "But take a break from the cases this afternoon and recharge. Starting tomorrow, get back at it. The hearing is just two weeks away. We're in an all-out sprint to catch the jewelry thief now."

Later in the day, Charlie arranged to have "36.3" imprinted on coffee mugs, baseball caps, pillowcases, tote bags, and a dog bowl (using a familiar third-party distributor of student art images) to memorialize the fundraiser. Charlie also commissioned a limited edition 500-piece jigsaw puzzle. The completed puzzle showed Stella dispensing medical advice to her half-sister as they ran side-by-side on the track. Charlie put in a rush order so these mementos could be quickly distributed to members of the expanded family. Arrangements were made to ship a tote bag, pillowcase, and jigsaw puzzle directly to Tay at her federal detention center.

* * *

For weeks, Charlie's two-foot-wide rotating loop antenna monitored the 52.350 frequency in the event the perpetrator of the dog crimes used this channel again. The antenna's receiver broadcast crackling static around the clock. From time-to-time, Charlie tried to find patterns in the background microwave noise, pressing headphones against her ears, like the Jody Foster character in *Contact*.

At 2:13 a.m. on Sunday, three days after the endurance test at Stella's high school, her receiver acquired its first steady 52.350-megahertz transmission since the late-night visit to the donut shop weeks before. In response, a high-pitched alarm sounded on Charlie's receiver, waking up the household.

* * *

After breakfast, Charlie and Clarke discussed their next move with their father. Fenton left on an international business trip the day before, with the girls arranging a short-notice video conference. Fenton's fifteen-foot head filled one of the displays in *Santa Maria della Concezione*. Charlie updated him on the repeating transmission on the frequency previously used to activate the dog collars.

Charlie rested her chin on pointed fingers. "My software located the transmission source: it's originating from a house about three miles from here. The broadcast is a two-second tone, repeating itself every two minutes and fifty-five seconds. It's as if the tone is functioning as a beacon."

Fenton leaned closer to his laptop camera, exposing the top half of his orange and pink Hawaiian shirt, one of his favorites. "Since the signal is repeating, I'd surmise the sender is taking pains to ensure that it *is* discovered. Have you girls considered my earlier counsel about the possibility of a retaliatory response to your investigative activities?"

Furrowing her brow, Clarke said, "You're saying the signal is leading us into a trap? Whoever's sending it doesn't even know we've picked it up."

Fenton rolled his gigantic head. "I disagree. If you're being lured into a trap, the sender already *knows* you've locked onto the signal, and you'll follow it to its source."

Clarke scowled. "But it's impossible to know who's listening to a radio broadcast."

"You're right, Clarke. There's no civilian technology that allows the broadcaster to know who is listening. But we are all vulnerable to power consumption surveillance."

"What's that?" Clarke asked.

"When Charlie's amplifier strengthens the broadcast signal, there's a tiny surge in our household electricity use. There are slight surges each time the amplifier refines and boosts a broadcast signal. Assuming the transmission is a trap, these minute surges have been observed by your adversary. They're waiting on your next move."

"How could a criminal know anything about our electricity use?" Charlie asked. "Our electric meter is housed in a locked cabinet, protected by our security gate and fifteen-foot concrete walls—reinforced by 120-grade hot-rolled steel rebar. And there are thirty-seven cameras, twenty-eight heat sensors, and 154 motion detectors monitoring our property."

Just as Lucy was unaware that her midafternoon visits to the family's property line were being monitored, Cosmo did not realize his visits to the estate triggered several silent alarms, alerting two heavily armed security guards who monitored the family's closed-circuit camera and audio surveillance system. Without Katherine's knowledge, Clarke uploaded Cosmo's performances from the security system to her phone. Her favorite recitals included: Bob Seger's "We've Got Tonight," Bobby Caldwell's "What You Won't Do for Love," and Jeffrey Osborne's "Stay with Me Tonight."

Scratching his beard, Fenton said, "Charlie, I'm sure you're aware that the power company uses an electric meter to monitor our home's power usage. There's a two-way radio system that exchanges information between a home and the power company using point-to-point network communications. Unfortunately, it's been shown this system is not secure. Cell towers can be tricked into rerouting signals from a home to another party. Once done, a home's meter can be attacked." Fenton took a deep breath. "Easily acquired software tools can be used to exploit weaknesses in the meter's technology. A criminal can initiate their own protocols to determine if a resident is home, away, or sleeping based on usage spikes and lulls. The attacker can also monitor more subtle power signatures to even ascertain the brand of an electronic component and identify a movie being streamed into the home."

Clarke frowned. "Shady stuff. How did we not know about all this?"

Rather than answering his daughter's question, the investigator pushed ahead with his discourse. "Our house uses several AI countermeasures, including ESTHER's Aegis routines, to frustrate this type of surveillance. Our power cloaking routine is called MYRTLE. But I'm afraid, Charlie, your receiver's repeated amplifications of the signals are hard to mask. I'd guess the signals *are* repeating to facilitate the acquisition of these small power signatures."

Charlie's shoulders slumped in response to an overlooked scenario.

Clarke's face reddened. "If the sender knows we've locked onto their signal, why do you think the bad guys know we're coming to get them?"

Fenton smiled. "It's likely your adversary has been observing you girls for some time now. Your pattern of unwavering pursuit predicts you will follow up on all promising leads. *Un oggetto in movimento tende a rimanere in movimento.* An object in motion tends to remain in motion. Although your enemy expects you to suspect a trap or diversion—especially after the relay system misdirection a few weeks ago—they *know* you must at least consider the possibility of a malfunction reactivating their broadcast. Your adversary knows you'd see a slip-up like this as a gift—and an irresistible temptation. *Una pedina passata deve essere spinta: A passed pawn must be pushed.*"

* * *

The girls and Lucy piled into Emma's car at 9:02 p.m. the following evening. Fenton was right: the temptation was too great to resist. They would investigate the signal source.

Fenton suggested that the group use Emma's car because if their adversary was monitoring their family's electricity use, they might also be intercepting communications between their vehicles and the household's technology infrastructure. The investigator reasoned that their opponent might exploit this vulnerability to pinpoint the timing of the group's visit to the broadcast site.

Charlie turned to her sister. In a quavering voice, she asked, "Do you think this is safe? What if this is a trap? What do you think will happen?"

With a smile, Clarke said, "You're asking me what will happen? Hmm... Only one thing I see clearly about the future. Very shortly, you, young one, will undergo an extraordinary trial that no human being can endure. That's it. The rest is foggy."

The group arrived at the signal source, a gloomy two-story Victorian. The mansion was set back from the street, shrouded in the shadows of deepening twilight. Lowering one of the car's windows, Charlie played her powerful flashlight beam over the dwelling's façade. The vacant windows, along with the withered gable pediments, corbels, and railings, gave the structure a foreboding skeletal aspect. Charlie's light moved to a Brazilian pepper tree, spreading its limbs over the neglected grounds. Spindly shrubs and vines crowded stone urns and entangled fallen statuary. All was quiet.

The girls reviewed their plan one last time: Starting at the rear of the property, the sisters would inspect the perimeter of the home for ten minutes while Lucy and Emma stayed in the getaway car.

Lucy looked out the rear window and started to snarl and bark. After Charlie quieted her down, the girls synched the stopwatch feature on their phones.

Charlie shook her head as she looked at Lucy. "My VMPFC conveys a dark presentiment of events to come."

Clarke scowled. "Pocket your phone, grab your flashlight, and pull yourself together." She jumped out of the car with Charlie in her wake.

The girls rounded the corner of the property and disappeared. Using the center console as a springboard, Lucy leapt to the passenger seat. The getaway driver confessed to Lucy, out loud, that it would have been better if she had joined the girls.

A minute later, Charlie ran up to the car.

Opening the driver's door, she asked, "What's wrong? Where's Clarke?"

"You need to follow me! Now!"

Emma jumped out of the car. Lucy would need to wait in the car.

As Charlie turned back to the house, she yelled, "Something's happening in there!"

The two reached the rear of the house. Somewhere within the dark mansion, a woman cried for help, followed by a bloodcurdling scream.

Clarke knelt, picked up a stone patio paver, and, in one motion, threw the paver through a picture window that had given the mansion's occupants a view of their patio. Sections of glass rained down on the interior floor and windowsill. Without discussing the need to call on law enforcement, Clarke pulled herself through this new entry point.

She opened a rear door from the inside, allowing Charlie and Emma to enter the house. Emma's words of caution were drowned out by the shrieks.

The house lights switched on.

They rushed into the room, where they heard the cries. No one was in the room—an unremarkable home office with a desk, standing lamp, bookshelves, and office supplies. Unremarkable, except for one detail.

That detail was inching its way up one of the walls. A three-foot mechanical centipede paused its climb, swiveling its bulbous silvery head to look down on the visitors. Its unseen mouth issued a piercing scream. From the sides of its swollen body, the insect sprayed a yellow-greenish jelly. The slime ran down the wall.

Clarke swiped a paper weight from the desk and hurled it at the centipede.

A new earsplitting, high-pitched mechanical whine filled the room. Their eardrums would rupture in seconds.

Emma grabbed the girls and pulled them into an adjoining room. They were met by three law enforcement officers. With arms locked in a firing position, they pointed their Glock service pistols at Emma. The screeching sound stopped.

One of the officers spoke into his communication epaulette: "We've got them. You've also found the jewelry in her car? Good."

Emma yelled, "Wait, you don't understand—"

"Stay where you are," shouted an officer who had moved behind Emma. His baton came crashing down on her head. Her legs buckled as she lost consciousness.

— Bonus Content: —
Recap of Jewelry Robbery Cases

Charlie's and Clarke's recap:

1. Both robbery victims are women who live alone.
2. Both victims live in close proximity.
3. The victims do not know each other and have not had any common visitors.
4. Both homeowners had premonitions involving their jewelry, experiencing anxieties even before they discovered the thefts.
5. Victims believe there will be a positive resolution of their losses, even without evidence supporting their optimism.
6. The thefts appear to have occurred within the past two months.
7. There is no credible evidence of forced entry.
8. High probability that both the robberies were committed by a common perpetrator.
9. High probability that the perpetrator of the Marcum robbery was the party who produced the replicas of her jewelry.
10. High probability that the perpetrator's scheme is to substitute imitation jewelry for the more valuable pieces in *all* robberies.

11. If jewelry substitution is the perpetrator's modus operandi, all stolen jewelry might be in the process of being duplicated.

12. The caller who asked Clara about creating low-cost replicas of various pieces of jewelry *might* have later commissioned the reproduction of jewelry. This possibility is supported by (a) the caller's interest in Clara's services (specializing in buying jewelry, then quickly melting the precious metals), (b) the improbability of the caller being an established professional (Clara's comment about the caller's questions more appropriately being directed to a manufacturer), and (c) the caller's interest in the timing of the melting of original articles, retention of images of the original articles, and reproduction services.

13. Since Clara thought the caller might be attempting to dispose of hundreds of pieces of jewelry, there is a high probability that there are other undiscovered victims.

14. *If* Clara's potential customer was associated with the Marcum robbery, the Huynh referral list could lead the Paretos to the manufacturer being used to produce the replicas and ultimately to the perpetrator.

Blockade

As handcuffs were snapped on Emma's wrists, she was told that she had been unconscious for a few minutes. The officers escorted the three out of the home. Walking behind Emma, an officer held an ice pack on top of her head. Police snipers, with their long rifles at their sides, huddled at the side of the property. A traffic jam of crazily parked squad cars with lights flashing and doors open clogged the street. The girls' unauthorized entry into the residence demanded immediate and overwhelming force.

The police response time had been exemplary on this night. Only four minutes elapsed from the time Emma dropped off the two young prowlers at the front of the Victorian to the girls' apprehension.

The burglars were separated to facilitate arrest procedures specific to their ages. Emma was advised of her Miranda rights and placed under arrest for burglary in the first degree, destruction of private property, possession of stolen goods, felony child endangerment, and resisting arrest. A female officer explained to Emma that if she had followed the officer's orders to stay where she was, the officer would not have been forced to use his baton.

The officer outlined the procedures for the girls' processing to Emma. As Charlie was under the age of twelve, she was afforded the protections of a "Non Punishable-Minor" (NPM). As an NPM, Charlie would not be arrested and would be treated as a legal witness. Charlie would be released from her handcuffs once her processing was completed. The girls' parents were being notified and Charlie would be released in their care. If the parents could not be located, a relative would be contacted. Clarke was arrested as a Punishable-Minor (PM), but the officer did not share the specific charges against her. Clarke would be informed of her arrest "in language understandable to her." In the next few hours, she would be brought before a judge. As a PM, Clarke would be held in a juvenile detention facility until the next morning.

Lucy would be held at the station until the parents or relatives arrived.

With arms cuffed behind her, Emma stood alone behind one of the squad cars. She wiped away tears with her shoulder as she waited for someone to deposit her in the back seat of the police car. Emma would not need to be reminded that this was her second felony arrest in ten weeks.

Two other police cars rolled up, reinforcing the municipal assets already committed to the scene. Although no sirens sounded before or after the girls' apprehension, residents gathered nearby. A local news van came to a quick stop behind one of the police vehicles.

Charlie and Clarke stood in the center of separate police officer scrums, illuminated by the squad cars' headlights. Charlie's head hung low, shrinking from the light and attention. Clarke's hands were cuffed in front of her. She looked over her shoulder in Emma's direction. Standing erect with her head held high, she clenched her jaw.

A tall fifty-ish officer walked up to Emma.

Running his fingers through his short silver hair, he said, "Before your booking at the station, I need some information. The older girl, Clarke, only shared her name.

She won't tell us anymore without her aunt or lawyer present or, she said, unless we take off her handcuffs so she can 'settle everything right here.' She has an attitude. The younger one seems to have a problem with her throat and can't talk. It would save time if you could tell me about your part in all this."

"All this? Can you be more specific?"

"For starters, a neighbor saw you break into the house. They said you were carrying two gasoline cans. This same residence was burglarized last week. When we arrived at the scene, we found the trunk of your car wide open."

"How convenient for you. Let me guess; stolen property was found in the trunk of my car?"

"You tell me. We found jewelry, several crystal vases, lock picks, gloves, glass cutting tools, and gasoline cans. I would guess you came back here to see if you missed anything the first time. You left your car trunk open so you could make a quick getaway. You were probably going to torch the place to cover everything up. There was no one home... not that you cared about that. You brought minors into your scheme. Worse for you. Is that *specific* enough for you?"

"I don't know what you're talking about."

"It'll go easier for you if you come clean now. But we'll be able to piece together everything soon enough."

"Then you don't really need my help."

"Have it your way, miss. Assisting us is just a way to help yourself. This is your last chance." Smiling, the officer said, "Later tonight, after my shift ends, I'm going home to my family. You? You're going to jail for a long, long time. You'll have plenty of time to think about the kind of role you played in those girls' lives."

* * *

Shortly after arriving at the police headquarters, Emma's handcuffs were removed, and she was escorted to a conference room where the girls were waiting. She passed a row of desks. A few were occupied by police staff. Lucy sat on the top of one of the desks, in the process of being interrogated by a female police officer in a black raid jacket.

As Emma was shown to the meeting room, a fast-talking clerk started with an apology. The clerk's right eye fluttered with a nervous tic. "I'm sorry. Mr. Pareto's message was delivered to the lieutenant just a few minutes ago."

"I don't understand. What message?"

"Mr. Pareto talked with a judge this morning about one of his investigations. The judge is a friend of his. Anyway, Mr. Pareto asked the judge to pass along a message to Commander Staunton earlier today."

"Again, *what* message?"

The clerk's eye twitched. "Mr. Pareto alerted us that there would be a caller, posing as a resident or a burglary victim, who would falsely report a break-in or home invasion either to 911 emergency dispatch or to this station between 9:15 p.m. and 9:30 p.m. The caller would give a description of a vehicle, which would contain stolen goods."

"Any more to the message?"

"Mr. Pareto recommended we dispatch officers to a particular residence by 8:45 p.m. to assist his daughters who would be arriving between 9:15 p.m. and 9:30 p.m. He suggested we canvass the neighborhood to find some type of camouflaged vehicle."

The clerk rubbed his eyes. "We just received this message. Otherwise, we would have approached the scene very differently."

"I'm sure you would have."

The police failed to deploy even one of Fenton's recommended countermeasures.

"We're sorry about the use of force. We need to reform a few industry practices."

"Industry? I've always thought law enforcement was a public service."

"Semantics. Since policing is a professionally provided service, it's a business."

Emma shook her head. "When I started my job with the Paretos, I thought Fenton was foolish to involve his children in dangerous criminal investigations. But do you know what was *really* foolish? Thinking law enforcement is even remotely functional. 'Protect and Serve.' Who? Yourselves?"

Emma made a pit stop before entering the conference room. A weary and battered face stared back at her from the bathroom mirror. There were bluish red crescents under her eyes. Her hair was tangled and clotted on one side with a sticky substance. Her skin looked decades older. After getting sick to her stomach, she neatened up as best as she could.

The girls were seated on one side of the conference table, texting furiously. Liberated from their manacles and rearmed with their phones, they updated friends and family on events that landed them in a small window-lined conference room in the heart of the local police station. The girls gave a quick acknowledgment to Emma before returning to their communications.

On the other side of the table, a swarthy police lieutenant observed the girls and their phones before turning his attention to Emma. With dark folds under his eyes and stooped posture, he had the look of a habitually underequipped public servant. As Emma sat down, the officer pronounced, "I'm pleased to inform you all charges against you, Ms. Dorner, and the Pareto sisters have been dropped."

"Where's Lucy?" Charlie asked, vigorously. Her throat problems were behind her.

"Your dog? She will be brought out in a few minutes after processing." The officer offered a weary smile. "After you make a brief statement, sign liability release forms, and retrieve your possessions, you are all free to go. We've called a caregiver to assist with the pick-up."

Fenton was traveling abroad. With the girls reluctant to draw their mother into their investigative affairs, this left Katherine to retrieve the girls.

"Unfortunately, Ms. Dorner, your vehicle has been impounded. Suspected stolen goods were found in your car. The department will contact you in approximately five to seven days about the retrieval of your vehicle."

The officer ran his fingers through his thinning hair. "Commander Staunton received intelligence earlier today about the residence you visited this evening. The commander left me a message about this intelligence earlier this afternoon. Unfortunately, I listened to his message just a few minutes ago." The officer shifted in his chair. "It's been chaos here. There's been a rash of accidents caused by the traffic signal malfunctions all over town. We've also had system problems in the station. Just a mess."

The girls continued to type into their phones, not offering any advice to the lieutenant on how to best prepare for the next unsympathetic Pareto visitor.

The lieutenant wiped his forehead. "Several of our officers received an anonymous text message at 9:02 p.m., advising them to 'ignore the Pareto intelligence and follow standard procedures.' We took the text seriously."

The young investigators had left the Pareto household at exactly 9:02 p.m.

Emma excused herself to revisit the bathroom.

The girls set their phones down and straightened up as their aunt strode into the meeting room. Katherine explained that she was briefed on the evening's events, just concluding calls with her brother and the police commander on her way to the station. Waving the girls away, she asked to spend a few minutes in private with the lieutenant.

Through the windows of the sound-proofed conference room, Emma and the girls observed the actors facing off at the meeting table without the accompanying dialogue. Katherine was doing the talking while ensuring that the sleeves of her stylish black St. John knit jacket were lint-free. The lieutenant slumped in his chair. After readjusting the kitchen cabinet key on her Gucci chain, she stood up and walked behind her chair. Putting her hands on the back of her chair, she continued to share her perspectives with the sagging public servant.

To add a dash of drama to this silent movie, Charlie selected Bach's dark and muscular organ masterpiece Passacaglia and Fugue in C minor, broadcasting this composition at a high volume on her phone. The conference room participants were insulated from this stirring accompaniment. There was also no indication that the station's personnel took notice of the reverberating plenum registrations.

The next day the girls learned about the tangible ways the lieutenant and his department demonstrated their remorse for the evening's events. These gestures were also intended to assuage the Pareto family's ire while mitigating legal exposures. Reparations included:

1. Emma was no longer required to sign the police procedure liability release forms.

2. The station agreed to give Clarke and Charlie an opportunity to dispense thirty hours of police-related community services over the next ninety days.

3. Charlie was extended a 15 percent discount at the local law enforcement outlet store on items selected by her aunt. Eligible items included advanced optics, survival tent, tactical dog collar, tactical dog leash, camouflage netting, shotgun earmuffs, water purification tablets, lapel microphone kit, women's light-weight tactical pants, infrared leggings, small women's tactical camisole tank top, and academy-grade high-gloss Oxford shoes.

4. The local law enforcement agreed to provide security services at one of Clarke's parties within the next six months at a yet-to-be-determined location.

5. The police K-9 unit would make a visit to Charlie's school during the upcoming term to educate the community's future leaders on the role of canine support in law enforcement operations.

6. Local law enforcement agreed to purchase and supervise the discharge of aerial fireworks–valued at no less than $17,500–for residents during the next Independence Day celebration.

7. The police fleet coordinator would personally supervise restoration of Emma's car, including deep interior cleaning, exterior detailing, scratch and dent removal, and a fifty-five-point mechanical inspection. All outstanding parking citations were forgiven. Fenton also arranged a non-mechanical inspection.

Despite some residual tenderness from the unpleasant negotiations with Katherine, the lieutenant and the station's staff quickly rebounded, responding to Fenton's requests for information over the next week. Staff members who interacted with Katherine, or just heard about her agreeable qualities, extended invitations to meet with her socially. The girls heard through their now regular interactions with police staff that Katherine did not respond to these requests.

* * *

Two days after what Charlie called the "Victorian's Secret," Fenton returned from his travels. Over dinner, the girls shared their experiences at the police station and Victorian mansion.

Clarke helped herself to a generous portion of flounder from a serving tray. Katherine prepared Flounder Amandine, one of the family's favorites. The fish had been baked in parchment paper, along with a layer of dough, creating a thin flaky crust. The wrapped fish was overlaid with amandine sauce, fresh Gulf shrimp, and crabmeat.

Like a Thanksgiving dinner, dishes rotated family style. Clarke surveyed the table in search of a side dish. "Auntie, you must've lowered the boom-boom on the police."

Katherine sighed. "There's no reason to dwell on this. I'm just happy this latest episode is concluded and that you all pulled through."

Clarke dug into the meal, her plate heaped with a jumble of fish, sautéed spinach, coleslaw, green beans, pommes frites, and risotto.

Frowning, Katherine said, "Clarke, eat more slowly. Charlie, you don't need all those potatoes. Honestly, Fenny, these girls are going to have digestive problems if they don't slow down and eat at a more civilized pace."

"But Auntie, we've just started to eat," Clarke said.

Katherine folded her arms. "By the way you two have started dinner, I know what you have in mind."

After Katherine's special Louisiana dinner, the girls and their father continued to discuss the events at the Victorian mansion. Fenton looked up at the cathedral ceiling of his home office as he pondered Clarke's question.

Turning to Clarke, Fenton said, "I imagine the Victorian ambush was designed to delay your pursuit of the perpetrator of the dog crimes. Our adversary likely reasoned that the consequential legal defense to the burglary, possession of stolen goods, and possibly other criminal charges would stall our investigation."

Shaking her head, Charlie said, "*Perciò è finita male.*"

Emma asked for a translation.

Forming a prayer gesture with her hands, Charlie said, "Emma, it's loosely translated as: 'So it ended badly.'"

Fenton continued, "With the new school year around the corner, this legal *deviazione* might have even suspended your investigation for months. *Ritardare intenzionalmente*. During this interlude, our foe would have time to adjust their strategy and launch further counterattacks."

Clarke nodded. "So, the criminals were just trying to put us back on our heels. Too bad the bumbling cops didn't act on your warnings. We might have been able to play a little offense. Can't wait to get my mitts on the perps."

Fenton frowned. "*Nulla può essere amato o odiato se prima non viene compreso*. Nothing can be loved or hated unless it is first understood."

Charlie brightened. "Admittedly, it could've been worse, Dad. Your preemptive efforts expeditiously resolved doubts concerning our innocence."

Leaning back in his chair, Fenton smiled at his youngest daughter and said, "And so, your adversary will not enjoy a respite from your determined pursuit."

Fenton explained he had, once again, employed his AI-enhanced game theory model to anticipate the specific tactics their opponent would use in the Victorian ambush.

* * *

BONUS CONTENT AT THE END OF CHAPTER

The following day, Fenton reconvened his conference with his daughters in the Golden Vault to share the preliminary police report related to their Victorian adventure and to review the girls' list of burglary theories. Fenton settled on an ornate chair which he pulled up to face his daughters, who were lounging on a sofa with their phones.

Nodding thoughtfully, Clarke said, "So, the creepy crawler was squirting lighter fluid to start a bonfire. Dad, do you know if the five-O found any sketchy chemicals near that propane tank fire a few weeks ago?"

The investigator crossed his arms. "I don't know. But I'll find out."

The conversation turned to how to remove jewelry from a residence by avoiding the use of forcible entry or by concealing the evidence of a break-in.

"Girls, thank you for sharing your list of 155 possible ways someone might cover up a burglary. Now, please set aside theories containing extra-terrestrial, divinely inspired, supernatural, or conspicuously conspiratorial elements. Also, exclude schemes requiring long planning horizons. As you whittle your list, Emma and I will play a game of chess, if she will do me the honor. I've brought in one of my sets."

Fenton unpacked a 1964 Man Ray chess set, with traditional chess piece shapes reinterpreted as elemental forms such as spheres, cones, and cylinders.

Over the next hour, the girls consulted their father from time-to-time to settle differences of opinion. Meanwhile, Fenton and Emma battled over the chess board. Fenton played aggressively, sacrificing pieces to create attacking opportunities.

Emma leaned back in her chair as she surveyed the board. "It seems, Mr. Pareto, that your motto might be: Attack at all costs. I don't know the Latin translation of that."

Fenton laughed. "*Impune impetum*. But I'm afraid, this time, my lack of restraint will lead to my undoing." He picked up a captured bishop and turned it upside down. Eyeing the piece, he said, "This game has made me happy in many small ways."

After Emma repulsed another attack, Fenton graciously resigned the game.

The girls' process reduced the original list to the most promising thirty-seven theories. Before going ahead, Charlie lodged a "formal protest" with her father. Scowling, Charlie said, "Dad, I believe several casualties of this sieving process included postulates worthy of further consideration." She described schemes involving powerful magnets, industrial-strength vacuums, tunneling systems, and psychically controlled pets.

"I understand, Charlie, but let's set aside these possibilities for now. Of the remaining ideas, I'd now like you two to create a ranked list of the ten most likely ways to avoid or conceal forcible entry."

After some bickering, the girls shared their list of mostly plausible theories:

1. Undetected human entry through an unlocked door or open window
2. Replacement of broken locks or concealment of other forcible entry indications
3. Admission of a trusted but dishonest visitor
4. Unusual entry point for a human or machine, such as through roof, floor or wall
5. Surveillance system tampering, such as video editing
6. Micro-technology or other robotics used to penetrate a home and evade detection
7. Trojan Horse (such as a large, delivered package), concealing an intruder entering the home

8. Small animal trained to perpetrate the crime and avoid detection

9. Projection system to conceal intruder and/or activities

10. Psychic control of the homeowner

Fenton suggested the girls revisit the two households that reported stolen jewelry to corroborate one of the likely entry methods. He would ask the owner of the Victorian for permission to inspect the premises.

*   *   *

Later in the week, Katherine met with Emma in the kitchen after dinner to discuss the counseling plan for Charlie. Katherine whisked away the house staff that had been attending to the post-dinner clean-up.

Katherine swept her shoulder-length hair back as she leaned against a kitchen counter. When she wore her hair down, she took off a few years. "The counseling is intended to give Charlie an opportunity to share her feelings about changes in the family. I'm not as concerned about Clarke because she's more grown-up. I've given Charlie a degree of latitude in selecting her therapist but encouraged her to select a 'network' specialist available through the family's health plan. She's chosen a credentialed therapist, but they're not in the carrier's network."

The two did not discuss the possibility that the selected "out-of-network" therapist's counseling methods would stray from generally accepted care practices.

"The therapist will conduct several private sessions with Charlie. Afterward, my brother, Ophelia, or I will join Charlie's sessions."

Katherine did not comment on the prospects of her brother joining any of these follow-up conferences.

"I'd like you to provide Charlie with transportation and help manage any insurance related matters. We've briefed the therapist and cleared the way for you to represent the family as required."

*   *   *

Emma turned her car into Dr. Willa Muschio's private cobblestone driveway. The long winding entry drive, flanked by a Mediterranean medley of valley oaks, stone pines, and olive trees led down a gentle slope to the house. The psychologist's large one-story ranch-style home came into view. The house was arranged in a "U" shape with a central courtyard.

During the drive to Dr. Muschio's house, Charlie had shared the therapist's curriculum vitae with Emma and Lucy. She neglected to mention that one of Dr. Muschio's patients was a gifted young art student who had made significant artistic contributions to her art club.

BONUS CONTENT AT THE END OF CHAPTER

To Charlie's delight, Dr. Muschio not only met the qualifications of a family counselor demanded by the Pareto adults but possessed the credentials of a preeminent psychic researcher. Charlie's hand-selected therapist was uniquely qualified to determine if a psychic agent might be at work in the jewelry crimes.

At the top of her agenda: What telepathic or other powers might induce a homeowner to make repeated yet uncalled visits to her vault during the middle of the night?

Bonus Content: How Fenton Used His Game Theory Model

After Fenton's daughters decided to investigate the source of the repeating radio signal, he used his AI-enhanced game theory model to predict their foe's next moves.

- Fenton's analytical construct used evolutionary game theory, anticipating sequential actions, non-symmetric pay-off, imperfect information (for all parties), and a zero-sum solution set.

- Fenton's analysis predicted the most likely opponent actions with the following case-specific parameters: (a) the repeating signal would lead the girls to an environment and time window where the adversary could best control or influence outcomes, (b) the selected environment and time window would limit local or outside assistance available to the girls, (c) the adversary would create a zero-sum (winner and loser) outcome, with no opportunity for mutual benefit to the parties, (d) the selected environment and time window would protect the identity of the opponent, (e) the girls would be unable to change the adversary's selected environment, and (f) the adversary's desired outcome would not jeopardize the welfare of any party (such as an action that might injure the girls, which would only fuel efforts to bring their adversary to justice).

- Fenton's model also tested his primary hypothesis: The adversary's desired outcome would be to restrict the girls' future movements, subsequent to the selected time window.

- Based on the case-specific parameters, the model predicted:

a) Most likely opponent goal: Delay the girls' further pursuit.

b) Most likely opponent strategy: Implicate the girls in the commission of a crime.

c) Most likely opponent tactic: Place incriminating evidence in the girls' possession.

Bonus Content: Dr. Muschio's Professional Background

Trained in experimental psychology, Willa Muschio conducted psychic research in the Institute of Perceptual Studies at UVA. She became a protégé of the founder of the institute, known for his unconventional work in child psychology. Her mentor's landmark research explored a "post-mortem survival" phenomenon, examining the cases of more than two thousand young children who spoke of people and circumstances that, upon investigation, were found to closely match the lives of recently deceased individuals.

Relocating to California after the death of her husband, Willa conducted psychic research at UCSB, investigating cases of telepathy, clairvoyance, psychokinesis, psychic healing, and precognition. Capping her long academic career, Willa led a research team at UCSB's Theoretical and Applied NeuroCausality Laboratory (TANC Lab), directing psychic experiments that blurred conventional notions of cause and effect.

The UCSB research team merged Willa's research with applied physics to test whether changes in subjects' brain activity signaled unconscious knowledge of future events. Quantum mechanics has long recognized "retrocausality," where the present is characterized by quantum states of the past and the future. Willa launched a second career in family therapy, often using hypnotherapy to treat a variety of psychological problems. Returning to her earlier work at UVA, she helped several young children interpret skills, memories, and obsessions incongruous with their juvenile experiences.

Disconnected Pieces

The psychologist's entryway door was ajar, revealing a sitting area with large picture windows and glass sliding doors on the opposite side of the space. The filtered late afternoon light from the opposing windows and doors gave the interior a gauzy aspect. Silhouettes of an adult and an adolescent passed through this space on their way to another part of the house.

As Emma rapped on the open door, Charlie supervised Lucy as she sniffed the foliage lining the entryway. A sleepy-looking young man came to the door, introducing himself as Dr. Muschio's assistant. He led Charlie, Lucy, and Emma to a small waiting room and departed. Seated abreast on a long sofa, with Lucy settling between the two, Charlie took a magazine out of her backpack. Showing off her good posture, she flipped through the pages of *Worth* magazine, with the headline: "Women and the Making of a Rich Life" and scanned articles titled: "How can you take your business's retirement plan to the next level?" and "How does the *Tax Cuts and Jobs Act* affect charitable-giving tax strategies?"

Charlie looked up from her magazine and surveyed the room. "Emma, I have this feeling I've been here before."

Willa came out to meet the visitors. She was an elderly woman with white hair pulled back to reveal a kind face and alert eyes. She was tall and long-limbed, moving with the fluidity that belied her advanced age. After introductions, Willa explained that the ninety-minute appointment would be divided into two parts: the first thirty minutes earmarked for a private session with her patient, with the remaining time devoted to a general discussion that, if Charlie wished, could include Emma, the family's designated caregiving representative. The therapist and Charlie withdrew for their private counsel.

Thirty minutes later, Willa led Emma into a small adjoining room. As Emma settled next to Lucy on a small sofa, Willa handed Charlie a signed emotional support dog certificate, giving Charlie's companion an expanded field of operations. Willa took a seat next to a small table stacked with papers and a small work lamp. Charlie sat upright on a Milo Baughman style wave chaise lounge.

As the therapist shuffled papers, Charlie recapped open questions about Ms. S's nocturnal activities, the principal topic of their initial thirty-minute conversation. Questions about Charlie's emotional state had been put on hold. There was no mention of the forum or timeframe for the young patient to share her emotional response to uncovering her family's secret—whether this subject would be covered in a future counseling session or in Charlie's memoirs.

"So, you're saying, Dr. Muschio, that it's not possible for a hypnotic suggestion to compel a person to do anything against their will?"

"That's right, Charlie." Willa formed a steeple with her fingers. "In a hypnotic state, the subject is *always* in control, never the hypnotist. The hypnotist makes suggestions, but the subject can always decide whether to comply. If a hypnotist suggests an act that is contrary to the subject's values, the subject will reject the suggestion."

Charlie frowned. "But what about hypnotism in stage acts? It doesn't seem like the subjects are in control in those situations."

"An audience volunteer is generally receptive to hypnotic suggestions because they are prepared for what will likely happen. Before entering a hypnotic state, the volunteer has *already* relinquished a degree of control to the hypnotist. Of course, there are many forms of hypnotism, including covert hypnotism, designed to disguise the presence of a hypnotic suggestion. But, whatever the technique, the subject cannot be induced to engage in an activity contrary to their values."

Willa leaned back in her chair and stretched her long arms. "Charlie, you asked if it's possible for a hypnotic suggestion to compel a person to do anything against their will. You might frame your question more broadly, such as: Could a skilled hypnotist introduce a covert suggestion that would manipulate a subject into performing an extraordinary action that would not violate a subject's value system? Or consider a more specific variation of this question: Could a subject be manipulated into believing that an unusual action could serve a desirable or even admirable purpose?"

"I can imagine possibilities along this line," Charlie said, using an erudite tone mirroring the venerated psychologist. "But still, it's difficult to envision how anyone could be convinced that it would be desirable to hand over their valuables to a criminal." Sighing, she said, "Perhaps it would be more likely for a victim to accept a hypnotic suggestion when weakened or vulnerable. Can someone be hypnotized while sleeping... and accept what is told to them as the truth?"

"It's possible to hypnotize someone during sleep, but the differences between sleep and hypnotic states are not clearly understood. In both sleep and hypnosis, our brain shifts into different brainwave states. In the deepest state of hypnosis, the brain exhibits a delta wave pattern from 0.5 to 4 Hz, the same pattern found in deep dreamless sleep. During hypnosis, the subject hears most of what the hypnotist says. In sleep, the subject may hear the hypnotist but not consciously. One cannot turn off hearing. And with respect to 'truth,' whose truth?" Willa did not wait for her pupil's answer. "We've found that the part of the brain that processes auditory information is active during sleep and responds preferentially to meaningful information. The brain continues to engage with verbal information even after one has fallen asleep."

"That's good to know. I sometimes talk to Lucy when she's sleeping."

"You should know, Charlie, that several research studies have tested the effect of drugs on hypnotic suggestibility. Drug-hypnosis studies have used mescaline, LSD, psilocybin, diazepam, cannabis/THC, nitrous oxide, and alcohol. The Stanford Hypnotic Susceptibility Scale and the Harvard Group Scale of Hypnotic Susceptibility indicate that cannabis, LSD, nitrous oxide, and alcohol produce the greatest suggestibility changes. Certain drug combinations produce up to a sixty to seventy percent increase in suggestibility. If you suspect a covert hypnotic scenario, liquid cannabis/THC could heighten hypnotic susceptibility while minimizing chemical aftereffects."

Tying up a couple loose ends, Charlie asked, "For now, can we safely rule out mind control or supernatural possibilities in the jewelry thefts?"

"I think so." Willa straightened in her chair and continued, "Advancements in transcranial magnetic stimulation coils will someday make remote mind control possible. But the science is too rudimentary to be deployed outside the laboratory. Also, I'm not seeing any paranormal influences in the case you've presented."

Willa discussed various applications of hypnosis. "You see, *subconscious expectations* determine a person's attitudes in life. Hypnosis is simply a medium through which positive subconscious expectancy can be programmed. Placebos have been known to cure illnesses by creating an *expectation* of healing. The subject's expectation that a placebo is a healing agent makes it effective. Although a placebo sugar pill has no healing properties, a sugar pill has been documented to reorganize cellular structures in a patient's body. The placebo effect is like a post-hypnotic response."

The psychologist shared inspiring stories of persevering patients whose career successes could be credited to strong subconscious expectations of occupational advancement. These expectations had been cultivated during hypnosis.

Since the therapist had not yet plumbed the depths of Charlie's nature, she was unaware of her young patient's money-making aspirations. Consequently, the good doctor did not know that she was all but telling Charlie that if she simply hypnotically aligned her subconscious expectations with her goals, vast riches were within reach. After several setbacks, the fundraising for Operation RECLAIM was behind schedule. For Charlie, the success of her initiative hung in the balance.

The two agreed to devote the remaining time to a hypnotic session.

Dr. Muschio explained that she would guide Charlie through a past life regression to help her confront any suppressed psychic influences. The young patient rubbed her hands together and asked, "Would it be possible if Ms. Dorner could be present during my hypnotic session?"

The therapist folded her arms. "Fine with me. But the subject must trust the observer; otherwise, they will be refractory to the hypnotic influence. If there are difficulties, I will ask you, Ms. Dorner, to excuse yourself." Shuffling some papers, the therapist said, "This would be a good time to share a little information about hypnotic induction. Our memory mechanism is not well understood. For example, rats that are given even a mild shock somehow transfer the fear associated with an identifiable stimulus on to their pups, and even to their pups' pups."

"Is the same kind of thing true in humans?" Emma asked.

"This is being researched. With respect to recollections of past lives, it's unclear if these are invented or actual narratives, perhaps built upon latent knowledge. Either way, past life regressions have proven to be a powerful therapeutic tool. Therapy is the goal of our upcoming session. But, be advised, in many cases, the person being spoken of in a past life regression has died violently or unnaturally."

The therapist did not share any theories about how the experiences of a deceased person could be found in the memory of a stranger.

Willa turned off all lights except a small Tiffany-style table lamp next to her chair. The light illuminated the scientist's hands as she adjusted the settings on a small recording device. Using relaxation techniques, she placed Charlie into a hypnotically regressed state. Emma did not follow Charlie into her own hypnotic trance, which Willa had described as a "free ride."

"Where are you?" Dr. Muschio asked.

"Outside the barn," Charlie answered in what sounded like a heavy rural Midwestern accent. Charlie's eyelids fluttered.

"What is your name and how old are you?" Willa asked.

"Name's Arch Hobson. I'm thirty-eight," the voice answered. Arch spoke through Charlie.

"Where do you live?"

"Down the road from Plainfield, near the mill."

"What state is that?" Willa asked, trying to learn more about this rural location.

"The Prairie State. Illinois."

"When is this?"

Emma sat up in her chair.

"Well, ah..."

"Arch, what year is this?" Willa clarified in a firm tone.

"Year of our Lord 1891... D'cember."

"What are you doing outside the barn?" Willa asked, returning to the starting point of the conversation.

"I'm ponder'n what to do. The bottom fact is I need to git out and leave this farm. Been here too long, a month of Sundays. My brother done left us here. He alighted this train." Changing subjects, Arch said, "No more moon. Snowing again. Cold night." Charlie's voice was unaltered, but there were shifts in her diction, syntax, and intonation.

"Arch, why do you need to leave the farm now?" Willa asked in an even tone.

"I'm ah goin' crazy here, off my chump, but mama needs me to help run the farm. I can't never leave. I need to start my life in the city but can't never leave her."

"Why can't you leave?"

"Mama can't manage this by herself. My brother's not here anymore to help. Left us last year. And there's a twisting shadow that moves on the ceiling. I c'n sometimes catch it in the corner of my eye when it don't think I'm look'n. It's alive... evil."

Charlie's face twitched. "Anyhow, Mama's a'feard I'll be goin' on a wake snakes sort of a spree if I go'n to the city. But I'm witherin' here and sc'rd of the shadow. It watches me."

"Tell us about the shadow, Arch."

"I won't! I can't! It's time to lay down the knife and fork." Charlie repositioned herself on the chaise lounge.

"What do you mean by that, Arch?"

"To end it now. Just walk out and settle into... the snow. In the field. Peaceful. Quiet." Tears ran down Charlie's face. Lucy jumped off the sofa and looked up at Charlie from the side of the chaise lounge.

Charlie shuddered.

"Yes, I've done it. Walked out... deep in the snow. Just drifting. Night."

"Have you passed on?" Willa asked quietly.

"Yes... all over... now," Arch confirmed between Charlie's sobs.

"Arch, what have you learned in this life?"

Arch snarled, "Don't trust nobody. My brother left me here. Should've never trusted him. Gotta take care of yourself."

*   *   *

Charlie's head hung low, with her tears rolling off her cheeks onto her lap. The two had not exchanged a word since getting into Emma's car. Emma guided her car onto the highway.

She broke the silence. "I'm so sorry. I let that go too far. I was supposed to watch out for you. I let you and your aunt down. That farm, or whatever, wasn't a place to visit."

"It's inside me, Emma. It's been there all along."

"I don't believe that. That's not you. If any of that ever existed, it's someone else and somewhere else."

"I've never seen that place before, but I think it was real."

Emma relaxed her grip on the steering wheel. "What you feel is certainly real. But the farm and everything else might be how your mind is interpreting your emotions."

Emma kept her eyes on the road. The clouds on the horizon were crimson and yellow. "I don't know anything about past life regressions, but I have a theory."

She shivered. "The car is really cold. I'm going to turn on the heater. Anyway, what you remembered or experienced was Arch's struggle to break away from his mother and the family farm to begin a new life. That was the central conflict."

Charlie nodded.

"For you... you're moving onto a new school after next year. There's college and lots of other decisions ahead. Maybe you're ambivalent about taking over the family businesses with your sister—or something else. You might decide to take a different path. But the reality is there's no path that will spare us from problems and pain. This is the way of the world. But don't worry about the choices down the line. Take them as they come. You've got a lot going for you, including the love of your family."

"Do you really think so? Dad is so involved with business. I don't know if he really cares about Clarke and me. And he always seems like he's ready to blow up. If he was still with my mom, things might be different."

"I'm sure he cares about you both. He may not show it, but I think he's trying to give you both space to grow... and for you to discover, for yourselves, the 'small ways' to... find happiness."

"What do you...? Wait, why are you crying, Emma?"

Emma wiped away tears. "Sorry, it's been a long day. I guess all this is a reminder that we all have to move forward."

In Emma's last conversation with her mother, her mother made Emma promise that she would not let anything derail her dreams. In the wake of her death, Emma had broken this promise. She had been unable to break free from a prison of guilt and anger. Only an unfair world would steal one parent while destroying the relationship with the other.

After spending a few minutes with their private thoughts, Charlie restarted the conversation. "Why did Arch tell me not to trust anyone? Does this mean that my subconscious mind is cautioning me about someone? And what was the shadow?"

Emma sighed. "Honestly, I don't know what to make of those things."

Charlie blew her nose, using a tissue she had brought with her from Dr. Muschio's office. "I feel better after talking with you."

"I'm glad. Again, I'm sorry about the hypnosis."

"It's odd, but I feel like everything I experienced during hypnosis is already fading away. It's like recalling a dream now, drifting away from me, untethered to familiar and reliable reference points." Charlie closed her eyes.

"By the way, did you have an opportunity to talk with Dr. Muschio about Stella?"

"Only in the most general sense. Dad told me that I should not disclose Stella's name to others, at least until her mother is released."

"Does this mean that you haven't told anyone about your connection with Stella?"

"I haven't divulged our biological connection to anyone outside the immediate family. Willa, Jill, Roberta, and others don't know about Stella."

After a long pause, Charlie said, "This afternoon's experience has me reassessing Roberta's peculiar behavior. I wonder if there was a hypnotic influence there."

The two were left with their thoughts for the rest of the journey home.

Although the visit with Dr. Muschio raised new questions, Charlie had acquired the object of her search. The psychologist gave Charlie the key to understanding how a hypnotic suggestion could be designed to recruit an unwitting accomplice.

* * *

The next morning, Emma joined a conga line that included Karl and nine staff as they sang "Ran Kan Kan." Although she only knew the words of the song's refrain, for the first time in years, she sang with all her heart.

* * *

Stella and Clarke visited the third company on the Huynh referral list of additive manufacturers. Although neither of the first two operators had replicated Laura's unusual bracelet, both speculated that the piece was the work of Trứng Thối.

Trứng occupied an office at the back of an industrial building. The girls found him seated at a worktable at the side of his cramped office, pouring a red liquid from a small bottle into a large flask. Behind him, large bins containing bottles and electronic equipment were stacked from floor to ceiling.

Taking notice of the girls, Trứng leaned back in his high back chair, pushing himself away from his stained wood desk. Trứng was an obese man. The color of his bald head, resembling a gigantic egg, matched his cassock.

The Egg shook his head. "So, if it isn't foul-mouthed Little Miss Huynh. So often, you bring more trouble than good business. Perhaps your friend is more agreeable."

"Xin chào, Mr. Thối. If you've had trouble with me, it's your own fault. Don't bother to get up." The girls settled onto two stools in front of Trứng's desk.

Stella dropped the bracelet onto his desk. "I understand you've seen this before."

Not bothering to examine it, The Egg shook his head again. "Never seen it."

"Such a quick verdict." Stella smiled as she turned to Clarke. "I think Mr. Thối might be _____ with us. What do you think?"

The Egg scowled. "Too bad Con mắt hasn't taught you any manners."

Clarke remained quiet while looking down at a box next to the proprietor's desk filled with gold computer connector pins and circuit board fingers.

Stella scowled. "I'm not polite to cheats. And I'm not as nice as my aunt. I assay everything we sell. You've tried to _____ us on your purity tests. I didn't tell my aunt about your little _____attempts to swindle us. But I'm having a change of heart."

"If you and your aunt aren't happy with our services, you can take your business elsewhere. I couldn't care less. And I'm not afraid of Bàn tay, either. She's locked away tight. You and Nancy better run along before you're sorry."

"Oh, we'll *run along* alright, but not before we turn everything upside down in this pigsty. You've seen this bracelet. Maybe we'll find something that'll jog your memory."

"You won't touch anything," Trửng growled. He reached under his desk and pulled out what looked like a squirt gun. He aimed the gun at Stella who laughed and said, "I haven't had a squirt gun fight in *ages*. Are we going to have a duel to decide this? Where's *my* gun?"

"Maybe I should point out a few differences between this weapon and a toy. This gun is made of glass, manufactured to exacting standards. Plastic guns tend to leak. Why's this important? Because I don't want this thing leaking on my hands. Why? Because it's filled with aqua regia. You know what this is, Little Miss Huynh. But I'll explain this to Nancy. AR is a mix of nitric acid and hydrochloric acid. It's so corrosive, it melts gold." The Egg turned to Stella and continued, "I've set the gun on medium dispersal. You'll have wished you would've worn long sleeves before you decided to traipse into my office, making your little demands. AR won't melt your skin right away. But you'll just have a few minutes to wash yourself off and get medical attention." Sneering, he said, "That'll be *your* priority, not touching anything in this office."

Stella leaned back and folded her arms. She stared at The Egg, pursing her lips. "So, Mr. Exacting Standards, you think you're beyond my mom's reach? Let me remind you, you fat _ _ _ _ _, why she's called The Hand. She's like an old-school clock. You'll be looking over your shoulder until the hour she chooses to deal with you. Days. Months. Years. Or you can give us what we want. Right _ _ _ _ _ now!"

The Egg pulled on the neck of his smock. Sighing, he lowered his gun. "Hold on. No reason to get bent. Just protecting my stuff. How should I know if we made this bracelet? We make hundreds. Not like I have a customer list. If word got out we had one—"

Stella scoffed, "Puh-lease. You know who comes in and out of here. You have security cameras inside and out. If you're curious, you can check the recording from a few minutes ago and see how I said hello to one of your outside cameras."

"The outside cameras record. But the inside one here is a dummy, just for show."

Stella smiled. "You don't say—the inside one is a *dummy*, just for show? Anyway, you could have told us about the outside cameras from the start instead of wasting our time."

After the half-sisters spent an hour reviewing the recordings, they hit pay dirt. Although the recording was grainy, it was clear enough to show a young man exiting a black van. As he stepped out of the van, he lowered his head. He was wearing a San Diego Padres baseball cap.

The girls shared the recording with The Egg. "It's too _____bad you don't remember this guy's name," Stella said. She pointed at Clarke. "But if he comes back, text my friend at this number. And don't _____ with her, either. She knows karate."

* * *

The next day, the sisters received a text message from their father. Fenton reported that investigators found an incendiary at the propane tank repository fire. The agent was chlorine trifluoride, the highly reactive jelly found at the Victorian.

Three formerly disjointed criminal threads were now woven together into one puzzling plot. Whoever destroyed the cell tower, presumably to conceal evidence of the cell jamming, was also responsible for the dog offenses and the jewelry robberies. The girls only had one week to determine how the crimes were connected.

En prise

Raising two Sweet Snowball doughnuts high over her head, Charlie triumphantly quoted Jameela Jamil: "With a doughnut in each hand, anything is possible!" She arranged an early morning outing to Chuck's Donuts with Clarke and Emma to share excerpts of her session with Willa. Clarke asked her sister if her upbeat disposition could be credited to the therapeutic session.

Charlie puckered her lips professorially and said, "My consultation with Dr. Muschio has strengthened my suspicion—nay, my belief—that a master puppeteer is dangling the robbery victims on the strings of hypnotic control. Somehow, our foe has hypnotically transformed our neighbors into insentient marionettes, manipulating them to plunder their own homes. Two questions for consideration: How are residents convinced to act in a manner contrary to their interests? And how is this puppeteer able to exert influence over so many while artfully concealing the strings of control?"

Stretching her arms behind her back, Clarke yawned. "I don't know about this puppet and string gibberish, but maybe we'll find answers by going over the clues we've collected the past few weeks. Seems like we've been looking at all this from different angles. To start with, the cell phone blocking was probably meant to raise stress levels, particularly in women. This stress, in turn, made them extra-sensitive to sounds, including the nighttime barking. Maybe the perp used this sound sensitivity to somehow make them more susceptible to being hypnotized or controlled in some way." Rubbing her eyes, Clarke continued, "Charlie, why don't you look for connections between noise sensitivity and hypnotism. Better get on it. No time to waste." She then leaned back and closed her eyes.

As Clarke napped, Charlie conducted internet searches aimed at finding connections between sound sensitivity and susceptibility to a hypnotic suggestion. After an hour of research and discussion, Charlie threw up her arms. "This is like trying to piece together fragments of Forma Urbis. I'm not finding a connection between noise sensitivity and hypnotic receptiveness."

Leaving the donut shop, Charlie pulled Emma aside. In a low tone, she said, "I've decrypted the data captured on the storage device."

"The data in the school's copy machine?"

"Right. There are dozens of documents with 'pick-up' and 'drop-off' schedules with lists of jewelry items and addresses. One list includes Laura's stolen jewelry. There are photographs of hundreds of pieces of jewelry. Three of the pictures captured part of a lady's hand with blue-green nail polish. The forefinger of that hand has pointed at me so many times it's easy to recognize. It belongs to Stiglitz. I found meeting notes referring to five names: Mr. Green, Professor Plum, Mrs. Peacock, Miss Scarlet, and Mrs. White. The notes indicate Mr. Green was involved in the jewelry exchanges. I think Mr. Green could be San Diego because Stella and Clarke discovered he visited the AM. There are references to acoustic equipment work conducted by Professor Plum. Given Silas' strange behavior and his expertise, I wonder if Professor Plum is Silas. That means Stiglitz is either Mrs. Peacock, Miss Scarlet, or Mrs. White."

Emma smiled. "What, no mention of Colonel Mustard?"

"Not that I saw."

"Maybe he's out of commission after getting smacked by a lead pipe in the conservatory. Have you talked with anybody else about what you found?"

"Not yet. I'd like to talk with my dad, but he doesn't know I also have the copy machine data. He may have already looked through the data. I'll need to find a way to drop a few hints about this without divulging the source."

Clarke walked up to Charlie and Emma. She rapidly blinked her eyes, adjusting to the midmorning light.

"I could use more sleep." Clarke rotated her torso. "Anyway, me thinks we should look into something else. Dad suggested we check around for single ladies who're stressed about their bling. They might have been ripped off or be the next targets. Pretty thin, but we gotta try everything. We're almost out of time."

The next two days, Clarke, Charlie, and Stella conducted door-to-door interviews of neighbors, asking residents if they had any dreams or premonitions about their household valuables. On a hunch, Clarke also asked if there had been any recent changes to exercise routines, unexplained feelings of wellbeing, or improved sleep. The girls found three households meeting their criteria. Notably, dogs in these three households had been victimized by high-frequency collars. One of these residents, Desiree Jones, agreed to submit to a more comprehensive follow-up interview.

Emma accompanied Clarke and Charlie on their second visit to Desiree's home. Desiree greeted the visitors as if they were relatives arriving for a Thanksgiving dinner. Desiree, mid-forties, was tall and thin. She had a friendly round face, and brown eyes, with her hair wrapped in a patterned tan scarf. A young

Golden Retriever, Baley, ran circles around the group. Baley jumped up on Charlie, putting his paws on her waist.

The three looked for a place to sit. Their only option was the living room sofa blanketed with clothing. As the guests fought for space on the couch, the host explained she was housesitting for her sister who was taking a one-year sabbatical.

Desiree tossed a dog toy in Baley's direction. "Since starting my exercise routine, I've been feeling really good. About a month ago, I started to use my sister's bike trainer. Before that, I never did any cycling. I'm totally hooked now. I cycle two hours a day. I've lost twenty-seven pounds."

Charlie said, "That's fantastic, Ms. Jones! What sparked your interest in cycling?"

"I woke up one morning and *just knew* this was something I needed to do."

Clarke pushed away a pile of clothes to give herself more space on the couch. "My sister and I have been helping our dad with a stolen jewelry case. We're just asking neighbors if they're missing any jewelry."

"I only brought a few pieces of my jewelry with me this summer—three rings and a necklace, I think. To be honest, I haven't seen any of my jewelry for a while. The house is a mess. I'm sure they will turn up after I tidy up."

Charlie glanced at her sister. "Would you mind, Ms. Jones, if we helped you look for your jewelry now? In doing so, we can assist you in organizing your belongings."

Charlie's offer would involve a significant expenditure of time: Boxes, containers, clothes, books, jigsaw puzzle boxes, shoes, dog toys, blankets, sheets, clothes, hangers, and beauty supplies were scattered throughout the house. There was an opportunity to pick up a few community service hours.

"I'd be delighted if you girls could help me restore some order. Your timing is perfect. I've scheduled a pest control visit on Monday. I have a rodent problem."

"Rodent problem?" Charlie asked absently.

Desiree frowned. "I think this mess must attract them. Last week, I found the lid of a cookie jar in one of the bathrooms. I'm afraid a rat must have raided the cookie jar in the kitchen and carried the lid to the bathroom over there." Desiree pointed to a powder room next to the entryway.

Raising her eyebrows, Charlie said, "Certainly a stalwart rodent to accomplish such a feat. If you still have the cookie jar lid, I'd like to examine it."

"The jar is in one of the cupboards." After briefly leaving the room, Desiree returned with an empty plastic beehive cookie jar. She handed the vessel to Charlie.

Charlie did not disclose that one of her associates sold her the cookie jar.

She lifted the lid of the jar. "May I borrow the cookie jar?"

Desiree shrugged. "Of course. You can keep the jar if you like."

Charlie rose from the sofa and walked to the powder room. After peeking into the bathroom, she opened and closed the door several times.

Charlie turned to Desiree. "Do you always keep the small window in the powder room open? Also, do you keep other windows open during the night?"

"I always keep the powder room window open, but it has security bars. I've also been leaving other windows open on warm nights. They have security bars too. What are you getting at, Charlie?" Desiree asked, with a tone of concern.

"I'm not sure yet. Just trying to piece something together."

"By the way, Charlie, I was talking to a neighbor about your visit today. They mentioned something about a science fair project. That was you?"

Answering for Charlie, Clarke said, "I'm sure whatever you heard is true. We'll get to work on your living room first."

The girls spent the afternoon organizing the house. Although Desiree's jewelry had not appeared, she was thrilled with the tidier home. Perhaps sensing a bank of good will, Charlie asked Desiree if the sisters and Emma could spend two nights in her home to rule out any foul play involving her jewelry. She consented, subject to caregiver approval.

After gaining Katherine's approval, Charlie arranged to have the group spend the next two nights in sleeping bags on her family room floor. Meanwhile, Baley would board with a dog sitter. The parameters of Emma's employment with the Paretos remained ambiguous. She asked Charlie to clarify the purpose of the sleepovers. Charlie told her that she was working through a theory but could not share more.

Two Pareto staff members delivered prepared dinners in the evenings. The staff set up the dinner table with crisp white linens and beeswax candles. After the staff cleared the table following each meal, they departed. The company spent the evenings playing *Clue, Exploding Kittens, Scrabble*, and *Cards Against Humanity*.

The first night passed uneventfully. On the second night, the investigators were woken by the tinkling of a small bell that Charlie had placed on Desiree's bedroom doorknob. She attached a bell to each household doorknob to alert the group if there was passage through any closed door.

Desiree trudged past the girls on a path to the front door. Her arms were stretched in front of her, with her palms facing the floor. Charlie called out to her, but she did not answer. After fumbling with the door lock, Desiree let herself out of the house. It was 2:06 a.m.

Charlie screamed, "Ms. Jones! Ms. Jones! Ms. Jones!" as the group followed Desiree down her driveway to the street. Stopping abruptly, Desiree stood motionless. The glow from a nearby streetlamp revealed her unblinking eyes and open mouth. With outstretched arms, she rapidly clenched her fists and straightened her fingers. Desiree turned around, letting her arms fall to her side, and walked back to the house. She knelt at the base of her mailbox to pick up a nine by twelve-inch clasp envelope. As she reentered her house, Charlie pleaded, "Ms. Jones! Ms. Jones! Can you hear me?" The mesmerized woman did not respond. Before returning to her bedroom, Desiree came to a sudden stop in the family room. Still in a trance, she turned over the pouch to liberate its contents. Three rings and a necklace fell onto the carpeted floor.

* * *

Over breakfast, Clarke asked Desiree how she slept. Desiree smiled, recalling a pleasant dream about strolling on a seashore. On the beach, she found an abalone shell that she brought home. For her, the night had passed unremarkably. Not wanting to upset Desiree, the girls chose to delay discussion of her nighttime activities, including the jewelry. Charlie inspected the articles. They were implausibly pristine.

* * *

Waking from a fitful sleep, Emma switched on a lamp next to her bed so she could record another dream in her journal. She had read that immediately writing down dreams was the best way to capture their details for future analysis.

She wrote quickly, not bothering with her penmanship. The journal documented that the ghostly shadow visited her dreams again. In this nightmare, as others before it, she wandered through an abandoned warehouse. She was alone. A late afternoon wind blew through broken windows lining one of the ice encrusted walls. As she walked through the icy space, she detected movement above her. She caught a fleeting glimpse of an amoeba-like shadow, an amorphous apparition, skimming the top of the wall. The three-dimensional shape, like a coil of smoke, possessed an animal intelligence. It was on an errand. As she swung around to confront the shadow, it dissolved into a crack in the wall. Its instant reaction to her perception of its presence, along with its unnatural shape, was repulsive. She tried to run but lost her footing on the icy floor. As she searched for a way out of the building, the shadow followed her. Each time she turned to her stalker, the specter darted into a dark corner or hid behind heaps of rubble. There was no escape from the frozen prison.

Returning her journal to the bedstand, Emma rose with the first dawn light. After throwing on some clothes, she walked down a long hallway to reach the back of the house. All was still except for the echoes of her footfalls on the marble floor and ESTHER's soft hum. Parts of the hallway were illuminated by glass-enclosed niches, displaying a collection of colorful Asian cloisonné vases and Egyptian gold pectorals. She let herself out of one of the doors leading to the veranda. A low fog hung over the gardens. From this vantage point, she surveyed the foggy pre-dawn outlines of the gardens just coming into view.

As she descended the stone staircase that led to the rear of the property, a shadowy form emerged from the formal section of the garden. As the figure approached the house, Emma waited at the foot of the stairs. Fenton smiled as he strode up to Emma. "I saw you on the veranda, Emma. Do you wish to join me in the garden?"

Emma nodded. Although she had lived under Fenton's roof for more than three months, she had not spent any time alone with him.

The two walked in silence along a crushed stone path leading to the formal section of the garden. The Paretos' garden was divided into two irreconcilable sections: a formal Renaissance garden and an untamed woodland. Reminiscent of the sixteenth century gardens found at Villa Farnese, the Paretos' Renaissance garden was divided into rows of manicured hedges, organized in geometric patterns. The symmetrical hedge designs formed numerous compartments containing topiary, flowers, and marble statues. The garden's design represented balance, order, and formality. The scale and design of this garden exuded power and control: a domain of determinism, logic, and confidence. Had the garden been found in Rome, it might have been created for an ambitious sixteenth century cardinal vying for the papacy.

Fenton stopped to examine a finely manicured hedge. "Ophelia always liked the precision of this part of the garden."

As the two walked through the maze of hedges, Emma updated Fenton on the direction of the girls' investigation of the jewelry thefts, including their suspicion that technology was being used to control the minds of the victims as they slept. She asked him how residents might be convinced to part with their valuables.

"It's unlikely the victims are being coerced to part with their belongings. More likely, a person will relinquish objects they value if they see such a forfeiture being virtuous, retrievable, tolerable, or inevitable. The first two reasons are usually the most powerful. Often, individuals have difficulty in assessing whether a sacrifice serves a higher purpose. Consequently, our virtue can be exploited by those who place their interests before our own. This reasoning would lead me to conclude that the victims have surrendered their valuables because they believe, in doing so, they are helping another or serving a greater good."

BONUS CONTENT AT THE END OF CHAPTER

Emma nodded. "Charlie's been working out a theory along this line. Whoever is behind all of this seems highly motivated. It's as if they're trying to settle a score."

Scratching his beard, Fenton said, "Indeed, in most cases, I find a motive like this: revenge, greed, protection, prestige... I've been able to solve these types of cases. But if the person's intent is simply to carry out evil, that's another matter. These cases can never end. The past, present, and future harbor this evil. We've all seen it, even if only in our dreams."

As they returned to the house, with the sun peeking over the trees at the perimeter of the property, the first measures of Mahler's Symphony No. 5 rolled across the gardens.

After a long pause, he said, "Thank you for your support of the girls. I understand the challenges on that front. Perhaps more than you might realize."

Scanning his garden, he said, "The valley oak branch twists and turns as it grows and reaches for the sky. There are no straight lines in its growth. So it is with us. While schools, employers, and societal institutions penalize our mistakes, we must give ourselves and others the latitude to make them. Our errors pave the true and only path to growth. Often this leads to suffering. Other times, life just delivers misery. It's no one's fault, Emma. Suffering isn't to be avoided at all costs or seen as the sole source of religious redemption. It's to be embraced and mastered. To live life fully, one needs to risk misery and grief. But, even in our suffering, we are never truly cut-off and alone. We are part of a larger family that reminds us to forgive others and ourselves. I hope you consider us as your extended family."

Emma said, "I've certainly made mistakes here."

"We all make mistakes. As a parent, I've reminded myself of the difference between influence and intervention. Knowing the harsh world in which we live, it's tempting to keep our children from falling and quickly rescuing them when they do. But by doing so, we only sow the seeds of fear within them, implanting the dread of unthinkable failures." Gazing at the colorful morning sky, Fenton quoted Virgil's *The Aeneid*, inviting Emma to consider the painful paradox of the human condition: "Dawn at that hour brought on her kindly light, arousing mankind to labor and distress."

Emma did not have to ask Fenton if his relaxed parenting approach was intended to give his daughters the latitude to make mistakes, positioning them for personal growth and fulfilling lives. His detachment did not mean indifference. Fenton was aware of her judgment errors involving his children. However, he had not second-guessed her ability to care for them.

As they parted ways, Emma asked, "Why did you hire me? Didn't others figure out the career fair challenge?"

"We considered your choices in the challenge, Emma, but it came down to your father's endorsement. We were able to contact him through the information you provided at the end of the challenge. He shared that you are a wonderful person—and talented. Of course, everything we now know. Your father told us that it would be a mistake not to hire you. He said your family has suffered a tremendous loss, but he is proud of you and you shouldn't be judged by the ways you've been dealing with what's happened."

After a pause, Fenton said, "I also know a good bet when I see one."

They walked back to the house without exchanging another word. Not wanting Fenton to see her reaction, Emma focused on the villa as tears rolled down her face.

* * *

The next day, Emma ran down a hallway leading to the girls' quarters, from which she had heard a blood-curdling scream and Charlie's unmistakable cries of anguish. As she stepped into the bottega, Charlie let out a final mournful howl: "Noooooooooooooooooo!" Clarke arrived a moment later. On the table in front of Charlie was the cookie jar lid Charlie borrowed from Desiree the preceding week. However, the lid was now dissected. From the belly of the cookie jar lid, Charlie had opened a cavity, containing two rows of matching foam earplugs of different colors. The rows of earplugs gave the appearance of insect egg sacs. What was once a smooth surface of the lid, now extended four rotors. Limp grasping claws also protruded from the sides of the lid. The beehive cookie jar lid was a drone. Charlie's mouth hung open. She had just absorbed the implications of distributing a record-setting 428 beehive cookie jars to her neighbors.

——— Bonus Content: World Garden ———

"As you might have surmised, Emma, the design of these gardens is intended to stimulate our thinking about the world. Therefore, this might be an opportune time to reflect on your question from a *societal* perspective. In every era, including the present, mankind struggles with forces that ask us to relinquish our interests. History shows us even entire societies can be duped into abdicating their sovereignty. We forfeit our interests and moral authority because we believe we cannot resist the will of powerful, complex, or inscrutable forces. How can we challenge what we do not understand? Time and again we blame our inept leaders for the failings of our formidable institutions. Who else is to blame? Yet, the truth lies within our gut: The apparatus of power is the essential problem. Each civilization faces the test of confronting its central power structure. While our seemingly all-encompassing technological domain produces countless benefits, it represents the crucial test of this age."

Emma did not ask the investigator to elaborate on this "crucial test" or ask why he chose to refer to the present as *this* age rather than *our* age.

They entered the untamed territory, containing large trees, shrubs, twisting paths, and colossal weather-worn stone carvings of indigenous animals and mythological creatures. A bear, wild boar, eagle, and horse were mixed with serpents, fanged bird-like creatures, and other monsters. Many of the sculptures were entirely covered with moss. These enormous carvings were rendered from granite boulders originally found at the site. The ground was uneven, creating natural terraces and embankments.

"So, how old are the stone carvings in this area?" Emma asked. "Roberta said some parts are ancient."

"We don't know the precise age of this forested garden. But there are plantings in this section that are over four hundred years old."

"Amazing. I thought the forest was nature's creation."

"The valley oak trees found within this part of the garden are grouped in arrangements not likely found in nature. The trees were probably planted in the early seventeenth century, the period when Spanish explorers first made contact with the Ohlone."

Fenton stopped to look up at the canopy of an ancient oak tree. "The oaks are approaching the end of their lifespan. Their time has been fulfilled. This transition marks the twilight of this era and the dawn of a new age."

"Isn't there anything that can be done to save them?"

"No, Emma," he said firmly. "The New supplants The Old. The Corinthian columns of St. Peter's Basilica were quarried from the pillars of the Temple of Vespasian."

Fenton ran his fingers down one of the ridges of the deeply ribbed oak trunk. "There have been many systems of power. Historically, these systems have operated within byzantine manmade religious, political, mystical, or ideological constructs. The contemporary cloud—and the central metaphor of the internet—is only the latest system of great power. Although it is a new type of power structure, one that is indifferent to human concerns, it is no less influential on civic affairs. Like other clouds of power, it retains the aura of something luminous, almost impossible to grasp. The present-day cloud is composed of an infrastructure of satellites, cables, wires, electronics, and buildings filled with machines. Like other structures before it, the cloud's inner workings, design and most importantly its implications, seem far too complex to understand. What do we see in this latest paradigm? An impassive medium? A manipulative tool? Like all great systems of power, the cloud informs the most important edifices of our civic sphere, including the manner of economic exchanges, social interactions, and daily decisions. But the challenge of this system, like all others before it, is that its unfathomable design obscures the activities that reside within it. The technology cloud's unpredictable path reveals all the attributes of indeterminism, producing events and outcomes not dictated by antecedent causes. Nevertheless, society is convinced that this unpredictable evolutionary path will promote prosperity, understanding, and peace."

The two set off again on a winding trail, leading to higher ground.

Emma stumbled on a tree root that crossed their path.

After reaching the crest of the poggio, the two followed the rocky path into a ravine covered by ferns. Emma lost her sense of direction as they descended into a shaded cathedral of valley oaks that bordered each side of the natural nave. A bubbling stream joined the trail, then turned away as it found lower ground. This domain was a paean to the spirits of magic, charm, and wonder—a repudiation of logic, order, and sophistication.

The air under the woodland canopy was heavy and still. But high above, leaves fluttered from a light breeze.

As the two followed the trail up a slope, Fenton asked a series of rhetorical questions to stimulate Emma's thinking about the technologically driven world. "Is this latest power structure casting an emancipatory light on the world, or are we entering a new dark age characterized by ever more bizarre and unforeseen events? Is technology helping fulfill the Enlightenment ideal—in which a wider distribution of information will lead to growing understanding and peace—or is it fostering social divisions, distrust, and fear? Does our technology help us understand who we are and what we need, or simply distract us with its dreamy diversions and anesthetized fantasies, forestalling the marvelously painful comprehension of our true selves? Most importantly, can we conceive that, like a natural cloud of water vapor drifting across the sky, the current power structure, like all human creations preceding it, is impermanent?"

Emma admitted that she was unable to see beyond the current technological paradigm. She asked how he thought we, individually and collectively, should respond to the challenges presented by our technological age.

Fenton paused his climb and turned to her. "We should continually ask ourselves the most important question spanning *all* ages: Are we awake or dreaming?"

"How do we know if we are awake?"

"You are awake if you feel the pain of your struggle. Life is full of pain. Anyone who tells you differently is trying to sell you something or is about to take something from you."

"So, we're only awake when we are suffering?"

"Suffering and sleep are incompatible. When we're comfortable, we're likely living in a dream constructed for us."

Mating Net

Charlie looked over Owen's shoulder as he dissected the earplugs found in the belly of the drone. Once again, Owen agreed to assist the girls with technical aspects of their investigation. Using a jeweler's lighted magnifying visor, he teased apart the earplugs with a small scalpel, tweezers, and a long needle. Charlie played the role of a surgical assistant, exchanging Owen's instruments with unerring efficiency.

The dissected drone held a collection of everyday foam earplugs. But there was another class of earplugs that contained a communication device that relayed broadcasts into the resident's ear.

Owen raised one of the devices to eye level with his occluding clamps. "Charlie, can you scoot back a bit? A little further." Owen pointed to Emma. "Plop yourself next to that enchanting girl. Anyway, an earpiece is turned off if another gizmo is turned on. This probably prevents a person hearing a neighbor's message."

Clarke smiled. "It would be confusing to get a different message in each ear! But if the hearing in my left ear gets any worse, it wouldn't be a problem for me."

Owen pulled back his hair. "These devices also have a sensory pad. I wonder if these pads monitor heart rates through the ear canal, transmitting data back to the operator. These sensors might even monitor breathing and sleep cycles." Owen leaned back in his chair. "Amazing little beasties."

Adjusting her tinted glasses, Charlie chimed in, "Undoubtedly, the drone was designed to substitute these special earplugs for the regular earplugs. Perhaps the substitution was done during the day when the earplugs were on a bedstand. I'd surmise each drone is stocked with an inventory of facsimile earplugs, offering a selection of hypoallergenic styles across a spectrum of colors."

Owen nodded. "You're probably right, Charlie. After the claws scoop up and ditch the real earplugs, the drone ejects the lookalike ones. I've found a spring under the auditory earplugs in the drone's storage compartment."

"Can you help us trace the source of transmissions?" Charlie asked.

Owen lowered his head, allowing his overflowing locks to fall forward. In a quick motion, he pulled his hair back and lifted his head. "There're actually two transmissions: one sent to the drone, another to the earplug. The drone's tech is pretty advanced. Never seen anything like it. The earplugs might be easier to work with. If a bunch of devices are receiving messages on the same band, that'll also help. But no promises."

The operator used a relay link at the tented house. If this was the case again, the earplug transmission source would jump from place to place.

Emma said, "We'll be grateful for whatever you can do, Owen."

He shook his head. "I don't know. I'm probably over my head."

Tucked into a compartment in the cookie jar lid, Owen discovered an optical system, allowing the operator to maneuver the drone. An electronic eye rotated on a short stalk, giving the drone a 360-degree view. The eye was equipped with its own light source.

He examined the lidless eye. "It looks like the eye is divided into two independent visual systems, creating binocular vision. The overlapping fields of view give the drone depth perception." He turned his attention to the mechanical grasping claws. "Yep, these are probably used to switch out the earplugs."

Looking up from her phone, Clarke added, "I think I found the brand and model of the grasping claws. It says here they can lift up to seven pounds."

Charlie nodded. "That would give the drone the ability to undertake many tasks, such as opening drawers and performing other light duties."

Owen found how the optics, rotors, and claws could be remotely extended and retracted. When retracted, the presence of these limbs was unnoticeable. Owen commented that the drone was constructed with skill and precision.

Charlie rested her chin on her extended index fingers. "I concur. Not only am I impressed with the craftsmanship that went into concealing the appendages, but this was accomplished while faithfully preserving my school's colors."

Charlie's phone had once argued that the plastic cookie jars were poorly made.

Owen said, "Look at the propeller shrouds. Probably meant to make them quieter."

Charlie said, "Owen, I'd like to re-task the drone for my own surveillance activities. Can you get it working again for me?"

"I should be able to get it flight-ready tomorrow. Need to check the motor, which looks pretty powerful. I'll give you a controller you can use."

It was now clear how the puzzle pieces fit together. The cell phone interruptions were designed to create higher levels of stress and, particularly for women, sound hypersensitivity. The nighttime dog barking encouraged the use of earplugs for those residents sensitized to noise. Each cookie jar was a snack-filled Trojan Horse, with the drones making the earplug substitutions. The new earplugs conveyed nighttime suggestions to the wearer, somehow persuading the victim to relinquish their jewelry. Days or weeks later, replica jewelry was introduced into the household to conceal the theft of the original articles.

* * *

That evening, the girls and Fenton lounged in one of *Volta Aurea's* seating areas. The girls briefed their father on the discoveries made at Desiree's house and the results of Owen's analysis. The FBI hearing was just two days away.

Rubbing her hands together, Charlie said, "I suspect the cookie jar lid—the drone—found in Desiree's powder room lost its way. Her house was cluttered, and perhaps the drone got confused, flying into the powder room by mistake. Since the bathroom window was open, along with other windows on the other side of her house, it's likely a gust of wind caused the powder room door to slam shut, trapping the drone. This event led to our discovery of the drone."

Nodding, Fenton said, "A reasonable theory, Charlie. Well done."

Charlie grinned, placing her clasped hands on her lap.

Fenton leaned back, gazing at the Cyclops oculus above. "I suggest you girls return to Desiree's house. You'll want to brief her on this case; she shouldn't be kept in the dark any longer. Perhaps Owen can examine her earplugs. No doubt he'll find a transmitter in at least one of her earplugs. You might be able to convince Desiree to wear her earplugs a little while longer and to permit an overnight stay again tonight. It wouldn't be surprising if she continues to receive messages, perhaps aimed at keeping the secret."

Clarke nodded. "Okay, we'll talk with Ms. Jones. Also, Owen is working out a way to find the source of the earplug transmissions." She clenched her jaw. "This time we'll get our hands on... we'll better understand what's happening."

* * *

As their father suggested, the girls briefed Desiree on the case, including their observations while visiting her home. Although shocked by the girls' account of the night's events, Desiree pledged to help the girls bring the perpetrators to justice. She lent Charlie her earplugs for inspection. Owen discovered that each one of them contained a small transmission device.

Desiree allowed another overnight stay in her home. This sleepover would include Stella. Owen constructed a small receiver, allowing them to eavesdrop on transmissions sent to Desiree's earplugs. The receiver, tuned to the frequency of Desiree's ear pieces, was also paired with a second receiver to acquire the location of the transmission.

Emma questioned why they needed to spend another night on Desiree's floor. Now that the jewelry exchange was complete, wouldn't the criminals move on to their next victim? She also reminded the girls that, before reassembling the drone for Charlie, Owen took it apart, piece by piece. No doubt, this dissection elicited repeated HAL 9000 appeals to the drone's creator. Their adversary was likely planning their next ambush."

* * *

Before turning in, Desiree told the visitors that she would leave the door to her room open during the night. "I usually close my door when I have overnight guests. But in this case, I'll leave it open, like I'm alone." With hands on hips, she said, "I'm ready for anything." She pointed to a baseball bat in the corner of her room. "And I have this." She opened her nightstand drawer and removed a nine-millimeter handgun. She racked the slide, loading a round in the gun's chamber, before returning it to the drawer.

"I see, Ms. Jones, you have a Beretta M9A1. I have it on good authority that your gun nicely balances firing ease and stopping power," Charlie said.

Emma shook her head as she turned to the girls. "Here's what I see: A dangerous adversary, countless unknowns, and a roomful of jumpy underage females with access to a loaded gun."

Clarke smiled. "And what could possibly go wrong?"

At 2:06 a.m., the visitors woke to music being broadcast over Owen's receiver. They were listening to the broadcast in Desiree's ear. The bland and repetitive music—like a telephonic on-hold composition—ebbed and flowed. A female voice replaced the music.

"You are relaxed... you are relaxed... you are relaxed... you are feeling well... you are relaxed... you are feeling well... you are well... you are well... you are relaxed and well... you are relaxed and feeling well..."

Combinations of these phrases continued for a few minutes. The group was glued to Owen's receiver. Charlie whispered that the voice sounded familiar.

"You will stay asleep. You will stay asleep. You will stay asleep."

The voice continued, "You are descending a staircase. With each step, you will become more relaxed. You are ready to take your first step. Relax. You are well..." The hypnotic induction covered five imaginary steps.

The voice continued, "You will stay asleep. You will stay asleep. You will stay asleep."

As they huddled around Owen's receiver, Charlie whispered that she would stand at Desiree's open bedroom door, so she could look in on her.

"You have done well. You have done well. All is well. All is well. The charity event is over, and your jewelry has been returned. The charity event is over, and your jewelry has been returned. Your friend looked so grateful. So grateful."

Clarke whispered, "What charity event?"

"You are so generous to lend your jewelry to your friend. They are appreciative. They couldn't have attended the event otherwise. You are so generous to lend your jewelry to your friend. They are appreciative. They couldn't have attended otherwise. You're a good person. You feel good about yourself."

Clarke nodded her head. "Now I get it. People have been tricked into thinking they're loaning their jewelry to a friend."

The fairy tale had been constructed to induce residents to "loan" their valuables to support a friend and a worthy cause. Victims received suggestions built on an altruistic theme.

The voice extolled Desiree's generous act, as if praising a pet: "You are *so* good. You are so *very* good. Good *girl*. You are so good. You are so *very* good. Good *girl*."

Clarke shook her head. "This just goes on and on."

"You are feeling good. You are exercising. You are loved. You are exercising..."

Turning to a new topic, the voice informed Desiree: "Your friend needs you again. Your friend needs you again..."

Charlie frantically motioned for the group to join her in Desiree's bedroom.

Clarke was the first to join her sister. Charlie pointed to the corner of the room, where a drone was hovering above a tall bookshelf. Its illuminated eye swiveled back and forth. Charlie ducked to avoid detection. Four rotors extended from the drone's body. Its claws limply hung under its body, like a flying wasp.

The group had not considered the possibility of a second drone infiltrating Desiree's house.

The drone noiselessly skirted the ceiling before approaching Desiree's bed. It stopped, hovering above Desiree's head. The machine's eye swiveled downward to study her face. Like a cat's eye, the yellow eye had a thin-slitted vertical pupil. The drone tipped forward, its claws opening and closing. An appendage, resembling a straw, extended from the body of the drone. The straw moved closer to Desiree's lips.

Charlie approached the bed. She reached out and touched the straw. In an instant, the eye swiveled in her direction. Charlie froze. With her hand still touching the straw, one of the claws clamped down on her fingers. She cried out in pain as she pulled away.

Clarke strode to the corner of Desiree's bedroom. She returned with Desiree's baseball bat. After measuring the distance between herself and the drone, she unleashed a full swing. Clarke went yard. What parts of the drone that did not atomize crashed against the opposite wall of the bedroom.

Desiree opened her eyes. She was now fully awake.

She would not learn why her friend needed her again.

Yawning, Clarke said, "That was exciting. But it's been a long night. I'm beat. I'm going to turn in." She returned Desiree's baseball bat to the corner of the room. Pointing to what was left of the drone, she said, "We can clean up this mess after we get some sleep." She rubbed her eyes. "Good night, all."

With hands on hips, Charlie said, "I would advocate for an immediate team debrief and a thorough evaluation of the remnants of the drone."

Emma was able to coax Desiree back to sleep. The three spent the rest of the night recounting what they had witnessed. Stella talked a mile a minute, punctuating her reflections with an assortment of profanities. The drone's claws were troubling to Charlie. More than once, she asked Emma why the drone's pincers opened and closed. Charlie was also concerned about the possibility of more drones in the house, confessing that she did not have a reliable record of the number of cookie jars sold to the household.

*   *   *

The group left Desiree's house at six o'clock, catching a few hours of sleep after returning to the Pareto compound.

The three girls and Emma enjoyed a late-morning brunch prepared by Katherine. The meal featured large slices of cantaloupe, honeydew, watermelon and pineapple, grapefruit and nectarines; double-dipped thick slices of French toast; and Belgian waffles with strawberries and turkey sausage. The meal was topped off with a double cappuccino.

The group complimented Katherine on the meal. They also commended her on her fashionable attire. Katherine modeled a recently purchased St. John chocolate stretch silk blouse, glossy leather skirt, and wide artisan belt for the girls, explaining that this ensemble represented her kick-off to the fall fashion season. Touching her pearl necklace, she said that she had arranged to meet with Cosmo over coffee in the afternoon to discuss his performances at the perimeter of the property.

Katherine had learned that Cosmo's visits were not a secret.

She assured the girls that there was no romantic motive for this meeting. Clarke smiled, pointing out to her aunt that her attention-grabbing outfit did not square with her platonic agenda. Katherine did not respond.

As Emma finished her cappuccino, she received a text response from Owen. He had traced the night's audio transmission.

Emma stepped away from the table to call him.

"Before I give you the transmission location, promise me that you'll be careful."

"Of course. I'll ask Mr. Pareto what to do."

"Seems like the police should take it from here."

"Probably right."

"By the way, we haven't talked about what's happening between us."

"What do you mean?"

"You know I have feelings for you."

"You've hidden them pretty well, Owen."

"I thought you knew..."

"This isn't the best time..."

"Okay, let's get together tomorrow. Ready for the coordinates? I'll text them to you. 37.428650 latitude, -122.193660 longitude."

* * *

The three girls met in *San Lorenzo Fuori le Mura*. Stella and Charlie looked over Clarke's shoulder as she entered the location coordinates on her laptop. Clarke surveyed a satellite map, zooming in and out of an aerial view of a residential area.

"Isn't that Roberta's place? Charlie, you said her place is a jungle. See, you can barely see the house."

Charlie nodded. The coordinates confirmed her theory about the connection between the odd events in Roberta's cluttered home and the hypnotic techniques used by the jewelry thieves. Clarke texted her father, who was meeting with a former colleague at Filoli—a historic garden in Woodside. Her text informed him that Roberta's house was likely the signal source. She asked him to call her right away.

A few minutes after Clarke's text, the three girls simultaneously received an identical text message from a blocked number.

"DO NOT enter Silas basement. DOORS/WALLS ELECTRIFIED."

Frowning, Clarke asked, "You both got the same message?"

"What does it mean?" Stella asked.

Charlie shook her head. "And who sent it? Do you think Roberta is in danger?"

"Oh, good. Dad's calling," Clarke said. She put her phone on speaker mode.

The girls updated their father on the source of the signal and the text warning.

Fenton cleared his throat. "Thanks for the update. I'll alert the police and suggest they send someone to Roberta's house. The police should take it from here."

Charlie removed her tinted glasses. After studying them, she put them back on. "Dad, don't you think it's odd the very morning we pinpoint Roberta's house as the signal source, we receive a text warning us not to enter this *same* house? Could the text be a diversion, just like our adversary used to misdirect the police at the Victorian? Maybe we should ignore the text and investigate the basement of Roberta's house."

"Charlie, I think it would be best if the police look into this. I must be going. I've received some intelligence that one of our suspects is a flight risk. Every minute counts."

Minutes after the girls wrapped up their conversation with their father, Clarke received a text from The Egg. A man matching San Diego's description just arrived at his office demanding final payment before closing his account.

Clarke jumped up, motioning for everyone to follow her. Hurrying out the door, she texted: **"DON'T allow him to leave!"**

* * *

Emma drove the girls and Lucy to the manufacturing site in record time, making wild maneuvers along the way. She called the police as they pulled into the rutted parking lot. A familiar black cargo van was parked in the middle of the lot, bordered by a municipal airport and a busy highway. As Emma pulled up alongside the van, Lucy looked out the window and barked.

After the group exited the car, Charlie launched the drone that Owen had rehabilitated for her, allowing the young detective to survey the surrounding area. As she used the controller's stick to position the drone high overhead, she whistled "Che Vuole Questa Musica Stasera."

Emma overruled Clarke's plan: "No, you need to stay here! *I'll* look for San Diego. I'll hold him here until the police arrive. You all can stand guard next to the van if he gets past me. If things go wrong, be careful. He's a violent man." Stella looked tough, with her sleeveless crop top exposing sculpted shoulders, biceps, and a taut midsection.

Emma's plan immediately unraveled. As Emma approached the entry, she was joined by Clarke, who caught up with her.

"You don't know what you're up against. You need me," Clarke said. Before Emma could respond, San Diego pushed through the swinging entry doors. His trademark cap was pulled down low, hiding his eyes. He had an angular unshaven face with a prominent jaw. His bronze tank top showcased a muscular frame, with intersecting ring-patterned tattoos extended from his shoulders to the hands of both arms.

He tilted his head to one side, puzzled as to why two young women were obstructing his path. Turning to Clarke, he reacted as if he had received an electric shock.

The Padres fanatic snarled through his clenched teeth: "You... but first..." With surprising speed, San Diego lifted Emma by the throat. Clarke struck San Diego's forearm, forcing him to drop Emma. Emma fell to her knees. He whirled around and swung at Clarke. Using her martial arts training, Clarke dodged his punch. But San Diego landed a follow-up left jab, striking Clarke's shoulder. He turned and sprinted toward his van. Emma struggled to her feet.

Shaking off the blow, Clarke took off after him, reprising their amusement park encounter. As the two sprinted across the parking area, a high-speed object, plunging from high above, struck San Diego on his forehead with a thump. He staggered but remained on his feet. After shaking off the blow, he resumed his flight, veering off course before correcting himself. He was hurt.

San Diego slowed, realizing that Stella and Charlie guarded the van. Stella stood her ground with arms folded. Charlie dropped the drone controller and picked up Lucy. She placed herself behind Stella. Rather than confronting the two sentries and their dog, San Diego sprinted to the airport fence. A moment later, Clarke reached the van, hesitating to share an unspoken thought with her half-sister.

Nodding in agreement, Stella pointed to San Diego, who just reached the airport fence. "So, you want a piece of the champ? Then go get him."

Large commercial airports are protected by towering fences, masses of barbed wire, and hardened defenses, such as blast walls, barriers, and bollards. By contrast, municipal airport security is more symbolic than protective. This municipal airport relied on a chain link fence for the security of its airfield. This obstacle did little to slow the panicked and athletic perpetrator of numerous crimes.

Lucy leapt out of Charlie's arms and raced across the parking lot in pursuit of San Diego. Reaching the fence, Lucy paused. There was no stair of boxes stacked against the fence to test her courage. After a quick survey, she squirmed under the fence.

As Clarke scaled the fence, San Diego ran toward the runway. His escape route crossed the path of aircraft. Clarke was highly motivated to bring this villain to justice. For her, San Diego represented the source of her cell phone torments, electrocution on Cell Tower 2173, injuries sustained in the amusement park struggle, permanent ten percent hearing loss in her left ear, and Victorian arrest.

Reaching the top of the fence, Clarke allowed herself to drop to the other side. San Diego staggered onto the runway. His legs were shaky, and he leaned to one side. Lucy latched onto San Diego's ankle, further slowing the fugitive.

The control tower personnel, surveying the airstrip and surrounding area, became aware of the two adventuresome visitors and a dog on the west side of the tarmac—visitors unaware of the airport's flight center motto: "Safety. Community. Adventure."

This runway extended twenty-six hundred feet, accommodating light aircraft. In recent years, an increasing number of small jets were using this airport.

Many of these jets were faster but not lighter than earlier generations of aircraft, now needing more runway.

A Cessna Citation CJ2 jet was approaching the south side of the airport for a landing. This jet would use most of the available runway, touching down at ninety-three knots.

The jet was coming in hot.

Clarke, San Diego, and Lucy were now settling their differences on the north end of the runway, directly in the plane's path. San Diego shook Lucy off his leg before continuing his flight. She landed hard on the runway and was not moving.

San Diego spun around and landed a hard right to Clarke's forehead. As Clarke slumped, he brought a crushing blow down on her back.

The Cessna touched down on the south end of the runway.

Clarke reeled from these punches but stayed on her feet. Somehow regaining her balance, she flung herself at San Diego. They landed hard on the asphalt runway, rolling away from the Cessna Citation CJ2 jet that sped by, narrowly missing the two.

Stunned by Clarke's tackle and suffering from the residual effects of the mysterious projectile, San Diego struggled to get to his feet. After settling into a crouched martial arts pose, Clarke delivered three punches to his neck and jaw. When Clarke connected with his jaw, she fractured the fifth metacarpal bone in her right hand. San Diego collapsed, pitching forward on his stomach. Now subdued, Clarke pinned him on the ground with one knee, pulling the villain's arms behind his back. Watching Clarke's triumph through the fence, Charlie yelled, "Yes!"

Two minutes later, and three minutes before the next aircraft landing, the airport's security team intercepted the two trespassers, slapping handcuffs on both.

There was movement in the high grass at the far end of the runway.

Emma drove the girls to the airport entrance on the east side of the airstrip. As she pulled up to the entrance, six uniformed guards escorted Clarke and San Diego into an airport building.

On the verge of tears, Charlie asked, "Did either of you see what happened to Lucy? She was on the runway and now she's gone."

Neither Stella nor Emma answered.

After a pause, Emma redirected the conversation as they pulled into the parking lot. "Did you see something hit San Diego when he was running?"

Stella said, "That was Charlie. She rammed him with the drone." Turning to Charlie, "You _____ nailed him—hit his forehead. You _____ him up. Hardcore."

Charlie lifted her tinted glasses and wiped her eyes. Looking at Emma, she said, "Given the available options, I used my intuition to find a provocative move with strong continuations. I conjectured that if I could get the 250-gram drone up to eighty miles per hour, it was capable of delivering approximately two thousand Newtons of decelerated force.

Emma... I can review the math later if..."

Charlie did not finish. She was sobbing.

A police car entered the manufacturer's parking area.

As the three walked to the airport administration office, Clarke, Fenton, and an airport official stepped out of the building. The famous investigator held Lucy in his arms. She was unharmed. Charlie raced ahead to meet Clarke, her father, and Lucy. As Stella and Emma joined the others, Clarke's handcuffs were removed. She flexed her right hand.

Putting his hand on Clarke's shoulder, Fenton reported that the other members of the criminal ring—Silas, June, and Ms. Stiglitz—had been rounded up. With one day to spare, the case had been solved.

With the joy only a truly proud parent can feel, Fenton knelt and hugged his daughters.

He then motioned for Stella and Emma to join the family hug, which they did.

Epilogue: The Black Queen

School resumed for the girls. Their already limited time was now consumed by homework and—for both girls—new social endeavors. Emma was seeing less of them, particularly Charlie. Emma talked with Katherine about scaling back her support role. The FBI charges had been dismissed. Due to complications involving the elementary school's former principal, the district allowed Charlie to advance to middle school. Except for a splinted finger, Clarke had recovered from her airport scuffle. Ophelia had left for Armenia, preparing for her permanent relocation the following summer.

While there were no visible signs of autumn, the late afternoon heat was interrupted by temperate breezes. These light gusts foretold a change of season, carrying traces of dried flowers, grasses, and earthy notes.

Roberta and Fenton had taken a few evening strolls through the ancient oak grove. Afterwards, Roberta spent time with Charlie in the Golden Vault, each updating the other on recent undertakings. One windy evening, the investigator and his old friend revisited the Sacro Bosco. Fenton held Roberta's forearm for balance. Both walked slowly, accounting for Roberta's advanced age. Roberta's laughter and melodic voice mixed with rustling leaves and the choruses of thrushes, sparrows, and an anxious nightingale.

The family would not see Roberta again. Later that week, Fenton shared with the family that Roberta passed away, at long last rejoining the Great Spirit that had given voice to all animals and lifeless things.

* * *

The Saturday following Roberta's passing, Fenton called the family together for a late afternoon discussion. Stella's and Clarke's wild laughter in the entryway rang through the downstairs hallway, galleries, and rear terrace. Lucy gave a couple of warning barks to let everyone know that a visitor had entered the house. As the girls walked to the back of the house, Stella shared, for all to hear, that the use of her aunt's car gave her the independence that, in her view, should have been conferred much earlier in life. The two girls met Fenton, Charlie, and Emma on the veranda overlooking the rear of the property. Jonny Kemp's "Just Got Paid" gave the gathering a party atmosphere.

Charlie's head was engulfed in an enormous straw sunhat, borrowed from Katherine. As Charlie repositioned the rolled brim of her hat, her face was briefly visible. She wore oversized Jackie Onassis style prescription sunglasses. Her nose, cheeks, and arms were smeared with unevenly applied white sunscreen. Intercepted by her aunt only moments before, Charlie had made hasty protective corrections. She leaned against a marble balustrade, sipping from a large glass of grapefruit flavored water.

Lucy and her enduring love interest, Tank, frolicked on a stretch of grass below. After an afternoon play date, Tank's caregiver was on his way to retrieve him.

After Clarke and Stella updated each other on their undertakings during each of the preceding twenty-four hours, the group descended a stone staircase leading to the gardens. With the criminal ring in the clutches of the justice system, Fenton brought the group together to discuss the case of the purloined jewelry, drawing upon police reports, suspects' confessions, and his own deductions.

During his much earlier academic career, Silas specialized in the study of advanced acoustic technologies, including high-frequency communications. Over the years, his theoretical work, conducted at a prominent university, was commercialized and incorporated into consumer products. Toward the end of his tenure at the university, Silas tested hypotheses involving how the pitch of an auditory message affects one's ability to later recall the content of the message. One of his graduate research assistants—independently investigating how psychological receptivity might be affected by different communication styles—was June Hatcher. She would complete her master's degree and become a social worker. June remained in contact with Silas over the years, who she considered a lifelong mentor. Although she would have preferred immersion in her academic passions, June stayed current on scholarly research. By text and email, she and Silas exchanged views on experimental work, including a Stockholm University study that concluded women suffering from stress-related exhaustion often exhibit hypersensitivity to sounds. Desiring to reunite with his former student, Silas arranged to have Roberta placed under state guardianship and nominated June as the ideal caretaker for his foster sister. However, he chose not to disclose to Roberta the past association between the two or their shared areas of interest.

Roberta earned her doctorate in botany and became a celebrated horticulturist. Although profound differences in temperament contributed to their problematical relationship, they continued to share the same home over the years. Silas harbored ill feelings toward his foster sister, stemming from her transcendent academic achievements. Her successes spawned lofty levels of approbation, overshadowing Silas' accomplishments. There was, however, one point of academic convergence between these two: The foster siblings collaborated on a study involving the effects of music on plant growth. In their work together, Silas' truculent and erratic demeanor created friction between the two, presaging an even more acute emotional degeneration in later years. Roberta maintained a conciliatory tone with her foster brother; however, his hard-fought yet gallingly protean evaluative standards during the project brought the two to an irreconcilable point. Expressing his dissatisfaction with the academic mésalliance, Silas removed his name from an academic paper that documented their work together. Silas later reinterpreted his own decision as a betrayal by Roberta, accusing her of failing to properly recognize his contributions in her published work.

In his retirement, Silas' emotions became increasingly erratic, and he suffered delusions about exerting mind control over others to acquire wealth and influence (that the world conspired to withhold from him). June not only served as a superintendent to Roberta, assisting with the household duties, but as a research colleague to Silas, privately collaborating with him on a range of technological subjects. She introduced fresh ideas drawn from the field of hypnotherapy that, when combined with Silas' knowledge of high-frequency transmission, helped make Silas' vision of widespread mind control a reality. Overlooking Silas' unstable mental state, June saw an opportunity to collaborate with her beloved mentor, rekindle academic passions and, of course, reap great wealth. Her code name: Miss Scarlet. The two scientists simply needed a private laboratory to conduct their experiments. The basement was well-suited to their needs. However, Roberta possessed an inquisitive nature and a quick mind; she represented a potential threat should she divine their plan. Quite naturally, Roberta became Silas' and June's first experimental subject. (Although not confirmed, Charlie's school's former principal may have been the second subject, leading to his relocation to Luxembourg.)

Roberta was already wearing earplugs at night. After substituting Roberta's earplugs with their invention, the researchers were able to test the first generations of their monitoring and transmission device. Each generation became increasingly sophisticated, as the earpieces acquired additional information about Roberta's vitals and sleep cycles. Later generations were used to introduce hypnotic suggestions. These suggestions prompted Roberta to recall Wiwe, the Ohlone underground lord of the earth. Through hypnotic suggestion, Roberta was invited to consider the possibility of a malevolent force at work under her own house. From that point, there would be no threat of Roberta entering the basement laboratory. Silas would make trips upstairs to quietly listen to Roberta's stories. The man who did not talk.

Over time, Roberta was also convinced that, through several nighttime suggestions, it would be in her best interest to overlook modifications Silas was making to the roof of their home. The 1950s era antenna and the organic debris on the roof soon concealed the most sophisticated communication equipment on the planet. A nighttime voice also invited Roberta to reinterpret the image of a black cargo van that was occasionally parked on their property. Instead of a van, Roberta saw a sleeping black Labrador. The visiting dog, Astro, simply wanted a hiatus from Lady Bracknell, a devious feline in his home. A nighttime voice advised Roberta to give the large animal a wide berth, as Astro became cranky when awakened. The dog that did not bark.

During Charlie's and Emma's last visit with Roberta, June became concerned that Charlie was probing into Roberta's nighttime visions. Fearing the direction of this inquiry, June instigated the avalanche to discourage future visits to the Ru't household.

The next set of challenges involved how to encourage residents to use earplugs, substitute these earplugs, and manage the nighttime communications. June met Olivia Stiglitz, aka Mrs. Peacock, at a community class helping residents resist tobacco use. The two struck up a friendship, eventually leading to conversations about their aspirations. The acting principal was motivated to secure additional capital flows for her desperately underfunded school. She held the key to how the transmission devices could be introduced into the households. The beehive cookie jars would be an ideal Trojan Horse. The teacher controlled–or so she thought– the cookie jar distribution channel, composed of legions of students. She did not, however, account for one of her students going off script.

Using Silas' design, Olivia worked with an overseas manufacturer to produce 1,550 of the most versatile cookie jar lids in history. The manufacturing partner was paid $59,675 to produce the cookie jars. The teacher's misappropriation of $11,000 of public funds as a downpayment to manufacture the cookie jar lids carried the most serious legal ramifications for her. Olivia funneled her share of the criminal proceeds to the school through her invented "anonymous donor." The school's records indicated that the donations made by the anonymous patron far exceeded her own.

Reusable school envelopes were used for the jewelry exchanges and placement of the QR code boobytraps. A hypnotic voice emphasized that only the police could use what was contained in the envelope. Only Laura's QR code had been activated.

Olivia maintained meticulous records of the operation—a critical function given the complexity of tracking the original and replica jewelry flowing in and out of the homes. Her records indicated the operation involved fifty-seven households and 798 pieces of jewelry, representing precious metals and cut-stones valued at $3.3 million. Of the fifty-seven households that were infiltrated, thirty-eight contained at least one cookie jar purchased from Charlie or one of her assistants. The criminal planners failed to anticipate that a household would procure more than one cookie jar. This complication was a direct result of Charlie's special prize drawing. The true purpose of the principal's bond sweepstakes inquiry was to ascertain why multiple cookie jars were showing up in homes.

The families that purchased more than one cookie jar created technical challenges for Silas, arising from the complexity of locating and shutting off redundant cookie jar lids. Quite simply, there were too many cookie jars to manage. This difficulty was at least partially overcome by a hypnotic suggestion that cataloged the benefits of extra kitchen counter space. Fenton did not comment on whether the technical difficulties Charlie created for the perpetrators, on balance, offset her assistance in the placement of drones in thirty-eight households.

In a conference with the school principal, Charlie's phone argued that the cookie jars were poorly made, and the cookies were stale. Fenton suggested there was some truth in these claims. Since the plastic lid was designed to facilitate drone take-offs, the lid could not create a tight seal with the jar. Consequently, the cookies quickly degraded.

The low voice that asked Clara about ways to produce replica jewelry and sell the original articles belonged to Olivia Stiglitz. She arranged for San Diego to pick up and drop off the jewelry with the manufacturer.

San Diego installed devices under the dog collars. His actual name: Clayton (Clay) Campbell. June recruited Clay, whose résumé featured dog-walking experience and a wide-ranging criminal career. His success in both domains recommended him as an ideal addition to the team. He would become Mr. Green.

Pre-collapse surveillance records from Macro Cell Tower 2173 showed Clay making several unauthorized visits to the site. Clay was charged with installing the cell signal jamming device on the tower. Clarke had disabled the cell signal jamming device on the tower. The tower's surveillance records had been compromised the week of the propane tank repository fire.

Silas designed the booby-trapped box that housed the jammer. He also set a trap to electrocute anyone who tampered with the relay station on the roof of the tented home (and others). Owen might have been electrocuted if a curious squirrel had not first investigated the transmission device on the roof of the tented dwelling.

Clay confessed to tampering with Ms. S's window to mislead whoever might investigate the crime scene. He made his deceptive alterations after Fenton's visit.

Silas protected his basement laboratory with security devices that would electrocute unwelcome visitors. The laboratory contained equipment to monitor the earpieces, operate the drones, and deliver recorded and live transmissions. Clay and Silas faced first-degree burglary and destruction of private property charges. Clay was also charged with second-degree arson in connection with the destruction of the propane tank refinery and cell tower. Silas faced an additional charge of attempted arson at the Victorian. The screaming centipede was not only intended to lure the girls into the Victorian but to start a fire that would consume the dwelling. This conflagration was designed to frustrate the Paretos' investigation. During the late-night track meet at Stella's school, Clay confessed to planting stolen items and burglary tools in Emma's car. He also installed a tracking device which he road-tested. Only one tracking device was used; the others were backups. Clay and the other perpetrators contended they had not deployed drones at Stella's school or the cell tower.

Silas was charged with cybercrimes related to the manipulation of what had once been considered impregnable computer networks, controlling traffic signals, utility company power monitoring, and law enforcement communications. The prosecutor's charges would be reduced if Silas agreed to cooperate with public agencies and a cybercrime task force.

Clay was a resident of Santa Cruz. When the girls spotted him at the amusement park, he was enjoying time-off from the rigors of his criminal vocation. He was skilled at many midway games, having once worked for the park. His favorite attraction was the high striker. Silas asked him to minimize the use of the van, unless needed to commit a crime. Disregarding Silas' directive, Clay used the van for his recreational outing, culminating in the nightmarish ride for the girls.

The lead prosecutor had asked Fenton if his family wanted to press charges in connection with the deafening defense system in Clay's van. In turn, Fenton asked Clarke if she sought legal remedies for her damaged ear. As Silas shared the encryption key, Clarke saw no reason to add to the list of charges confronting Clay and the others. Fenton commended Clarke on her compassion: *"A fine partita, il re e il pedone finiscono nella stressa scatola."* Charlie translated: "When you finish the game, the king and the pawn end up in the same box."

Fenton shared additional details about the hypnotic inductions. Once a resident was found to be receptive to nighttime hypnotic suggestion, the drone deposited a small amount of distilled Tetrahydrocannabinol (THC) on the subject's lips during the subject's deepest sleep cycle, strengthening their receptivity to messages delivered through the ear transmitter. Of course, THC is the principal psychoactive constituent of cannabis. Many of the victims reported premonitions and a wide range of other feelings involving their jewelry, both before and after the robberies. June confessed that while the hypnotic suggestions, even those amplified by the administration of THC, were designed to keep the subjects from becoming aware of the nighttime messages, there were instances when the hypnotic suggestion was either not fully effective or the power of the suggestion dissipated over time. The victims' premonitions were examples of the hypnotic suggestions being less effective than June and Silas anticipated. The two scientists debated whether they should increase the drug dosage. However, they chose not to step up the THC dosing due to concerns about producing lingering and more detectable effects of the psychoactive agent. Until the last hours of their operation, the two were searching for ways to address this technical challenge.

Of the $3.3 million in jewelry taken from the homes, only $1.6 million of the original jewelry was recovered. The remainder was disassembled, with the precious metals sold as scrap and the cut-stones sold in secondary markets. Many victims were unaware of the loss of their jewelry until the articles were returned to them.

Ms. S's valuable necklace was returned to her, along with the rest of her jewelry. However, Laura Marcum's jewelry would not be recovered.

Fenton collected handsome rewards for the recovered jewelry, with a significant portion of these proceeds shared with Clarke, Charlie, Stella, and Emma. Drawing from her share of the reward money, Charlie awarded Lucy with a new collar, high-end dog treats, and a special "spa day" at a new dog grooming studio.

Charlie used her remaining share of the reward money to launch an animal rescue organization called "San Michele's Dogs" (inspired by Axel Munthe, a notable animal patron and one-time Anacapri resident). Clarke also contributed to this new organization, dedicated to rescuing abused dogs in tough urban environments. Dogs would be relocated to their "sanctuary city," placing them in loving homes. The girls learned about the sensitive cultural aspects of this undertaking and the dismaying pervasiveness of dog neglect and mistreatment.

Emma had not decided how to use the reward money beyond making a small withdrawal for a few nice dinners with Owen and purchasing an airline ticket so she could visit her father at long last. The Paretos had also collected open recommendation letters for Emma from a judge, a retired entrepreneur, a notable psychologist, and a Copley Medal winner.

An accounting of the criminal funds and stolen articles raised two important questions. After tallying all contributions credited to the "anonymous donor" and the significant expenditures made by the criminal enterprise, $233,157 was missing. Two articles of jewelry—a ring and a necklace—were not accounted for in the inventory of items dismantled or recovered. Olivia's records instructed that "the ring and the necklace should be set aside for her." The identity of the female recipient remained a mystery.

The sentencing of the conspirators proceeded on a predictable path. All would serve lengthy prison sentences (apart from Silas, who might choose to cooperate with the authorities). Olivia was expelled from the teaching profession. Silas was barred from conducting any activities regulated by the FCC. June was prohibited from providing social services. San Diego was forbidden to provide any "canine related services." None of the four agreed to turn state's evidence by testifying as a witness for the prosecution.

Although the burglary ring was brought to justice, investigators considered the possibility of a still at-large operational mastermind. Who was Mrs. White? Who bankrolled the operation? Where was the missing money? Who received the missing jewelry? Who texted the three girls to warn them about the hazards of entering Roberta's basement? The four perpetrators told investigators that they did not know Stella.

Fenton told the investigators that Charlie discovered irregularities involving the school's copy machine. He recommended that the police review the data on the eavesdropping storage device. Olivia confessed that she used her school's copy machine after hours to reproduce documents related to the jewelry operation. She used the copier to fake the hard-copy documentation of ownership demanded by the buyers of the loose cut-stones. To ensure that the in-person bi-weekly meetings with her fellow conspirators were productive, the teacher drafted detailed meeting agendas. She made copies of the agendas using the printer to sidestep more traceable electronic channels. Documents showed that the group held two retreats at lavish but remote locations.

Mysteriously, investigators found that the storage device was activated only when Olivia keyed in her password to use the copy machine. Someone had been monitoring her activities all along, presumably in connection with the criminal operation. Olivia was shocked when told she was under surveillance. Was the observer one of the other three accomplices or another party?

Another disquieting finding: The copy machine's hard drive revealed that five copies were made of every document related to the jewelry scheme. Was there a fifth member of the criminal ring whose intelligence and cunning continued to shield them from view? Olivia wouldn't say.

Following Fenton's garden briefing, Charlie met with Emma to share her theory about the possible involvement of a fifth member—and presumed leader—of the criminal ring. Charlie deduced there were only three suspects who could have possibly served in this capacity. To begin with, Charlie conjectured that the ringleader was female because of the likelihood that the recipient of the missing two pieces of jewelry ("set aside for her") possessed inside knowledge of the operation. Although speculative, Charlie concluded the recipient was important, likely the leader. Further, she suspected that the sender of the text message warning (to the three girls) was the fifth member. The sender would have known that Stella was a half-sister and involved in the jewelry theft investigation. This ruled out the sender being one of the other four conspirators (along with Willa, Roberta and others) who did not know about Stella's connection with the case. Based on Ms. Stiglitz's records of the group's in-person meetings and retreats, the ringleader must have met with the other perpetrators. Although Tay already knew about the half-sisters, her incarceration precluded in-person meetings. This left Clara Huynh, her aunt Katherine, and her mother as possible suspects.

Charlie further reasoned that only one of the suspects harbored a personal motive and possessed the means to assemble and oversee the component parts of the scheme. The ringleader likely understood that Fenton was directing many parts of the investigation. In Charlie's view, this ruled out Katherine, who was close to her brother, and Clara, who considered Fenton, a family member. This left her mother. Ophelia was a close friend of Olivia Stiglitz. Charlie imagined that her mother was sympathetic to the financial plight of Olivia's school. Ophelia must have expected that at least a few of the victims of the jewelry thefts would engage Fenton. If she and her co-conspirators outfoxed her former husband, the clever investigator, all the better. This would be further punishment for Fenton's deceitful placement of Stella. However, Ophelia needed to ensure her daughters were not harmed if Fenton brought them into an investigation. This daughter-endangerment line was about to be crossed when she texted the warning to the three girls.

Charlie suggested that a high-level chess match was being played out by her parents. If Charlie's mother had been involved in the robberies, several questions could be asked about her father. Had Fenton reached the same conclusion as Charlie? If he had, at what point did he suspect Ophelia? The morning of the text warning, Fenton was meeting with a "former colleague." Was this former colleague, in fact, his former spouse? Had Fenton convinced Ophelia that the game was over and that the girls needed to be protected?

Emma told Charlie that she would reflect on her theory but suggested there might be another way to piece together the puzzle. She asked Charlie to promise that she would not share her theory with others until giving her a chance to consider it, along with another hypothesis. Charlie agreed but asked to talk again soon. Emma suspected this pause would give Charlie time to inventory her mother's jewelry holdings and research laws concerning the extradition of Armenian citizens.

Charlie's role in the stolen jewelry affair could be considered problematic. She unwittingly contributed to a criminal scheme by distributing the drones. When she helped bring those criminals to justice, she removed a much-needed funding source for her former school. Had she also discovered her mother's involvement in a criminal plot? Regardless, Operation RECLAIM had been put on hold. This case could be titled: *The Case of the Unintended and Disturbing Consequences*. Alternatively, since the Pareto girls ruined the gang's plan to redistribute wealth from well-to-do jewelry owners to an underfunded public school, the case might be called: *The Sheriff of Nottingham Brings Robin Hood to Justice*. Charlie liked the title: *The Stale Cookies Mystery*.

The equivocal aspects of the case led to equally uncertain implications for the Pareto family. Charlie's stunning theory was only the latest turn in an unpredictable summer. Charlie suggested that there might never be a definitive resolution to *The Invisible Hand affair*. "Adam Smith asserts that 'our superior reason and understanding, by which we are capable of discerning the remote consequences of all our actions, and of foreseeing the advantage or detriment which is likely to result from them,' is one of mankind's greatest gifts. I'm beginning to wonder if this is true. I've come to appreciate that our actions create a ripple of infinite and increasingly ambiguous effects."

As Fenton wrapped up his briefing, he looked down at his phone. "Katherine has been trying to reach us. Dinner has been ready for some time now." Kool & The Gang's wistful instrumental "Summer Madness" was being broadcast from the loggia.

Katherine looked upon the group from the veranda as they walked back to the house. In her usual manner, she stood erect with her head held high. She held Lucy in her arms. As Katherine gazed upon her enlarged family, she smiled with satisfaction.

Author's Annotations and Disclaimers

When I first approached Charlie about sharing her family's adventures with a broader audience, she expressed some reservations. She pointed out that many of the Paretos' investigative methods are proprietary. If divulged, there would be no means to compensate her family for use of these techniques. Further, Charlie shared that she abhors the public spotlight, preferring to maintain a private existence. She also acknowledged there were one or two incidents in the stolen jewelry case that, on their surface, might not be entirely flattering to herself. Nevertheless, after an extended negotiation, Charlie acquiesced to my retelling of these events. However, she imposed several conditions, including a variety of omissions that should be inconsequential to the narrative. Charlie also requires the publisher to extend to readers valuable merchandise that will be offered for a limited time. These items are listed on the following page. The proceeds of these sales will be divided between a 501(c) nonprofit dog rescue agency and Charlie's family. She is not raffling bonds or other securities at this time.

Charlie predicts that a few misguided English teachers will compel students to not only read this book but supply its "moral." If a reader is caught in this unhappy situation, Charlie discourages a theme like: "Don't trust your mother." While acknowledging that this may be good advice for some, she is giving her mother the benefit of the doubt at this time. Every mother deserves the same consideration. Charlie offers these valuable lessons: "Don't hire a dog walker before checking references," or "Don't use earplugs unless absolutely necessary," or "Don't enter into unfair contracts with siblings."

I am forever indebted to Emma, who provided invaluable insights and critical details.

Finally, the Pareto family and the publisher discourage the employment of methods, techniques, technologies, and tactics described in this book, making no warranties concerning their effectiveness and discharging any and all liability for their use.

—P.E.K.

Official Pareto Merchandise

Limited offer, subject to availability of stock, available through the publisher U.S.A. prices exclude tax shipping charges and are subject to change

"36.3" Plastic Dog Bowl	$19.95
"36.3" Coffee Mug	$9.95
"36.3" Pillowcase	$9.95
"36.3 Bumper Sticker **(NEW!)**	$6.95
"36.3" Women's T-Shirt: S/M/L	$19.95
"36.3" Men's T-Shirt: S/M/L	$19.95
8" X 10" Glossy Photo of Lucy **(NEW!)**	$7.95
Lucy's dog collar: XS/S/M/L	$16.95
Lucy: The Early Years - Streets of Santa Ana (eBook by Charlie Pareto)	$14.95
Sample Nondisclosure Agreement (NDA)	$4.95
Charlie's Science Fair Project: An Unapologetic Review (5 Pages)	$3.95
24" X 36" Poster-Diagram of Charlie's Commercial Interests	$19.95
Charlie's Online Newsletter and Chat Portal (one-year subscription)	$29.95
Katherine's Culinary Triumphs (Ten recipes compiled by Charlie Pareto)	$9.95
The Invisible Hand Differential Equations (16-question calculus problem set)	$8.95

DID YOU KNOW? Your business can feature its product or service in this book. Contact the publisher for exciting placement opportunities!

Afterword

The most common question I've received from readers—aside from how to contact one or more members of the Pareto family—is how Emma applied for the Pareto job at the career fair. Since this seems to be a topic of interest, I've reconstructed the career fair challenge from what Emma has shared with me.

* * *

Sitting on the booth table was an expensive looking virtual reality headset and large headphones. A note was taped to the top of the visor which read: "Apply here." Emma put on the headset and headphones and took a deep breath.

The VR system translated hand movements into the virtual environment. The headset showed a virtual representation of Emma's hands as they made impolite gestures.

Another image came into view.

Emma stood outside a small cottage. Around her was an expansive vineyard, shimmering under a late afternoon sun. The advanced VR optics made the scene appear life-like. A small swarm of gnats gathered a few feet away. A handsome middle-aged man with closely trimmed salt-and-pepper hair and beard emerged from the cottage and walked toward her. He wore a vintage white pull-over style work shirt and brown canvas high waist trousers with suspenders. He could have belonged in the nineteenth century.

As he walked up to her, the man started to speak rapidly in Italian. Emma did not speak Italian. There was no menu or helpful language option in her field of view.

The virtual man showed Emma a grape vine cutting with shoots, leaves, and roots. The underside of each leaf was dotted with numerous small bumps, each about the size of a half a pea. The roots were deformed and stunted. The man made a broad sweeping gesture as he shook his head in dismay, suggesting the presence of a widespread problem affecting the vineyard. A thick cloud of black smoke filled the sky from a nearby area.

He unfolded a large map and handed it to Emma. The sketch showed elevations, flat and rocky areas, and a cottage corresponding to the vineyard. After comparing a few topographical features to the position of the cottage, Emma concluded that the map was a representation of the area around her. A writhing column of black smoke rose from a low area at the north side of the vineyard. The plume flattened as it rose higher, with a dislocated smoky patch sliding in their direction.

The man gestured to an area to the left of the cottage. Arranged in countless rows were thousands of juvenile bare root plants. The vineyard needed to be replanted, replacing the defective vines with these young vines.

The eye-tracking technology in the advanced display system created a scene indistinguishable from reality.

There were several planting areas on the map. Touching the center of the map, a pull-down menu of options was revealed. Although the planting areas were predetermined, there were options on how to cultivate the plants. Symbols helped Emma understand her four choices: nutrients added/no nutrients, tilled/rocky soil, irrigated/dry soil, and closely spaced/widely spaced planting. Her selections would determine the cultivation plan for the next generation of young vines.

A two-minute countdown started at the corner of her view. Emma did not have a background in growing grapes, but she needed to make some quick decisions.

Emma decided to give the vines nutrients, plant them in tilled soil, irrigate them and give them plenty of space to grow. These were safe choices.

After handing the virtual paper back to the man, the scene dimmed. The sun made rapidly repeated arcs across the sky, suggesting the passage of years. After time passed, the scene reappeared. The nineteenth-century man stepped out of the cottage, but his hair was grayer and a bit longer. He spoke angrily in Italian as he shoved a large clump of vine clippings in front of Emma for inspection. The leaves and shoots were large, green, and lustrous. He opened his other hand and showed her a few large juicy looking grapes.

He then thrust a piece of paper at Emma, which included an English translation.

Raccolto 1: nutrienti (nutrients), lavorato (tilled), sporco umido (moist dirt), distanziati/widely spaced

Raccolto/ Crop	Ettaro/ Hectares Planted	Produzione/ Total Yield Tonnellate/ Tons	Reddito/ Total Income (1000 £)	Spese/ Expense (1000 £)	Reddito Netto/ Net Income (1000 £)
1	10	60	120	80	40
2	10				
3	10				

Emma did not recognize the currency. While the net income was positive, the Italian man's unenthusiastic reaction told her that she should try something different in the next planting cycle. The chart suggested that she would have only three cycles to get this right. There were sixteen possible planting combinations. She had tested only one of them.

The lush vines and plump grapes from the first planting cycle appeared healthy. Emma had missed something.

The safe choices were not the right choices.

Logically, the vines needed less assistance in one or more ways. The timer showed forty seconds remaining for Emma to choose her approach for the second crop. Without knowing the problem with the first crop, she did not know how to make good choices for the second one. She did not have a theory.

Ten seconds.

She changed just one of her selections from the first planting. The second-year cultivation plan withheld the nutritional supplement.

The sun made many arcs across the sky.

The Italian man trudged up to Emma. He was slightly stooped. His beard was now entirely gray and a few more lines under his eyes. He held a large clump of vine clippings. Looking down at the leaves and shoots, he shook his head sadly.

Without a word, he handed Emma a piece of paper:

Raccolto 1: nutrienti (nutrients), lavorato (tilled), sporco umido (moist dirt), distanziati/widely spaced

Raccolto 2: senza nutrienti (no nutrients), lavorato (tilled), sporco umido (moist dirt), distanziati/widely spaced

Raccolto/ Crop	Ettaro/ Hectares Planted	Produzione/ Total Yield Tonnellate/ Tons	Reddito/ Total Income (1000 £)	Spese/ Expense (1000 £)	Reddito Netto/ Net Income (1000 £)
1	10	60	120	80	40
2	10	40	140	90	50
3	10				

While eliminating the nutritional aid reduced the yield, the gross income from this smaller crop was higher. Emma calculated that the nutritionally assisted crop produced £2,000 per hectare (£120,000 divided by 60). The nutrient-starved crop produced £3,500 per hectare (£140,000 divided by 40).

The expense increased, suggesting higher maintenance costs associated with plants that had to work harder to find nutrients. However, the increase in expense did not entirely offset the net income gain. Emma reasoned that the grapes were higher quality and could fetch a higher price. She had thirty seconds to select the plan for the next and final planting cycle. Was it possible that the more the grape vine struggles, the lower the yield but higher the quality of grape? With ten seconds left, Emma took a gamble.

The man emerged from the cottage. The third planting cycle had been kind to him: he had regained his youth. His hair and beard were closely clipped. He wore a stylish navy linen blazer and white trousers.

With a broad perfect smile, he said *"Congratulazioni! Congratulazioni!"* He handed Emma a piece of paper.

Raccolto 1: nutrienti (nutrients), lavorato (tilled), sporco umido (moist dirt), distanziati/widely spaced

Raccolto 2: senza nutrienti (no nutrients), lavorato (tilled), sporco umido (moist dirt), distanziati/widely spaced

Raccolto 3: senza nutrienti (no nutrients), terreno rocciosco (rocky), sporco secco (dry dirt), naturale/ natural, affollato (crowded/closely planted)

Raccolto/ Crop	Ettaro/ Hectares Planted	Produzione/ Total Yield Tonnellate/ Tons	Reddito/ Total Income (1000 £)	Spese/ Expense (1000 £)	Reddito Netto/ Net Income (1000 £)
1	10	60	120	80	40
2	10	40	140	90	50
3	10	20	170	95	75

As Loose End's "Stay A Little While Child" played in the background, the screen prompted Emma to share her contact information, including a family contact.

After she entered the information, everything went black. She tapped the headset with two fingers. Perhaps there had been a glitch in the software.

The simulation had not revealed how the vineyard revenue-optimizing exercise tested her ability to care for the Pareto children or gauge her competency in any pursuit not directly related to viticulture. Emma was left to consider how her selections for the third crop aligned with the philosophy of the game's creator.

TO MY READERS

Thank you for reading The Invisible Hand. Book reviews are often overlooked, but they are critical to helping authors gain visibility. Your feedback is important to me. Please take a moment to write an honest review on the e-retailer of your choice. Every review makes a difference. Have a great day

–P.E. Klein